Penguin Books
A Horse of Air

Dal Stivens, born in 1911, is an internationally known
author who has published eight collections of short
stories and five novels. He has contributed to many
newspapers and periodicals.

From 1944 to 1951, he was on the staff of the Australian
Department of Information. He was Foundation
President of the Australian Society of Authors and is a
keen amateur naturalist. Since 1970, he has been
painting almost full-time.

He won the Patrick White Award for 1981 for the
contribution of his novels (*Jimmy Brockett* and *Horse of Air*)
and his short stories to Australian literature.

Other books by the same author

Novels

The Wide Arch
Three Persons Make a Tiger
Jimmy Brockett
The Bushranger

Stories

The Tramp
The Courtship of Uncle Henry
The Gambling Ghost
Ironbark Bill
The Scholarly Mouse
Selected Stories 1936-1968
The Unicorn and Other Tales
The Demon Bowler and Other Cricket Stories

Non-fiction

The Incredible Egg
A Guide to Book Contracts (with Barbara Jefferis)

DAL STIVENS

A Horse of Air

PENGUIN BOOKS

ACKNOWLEDGEMENT

The passages quoted on pages 2 and 43 are extracts from 'My Sister and I' by Frederick Nietzsche, published in *The Scarlet Treasury of Great Confessions*, edited by Whit Burnett (Pyramid Books, New York, 1958). This translation was previously published by Bridgehead Books, © 1951 by Boars Head Books.

Penguin Books Australia Ltd,
487 Maroondah Highway, P.O. Box 257
Ringwood, Victoria, 3134, Australia
Penguin Books Ltd,
Harmondsworth, Middlesex, England
40 West 23rd Street, New York, N.Y. 10010, U.S.A.
Penguin Books (Canada) Limited,
2801 John Street, Markham, Ontario, Canada L3R 1B4
Penguin Books (N.Z.) Ltd,
182-190 Wairau Road, Auckland 10, New Zealand

First published 1970 by Angus & Robertson Publishers
Published in Penguin, 1986

Copyright © Dal Stivens, 1986

All Rights Reserved. Without limiting the rights under copyright reserved above, no part of this publication may be reproduced, stored in or introduced into a retrieval system, or transmitted in any form or by any means (electronic, mechanical, photocopying, recording or otherwise), without the prior written permission of both the copyright owner and the above publisher of this book.

Offset from the Angus & Robertson Publishers edition
Made and printed in Australia by
Dominion Press-Hedges & Bell, Maryborough

CIP

Stivens, Dal, 1911- .
A horse of air.

ISBN 0 14 009216 1 (pbk.).

I. Title.

A823'.3

with an hoast of furious fancies
whereof I am commaunder,
with a burning speare, & a horse of aire,
to the wildernesse I wander.
By a knight of ghostes & shadowes,
I sumon'd am to Tourney.
ten leagues beyond the wide worlds end
mee thinke it is noe iourney.
    yet will I sing, & c:

Mad Tom o'Bedlam's Ballad (Anon.)

Of the gladdest moments in human life, methinks, is
the departure upon a distant journey into unknown
lands. Shaking off with one mighty effort the fetters of
Habit, the leaden weight of Routine, the cloak of many
Cares and the slavery of Home, man feels once more
happy. The blood flows with the fast circulation of
childhood . . . Afresh dawns the morn of life . . .

—RICHARD BURTON, Journal entry, 2nd December 1856.

Our lives were wild, romantic, and solemn.

—ISABEL BURTON, on their stay in Damascus.

"To know how to free oneself is nothing; the arduous
thing is to know what to do with one's freedom."

—ANDRÉ GIDE, *The Immoralist*

I have been cunning in mine overthrow,
The careful pilot of my proper woe.

—BYRON

v

"But is analogy argument? You are a punster."

"Punster, respected sir?" with a look of being aggrieved.

"Yes, you pun with ideas as another man may with words."

"Oh well, sir, whoever talks in that strain, whoever has no confidence in human reason, in vain to reason with him. Still, respected sir," altering his air, "permit me to hint that, had not the force of analogy moved you somewhat, you would hardly have offered to contemn it."

—HERMAN MELVILLE, *The Confidence Man*

PREFACE

I am the author and amateur naturalist mentioned in the first chapter of this rather unorthodox autobiography by Harold Craddock. I had known and respected Harry Craddock for some years—his contributions to Australian ornithology have been outstanding—but I was never a close friend. Accordingly, I was a little surprised when he asked me to act as his literary godfather, as it were, and handed me the manuscript which with only slight editing appears on the pages that follow. His original idea was that I should use his autobiography as part of the source material for an account of the expedition he led to central Australia in 1967. His manuscript, as he was at pains to point out, was a subjective account and was deficient in many details. "Moreover, it's a bit wild in places—you'll need to get people to corroborate some of the things I've written," he said. This was my own first reaction, and I, accordingly, spent several months interviewing other people who had accompanied Harry Craddock and gathering the mass of material necessary for a straightforward account of the Craddock and Drake Expedition to find the rare night parrot. It was only when I had accumulated a mass of material that I realized that the finest memorial to my friend was to publish his autobiography much as he had written it, with only minor interpolations by others where accounts differed. Who was I, for instance, to judge whether Harry Craddock, or someone else, was being truthful? The truth about anything must be disputable. As he asks in the autobiography, which is the reality and which is the dream? Most of the people mentioned have consented to the references made to them even though they did not always agree that they acted as Harry Craddock said they did or from the motives he imputed to them. They have, in fact, behaved with extraordinary magnanimity. In a few places only they have interpolated mild demurrers. Occasionally it has been necessary to use invented names and alter details.

I have called this autobiography unorthodox and so in a sense it is. Harry Craddock was a man of great originality and directness. His originality sometimes took a form which others thought eccentric. He would, for instance, rarely kill an insect. The ants troubled him greatly in central Australia, but he fails to tell you he wouldn't crush one even when it got inside his shirt and was biting him. I once saw him contemplate a troublesome house-fly, which kept perching on his arm, for several minutes before he finally did kill it. "I couldn't run the risk of parodying Uncle Toby!" he explained with a grin. Sterne was one of his favourites. (I sometimes think his life was rather Shandeian.) Another of his heroes was the English naturalist and eccentric Charles Waterton (1782-1865) who also (coincidentally?) loved Sterne.

He was gentle in his dealings with his fellows—so much so that some took undue advantage of him. He had his limits. "I seem soft," he said once. "But I'm not —if they chop in too far, they gap their axe."

He was courteous, and witty, too, but never malicious. What he doesn't tell us about is his generosity. He'd have helped everyone who asked him for money if he could. His mother may have realized this because, although he was only thirteen when she died, the great fortune she left him and his sister was tied up in a trust.

The only person who raised any serious objections to publication was the doctor at the mental home. He insisted on the interpolation on page 170. He also tried to persuade me that the autobiography should not be published because, he said, it was a tangled complex of falsehood, truth, half-truth and phantasy, which only a psychiatrist such as himself could unravel. As an example of what he called sheer phantasy, he cited Harry Craddock's account of his revenge on Swinburne. He added that he much regretted having ever suggested to Harry Craddock that he should write his memoirs. Moreover, he requested that I should make it clear in this preface that he was not as ignorant of German and other literatures as Harry Craddock claimed.

THE EDITOR

I

My big trouble is that I've never grown up. At fifty I ought to know better, but the psychiatrist annoys me. He knows all the answers. "Now, we want to get to the bottom of this," he says. His tongue—I notice it is furred—runs over his lips. But I don't care whether we ever get to the bottom of it. He sits there beaming at me. He should be selling motor-cars in Parramatta Road; he has the same persuader look you see in public relations men and priests. He is a thick-set man with a smallish, round reptilian head, but with big lips and moist brown eyes. I puzzle over what he reminds me of—a Centralian bluetongue (*Tiliqua occipitalis multifasciata* Sternfeld)? "If you shot this strange man, you must know why," he insisted today. I said: "I often get impulses to do something outrageous. I don't always know the reasons." I was thinking of one night at a party when I got drunk and tried to stake out my territory the way a dog does. There was a reason, but I didn't discover it until later.

My room in the mental hospital is pleasant enough as such rooms go. By accident, no doubt, it is a fashionable white. There's a table and a comfortable chair, and our motor-car salesman friend has set out pens and pencils and paper and even a dictation machine. He wants me to write my autobiography.

"Just write anything," he urged yesterday. "Free associations shouldn't be hard for you. Moreover, you come from a literary family."

1

"Literary? The Craddocks are merchandisers of words."

He laughed as one might humour a child. "Think of a number," he shot at me.

"Eight," I said, to be agreeable.

"What happened when you were eight?"

I stared back at him. He tried me with some more. I won't bore you. Blue was the colour I gave him. It seemed to fascinate him but didn't mean anything to me. After he'd gone I did try to write something, to doodle as he put it, to let thoughts flow. I thought I might as well do that as anything else. But nothing came. I drew a few figures—triangles and squares imposed on each other—and a tortoise. He was welcome to them, if it kept him amused. And I tried the dictation machine. A neat little toy and a different make from the one I was familiar with; I gabbled a lot of nonsense to it, including a free version of my interview with the psychiatrist. The tape disappeared last night. I hope it gave him something to keep him amused. When he talked to me today he didn't mention the tape recording.

"Write anything," he said. "Write about your father, or your sister, or your mother, or your first day at school. Anything. We've got to get to the bottom of this."

"But why?" I said. I enjoyed tormenting him. And after he'd gone I got an idea. I wrote with absurd ease, but it need not strike you as remarkable. I didn't have to think of a word as I wrote:

It first happened between Elisabeth and me the night our young brother Joseph died, though we had no idea that he was dying when she crept into my bed, pleading that it was cold where she was, and she knew how warm I always was. As a matter of fact, this was not true. Even in these early days, chills seized me and held on to me at the oddest and most unexpected times. And I was particu-

2

larly cold that night. . . . All afternoon little Joseph had kept the household in turmoil with his screaming and gasping. . . . Suddenly I felt Elisabeth's warm little hands in mine, her hissing little voice was in my ear, and I began feeling warm all over.

I both loved and resented that wealth of warmth which Elisabeth brought to me in those unexpected hours of the night. I was usually in the midst of a sound sleep when she got into my bed, and thrilling as I found the ministrations of her fat little fingers, it also meant my being kept awake for hours and hours. Besides, though in my conscious nature I knew nothing about what was going on, I must have had a feeling that my sister was bringing into my life as an accomplished fact sensations whose real value to a boy was in their being discovered as part of the experience of growing up. She was presenting me with triumphs I should by right attain only by my own efforts in a much more restricted world.

My main task from now until death day is to keep these notes from falling into the hands of my sister who best exemplifies the saying of Matthew, By their fruits ye shall know them. Fearing temptation, she has been tempted beyond what is common to mankind, and has drawn me irresistibly toward her incestuous womb. But I urge the reader to remember the parable of the tares: the rank weeds of our being, if gathered up, may cause us to root up the wheat also. Despite her incestuous leanings, Elisabeth has been both a mother and a father to me. Without her strict discipline, my genius might have been blighted in early youth when I first realized that God was dead and that we were trapped in a whirling void, a meaningless chaos of being. . . .

There were several more pages in this vein. I shan't bore you with them.

He pattered in to see me the next day, head thrust forward and licking his lips. Slightly bald, he made me think suddenly of *Pseudemydura umbrina* Siebenrock, the short-necked swamp tortoise of Western Australia.

3

I don't mean this unkindly. For some years I have found myself identifying more readily with animals than with people. I have more sympathy with animals and I think I like them better. They conduct their lives more sensibly than we do. They curb their aggression. Animals, for instance, never make war. War, as defined by Malinowski, is the use of organized force between two politically independent units in the pursuit of tribal policy. Thus war enters fairly late into the development of human societies. But I am being diverted again. That's the trouble with me. I must be an oral type. I spout words. I envelope people in words, I spit words at them, I want to swallow them with words.

"Ah, you have something for me," he observed.

I passed it over to him and he pretended to read it cursorily. But I could see he was taking much of it in because there was a sudden gleam in his eyes—particularly when they lit on the passages about my sister—or what he thought was my sister.

"There, who said you couldn't write? This is very gracefully written—of course, I've only just glanced at it, but anyone can see you're a skilled writer."

"They tell me my German translations are even better," I said.

"Have you published in Germany?"

"A little," I said, with pretended casualness.

"Well, keep it up! Do a little more today. I'll take this away and read it at my leisure."

After he'd gone I went to the bookshelf and picked out a few books. I leafed through them for half an hour. Then I sat down at the table and copied for a good hour and a half. I can't help it. I am a buffoon. Give me a role and I'll play it. That was part of the trouble with my first wife, Jessica. When we'd been married about two years I started drinking, not seriously, but it was enough to start her complaining, so I played the

4

alcoholic, thickening my voice and staggering about when I came home. At other times I hadn't touched it, but she never knew. I'd be having one of my fits of exhilaration, of hypomania, and it was all the same to her. But there was more to it than I realize. My poor behaviour was a symptom of more serious differences.

After I'd done my set piece for the psychiatrist, I started work on my genuine memoir. At first I had no conscious thought of gaining some knowledge of myself. That came later when I'd covered several pages. I had a momentary impulse to seek some advice from a friend who was a novelist and a keen amateur naturalist, but to my surprise I found I had no difficulty in getting started and my autobiography or memoir flowed with astonishing ease. Chekhov used to say that when he had a block he'd write nonsense for two or three pages and eventually something would come from his subconscious. Or should it be pre-conscious? I am over fifty and perhaps, as my children say, I am a product of the thirties. The books on my shelves in my former home betray me—so many Gollancz Left Book Club volumes! My thinking has been influenced by Marx, Freud, Bertrand Russell, Christopher Caudwell, Fromm, and even, shamefacedly, D. H. Lawrence! and I am adrift in the modern world without the tools to apprehend it correctly. Or maybe the intellectual fashions have changed.

2

I think it all started with the search for the night parrot (*Geopsittacus occidentalis*), the rare night parrot* of outback Australia. You probably read something about my search in the newspapers. This was germinal, and so, too, I think, was turning fifty. Turning fifty worried me. It was a watershed with a quick descent. Turning thirty, too, had been a bad moment in my life. Strangely, I'd slid past forty without depression. But reaching fifty was a bad time. I realized suddenly the significance of a remark of Jorge Luis Borges, "Death reduces me incessantly." There were books I'd never read again—or want to read—and places I'd never visit—or want to see—and women I'd never love—or, worse, want to love. Hemingway had the right idea. Old age is a shipwreck and Hemingway saw the reefs and shoals ahead; his health was failing; his talent had deserted him, or so he feared. He made his separate peace. (When —or if—I tried to make mine I'd probably be plagued by that Piper propensity for bungling or indecision.)†
When I turned fifty I weighed twelve stone and was five feet eleven high. I have kept fairly fit. I have most of my hair (dark brown). I have, as yet, only a small pot belly. Every few months I start to worry about it and then I do exercises for a fortnight or so. I lie on

* EDITOR: The MS. has "Night Parrot" throughout which is the correct scientific style. Other birds and mammals, etc., are also capitalized. Capitals have been dispensed with in this publication to conform to popular practice.

† EDITOR: This is presumably a reference to the unsuccessful suicide attempt of John Piper (1773-1851), Harry Craddock's ancestor, Rum Fleet officer and later, Naval Officer for Sydney. When discrepancies were found in the customs accounts—no dishonesty was involved—Piper had himself rowed out between the heads and leapt overboard. The crew rescued him.

Feedback
Theatrebooks
&
Prospero
Press

Specializing in
Pre-World War I
American Plays
and Anthologies

P.O. Box 220
Naskeag Point
Brooklin, ME
04616
(207) 359-2781
Fax (207) 359-5532

the floor and raise each leg and lower it slowly to the floor. It has a very good effect on the belly muscles. I'm always intending to exercise regularly. I know I should. There is a rebellious streak in me, dating back to my schooldays, which makes me dislike any regimented exercise. The thought is boring—to stand and go through the exercises like an automaton. So in the past I preferred to play golf and tennis and squash. But after forty I'd lost interest in these games. Once I bought a book about 5BX and I did the exercises conscientiously for three weeks and felt a lot better. I even took the book with me on a trip to Adelaide and did them every night in my hotel room. And then I came home about midnight and I was too tired to do them —or thought I was. And something happened the next night and the night after that. And so I stopped. My attempts to give up smoking always fail. My only health problem, and it's minor, is a form of dermatitis. I scratch my head and chest when I'm asleep.

The bald facts of my life are in the Australian *Who's Who* and are reproduced on the following page. Being born on the 31st December 1916 was an odd chance, but I think it had some effect on my life because I always missed out a little on presents as a child. After they'd made the effort of choosing a Christmas present for me, it required a special effort to rise to the occasion of my birthday. My grandmother Piper always remembered me. She sent all her grandsons braces. As she had over twenty grandsons, I assume she bought the braces in bulk from Dalgety's. The year of my birth was the Year of the Dragon, of Fire-Dragon in the Oriental Calendar. I wondered if that mattered—I should have preferred to have been born in the Year of Earth and Monkey, which would have had to be 1908 or 1848. The Year of Earth and Monkey is considered particularly lucky. Australia was founded in the Year of Earth and Monkey (1788)

CRADDOCK, Harold Piper Vincent, M.A., M.Sc., F.R.Z.S., naturalist and author; son of Sir Charles Craddock and Janet Craddock (*née* Vincent) decd.; *b.* 31st December 1916; *ed.* King's School, Parramatta, Christ Church, Oxford, M.A.; Hon. Ornithologist Aust. Museum, Sydney; contributor to the *Emu*, etc.; past president of Royal Australian Ornithologists' Union; Corresp. Memb. German Ornithologists' Society; Memb. Bd. Aust. Elizabethan Trust; *publications*, The Company of Blue Wrens, Eastern Spinebills, Dying Australia; *m.* (1) 1940, Jessica, d. Sir Henry Basedow, 1 s. 1 d.; (2) 1946, Martha, d. H. Cunningham; (3) 1962, Joanna, d. Stephen Macleay; *recreations*, music, theatre, talking, photography; *clubs*, Athenaeum and Travellers (London), University, and Journalists (Sydney); *address*, Chisholm, Bellevue Hill, N.S.W.

but it wasn't lucky for the Aborigines. That bout of gastro-enteritis, too, was probably important. As a small child I wasn't allowed to eat things which they said would upset me. I remember with distaste prunes and junket and having to pick the sultanas and raisins out of cakes and buns to throw them away! Once we all picked cherries in an orchard at Orange. Margaret and the other children could eat as many as they liked but I wasn't allowed to eat any. In spite of the Craddock money, you'd say it was a deprived childhood.

My secondary education was at King's School, Parramatta. (I should mention I had some earlier education from private tutors on the Continent when my mother was living in France and Italy after she separated from my father. When I was ten I attended a rather disastrous prep school in England.)* From King's I went on to Christ Church, Oxford, where I took my M.A. with first-class honours in philosophy, politics, and economics. My father, Sir Charles Craddock, intended that I should enter the family newspaper business–the Sydney *Clarion* group. After coming down from Oxford I spent two years in London working on various newspapers. The door was opened to me by letters of introduction from my father.

This is not very interesting. To me, anyway. It might interest you; people like to pry into your adolescence and young manhood when you're rich and born with a silver spoon in your mouth. There's a theory the rich get plenty of women. I suppose they do. (My two divorces are thrown in my face. I could afford them and other men can't, and they resent it.) I hate to talk about the money, but it's a fact of life and I'm what I am because of it. I think differently from the way a poor

---

* EDITOR: Harry Craddock was brought back to Australia by his father after his mother's death and entered at King's School when he was twelve.

man does. Scott Fitzgerald. I sense this to be so but at the same time I don't like talking about it.

Once I felt guilty to have inherited so much. I've largely outgrown that. Great wealth has given me freedom. The mistakes I've made—and they're many—have been mainly of my own choice. I've never been compelled to labour at something I didn't like and to defer to anyone—people who work for my father crawl to him. All the same, having $4,000,000 doesn't leave you completely free. You tend to become a little paranoic in your relationships with others. "Does he like me or does he want something?" Once I was in a car smash and a paper headline ran: CRADDOCK SHAKEN UP. The rival Sydney morning paper wanted to tell readers that that drunken playboy Craddock had been in another scrape. I cracked to a friend: "It's an improvement on CRADDOCK SHAKEN DOWN." When I heard myself talking that way I began taking stock—I didn't want to get as alienated as the other Craddocks. I thought I could avoid the dangers and meanwhile be relatively free:

"I'll be judge, I'll be jury," said cunning old Fury.

I'm out of sympathy with the young man down from Oxford. He's a stranger whom I don't understand very well. I don't approve of him—but that's too strong. He's a rather boring, foolish young man.

I keep wanting to race ahead with my story. But Oxford was important. You could say that some of my troubles started there. King's School in my day was a philistine school—*Fortiter Et Fideliter** tells you enough. It may be better now, but I don't know because I'm a lapsed King's School Old Boy. In my day no one thought much beyond rowing, cricket, football and athletics. The interest in verse did not go much beyond the doggerel the seniors used to sing under the showers

* EDITOR: "Bravely and faithfully".

10

(cold for reasons of morality) to the tune of "The Prisoner's Song":

> *If I had a prick like a crow-bar*
> *And the balls of an old kangaroo,*
> *I'd fuck all the girls in creation*
> *And send the results to the zoo!*

Suddenly, at Oxford I found myself in the company of young men who cared about music and poetry. They accepted these things naturally and I, the impressionable young Australian feeling himself to be undereducated and even barbarous, took to them as easily as I had earlier to cricket, football and boxing. I even tried to write verse and published two small books, *Thoughts* and *William Charles Wentworth*. Some of this juvenilia was recently reprinted in a satirical weekly in Sydney—needless to say without my permission. I suppose they wanted to make me look foolish. They probably succeeded because it was poor verse, as I acknowledged in a letter to the editor (printed) informing them that whereas other youthful mistakes were forgotten, literary ones never were, and adding that I did not propose to sue for breach of my copyright.

I've tried a lot of things in my life and writing was one of them. "The trouble with you, Harry, is that you're a bad case of genius without talent!" said one of my Oxford friends. It wouldn't make a bad epitaph. I flirted with socialism, too, while remaining obstinately a rich man. Many of my generation did from the generosity of youth and because we had in Orwell's words "developed a new sort of compunction which our parents did not have, an awareness of the enormous injustice and misery of the world, and a guilt-stricken feeling that one ought to be doing something about it". I became an agnostic—and remain one—and experienced the "intolerable burden of selfhood". My verse

11

was poor, but this doesn't make me ashamed. Most young men write poor verse. How could I be affected by what this stranger, this young provincial, had written at Oxford nearly thirty years ago? He meant nothing to me. He had hungered after a girl with long legs and a voice that gave him an erection whenever he heard it over the telephone—or so one poem—verse—said. The House (Christ Church) taught me some of the civilized virtues, including tolerance. (Its war memorial lists its German dead with its English dead.) But I can't go on like this, partly because I didn't notice everything at the time and some of what I did notice I've forgotten, or confused it with something I wished, had happened or hadn't happened, but more particularly because I can't put it all here.

The search for the night parrot interests me more. I became obsessed with finding this rare bird. Something takes charge in me at times and I can't stop myself. After I opted out of the family newspaper business, the obsession was breeding stud sheep, and later it was breeding Arabs. Then I went abroad and lived in London and Italy for the best part of ten years, always having love affairs with something or another, collecting modern paintings, even trying to write novels. Back in Australia it was azaleas and then natural history. There's a long list of my obsessions. Joanna came to hate them. She didn't say much—these dark-haired women with white skins smoulder inside with an occasional splutter of sardonic wit. Once when I went to Kenya to study the "farming" of game—notably that of elephants by the Waliangulu tribe where the people could shoot a number of elephants each year under strict supervision and retain the meat and ivory—well, when I got home most of the twenty thousand azaleas had died. I admit there'd been a drought in Sydney and severe water restrictions but, none the less, I think

Joanna could have done a lot better. There was art水
water all the time on the Mona Vale property, as
told her in two letters from Kenya which she claims s
never received.

"Reynolds knew," I told her.

"I had to sack him," she said. Her moist red lower
lip seemed to hang lower than ever as she spoke. "A
week after you left."

That gave it away. She hadn't wasted any time getting rid of one of the few people in Australia who
knew anything about azaleas and hiring a fool in his
place. I suppose she'd had enough of my quirks. And
that was why she'd said no at first to accompanying me
to central Australia to look for the night parrot.

3

The notion of searching for the rare night parrot which
no trained observer has seen for over fifty years must
have been lurking in my head for a long time before
a bubble popped up into my pre-conscious and set me
in full cry. I remember I was rereading my friend C. P.
Mountford's book *Brown Men and Red Sand* one night
in 1967. There's no mention of the night parrot in it,
by the way, but something must have started it up—
perhaps references to spinifex—because I put the book
down and the resolution was firm in my mind: "I'll
look for the night parrot!"

To fill you in about the bird there's this entry in
Cayley's *What Bird Is That?*:

Night Parrot *Geopsittacus occidentalis*

Gē-o-psit'-ta-cus—Gk, *ge*, earth; Gk, *psittacos*, parrot: *oc-ci-den-tā'-lis*—L., *occidentalis*, western.

DISTRIBUTION. Restricted and scattered localities in Central Australia, northern South Australia, and inland Western Australia; probably also western Queensland and western New South Wales.

NOTES. Also called Spinifex Parrot. This extremely rare species inhabits sandstone ranges, spinifex country, and shrubby samphire flats. It is nocturnal, seeking cover in tussocks of spinifex during the day and emerging at dusk to drink and to feed on the seeds of grasses. Only rarely has the bird been kept in captivity: one was studied in the London Zoo for two months in 1867-8. The voice has been described as "a double note, loud and harsh".

NEST. A depression in the ground, usually under spinifex-grass.

EGGS. Four or five; white. Breeding-season: not recorded.

Five specimens of this small green parrot—about ten inches long and the size of an eastern rosella—are in the Australian Museum in Sydney. One of the best was taken in 1870 in the Gawler Ranges, in South Australia. I had colour photographs taken of them which would be useful to show to people when I got outback, even if the birds in death looked dull and scruffy. The feathers of stuffed birds soon lose the oily lustre they have in life. None the less, the bird was distinctive even in its parodied immortality with a greenish-yellow throat and brown arrow-shaped flecks on its breast and wings and black spots on its tail feathers. Its legs were short and pink and its toes were stout—doubtless an adaptation to life on sandy ground. You find broadened feet, for instance, in the desert larks of the Namib Desert of South-West Africa.

My studies of the night parrot led me to think that I might find it in association with spinifex (*Triodia* spp.). Before I go any further I'd better clear up a little

14

point about this spinifex or porcupine grass so that I won't have to be a pedant and continually refer to "the so-called spinifex". The genus *Spinifex* is for the most part a grass which grows on coastal sand dunes. The popularly named spinifex of the desert, spiky and formidable, belongs to another genus altogether. But spinifex is what most people call it and I'll do the same. The association of the bird with spinifex was described about forty years ago by a Western Australian ornithologist, Lawson Whitlock.

Whitlock had the tantalizing experience of almost seeing a night parrot. He was camped five or six miles west of Hermannsburg Mission, in central Australia when, about sunset, two boys arrived with a note from Mr Heinrich, the mission superintendent, asking him to come at once because he had important news about the night parrot. Whitlock walked to the mission by moonlight. "I was told that some young boys and girls playing about in the *Triodia* less than a mile from the mission had set fire to the Porcupine grass," he wrote later. "A parrot had been driven out and chased into an isolated clump, when it was again driven out, caught, cooked and eaten. Most unfortunately, it was cooked without being plucked. A search was made for the mate of the victim."

The superintendent, Mr Heinrich, heard of this and took over. The Aborigines found some tunnels going into the spinifex; the prints of what looked like birds' feet led into them. Mr Heinrich smoothed these out and then sent word to Whitlock. Next morning Whitlock, Heinrich and some natives saw fresh bird tracks at the entrance to one tunnel, and the Aborigines uprooted and overturned the spinifex clump, but found nothing.

"We searched high and low, the Aborigines vigorously prodding the adjacent *Triodia* with sticks," wrote

15

Whitlock. "We even went so far as to set fire to a small tract of *Triodia*, but all without success."

I proposed to look first for the bird in regions which had not been grazed by cattle or horses and where, I hoped, domestic cats gone bush had not reached. Feral cats have reduced the numbers of our ground-dwelling birds and smaller marsupials—and, probably, aided the extinction of some. As a consequence, I'm not a cat lover and do not share the enthusiasm of Margaret and her friends for Siamese, even if they're so pampered they never get the chance to hunt birds. At my former house on a bushland reserve I'd kept a kelpie to chase away the cats. That was before I "owned" Red, the dingo pup—I'll tell you about him later.

The fact that one bird had survived the long sea voyage and lived for two months in London led me to hope that if I found the bird I might be able to breed it for later release in areas where it would be reasonably secure. In successful breeding and seeding lay the only future for so many of the world's threatened creatures. Perhaps for man himself? A whimsical thought. But the decision to embark on a breeding programme would depend on how many birds I found. I was not trying to capture the bird for a zoo triumph, but to find it, study it, and preserve it. I stress this because as soon as the news got out I was misunderstood.

As I've found all my life, I can't keep the money business out of it—or other people can't.

First, X——, a professional ornithologist. "You can afford it," he said. "It's more newsworthy than studying lyrebirds."

"Or blue wrens," I said, smiling.

"Ah, yes, blue wrens," he said. I watched his thin lips groping for something waspish to say—like an elderly parakeet nibbling at someone's finger. But he couldn't. I spent three years on that blue wren study and I knew he couldn't fault though he wanted to . . . "rich dilettante" wouldn't wash any longer and he knew it. On the strength of the paper I'd been made a Fellow of the Royal Australian Ornithological Union and the Royal Zoological Society of New South Wales and asked to contribute to the definitive *A New Dictionary of Birds* edited by Landsborough Thomson—along with two hundred others!

"I'd thought you might have done something on silver-eyes—some work is needed there," he said.

"It's an idea," I said. "I'll do it later."

Joanna, too. I sang under the shower:

"I am not Prince Hamlet nor was meant to be . . ."

It was meaningless, but I liked the sound.

Joanna came into the bathroom. "The Craddock theme song," she said.

"I have some affinity, no doubt, with Prufrock," I said.

"What is it now?"

"The night parrot."

There was a lot of organising to do before I could start after the Grail—night parrot. I was kept busy for a month. During that time the affair of my dingo pup, Red, developed. I'd better tell the story about the dingo consecutively because it will make more sense if it's not broken up with accounts of my problems in getting the right kind of nets to trap the night parrot and other gear, my research at the Mitchell Library and at the Australian Museum and the planning of the expedition —what vehicles, how about petrol supplies, tyres, two-way radio, kerosene-operated refrigerator, cameras, food, etc.? Whom should I take with me? Where should I start? The problems were endless. Most modern exploration expeditions, including my modest ones, are romps. The biggest worries and problems are solved before you start. Adventures, said Stefansson, are a sign of incompetence.

The story of my dingo pup, Red, seems to me to be significant and to explain in some way, not quite clear to me, what happened afterwards including the shooting of R.H. at Parramatta. He has a name and you possibly remember it. I do. But it might as well be R.H.

I referred to Red as my dingo pup, but I flinch from the word "my"—he wasn't mine or anyone's. A zoologist friend had brought Red to Sydney and then found his wife wouldn't let him keep the dingo. I'd accepted him —I know now I shouldn't have. It was selfish of me.

I should explain we were living in one of the outer North Shore suburbs on the edge of a mountain gully leading to a bushland reserve. We'd chosen it hopefully for its unspoilt character.

Trouble had started fairly soon, when Red was no longer the tiny bundle of fur for the sentimental bourgeoisie to gush over—and dominate. Red, growing steadily, was soon no longer an object, an acquisition. It began on a Saturday afternoon. I had a shower and after I'd dried myself, noting that my belly was rounding out like a small cupola and shrieking that I'd neglected 5BX, I went outside. I remember telling myself I should cut down on my smoking—or even give it up.

"You'll have to get rid of that dingo before long," my neighbour Swinburne said to me across the fence the moment I appeared. He's aggressive in the way so many Australians are. "Why, he's an Asiatic wolf—"

"No one of any authority says that the dingo is an Asiatic wolf," I said. "The Curator of Mammals at the Australian Museum classifies the dingo as *Canis familiaris* variety *dingo*—that is, a variety of the common dog. Another eminent authority says it's most unlikely that the dingo is descended from the northern wolf—"

18

"I know a wolf when I see it," this classic pyknic said. (He was the managing director of a small confectionery factory.) "I don't care what some long-haired professors say—I was brought up in the bush."

As Joanna says, I can be insufferable—particularly when I'm provoked. I said: "So much for your fears of this animal attacking you—it's most unlikely as long as he continues to look on you as the *gamma* animal. Of course, you need to act like a *gamma* animal at all times."

I thought for a moment he was going to climb over the paling fence that divided our properties and throw a punch at me. (I'd been planning to replace that fence with something less hideous.)

"You be careful who you call an animal!" His big red face and neck were swelling like a frog's. I was throwing pure Lorenz and Hediger at him.

"I'm not calling you an animal," I said. "I'm just explaining how the dingo sees you. He sees me as the *alpha* animal—*alpha* is Greek for A. I'm the pack leader in his eyes. He sees my wife, Joanna, as the *beta* animal. *Beta* is B and *gamma* is C. He probably sees you and your wife and kids as *gamma* or *delta* animals. *Delta* is D. While you behave like *gamma* or *delta* animals, you'll be okay. He'll defer to you."

He seemed a little reassured—or confused, anyway.

"This *gamma* stuff," he began uncertainly. "You're sure of it, now?"

"I'll lend you a book."

"All the same, he's got pretty powerful jaws," he said, pointing to Red, who was crouching at my feet, his eyes not leaving me. The jaws were, as he said, powerful and the white shining canine teeth rather large. The head was a little too large, the prick ears a bit too thick at the roots for Red to be a really handsome dog, but there

19

was a compact power in his strong tawny chest and limbs.

"No more than a German shepherd's," I said. There were two in Mansion Road—that wasn't the name, but it will do.

"I suppose so," he said doubtfully.

"If I hadn't told you Red was a dingo you wouldn't be worrying," I said. "I could have told you Red was a mongrel."

"Are you trying to tell me I wouldn't know a dingo?" he started in belligerently.

Before I could answer his own dog, a Doberman Pinscher and a real North Shore status job, came out and began challenging Red. Both dogs raced up and down on their sides of the fence, the Pinscher growling and barking and Red just growling. (Dingoes don't bark in the wilds. When domesticated some learn to do so, but Red hadn't.) Red ran on his toes, his reddish-brown coat gleaming and white-tipped bushy tail waving erect. His gait was exciting to watch: it was smooth, effortless, and one he could maintain for hours.

"This is what I mean," he said. "Your Asiatic wolf could savage my dog to death."

"Yours is making the most noise," I said. The Pinscher was as aggressive as his master.

"Noise isn't everything," he said. "Look at that wolf-like crouching."

"Innate behaviour," I said. "Dingoes have acquired that over thousands of years of attacking emus and kangaroos. They crouch to avoid the kicks."

"So your wolf is getting ready to attack, is he?"

"Not necessarily," I said. "No more than yours is. Of course, if one dog were to invade the other's territory, then there would be a fight. But they won't invade."

"Yours could jump the fence," he said. "I've seen

20

him. He could kill my dog and clean up my fowls."

"Not into your place," I said. "He wouldn't. He knows it isn't his."

"So he's moral, is he?" he shouted. "This wild dog—"

"They're all moral, although the term is anthropomorphic. Wild dogs or domestic dogs usually won't invade another's territory."

"So you say," he said. His face was purpling. "I warn you now yours had better not. If he does I'll shoot him. The law's on my side."

On an impulse I went inside and got a hammer. I started knocking palings out of the fence.

"Hey!" he shouted. "That's my fence. And I meant what I said about shooting that Asiatic mongrel."

"Pure-bred dingo," I grunted. I was out of condition and the nails were tough. "Our fence."

I got four palings out and, as I knew would happen, the dogs kept racing past it and ignoring the chance to enter and attack. I was still dishing out Lorenz.

"It's just bluff," I said. "You can see it for yourself. They talk big. After they've said their bit, they'll knock off."

"Perhaps," he said, doubtfully.

"Call your dog out into the street," I said. "I'll call mine. They'll meet in the middle and sniff each other's anal quarters but they won't fight. There's nothing to fight about—neither lays claim to the centre of the road. Of course, the footpath is different."

"I won't risk it," he said and he called the Pinscher and went off. "You may be right and your dingo ought to be at home in your garden."

It might have sounded conciliatory to you. But there was a sting in the reference to my garden. This was during my Australian native flora period. When I bought this block I had had the house built well down the hillside and left all the trees and shrubs. I wanted

21

a native bushland garden and I had left what the other people in Mansion Road called "that rubbish" in its near natural state. I had planted some more natives—waratahs like great red Roman torches, delicately starred wax-flowers and native roses, piquantly scented boronias, flannel-flowers, subtly curving spider flowers, and a red cedar which after seven years was fifteen feet tall. This was in keeping with my newly acquired feeling for *furyu*, which is often used to describe things Japanese. It can be translated as "tasteful", but the Chinese characters convey a fuller meaning of "flowing with the wind"—the acceptance of nature, of the material itself, and the patterns it imposes. Transferring the concept to Australia, I was accepting nature and learning to appreciate the muted beauty of Australian shrubs and flowers.

The neighbours didn't approve. They all had lots of lawns and terraces and beds of perennials and annuals. They'd chopped down most of the native trees and planted exotics. They thought my garden lowered the tone of the street. And they thought the same about our unobtrusive low-line house, blending with the slim eucalypts and the sandstone outcrops. They preferred double-fronted mod. bungs.

We'd have got on a lot better if we had lived in Mansion Road during my azalea and camellia period. At our last house Joanna and I had gone in for landscaping—vistas, focus points and the rest. Or, to be honest, I had. Joanna, I realize now, had gone along with me in the first dawn tenderness of our marriage. We'd used azaleas and camellias for much of the mass planting. I'd got engrossed in azaleas, particularly, and I knew as much as most about Wilson's fifty Kurumes and I once engaged in some learned discussion in a specialist journal as to whether some experts were correct in thinking Pink Pearl (Azuma Kagami) was,

22

indeed, the progenitor of all the pink-flowered forms. In case you're wondering about the entry in *Who's Who*, we'd rarely lived at Chisholm* during our marriage. Chisholm had its charms, but you couldn't plan a *new* garden there. Its grounds were eighty years old.

Although I still like azaleas, the love affair was over by the time we moved to Mansion Road. Not everyone appreciates Australian natives. We went away for a week once and when we came back someone had dumped two tons of rubbish into our place. We had no fence at the street level and someone must have thought it was a virgin block because the house was well down the slope and hard to see from the street. Of course, he should have noticed the rather heavy concentration of native flora. He had tipped the rusting tins, galvanized iron, mattresses, etc. on a thick stand of native roses, too.

We didn't really fit into Mansion Road for a number of reasons. They tried to cultivate us at first, but we were too off-beat. Joanna and I were in our abstraction and Miro and Chagall period—our earlier Rembrandt love affair might have been accepted. There was also the car business. They all had one or two cars, but we didn't see the need when there was a good taxi and hire-car service. When they got the idea finally that we could afford a car but wouldn't have one, it struck them as un-Australian or something.

The dingo business was merely another straw, though Swinburne seemed to be trying to push it a bit further.

"Why get yourself angry?" Joanna reproached me when I went inside.

"A conformist ass!"

"You can't educate him," she said.

* EDITOR: Chisholm, Bellevue Hill, Sydney, is an outstanding example of late Gothic revival style and was built in 1851 by the Colonial Architect, Mortimer Lewis, for Alexander Vincent, merchant and grazier. Mortimer Lewis also designed Randwick Racecourse and Bronte House.

C

"I know," I said. "I was having a bit of fun."

"Whatever you call it, we'll probably have to get rid of Red," she said.

"Where?" I said.

That was the question. I wasn't giving him to the Zoo as some in Mansion Road had hinted I should. Dingoes are far-ranging, lively, intelligent creatures and it would be cruelty to confine him. And I couldn't release him in the bush now when he was a year old and without any training in hunting for himself. Normally, he would have acquired this from his mother.

I didn't see Swinburne again until the next week-end. He called me over the fence.

"What you say about that dingo might be true at present but he'll revert to type," he said. "The hunting instinct is too strong. It will be someone's chicken run eventually even if it's not mine."

"He hasn't been taught to hunt fowls—or anything else," I said. "So why should he? He's well fed."

"Primitive instincts are strong," he said.

"We don't know what his primeval instincts are," I said.

"He's a wild dog."

I said, insufferably: "Professor Konrad Lorenz, who is one of the world's greatest authorities on dogs, says that the dingo is a descendant of a domesticated dog brought here by the Aborigines. He points out that a pure-blooded dingo often has white stockings or stars and nearly always a white tip to its tail. He adds that these points are quite irregularly distributed. This, as everyone knows, is a feature never seen in wild animals but occurring frequently in all domestic animals."

"Has this foreign professor ever seen a dingo in the wilds?" he asked.

I couldn't see what his question had to do with the paraphrase I had given him, but I told him that Lorenz

24

had not been to Australia so far as I knew, but he had bred and studied dingoes.

He changed the subject abruptly.

"You seem to know all about animals and birds," he said. "Perhaps you have a cure for a crowing rooster? Mine is upsetting some of the neighbours by crowing during the night. He answers other roosters across the valley." (There were farms there.) "In a street like Mansion Road, you have to fit in."

"I think there's a way to stop your rooster," I said.

"I'd like to hear it," he said, too sweetly.

"You have to get on with people, as you say," I said, also too sweetly. "Roosters can be stopped from crowing in a very simple fashion. A rooster, as you know, has to stretch its neck to crow. I'd suggest tacking a piece of hessian over the perch, a couple of inches over his head. When he goes to stretch his neck, he'll bump the hessian and won't be able to crow."

Swinburne and his fifteen-year-old son were engaged for most of the afternoon. I must say they were thorough. It took them ten minutes to catch that White Leghorn and then they held him with his feet on the ground and measured the distance to a couple of inches over his head. They measured the hessian meticulously and then they had a conference during which they kept looking towards me. I was sowing some flannel-flower seeds. I'd gone to the near-by bushland reserve several times to observe the soil and aspect of flannel-flowers so that I could plant the seeds in the right place in my garden.

Swinburne came over to the fence finally. "I'm sorry to trouble you," he said. This was a change. "But there are several perches in the hen-house."

"The top one," I said. "He's the *alpha* animal."

They fixed it there and Swinburne asked me to come and have a beer at his place. But he hadn't changed his

25

mind much about the dingo because he and his wife started telling me about the merits of budgerigars as pets.

"Now budgerigars make marvellous pets," he said. "Our Joey is a wonderful talker."

The bird, a male pied blue, was perched on his hand and while Mrs Swinburne smiled dotingly it displayed and then, with wings down-dragging, it tried to copulate with Swinburne's big red hand.

"Isn't he quaint?" asked Mrs Swinburne. "He does that by the hour."

Poor bloody bird, I thought.

"No wonder," I said aloud.

"What do you mean?"

"Nothing," I said. "I mean it's wonderful."

"And they tell me budgerigars don't talk in the wilds," said Mrs Swinburne.

"No," I said. "Only when they're caged." I refrained from saying anything about mimicry being due to starved sexuality, to banked-up energy.

I couldn't see Mansion Road letting up on Red— Swinburne was just the official spokesman, as it were, one of the *alpha* members in the street. I knew the others were saying the same things among themselves.

They said them to me a few nights later. Mrs Fitter called. If Swinburne was an *alpha* male, she was the *alpha* female. Her father had been a drapery knight and had built the big house in which the Fitters lived with a feature window and two cars.

"I've come on behalf of the mothers of Mansion Road," she started in. She was a large dark woman with a broad hint of a moustache. "They're very frightened that ravening wild dingo will attack their children. They have to pass it on their way to school and it crouches in the gutter."

26

She was laying it on. Most children were driven to school.

"It won't attack them," I said. "He lies in the gutter because that's his territorial boundary. Like ourselves, animals are land-owners."

"And what's more he barks at them," she said, going too far.

"Dingoes don't bark," I said gently, but I was getting angry. Joanna was making signs.

"And at cars, too," she said. "I had to swerve to miss him. And he slavers at the lips."

"He has well-developed salivary glands," I said. "I assure you he won't attack anyone, but in any case the solution is simple. Your Schnauzer owns your footpath, Mrs Fitter—or thinks he does. I respect his property rights and don't walk on his footpath and we get on very well."

It wasn't tactful, but I didn't want to be.

After Mrs Fitter had left, Joanna said, "Red has been going out after cars the last couple of days."

"But not barking?"

"No," she said.

Three nights later a young policeman called. Mrs Fitter had complained that Red had killed one of her fowls.

"Did she see him?" I asked.

"No, but she is convinced it could only have been the dingo," he said.

"Well, constable, you know the legal position as well as I do," I said. I didn't like it but I had to tack a bit. "Every dog is allowed one bite—but not two. I don't admit that Red did kill the fowl. It could have been any one of the dogs in the street. And, further, Red is not necessarily a dingo. He could be a mongrel. I don't know his parentage. He was found in the outback by a friend and brought to Sydney."

He went away but was back the next night.

"Mrs Fitter says that you have admitted that the animal is a dingo," he said.

"I admit nothing," I said, tacking again. "I have called the dog a dingo without any accurate knowledge and purely in a spirit of fantasy. I wanted to indulge in a little fancy. It has been fun to think of Red as dingo."

He was a bit shaken and I went on, "I'm no expert on dingoes nor is anyone else in this street. Have you ever seen a pure-bred dingo?"

"I think so—at the Zoo—" he said, uncertainly.

"Exactly," I said. "And how do you know it was a pure one, and even if it was, would you be able to point to any dog with certainty and say 'that is a dingo' or that another was a Doberman Pinscher—"

"A Doberman what, sir?"

"Mr Swinburne's dog is a Doberman Pinscher. Mrs Fitter, on the other hand, has a Schnauzer. Of course, the two have points in common, according to the experts. I am told that a Manchester terrier is even closer in appearance to a Doberman Pinscher and that only the well-informed can pick one from the other. Now when you come to mongrels, the question of identification is much more complicated—"

There was a bit more of it. He fled in some confusion and Joanna and I rolled round the floor, helpless with laughter, and went to bed earlier. But it was getting serious. If I didn't cure Red of going out on the road, Mrs Fitter or someone else, wasn't going to swerve next time.

What I did was undiluted Lorenz. If you want to stop a dog chasing cars you have to fire a small stone at him from behind from a catapult when he is in the middle of chasing. The dog is taken by surprise; he doesn't see you do it and it seems to him like the hand of God. That is anthropomorphic, but you know what

28

I'm getting at; it's a memorable experience for the dog and usually cures him. I stayed home the next day. It took me an hour to make a catapult that worked properly and I had to practise for twenty minutes. Then I was ready. I cured Red that morning with two hits, which, I hope, were not too painful. The gutter and the street were abandoned by him. Encouraged, I decided to cure him of establishing himself on the footpath. I achieved that, too.

I knew it only won a respite for the dingo. I had to return him to the wilds.

Swinburne came home early that day.

"I see you're still insisting on keeping that Asiatic wolf," he said.

"*Canis familiaris* variety *dingo*," I corrected. "But you're wrong about keeping him. I'm returning him to the wilds."

"But they're sheep killers."

"Not where there are no sheep."

"There are sheep everywhere," he said stubbornly.

"Australia's a big place," I said. "There ought to be a place somewhere where he can live his own life. But he'll have to be taught to hunt before I can release him."

"You mean on wild animals?"

"What else?"

"You'll soon have the Fauna Protection people after you."

"Rabbits aren't protected."

"They're vermin—and so are dingoes."

They didn't give me time to put my plan into operation. I had thought that they might give Red a bait. But I couldn't believe they hated him so much. Besides, it's an offence to lay baits and they were most law-abiding in Mansion Road. They didn't poison Red. What happened was that Red went wandering off one day through the bushland reserve and a poultry farmer on the other side of the valley shot the dingo, as he was legally entitled to do.

"Sorry to hear about that dog of yours," said Swinburne later.

"But why should he go off?"

"I know a bit about dingoes," he said and his eyes were gleaming. "Most likely he followed a bitch on heat. It's a question of studying animal behaviour."

I knew then how he'd arranged it with a farmer in on the job. They were legal in Mansion Road. But I wouldn't be able to prove anything.

"It's better to keep budgerigars as pets," I said, blazing inside. "You keep them sex-starved and they'll try to fuck with your hand. It's all nice and jolly and they'll talk, too."

I was sorry afterwards for losing my temper. Swinburne, that suburban Othello, wrung the budgerigar's neck the next time it displayed on his wife's hand.

We sold the house soon afterwards. I was caught up in the search for the night parrot and, moreover, I was coming to the end of my Australian native flora period. And my Joanna period, too. Put that way it sounds as though I initiated it. The truth is we drifted to separation and both desired it. I decided I'd provide the grounds for a divorce—and a settlement, if she wanted it.

4

I'm a manic-depressive. That early autumn afternoon in 1967 when I walked down the steps of the Public Library I was definitely euphoric. I caracoled along Macquarie Street, singing to myself without moving my lips. Singing in my mind, I mean. I'm going to look for the night parrot, I'm going to look for the night parrot. I'm a buffoon and a clown and I've never grown up. I'm fifty and an amateur naturalist and amateur everything. I am always searching. For what? What do you think of what? asked Mr Apple or Appel. Watt? asked Mrs Appel. Appel it is. What do you think of what? repeated Mr Appel, elevated. Which Watt? asked Mrs Appel, scratching her nose, her el. Elevated Mr Appel said . . .

The red "Don't walk" sign flickered and I attuned the tempo of my steps to its admonitory rhythm as I crossed the street. A diamond glint of sunlight from a turning taxi jabbed at my eyes. On balmy afternoons such as this when the sun shines warmly (70°F.) and there's no wind, all my senses are hyper-acute. Lance-points of light bounce off car headlights and from footpaths; the astringent smell of new tar from roadway tingles my nostrils; a small pebble infringes through the thin soles of my shoes; a woman's perfume steals through the chambers of my mind (I turn to look after her—the calves of her legs are classically symmetrical like those of the girl from *The Mercury* who interviewed me about my expedition: a nice lass with long dark-brown hair and green-grey eyes); I'm aware of the Harbour, light-shattered, behind me because I saw it earlier that day. Teetering on staccato, black-and-white wings over Sydney Hospital, a magpie-lark voices its sharp, territorial challenge. It's late for them to be

31

breeding—so I speculate and then on impulse hail a taxi and ask the driver to drive me to Chisholm.

Inside I changed into shorts and shirt. My house-keeper, Mrs Green, poised outside my study like a cat outside a mousehole.

"It's cracking the furniture," she said. "It's too dry."

"The humidifier will take care of that."

"I hope so." Doubtfully. She went off. I'd turned the old ballroom of Chisholm into a large flight where I could study a flock of Bourke parrots (*Neophema bourki*) under central Australian climatic conditions, which an air-conditioning firm had duplicated. These small pink-bellied parrots spend much of their time in the wild state on the ground searching for the seeds of grasses and acacia trees. They are to some extent nocturnal and visit waterholes after dark or before dawn. Their habits were thus close to the elusive rare bird I was seeking. Why should a bird become crepuscular or even nocturnal? No one knows. Most likely to avoid the day's heat and predatory birds. The openness of arid lands has meant the development of cursorial habits in certain species such as the roadrunner of south-western North America, which depends on its speed of foot to run down its quick-moving lizard prey. If most of the night parrot's food was on the ground, it might come in time to lose some of its flying ability just as some New Zealand birds had done, notably the kiwis, the kakapo, the takahe, the wekas, and the Auckland Island rail.

I spent the next three hours watching the birds. Their behaviour, I reasoned, might give me a clue to where to look for the night parrot. The floor of the ballroom was strewn with brilliant red sand and planted with mulga (*Acacia aneura*) and *Triodia* (spinifex). Because there is little rain in arid regions, there's no leaching and a fine coating of oxides of iron forms on the grains of quartz and gives their characteristic rich red colour. An unromantic geologist once observed to me that when you kissed a girl your lips caressed iron oxides, the chief ingredient in rouge. I was reminded of this, inconsequently, as I looked through the large sheet of one-way glass I'd installed at the entrance. The thermometer registered 95°F. in the phytotron and most of the parrots sheltered under the grasses and spinifex; some slept; on the edge of the largest clump of spinifex two fed sluggishly. I moved the controls and the "sunlight" began to fade slowly. In the "west" my artificial sunset splashed red and yellow. I was speeding things up because I wanted to watch the birds drinking at the pool in Craddock's Folly. With the fading of the garish red-yellow light the hundred birds began chirruping excitedly and moving out from under the grasses and spinifex, their yellow-green backs and pink bellies gleaming and flashing so that they looked like so many living gems, blends of opals and pearls. I watched fascinated and several minutes passed before I realized that I wasn't observing them with the intellectual part of my brain but in a kind of waking dream. This abstraction is probably as near as I'll ever approach to mysticism or to the vision of the artist. (In eucalypt-clothed Mansion Road I'd planted a red cedar and when it began to grow I'd stare and stare at it for minutes on end.) The birds hopped, staccato-style, towards the water-hole, calling excitedly to each other. They live at an emotional level we only approach when we're drugged, drunk or in love; their metabolism is at least 10°F. higher than our own. I watched them for an hour and made notes. At the end of that time the birds moved back to the plain. I took my notes to my study and read them. They told me nothing I didn't know. But I was determined to persist. The seemingly most innocent thing could be a clue to help my quest.

About this time I sometimes questioned myself about my motives—as I had done for some years. Why was I committed to this business? Was it exhibitionism? There were easier ways. Was I deliberately courting failure? After all, the bird hadn't been seen for fifty years. Why this absurdity? I came up with no answers except the knowledge that I was deeply committed.

In extenuation of my obsession with so "useless" an objective as the night parrot I can plead that curiosity has been largely responsible for man's biological success —or alleged success—just as it has been with the primates. Experimenters have demonstrated that curiosity among young monkeys is largely responsible for their early extensive learning. I recall that at the University of Wisconsin monkeys were shown two doors, one marked with a blue card and another with a yellow card. If a monkey pushed against the door with the blue card, it opened and the monkey could look out into the laboratories for thirty seconds. Then a screen was lowered. If the monkey pushed against the door with the yellow card, the experimenter lowered a screen, denying the animal the sight of the laboratories. The monkeys all preferred the door with the blue card. Three monkeys were put to the door-opening test hour after hour, with thirty seconds between trials, until they got tired. One monkey kept on continually for nine hours, another for eleven and the third for over nineteen hours! The experimenter observed that it was unlikely the animals would have worked so long and persistently for a food reward.

Something that happened before I left Sydney may give you some idea of the intensity of my desire to find the night parrot. You've got to get really jolted to know the truth about yourself, such as when someone you love dies suddenly. Now, I've got to admit I'm a worrier over my health. I accept my good health, but

I've seen too many people get stricken down suddenly —usually by cancer. So why shouldn't it happen to me? I tell myself, "One of these days, Harry Craddock, you may start passing blood with your stools and then it will be on." My grandfather Craddock died of cancer of the bowel and so did one of my uncles. About this time I pulled the chain and the bowl flushed pink. I stared at it, only a little bit shocked but appreciating it fully and thinking I'd better see my doctor and saying, "If it's it, I'll still have time to find the night parrot!" Then I remembered I'd drunk a lot of claret the night before!

God I had rejected—couldn't accept—and could not seek. At my centre is a despair and a passion for the something I seek. Interposed between this inner core and the outside me and the world are layers upon layers, like the silken shrouds of a cocoon: my pantheistic joy in nature, my affection (if Olympian) for people, my cheerfulness which I wear as a mask to hide not only from others but from myself. Melancholy Webster—and Darwin, too—knew the agony of the skull's grin and patrician Mozart knew he couldn't win.

"With your drive and ability you could be a tremendous success in business," said my father to me the next morning. He meant Hubert Craddock and Sons Pty Ltd. This was the first time for years he'd approached the subject. We were standing together watching the Bourke parrots. I didn't answer because there was no need. His words tugged at my heart. He was my father and I loved him. He was seventy-three and went to sleep each night knowing it could be his last. He wanted me to carry on his life and I couldn't do it, even though I loved him. He made me feel selfish and he had no right to make me feel that way. He was as big a clown and as obsessional as I was. I was a bloody sight better because I didn't try to impose myself on others and manipulate them the way he did. (I'd done that a little with my wives and I'm sorry for it.)

"I've got my own Hubert Craddock and Sons Pty Ltd," I said, feeling the skin on my forehead growing tight and hearing my voice getting on edge. "See, I can step up the heat and make them dance." I moved the thermostat to 110°F. "It'll be uncomfortable for them, but I won't let them suffer for too long. And they're well looked after—well, reasonably."

You were playing at God, Harry Craddock. My mind saw the ugly concrete block in which his parrots produced his newspapers—a commercial slum by the standards of other businesses—and in my imagination I walked along those dreary duck-turd-green corridors with their hot little cubicles: "The factory," they called it on the richly carpeted executive floor. If I'd taxed my father with deliberately degrading the journalists who produced "Australia's greatest newspaper" he'd have expressed genuine surprise. Yet I knew it was deliberate, even if it was below the level of consciousness. "My personal experience is that the more uncomfortable journalists are the more they whinge and the better is the work they produce," said one proprietor once. Bad conditions and fear were important ingredients in the Craddock empire. My riches—inherited from my mother and a maiden aunt—and my freedom had been bought with this ruthless exploitation of men and their idealism.

"It's very ingenious," said my father. He is tall, like most of the Craddocks, with the lean aristocratic face they'd acquired from great-grandfather Hubert's marriage with Amelia Vincent. "This is my Hubert Craddock and Sons Pty Ltd," I said, indicating the phytotron. He hadn't understood me and I cooled quickly, as I usually do. I set the temperature at 90°F.

"Glassop will come out to see you," my father said.

Glassop was the company secretary. The family business was going public, not before time. I nodded. The trouble was my father didn't understand me and I understood him only too well. My early flirtation with socialism—he'd never understood that. In the past, I'd asked myself, had all my life been a rebellion against him? Had I, for instance, opted out of the family business because I didn't want to compete head on with him? But I don't think so. The family business didn't interest me. It was as simple as that. It might have been different if I'd never been to Oxford. My years there left me neither Australian nor English. That's not correct, but if I had never travelled and been exposed to other standards I could have slipped comfortably into the mediocrity of *The Clarion*. "A first-class English provincial newspaper," said an Englishman who didn't know who I was at a London party when I had been working on *The Observer* for a year. How right he was! I came back to Australia full of ideas.

"They're lovely birds," said my father. "There must have been about one hundred thousand of them at a water-hole in Palm Valley. They covered every tree for half a mile. One dead tree looked like coral, it was so thick with them." The starved, shut-in poet that was my father.

I had ideas once for improving the paper both in quality and commercially. In publishing you have to be half whore and half artist to be successful. Hubert Craddock and Sons Pty Ltd wasn't—and isn't—one or the other. Some of the things I suggested were brought in about ten years later and then only to meet competition. In other words, they went through the motions, not from conviction. My great-grandfather Hubert, who came to Australia in 1832, had been a son of the manse —as good a background as any for a successful politician, publisher or film-maker. Publishing and film-making are studded with their names—Sir Keith Murdoch in Australia, Henry Luce (*Life*), DeWitt Wallace (*Reader's Digest*), Arthur Rank. (Both Wallace and Luce were the sons of missionaries in China which explains their messianic approach.) Hubert Craddock had a sense of mission, a strong streak of didacticism, and a dislike of poverty which he'd experienced in England.

The Craddock empire is like the Roman Empire in its decline. The people who control it care for nothing except profits. All that slows up its inevitable collapse is the work of dedicated proconsuls, the talented journalists, most of them over forty years old, who like their craft and try to do an honest job against the pressure of management. My conscience sometimes pricks me. Here is, perhaps, a responsibility from which I ran away. My father, puzzled, once called me "Shelley". This used to infuriate me for some reason that escaped me, unless it was that it showed the bourgeois's contempt for the poet. But then Shelley could never keep his sex life straightforward; he was always importing those sister-substitutes into it. The first was Elizabeth Westbrook, brought into his marriage with Harriet; and later there was another Elizabeth. And Claire Clairmont played the role during the marriage with Mary. And he was always wanting to share his women with Hogg. I wonder if Peer Gynt might not have been more apt—if my father had to be literary. I go round problems. But, unlike Peer, always I have sought, driven by a nagging restlessness. As well as trying to write verse, I tried to write novels. I didn't have the talent—or so it seemed to me. I wasn't arrogant or single-minded enough—I knew too much or not enough.

A male Bourke was wooing a female, offering her

seeds from his beak. She took them. He circled her. She crouched and he mounted, blue-green wings shimmering in the violence of his obliterating ecstasy. My father watched. I've been anthropomorphic. We don't know if birds have consciousness the way we have. Perhaps they have none at all and they live in what in our terms is a kind of dream—one that is chaotic, disordered and episodic. But we'd be foolish not to concede that it is a dream with intense, blinding pleasure. The sexual drive, instinct, call it what you will, always puzzles me. "It's innate," says one of my professional friends. This is a form of deception, because naming it doesn't explain it any more than when primitive man gave the name of God to things he didn't understand. The sexual drive exists. But why does it exist? "So that the race perpetuates itself." But why the drive? "Those creatures which developed it survived." I give up.

"It's what I've suspected about the Bourkes," I said. "They're said to breed from August to October. I think they will breed when the food supply is optimum. It's optimum here at Bellevue Hill."

My father laughed sardonically. I observed to myself that a deprived slum dweller or old-age pensioner might have laughed at my remark.

Before leaving my father suddenly turned to me and said, "Harry, be careful."

It surprised me. "About what?"

"This parrot thing."

With my talent for harmless lying or exaggeration I've referred to myself as an amateur naturalist. It's half true, but I did a B.Sc. at Sydney University when I was thirty-five. And took my Master's later. I had planned to work for my doctorate but hadn't. I am, perhaps, too easily diverted—to breeding Arabs or azaleas or looking for rare birds. Women, too.

I took Joanna to dinner that night. She'd phoned

about some legal matter and I was feeling lonely. Over the coffee in the little Italian restaurant she said, black eyebrows arching slightly:

"I'm not going to divorce you, Harry."

"Good Lord!" I laughed.

"I mean it." With moist, red lips smiling.

"Okay," I said. "It doesn't matter one way or the other."

"I thought you wanted a divorce."

"It's of no consequence."

"But you'd like it," she said. I saw her lips shaping again to a poised smile. "You always like your own way."

"It was an idea—that's all," I said. "If you don't want a divorce, that's the end of it."

"I want to just finish. Why go through the legal nonsense."

"None at all," I said. And I meant it. When I had offered her a divorce earlier I thought that was what she wanted.

"You're taking it well," she said. "You usually want your own way."

"You're typing me—like everyone else," I said. "I don't know who and what I am, so why should anyone else?"

We went to bed afterwards. I wanted her suddenly —I am easily roused by perfume, or the toss of the head, or the gleam of an eye, or the whisper of silk or the memory that she was what the Arabs call a *kabbazah**—and she agreed quickly enough. I spent the night in her apartment.

"I suppose I've spoilt your dream, Harry," Joanna said at breakfast. "If you were free you could seek for the perfect woman and marry her."

"I abandoned that one when I was twenty," I said.

* EDITOR: Literally "a holder", an artist in love.

40

Thirty, really—when Martha died.

"You've sublimated it, that's all. Later it was a vision of a rich life for all men."

"My socialist period," I agreed.

"And now it's conservation?"

"Yes," I said and thought, Let's leave it here, please. Another entry for your diary. Scribble, scribble, eh, Mr Gibbon?

I hadn't thought about that until then. My instinct to break with Joanna had been sound if I was to go on preserving my illusions. She is too perceptive.

My concern with conservation, I realized about this time, was linked with my concern about the bomb. It was a defence against the dread that lurked in the back of my mind. A nuclear holocaust is probably inevitable, men being what they are. As a half-scientist I accept this: as a half-artist, I reject it. Extinction has been the fate of most of the species which have evolved on this earth. They died out because they were too specialized to adapt to changing conditions, or because they could not adapt quickly enough. Only half a second ago, as it were, *Homo sapiens* had been a food-gatherer and hunter. The qualities of aggressiveness and group identity he'd acquired helped him to survive. His weapons had been primitive and the race could tolerate wars. But to-day his aggressiveness threatens his survival. It could unleash a nuclear or chemical-biological war which would not only destroy man but most of the other creatures and their habitat—Earth. I doubted if he had sufficient time left to adapt, to dilute that aggressiveness. Another mirror that sneaks up on you is the one behind bars in the Bronx Zoo with the sign, "You are looking at the most dangerous animal in the world." He was loose in Vietnam, and in the Middle East and Africa—and central Australia.

Man is an experiment of evolution and probably an

41

unfortunate one. He's such a foolish animal. Probably we won't need a nuclear holocaust. We may simply destroy ourselves by irredeemably polluting our fragile planet. We are burning so much oxygen that we may eventually cook ourselves to death beneath a blanket of carbon dioxide. Natural production in the United States is only sixty per cent of consumption. If the rest of the world industrializes along her lines, we'll all frizzle. And if we should accidentally kill enough of the diatoms (which produce most of our oxygen) in the world's oceans we may even choke before we burn.

One of my small triumphs has been to teach Joanna to accept spiders. Like most women she was afraid of them. I taught her to tolerate and even enjoy a large huntsman which lived in our drawing room in Mansion Road for seven months.

I've reported my night with Joanna as truthfully and factually as possible, uninformed by hindsight. On rereading my account, I have been struck by its detachment. I flatter myself that in recording some incidents of my life I have almost perfect recall, not merely of physical sights and sounds but of my own thoughts and feelings. There are, of course, inbuilt problems. Although I am at present an inmate of a mental home, I am still essentially that same Harry Craddock you saw walking down Macquarie Street fired with the elation of his Quixotish quest—and the same Harry Craddock that on other occasions (which you've not seen yet) was plunged in melancholia. Yet, although I am essentially the same, the Harry Craddock in this mental home is a slightly larger-than-life version of the earlier one. His moods of elation are wilder, his melancholia deeper. Standing off and looking at myself, I seem at times to look like a caricature of myself. I sometimes think I have no need of L.S.D. When my senses are heightened as they are now, I live intensely.

I have been looking at the elegant lemon-scented gum in the hospital grounds with a quicksilver trunk, straight as a gun-barrel for forty feet before it pushes out the first branch . . . and then on for another thirty feet to the feathery top spread fanwise against the racing clouds. If I look too long, run my thoughts, I'll sink into nothingness and never return, merge, perhaps, into the kindly tree or the soil in which its roots probe and thrust. My mind blanked out for some time. The pounding of my heart recalled me.

I am continually distracted from this memoir, which now fascinates me, by the demands of the doctor. To appease him I throw him from time to time small snippets which I did not trouble to invent at first, such as:

I have been trying to imagine what my sister is capable of telling the world about me.

Would she tell how early in childhood she made a practice of crawling into my bed Saturday mornings to play with my genitalia and, after a while, got into the habit of treating them as if they were special toys of hers?

Would she tell the world how for many years she haunted the world of my senses with those marvellous fingers of hers, driving me to a premature and hopeless awakening? So that for a whole spasm of my life I was unable to think of beauty or pleasure except in terms of her eyes and her damnably wonderful fingers? So refurbishing my life that in place of the strange goddess who visits the imagination of every normal adolescent I could only look forward to headaches and a sister?

But those are not the things Elisabeth would tell the world about me—if someone could be found who was foolish enough to encourage her to write about me. Then what would Elisabeth write about in the articles they are threatening to buy from her? I can't for the life of me guess.

Would she tell how eagerly she joined me in every hope but always fell back when it was sorrow which struck at me?

43

Would she tell how, whenever it appeared as if I were about to make a real friend of a man or woman, she would find some reason for my not having anything to do with him or her—usually a moral reason?

I filled several more pages with nonsense. I threw them together in a pastiche of literary styles, parodying D. H. Lawrence, Proust, Ernest Hemingway, and others. I even sprinkled the salad with a little very sub-standard Joyce. I hinted at such things as the sin of the Egyptians.

The idiot took it away happily, no doubt to gloat over in his study. I suppose it was a form of intellectual snobbery to have served him such a pot-pourri—I'm tired of trying to be reasonable and to make excuses for other people.

These and earlier snippets clearly delighted him, the more so because he knows I have a sister. But he forbears to question me about her although the weak hams of his mind exclaim "Still harping on his sister!" There is, of course, no rapport between us. I do not dislike him—the word is too strong. In his jargon I am resisting his analysis. I'm indifferent to his amateur probings and attempt to remake me in terms of his Rotarian insights. "I want you to relate to others."

I suppose our friend is looking for sibling jealousy. No doubt it existed, but not unduly. I was the second and fêted child—the longed-for son. My babyhood illness also helped to ensure my privileged treatment. But Margaret didn't resent my coming. I'm sure of that. On the contrary, she mothered me. And incest? I can't recall a single thing except that once Margaret and a friend and I showed each other our genitals in the harness room at Chisholm. Theirs (like mine) had no hair and I thought they looked ugly, very large, with red lips. Even on babies they look that way now. But not, of course, on mature women. I love them. I owe that to Modigliani, I think.

44

I never did find out until years later why my mother was able to take us abroad after she separated from my father; I used to puzzle over that when I was at King's because I'd read about other divorces in *Truth*—about custody and all that.

The day after I'd slept with Joanna I rang her flat. "Come to central Australia with me," I urged.

She burst out laughing. "You're incorrigible, Harry!" She paused. "No, it might all start again. I'm free now."

I argued, but I knew what she meant. We were both free but could enslave each other. I cannot live without women. I can go off the deep end over a woman as readily as I can over other things. Joanna fascinated me, even after five years, but, as I recognized in my saner moments, she was too sentient for the health of my ego-ideal. This wasn't one of my saner moments.

"It'd be fun," I pleaded. "You'd enjoy yourself and I promise not to talk night parrots all the time."

After some more exchanges she said she'd think about it. I hung up and dashed into town to pick up some mist nets. I needed to be able to use them expertly before I went to the Centre.

The paper work was growing about this time. I'd have to travel through several Aboriginal reserves and permits were necessaary. Also I had to pass through the Giles Weather Station on the edge of the Gibson Desert and I'd need permission from the Weapons Research Settlement. I was writing and phoning regularly to Ted Summers in Alice Springs, who took parties on safari into the Centre and who was supplying the Land-Rovers for the job. I realized I was drowning in detail. I needed a capable secretary. I put an advertisement in the morning papers.

Over the week-end I tried out the mist nets at Windsor. Mist nets, so thin as to be almost invisible, to catch low-flying birds were developed over three hundred years ago by the Japanese. The West began using them for bird-banding in 1947. My twelve nets were each forty feet long and stood nine feet, with a mesh of one and a quarter inches. Four cross strands horizontally supported the net when it was strung between two poles. At each cord there was a trailing pocket. Birds hit the net and tumbled into the pockets.

At this stage I planned to set these nets round water-holes before sunset. What I wanted now was practice in releasing captured birds swifty without harm to bird or net. My bird-banding friends had given me some coaching, but there's no substitute for experience. At first I had been too timid. Fear of hurting a bird could cause it to suffer through being handled too long. The first trapped bird I released under the watchful eyes of a friend—a silver-eye—pulsed with fright in my hand until I feared it would die. "Firm but gentle does it," he urged. I did better later. But I still had some way to go so I practised all the week-end, setting the nets before dawn and dusk and visiting regularly all four nets I'd rigged. In this way birds did not have time to entangle themselves badly. Some could even be lifted out of the pockets. Gaining skill on that Sunday afternoon, I left four eastern silver-eyes long enough to get well tangled before releasing them. There's a correct drill—I won't bore you with it—and I managed well enough. I returned to Chisholm reasonably content. But I had still to choose the personnel. I wanted to keep the party a small one for greater mobility. I needed a good orni-thologist and also someone who could collect reptile specimens for the Australian Museum. Although my major objective was the night parrot, it would be a shame not to make the most of studying some of the other creatures of the Centre.

When I'd turned the large ballroom over to the Bourke parrots I had to store some of my Australian paintings. This began to worry me. I'm selfish in many things, but it seemed wrong to put my Dobells, Drysdales, Olsens, Frenches and the rest where no one could enjoy them. I thought of presenting some to the National Gallery. Then I had a better idea. I put them up for auction and, as I'd expected, they brought good prices. I'd paid one hundred pounds for the Dobell and it brought six thousand dollars. My impulse was to send a cheque for that amount to the artist. But I hesitated—he might be insulted. Instead, I sent all the artists a cheque for twenty per cent of what I had received and then wrote to the newspapers saying what I'd done and expressing a wish that other sellers would do the same.

Few other sellers did the same. But I was also attacked by people who said I was trying to win praise at little cost because I was a millionaire. I got so carried away that I even briefed a leading silk to see what changes would need to be made in the Copyright Act so that artists would be entitled to a royalty of ten to twenty per cent on all sales of their work, and I sent a printed submission on the scheme to all Senators and Members of Parliament. Tilting at this windmill diverted some of my energies from my main objective, the night parrot. (All my life I've been inclined to go off on tangents.) Although I didn't know it at the time, other things were conspiring to keep me in Sydney.

Soon after the news was out that I was going to central Australia I was heartened to receive letters from three people claiming to have seen the night parrot. (I got over thirty letters, but some were too vague to be immediately useful, some were patently mistaken, and a

47

few were from the lunatic fringe.) The first letter was from a man four hundred miles west of Alice Springs whom I'd met and knew to be an accurate observer. "I saw a pair at dawn at a water-hole about a year ago," he wrote. "There's no doubt about it. I've studied the photograph you sent me and I know all the parrots in this area." The other letters come from White Cliffs in New South Wales and Eyre's Peninsula in South Australia. I knew the reputation of the first to be that of a sound man. The three letters were consistent—the bird's range in the past had been enormous, even though it was always scarce. It had been all through the vast semi-arid interior wherever there was spinifex. Then I got another letter, from Western Australia, where the writer had seen the birds late last year,* not in spinifex country, but among another seeding plant.

A pattern was emerging. The birds were seen either singly or in pairs. I suspected a pair bond throughout the year, even when they were not breeding.

I've not been quite frank about my concern with painters. As is usually the case in my life, there was a woman mixed up in it—a short-lived infatuation after my separation from Joanna. My interest in the welfare of painters was genuine enough, but Sadie's irritation when one of her pictures was sold for two thousand dollars—she'd sold it for a hundred—was the catalyst. Sadie was my typical Dark Lady type—I don't go for blondes. But Sadie doesn't really belong to this story.

At this time I was on the crest. I had a ferocious capacity for work; I needed only a few hours sleep at night. Experience has taught me that when I was seemingly on the crest, I was in fact descending swiftly into the trough of depression. When you are on a peak—or a seeming peak—you tend to forget that you are going to plunge into the bleak depths before too long. Your

* EDITOR: 1966.

48

mood is too elated to admit such truths. So I worked feverishly on the infinity of things to be done and never felt tired, even at two o'clock in the morning when common sense would sometimes drive me to bed where I'd not go to sleep for a couple of hours. One night I got out of bed three times to make notes of things I had to do. My brain seemed lit up at such times as with white flashes of light. It was near enough to insomnia. One night I did not go to sleep until about five in the morning. I would not have been quite so euphoric if I'd known what lay ahead.

My reading has always been eclectic—undisciplined, if you insist. But I realize now that it has been part of the pattern of my living, of the quest on which I have been engaged all my life. Today I was rereading *Principles of Psychology* by William James and came upon this famous passage:

> I am often confronted by the necessity of standing by one of my empirical selves and relinquishing the rest. Not that I would not, if I could, be both handsome and fat and well dressed, and a great athlete, and make a million a year, be a wit, a *bon-vivant*, and a lady-killer, as well as a philosopher; a philanthropist, statesman, warrior, and African explorer, as well as a "tone-poet" and saint. But the thing is simply impossible. The millionaire's work would run counter to the saint's; the *bon-vivant* and the philanthropist would trip each other up; the philosopher and the lady-killer could not well keep house in the same tenement of clay. . . . To make any one of them actual, the rest must more or less be suppressed. . . . So the seeker of his truest, strongest, deepest self must review the list carefully, and pick out the one on which to stake his salvation.

His words struck me with particular force. My mistake, it seems to me, is that I have never stood by one of my empirical selves and relinquished the rest.

These thoughts have been provoked by a visit yesterday from Joanna. Just before she left she asked me if there was anything I wanted.

"Yes, Rousseau's *Confessions*."

"I didn't know you were an admirer of his."

"One of the great autobiographists."

She looked at me shrewdly.

"What are you up to, Harry?"

"What do you mean?"

"You're incorrigible," she said. She laughed quietly. "Dr Sullivan says you're making good progress."

"That's nice to know," I said. "Well, nice for him."

She started to bubble with laughter. "I know you're up to something, Harry. You haven't changed a bit."

Once I would have shared my joke with her but not this time.

"Sullivan's a fool," I said.

"He's trying to help."

"I don't want to be helped," I said. "I killed that man and should be punished."

She put a brown-paper-wrapped parcel on my desk. "Don't lose it, Harry."

After she'd gone I started to read her journal, which she'd brought at my request. The entries I wanted to see particularly were the ones about the time I'd started on the quest for the night parrot. In that decision of mine and the events that followed lay something I was seeking. When I married Joanna I'd been surprised to find she kept a diary. It's a measure of my insensitivity to others that she couldn't tell me for some months. She'd thought I'd laugh. I didn't, but I'd been unable to imagine that she would keep one. I couldn't imagine myself keeping a diary and so I'd been unable to think that someone else might do so.

After I'd finished reading her diary, I saw that I could incorporate some excerpts in my narrative, provided I inserted additions or corrections of fact when necessary. In this way, I'd save some work and be released from some of the inevitable boredom of narration. There's a more important reason. Writing of past events, I tend to telescope them—I cannot give you the day-by-day immediacy of Joanna's journal. Moreover, I'm trying to tell the truth and, even when your vanity is not involved, human memory is fallible. I remember that a famous biographer said that the more detailed an account of an event was, the more accurate it was liable to be. He added that the closer the account to the event the greater was the accuracy.* On this last score Joanna's journal would appear to be more accurate than my version recollected much later.

5

JOANNA'S JOURNAL

5th April 1967. This is my first entry for three days. We have been looking for Red until late at night. I thought Harry might do something violent to them when he found out. Instead he put the house on the market. We are going to Chisholm. Or so Harry says, but I think he will be going alone. The significance of his choice of Chisholm, which had been his mother's family home, does not escape me. Harry is going home, back to his world which he has never quite left. It's too dramatic to say our marriage is breaking up—we're drifting apart, amicably.

* EDITOR: John A. Garraty in *The Nature of Biography* (Cape, London, 1958).

Tom Freedman was here tonight. He wants Harry to join the Liberal Reform Group.

"No," said Harry. "I don't like to join anything in which I can't take an active part."

"Your name would help us," Tom said.

Harry laughed. "You want a respectable image, but I'm not respectable—or even respected by the respectable middle class you want to impress."

"We want more than middle-class votes. We want an alternative party."

Harry was not to be persuaded. He said later that night, "I didn't want to get mixed up in it. You know me, I can't do anything by halves. I like some of their policy—opposition to the Vietnam commitment—but to hell with their talk of universal conscription." He was a long time getting to sleep. The dirty, cowardly Australian commitment in Vietnam distresses him although he rarely speaks of it. He won't discuss it. It's as though he's ashamed, not of failing to declare publicly his opposition, but of an earlier fancied betrayal. Harry blames himself for not persisting in trying to make *The Clarion* a great liberal newspaper. For all his shrewdness, he is often naïve. He couldn't have won. The family, the family friends, the advertisers, the Establishment, if you like, would have licked him. I tried several times to make him see it but I couldn't convince him. He bears this burden of guilt. His obsession with conservation is an expression of his concern over a world where men are heading for nuclear destruction. He affects not to worry. "A year, perhaps five or ten," he said recently at a party. "And then. But what does it matter? Ninety-nine per cent of the species that have lived on this earth have become extinct. If man can't channel his aggressive instincts quickly enough then he is unfit to survive."

52

"Social Darwinism," sneered a young anthropology tutor.*

"Giving it a label won't alter it," said Harry.

6th April 1967. It's over with us. I've known it for sometime. I accept it. I disappoint Harry which means that the real Joanna Craddock isn't the illusory one he thought he was marrying. People have been out to look at the house all day and Harry is ill-tempered. Then there was the girl from *The Mercury*. Having been one himself, he's wary of journalists. "If you want to, you can make anyone look a fool," he said after he hung up. "Why see her then?" "If you don't give an interview you've had it, too, if they want to be smart. They have you either way."

She got an interview. She'd done her homework and knew something about the night parrot. Harry warmed to her. He can be charming when he's at ease. I'm quite sure he turned the poor girl's head. He has a flair for dress. Mod with taste. And handsome with it, too. Someone once twitted Harry. "You can dress well if you have the money," he said. "Italian shoes and ties. And Savile Row." "You don't need money but you need courage," Harry retorted. And that voice which can charm me still had the lass quite bewitched. And he was generous, too, feeding the story to her in little snippets like a parent bird with a fledgling. Her little bill gaped greedily—Harry has a gift for the telling phrase. He's generous but like other rich people, sometimes suspicious. Afterwards he wondered if he'd said too much, but I thought the girl would write an honest and probably a good piece. "I'll read the tricky bits about the night parrot back to you," she had said when leaving. She was a tall, leggy girl with shoulder-length

* H. CRADDOCK: It was no such thing, but I saw no point in arguing with him.

53

hair which got mixed up with her pen while she scribbled.

My diary entries often seem to be mainly about Harry. That's the trouble. He engulfs you.

8th April 1967. Margaret came out for dinner last night. She still tries to dominate Harry—the elder-sister role she played forty years ago. At fifty-three she's well preserved and looks a good ten years younger. She was quite a beauty and the father's darling. She said the bright—right—things. I notice an asperity creeps in whenever I discuss Margaret. She was excited about something, like a child with a secret she wants to unburden. Her hazel eyes—her best feature—would gleam in the most lively, innocent fashion and then the lids of the sophisticated woman of fashion would veil them. Harry seemed to notice nothing. His sister amuses him —interests him like one of his blue wrens. He's not quite sure what she'll say or do next. "But then, Margaret is a tiercel," he observed once. A tiercel is, of course, the female falcon, one-third bigger than the male, but I'm not sure what he meant.

"How could you stand this dreadful suburban street so long?" she asked after dinner. "My God, it's terrible!"

"We wanted to grow Australian native plants."

"You could have done it at Chisholm."

Harry wouldn't be drawn. "It is terrible and we're leaving." He started rolling a cigarette—something he started doing during the last month. He'd bought a machine for the purpose.

Margaret started to laugh when he shut the case and the first cigarette popped out. "Grandfather had one like that. He started using it after Grandmother died. It gave him something to do with his hands."

"It's the same machine," Harry said. One of his jokes.

"It's n—," she began and stopped. "I have some

54

documents I'd like you to witness, Harry. May I bring them out in a day or so?"

"If I'm—we're—still here," he said. He walked out on the terrace. "I'd like to try moving that red cedar." He pointed. Harry had planted it when we first bought the house and it stood fifteen feet high. "We might get away with it but they tell me it would probably die. We'd better leave it."

"*Toona australis*," he said softly to himself. "*Cedrela australis*." *Cedrela* was the earlier generic name. Harry is a pedant sometimes.

I couldn't sleep after Margaret left. About two thirty in a half-sleep I heard those ludicrous roosters crowing across the valley, quite faintly at first, and then, as my senses grew acuter, they seemed quite loud. They angered me. At perhaps the same farmhouse where the higher-pitched one challenged in his male arrogance, Red had trotted trustingly into the searing blast of a yokel's shot-gun. The greed and cruelty burns me. Ten or twenty dollars changing hands in a wink-sealed deal.

I'm surprised Harry takes it so calmly. He took his revenge on Swinburne. A deadly remark, I admit, but I'd have liked a little violence. It's bottled up in me now and I couldn't get off to sleep last night. Four o'clock came before I slept.

9th April 1967. Sunday night. Harry is depressed. He asks too much of himself, sets too high a standard, and so inevitably he exhausts himself. Harry has accomplished a lot; professional ornithologists respect him. He's his own worst taskmaster. That's the superficial view, anyway. I think it goes deeper. Perhaps it's the tragedy of his second marriage. It hurt Harry terribly at the time. He felt he had failed, that he could have averted Martha's suicide. No one could.

He rarely talks about his childhood—"I have a shock-

55

ing memory," he said once. "Margaret, now, she remembers everything. This, perhaps, accounts for her dullness."

Some young man rang tonight and gabbled out his gratitude to me. A conscientious objector. Learnt that Harry has been giving money to some group so they can get legal advice. Harry shrugged it off when I passed on the message when he came home.

"Oh, I sent him on to Armitage," he said. "I'm getting Armitage to screen appeals for help." He put on his glasses and began reading his mail. "Didn't I tell you? You get too emotionally involved otherwise—wives who've been deserted, young couples who can't raise the deposit, pensioners, and the rest." With an apologetic smile he added after a pause, "Cowardly, perhaps, or self-preservation. I've got to channel my energies at my age. Fifty. I think if I could start again I might have gone in for . . ."

He didn't finish.

Was it medical research? But there had always been that animal thing from the time of the small boy who made natural history collections.

Fortunately I'm not tortured by the Protestant ethic the way Harry is. I'm content to drift along in a moral vacuum—or have been since I met Harry. Now that it's over I might take up my painting. Years ago—when I was thirteen—my father said to me I had a great talent for painting and could accomplish much. "I haven't the dedication, daddy," I said. Even then I knew my limitations.

I was tempted to write earlier that Harry was on the verge of falling in love. I've noticed that falling in love doesn't just happen, but is preceded by a sustained period of unhappiness. So is religious conversion. Harry has been depressed for some days. Perhaps Harry has fallen in love symbolically—in his quixotic quest for the night parrot? Or perhaps it is Harry's night journey in the belly of the whale? Harry wouldn't go to Nineveh, that great city, and cry against it—or so he believes in his guilt-heavy soul—and, usurping God, creates his whale, the sojourn in the ancient pre-Cambrian sea of Australia's centre. Harry has taken many ships to Tarshish.

With growing depression, Harry becomes increasingly irritable. He blew up when Dalgety's rang to say there'd been a hold-up with the mist nets, which had been off-loaded at Fremantle. "This damned country!" His dislike of Australia grows daily. Harry's outburst is linked with his contempt for Australian materialism. Although he'd be surprised if he heard me say it, Harry's "father image" is probably Captain John Piper, that "Prince of Australia" as his contemporaries called him. He was certainly an oddity among the great predators of the Rum Fleet, earning the praise of the rebel Joseph Holt for his mild rule as Governor on Norfolk Island, and dying a comparatively poor man because, some said, "he lacked business sense and the ability to resist spongers . . . too noble minded to desire to make a fortune from the labour of the settler, the plunder of the soldier, or the sweat of the convict's brow". Is it significant that John Piper bred horses at Bathurst—as Harry did a hundred years later? Admittedly, some of Harry's ancestor worship is a defence against those at Bathurst—and elsewhere—who thought he was a "Pommy". "I'm a fifth-generation Australian," Harry will say when he is baited for allegedly un-Australian attitudes, "and I'm tired of having to be a pioneer."

I was amused at the time—and laugh now as I recall Harry's assertion at a dinner party one night that the quarters of the Australian Coat of Arms should be a home (not house), a Holden, a motor lawnmower, and a Jno. Baker castrating knife (for Australian wives).

Harry is usually good-tempered but in his present mood he can explode suddenly—and subside quickly with instant apologies. Once just after we were married I was combing my hair and he came up behind me. I said, pointing in the glass, "We look just like brother and sister." (There was a similarity in our features; I speculate that there's some inbreeding among the older Australian families. Probably there's even a connexion between our two families. Such things don't interest me, but some of my aunts have it by heart to four or five generations.) Harry said nothing, but there was no mistaking his anger.

Harry's error, if it is one, is to think other men are as rational as he is. The case for conservation is obvious to him and he's bewildered because others do not see the obvious.

10th April 1967. Harry came home tonight with plaster on his nose! He'd had the septum of his nose pierced.

"Giles did it," he explained grinning. "So he could fit bones through his nose and get on side with the Aborigines. I thought I'd better do the same."

Is he serious? Or is this one of his jokes?

A combined British Services expedition has been in the Centre since February. Sponsored by the Royal Geographical Society, it will test methods of desert survival—and look for the night parrot. Harry affects not to be concerned. "Good luck to them," he was quoted as saying in *The Clarion*. "All that matters is that someone finds the night parrot." And he told me, "There are plenty of other things to seek in the Centre." Harry is not merely being "sporting"—a natural hazard of his background. None the less, he is worried and he'd be less than human if he wasn't. The expedition has been west of Alice Springs and returns to Adelaide next month.

58

Tom Drake is keen to join Harry's expedition. I admit I don't know him well, but I don't care for this young man. Odd I should write that, because he's thirty-two and only four years younger than I am. It's as though I'm seeing things through Harry's eyes. Tom rang and Harry ended by asking him out for dinner.

"I suppose I'd better let him come," Harry said, frowning, after he'd hung up. "But you can move easier and faster when you don't have to consider others."

"Consider Tom?"

"He wants to help find *Geopsittacus occidentalis* but he also wants to study other birds."

"Don't take him then," I said.

"I made him a half-promise," said Harry. "It's a big chance for him."

Tom is one of Harry's "lame ducks"—one of many he's helped either professionally or with money. He arrived about six thirty—tallish, thick-shouldered, with close-cropped hair, more like an Olympic swimmer than my idea of a university zoologist. He stood in the drawing room, looking round and taking everything in, like a dealer in second-hand furniture, I thought, or perhaps I was ready to look for offence. And goggling with suburban contempt at Harry's alabaster eggs!

"Nice house you've got here," he said. His lower-middle-class origins showed. "It's a wonder you can bear to sell it."

I wasn't prepared to tell him the reasons.

"Harry's in the garden," I said. "He'll be in shortly. He's trying to move a young cedar tree to Chisholm."

"He's a man of parts." He walked over to the french windows. His face is strangely mask-like, even when he smiles. "I was born in this suburb—not in this posh part. In Sydney Street. My father was a railway shunter."

Was I expected to feel sorry for him? Or was he being aggressively assertive? I'm more interested in people than in their social backgrounds—though I suppose few people escape them.

"What started you on zoology?" I asked.

"It looked a soft way of making a living," with a shrug of wide shoulders. "I had to make a living." Unsaid was, "Unlike Harry."

He could play it close to his chest, if he wished, but I could think of more pleasant companions on a trip to central Australia. My father used to say that the best way of putting a finish to even the best of friendships was for two people to be thrown closely together for a few weeks on a holiday. But nothing I might say will influence Harry.

Harry came in then. We had more drinks and then dinner. The conversation was professionally ornithological. Tom showed himself in a better light when he became absorbed in a subject and forgot himself.

I had some packing to do so I excused myself and left them to it until it was time to serve coffee.

"He'll be useful—he's a good ornithologist and besides it would be selfish for me not to take him," Harry said after Tom had left.

"Have you agreed then?"

"Yes, but he's to let me know. Some question of getting leave."

That struck me as odd after Tom's earlier keenness to go.

"And he wants to call it the Craddock and Drake Expedition."

"That's rough," I said.

"He's just ambitious."

I didn't argue. We're going our own ways and I've got to let up on trying to protect Harry.

"What about you?" Harry asked suddenly. "Will you come to central Australia with me? You'd enjoy it."

I was tempted but said firmly that I couldn't. I had to let go.

11th April 1967. Harry suddenly in high spirits today. A dealer in New Orleans has sent him a veritable clutch of alabaster eggs—twenty Victorian alabaster eggs—each about the size of a hen's egg but elliptical in shape. They were in soft tints of pink, cerulean blue, lilac, turquoise, champagne, ivory and many other shades. One was a lovely pale pink with a smoky veining. Another was a declamatory shocking pink. All, too, had "feel" as well as eye appeal and were cool to the touch. Most had been made in Italy, Harry said. He spent the whole afternoon arranging the acquisitions with the thousands he owns in cabinets and on tables.

When things are no longer utilitarian they become objects for collectors. Thus vintage cars, steam engines —and Victorian alabaster eggs. For Victorian upper-class women alabaster eggs were mainly utilitarian. When visitors knocked at the front door, Great-Grandmother Macleay, I was told, would wash her hands and then walk to the front door clutching an alabaster egg in both soft white hands. By the time she got there the egg would have drawn off the heat from her hands and she'd greet her visitors with cool long fingers! The egg she'd put down on a table before doing so.

I mentioned this to Harry and he said, fondling a moss-agate-coloured egg, "I think they had something!"

This egg was the pick of the collection; its filmy veining evoked spiral nebulae, of vast clouds of swirling interstellar gas, of luminous hot blue stars, a universe held in your hand.

14th April 1967. No entries for several days. The prosaic, trivial routine savagely broken. Harry is out of danger. It was only chance I found him in time. . . .

6

Joanna's Tolstoyan gesture of giving me her journal to read has interrupted my narrative and introduced a new perspective, as it were. I write now with her eyes as well as my own. Why did she give me her diary?* To help me? To curb me? I've reproduced some of her entries in this narrative with, I assure you, no censorship by myself. But I see no reason why I should reproduce them beyond the break I've made on 14th April. She is entitled to her false interpretation of the events of that evening, but I'm not obliged to reproduce it here. Who tells the truth, anyway?

The glass in the window is flawed and the silvery, slim trunk of the lemon-scented gum is refracted as though I'm looking at it through water. It bends sharply at an angle of 120 degrees. You've observed that Joanna wished I'd taken a more severe revenge on Swinburne. . . . That classic pyknic, as aggressive as a game-cock, strutted into Armitage's office when he was phoned for.

"Sit down, Jim," says Armitage. (I didn't know what was Swinburne's Christian name until Armitage told me.)

Swinburne all smiles.

"Some organization is involved, as you can realize, Jim," says Armitage, "now that we've taken over."

"Of course," says Swinburne, not suspecting anything. "I've been giving it some thought. You can rely on me to co-operate in every way with the new board."

"Thank you, Jim. We appreciate that. That will make it easier . . ." The slow pause. Armitage, the tool, the hatchet man. My creature to buy out the small con-

---

* EDITOR: There is a contradiction here. Earlier Harry Craddock said that he asked her for her diary.

62

fectionery factory of which Swinburne was managing director. "Major re-organization is needed to put this company on its feet. Not your fault, Jim, but it's run down. We need first of all, a young team." More exchanges and slow realization by Swinburne that he is being sacked, all very gentlemanly, with lavish severance pay. He takes it well, but he is broken. His assurance is gone. "I've always given every satisfaction . . . built this business up from scratch . . . the former board was always well satisfied . . . I turned down several attractive offers." The voice is quavering and the eyes glassy. He may recover and because he's a good man get another position, but he's no safer there. Another Armitage is there again with gentle words.

I saw Swinburne in Pitt Street not long ago. I scarcely recognized him. He looked shrunken—he'd lost about three stone, I'd say. And he looked toothless but wasn't. Meeting me, he assumed what I'd call a subordinate posture. By now I think he knew I'd been responsible. His manner was mousy. (A subordinate mouse, when approached by a dominant one, rears up on its hind legs, raises a foreleg, closes it eyes and draws back its head.)

I said, "Shot any dingoes lately?" and walked on while he pleaded with me.*

I couldn't shoot the farmer who had shot Red, which was the first idea that occurred. I spent a lot of time pondering on what would be a fair revenge. I wanted to punish him, but not his wife and children, so any economic retribution was out. I had thought of spraying one of his crops with a defoliant—after all, he prob-

* EDITOR: These are presumably the incidents which the psychiatrist claimed were "sheer phantasy". H. F. Armitage, company director and business associate of Harry Craddock, refused to answer any questions. Nor would Swinburne when I finally tracked him down in the small business where he was company secretary. As my main interest was in the expedition to central Australia, I did not pursue my inquiries.

ably supported the war in Vietnam. You could do this easily from an aircraft. But that would have penalised his family. The Cessna turned over the eucalypt gorge and we came in low in the run towards the farm. I'd picked a large lettuce patch well away from the house. I pressed the button and the weedicide (what was it?) rushed out behind the plane in a widening V and settled down slowly, irrevocably towards the gleaming green hearts. Only, of course, it never happened at all. It would have been so easy that way. I racked my brains for hours seeking the precise and equitable punishment. I even toyed, only momentarily, with the thought that I might import a few dingoes and train them to attack his fowls and a few sheep. But again this would affect his family and, moreover, the dingoes would probably be killed. No good. I could have waylaid him and horsewhipped him but found the idea unpleasant. Finally, I had to put it aside.

7

Freedom, even in so simple a matter as the narration of events, is difficult. I write now with Joanna, as it were, leaning over my shoulder. But it goes further. I am myself, but today I caught sight of myself in a mirror. That's badly put, but Harry Craddock—or one Harry Craddock—caught a glimpse of a stranger called Harry Craddock. The sight startled the Harry Craddock who observed it. The man in the mirror looked like my father, Sir Charles Craddock. Basic bone structures emerge with age. Your identity, heredity, life pattern are perhaps something you can't evade. Mirrors in shop windows are always lurking in ambush to confront you with the truth about yourself. When you look in your own mirror your mind remakes the image to present the one you want to see—you make an acceptable compromise between reality and fantasy. That's why most of us don't like photographs of ourselves. I don't even like the ones I take of myself.

I wish to clear up a point here. Joanna said I was coming to hate Australia. Like other cosmopolitan Australians I have a love-hatred relationship with my own land. Because we've lived elsewhere we see it with more detachment. When I'm living in Italy a time comes when I start wanting to return to Australia—and when I'm in Australia it works the other way. When I was younger I used to get annoyed when they referred to me as "the expatriate something or other". We Australians take it as a deep insult if any Australian prefers to live anywhere else, even temporarily. I am interested that I wrote "we Australians". When Jessica and I came back from living in Europe we used to think of Australians as "they" for several years. Even now I sometimes use the term.

The agony of Vietnam, as Joanna surmised, was like a jagged flake in my heart. In Sydney before I went to central Australia I pushed my thoughts away, recalling how we'd sorrowed over Spain in the thirties, and hoped the agony would end so that I'd no longer feel shamefaced.

To return to my memoir: I'd advertised for a secretary—too much was piling up and I'd fresh troubles. The museums couldn't spare anyone to collect reptiles. Among the first who answered my advertisement was the lass who'd interviewed me for a newspaper article a few weeks earlier. I was surprised. I wasn't vain enough to think her bosses were sending her along to spy on me.

I wasn't worth their shot—I didn't rock the boat enough for them to worry about. Still I was careful when she came to Chisholm. I hadn't taken much notice of her when she'd interviewed me, a mini-skirted lass with elegant legs—I searched my mind for an animal simile, perhaps an impala—and undisciplined brown hair. I saw now a striking but not beautiful face—the slightly aquiline nose was too long. She had brilliant blue-green eyes and well-moulded lips.

"You're serious about wanting this job?"

She nodded.

"What grading are you on?"

"B plus."

"I wasn't planning to pay as much," I said. B plus was probably over $100 a week.

"I know."

"I could pay it, though," I said.

"I won't take it." Her teeth were largish, gleamingly white.

"That's for me to decide. You'd probably be worth it. But the job is a dull one."

"Let me decide that."

"You're an independent type."

She smiled. She was about twenty-seven. The legs, I decided, were those of the lovely and rare white oryx of the Rub' al-Khali of Arabia and perhaps the original for all those stories of unicorns whose fierceness could only be tamed by the touch of a virgin.

"You're independent, too," she said. Her voice was well modulated with little hills and dales. She stood up, suddenly. "You have an impulse to look for the night parrot. Let me be impulsive, too, and work for you."

"All right," I said. I realized then that I didn't know her name.

"Elizabeth Trumbull. T-r-u-m-b-u-l-l."

"One hundred and ten dollars a week," I said. "If

you're any good—and I'm sure you are—you're worth that. If you want to write anything about the expedition it will be okay, but clear it with me first. I have a contract with *The Times* and *The Clarion*."

"I don't think I want to write anything," Elizabeth said. "I don't see why you should pay me one hundred and ten dollars—"

"There are no strings."

She blushed.

"Do you know anything about ornithology?"

"Not much," she said. "I have some interest, though." She looked at me for several seconds before adding, "I have a science degree."

"That is handy." I meant it. I was playing my father role—she was only five years or so older than my daughter, Rosemary. Something clicked as soon as she mentioned her science degree. I have a bad habit of organizing people's lives and putting them to work for me. Elizabeth's science degree and intelligence solved one of my problems. She could collect reptile specimens with some help from the men members of the expedition. It'd be necessary for her to take a crash course in preparing specimens. She was ready to start work immediately so I set her to work dealing with some of the piled up correspondence. I said nothing about the reptile chore—that would have to wait until she'd settled in a little.

I went up to the ballroom to spend an hour with the Bourke parrots. Three electricians were installing blue lights. When I was in New Zealand the director of one of the zoos had shown me his successful experiments in studying nocturnal kiwis under mild blue lighting. The birds were not upset by it and carried on normally while being clearly visible. "I assume they think it's moonlight," he said. Later when I'd returned home it had struck me I could try blue lights round water-holes in

67

the Centre and for a dry run I was going to test it on the Bourkes. The electricians, solid, practical chaps, choked back slightly indulgent smiles when I discussed some of the problems with them. I could have told them I'd seen the same expression on the face of New Guinea highlanders when I offered them money to bring in some birds alive and with plumage undamaged. Why all the fuss over something which, after all, is only good for eating? This rich bastard wasting his money on blue lights for birds—bugger you, it takes all sorts.

I got the lights fixed the way I wanted them and then Armitage was on the doorstep, almost to the second of the appointment he'd made. A careful, grey man, but necessary to look after my affairs. Some of my estate is in property but most of it is in industrials—I'd been moving it there for years.

"Very wise, too," he commended. But my reasons weren't his.

"Mining shares would be good—picked carefully," he said, lean face swivelling atop his long neck, yellow eyes glinting. Some creatures are over-specialized: the Everglades kites live on freshwater snails and with swamp drainage the snails are getting fewer and so are the kites. Close the Stock Exchange and he'd become extinct, too.

"No," I said. "I don't want the worry of them."

"And probably wise, too." And I read his thoughts: the noted caution of the Craddocks and the motto on their coat of arms, *Je respondray*—I will answer for what I say or do. I will be responsible. Or so I was told when a child.

But I just wanted to reduce my worries. I have too much money—or had too much. At that time I was thinking I should put some of it to better use by setting up a foundation or two.

Pseudemydura umbrina—my abuse of the analyst follows a monotonous pattern, I admit, but I'm only the analysand to be remoulded in his Rotarian and Returned Servicemen's League image, so any defence I assume, however vulgar, is justified—the analyst, if that pleases you more, has a not very distinguished print of the Mona Lisa behind his desk. While we talk I speculate about which is the "true" background in this enigmatic picture. The dream landscape behind her left shoulder has a lower horizon line and appears nearer than the quite different dream landscape behind her right shoulder. Where is she, therefore? What is she, because the two sides of her face do not quite match? She changes constantly as I look at her. Where am I, I ask myself. Here? In central Australia? At King's School? In Venice? Which is Harry Craddock?

Elizabeth called me twice to answer the telephone. After the second call she looked at me, smiling. "You want to fuck me," she said. "Well, you can." Her voice gentle, lilting. Mrs Green was out and I took her to my bedroom in the north wing. She let me kiss her and then she broke away and began undressing, not wanting me to help. I shed my clothes and went towards her, embracing her and seeking her mouth with mine. Her body was silky, firm. I cupped her breasts and the purple nipples stiffened between my fingers. My breath was coming quickly as she drew me down on the bed and her fingers, not fat and stubby but slim and silky, were caressing tenderly the strong, upright, tight flesh sprouting from my thighs. Throbbingly painful and pleasurable at the one instant.

"I want you. Don't talk." And her slender fingers guided me into her silky, voluptuous, warm, moist cave and I was thrusting gently and withdrawing and thrusting and she was moving with me and we continued for minutes and then we both quickened our thrust and

69

counter-thrust, faster and faster, and she screamed and bit my shoulder and I got my hands under her firm buttocks and held on and we rammed our bodies together and her oryx legs clamped over my back and I felt the exciting clasp of her heels. And she was soft and wet and wide and I spurted wanting to fill her utterly with my seed. She felt it splashing and my throbbing and she screamed, "Darling!"

Afterwards we lay there, not talking. Only it didn't happen like that at all. Not there and on that first day. I have been day-dreaming. I got to thinking about Elizabeth while recalling the past. Dreams can be as real and as important as what actually does happen. Where, indeed, is the dividing line? In the Mona Lisa?

As I said when I began writing this portion of my memoir, Joanna's journal has introduced a fresh point of view. I have difficulty in returning in time to May 1967. (I realize for the first time that my quest was exactly one hundred years after the capture of the bird in the Flinders Ranges.) When I began this memoir I could live happily and easily in past time. Now I continually introduce the present, including a masturbatory day-dream of bedding with Elizabeth. And I'm nagged by the thought that I must produce another instalment for Dr Sullivan.

Early in May I was almost ready to leave for the Centre. I wasn't able to sleep at night but kept getting out of bed to make a note of something to do. I'd do it three times or more before I'd settle down to sleep.

About this time Margaret phoned and insisted on coming out to see me.

"I have some news for you," she said.

"Tell me now."

"No," she said. "I want to see you. Are you all right now, Harry?"

"Why shouldn't I be?" I asked her, a little tersely I realized as soon as I'd spoken.

"I wondered."

When she arrived I took her up to the ballroom to show her the Bourkes. She giggled when she saw what I'd done. "What would the Vincents say if they could see the ancestral home!"

Her news was that she was marrying again. I congratulated her. I remember my mind groped to identify the perfume she was wearing. Delicate like a Debussy chord.

"You don't mind?"

"Why should I?"

"I wanted your approval, Harry." The intent way she was looking at me made me uncomfortable.

"You're free to do what you want with your life," I said. "I'm happy for you. Bring him out before I leave."

Our tortoise friend once asked me how I reacted to this news.

"I was pleased for her sake," I said.

"Are you sure you were?"

"Of course," I said, looking out through the window into the garden. When I shifted slightly in my chair, the trunk of the lemon-scented gum bent about fifteen feet up at an angle of 120 degrees, owing to that flaw in the glass.

As soon as Margaret had gone, I picked up the phone. When the inquiry agent arrived I kept him standing while we talked. He had the wary, suspicious eyes of an ex-policeman with a low opinion of human nature. Blue suit and the inevitable R.S.L. badge. He'd put on a bit of weight since he'd left the force—or it had left him. Repressed and with violence coiled ready to spring out. I didn't like myself for using his dirty talents. There's no animal I can liken him to; animals, even the

71

F

largest and most powerful, use their teeth and talons only to eat.

"Get everything you can on Laurence Jordan. I want it in three days," I said.

"There mightn't be much," he said.

"There has to be," I said. "He's marrying my sister for her money—he's eight years younger."

When I'm absorbed in anything I lose count of time. My demands on Elizabeth Trumbull during the next couple of days were high, from nine in the morning to late at night. I realized it suddenly and was contrite because others don't necessarily share my obsessions.

"Take tomorrow off," I said at eleven o'clock and called a taxi for her.

"I'm enjoying it," she said. "I don't need a day off."

"I insist."

"No. I knew—"

"What?"

"What I was in for." Smiling.

"When you came to work for me?" Nodding. Smiling.

"Why did you come to work for me?"

"I thought—I thought you were beaut. When I interviewed you."

It was dangerous ground but probably, I thought, a young girl's delightful frankness. Was I a father figure? It was something I didn't get from Rosemary. Jessica saw to that. In time, Rosemary would come round.

I was suddenly excited that Elizabeth liked me, but I continued to play my father and eminent ornithologist role. We create ourselves. Balzac on his deathbed called for Biancon, the doctor in one of his novels.

Art creates us, too. I see so much of our landscape through the eyes of Drysdale, Nolan and Tom Roberts —even Streeton and Gruner. And people through the mind of Cervantes, Shakespeare, Fielding, Joyce and Hediger, Tinbergen, Lorenz. Is there a danger here? St Augustine lamented that he had lived in mortal sin, yet "all this I wept not, I who wept for Dido dead".

I told Elizabeth about the reptile problem and she grew keen on the idea.

23rd April 1967. The Vincents are furious with Harry. "Janet should never have left Chisholm to him!" It's the best use the ballroom has been put to in years. I don't know whether Harry did it to spite the Vincents or whether he simply didn't think about it all. ("They're peasants even if they call themselves graziers.") He wanted space for a large phytotron so he could study the Bourkes, and what could be better? So he would have reasoned. And yet I don't know. Harry is unpredictable. Sometimes when you're talking to him a part of him switches off and operates separately.

He's stalling on central Australia now. Something about his sister and her new lover? Or is there a new love interest? I'm desperately afraid—I sense that Harry's sanity hinges on his going to central Australia. Alan said to day, "You've got some influence with Harry. He's got to succeed with something—find that bird even." Alan has been Harry's doctor for years and knows more about him than I do. Where does Margaret figure in Harry's story? "That recent business now—" Alan said. "He told me he did it because he'd failed Red." Someone said once that all travel was a quest, a conscious or subconscious searching for something that was lacking in our lives or in ourselves. With Harry it is perhaps a search for identity. As a child he was a prodigal liar. Margaret told me this once. After the separation or the divorce Janet Craddock went abroad. Up to that time she'd been a devoted mother; then in Paris she'd met the first of her lovers and the children

73

were left for some months with servants. "I learnt not to miss her," said Margaret. "Harry fretted at first but soon got like me." But from somewhere there's printed sharply in my mind—where does it come from?—a picture of a small boy who on her return clung to her and wouldn't let her out of his sight and was constantly demanding. And who would storm and rage at her. And refused his food. "It made us independent," said Margaret once. She was his refuge from that brilliant and erratic mother who alternately screamed at him and smothered him with kisses. At Oxford there was poetry and amateur theatricals. Disguises? Roles? And fantastic learning of an esoteric kind. All that work on birds' gonads which he hasn't published yet. That party in London at Norman Haire's and the Welsh girl, sodden with drink and Marxism. "What's the matter with you?" she demanded. "Are you impotent?" How Harry laughed. She was astray but sensed something. You could say that Harry has never had a profession, perhaps not even a nationality.

Harry must go to the Centre, idiotic as the venture seems to some and, sometimes, even to himself. Harry is a Great Victorian born out of his time. One hundred and thirty years earlier he'd have been a Stanley or Burton and plunged into Africa or Arabia. When tonight I knew Harry wanted me to go with him, I set a time limit and felt arbitrary and bitchy.

25th April 1967. Rosemary came to see me and had some trouble in getting a taxi on this national totem feast. Like many of the young she is scornful and without understanding that men might cherish the memories of a time when they'd been bound together in a common peril. They were once united, with their aggression channelled against official enemies and approved by Church and State. A Golden Age of mateship to which, ageing, they look back nostalgically.

"Licensed drunks everywhere!" she cried. "Mummy wanted the car." Her father's colouring and vehemence. Last year Harry deleted his war service details from his entry in *Who's Who*.

"I hope you don't mind me dropping in at short notice," she said and, taking my agreement for granted, went on, "Now that you're separated, it's all right for me to call on you."

I wasn't buying in on this; I'd trod a circumspect path, and I don't know her well. A nice, coltish child but shy about her mission. She wanted, as I'd guessed, to build a bridge to Harry.

"Telephone him," I urged her. "He'll be pleased to hear from you."

Tom Drake has now gone cold on joining the expedition . . . or the university has. Harry told me this at lunch. That solves things, was my relieved reaction. Harry caught me looking at the scars on his wrists. He teased his shirt sleeves down gently, calling to the waiter for the bill.

26th April 1967. Lunched with Margaret and Laurence (Larry) as she'd arranged. People marry for a complex of reasons, so I choked back speculations on why a man should marry a woman eight years older than himself; men in their late forties or fifties usually choose younger women. It's not for money as Harry seems to think—or so he says. Harry told me once, "I married you because you were rich. Rich women can follow their heart. Middle-class girls are usually whores and sell themselves for financial security." I remember I said, "Why not a working-class girl? They're free, too." He didn't answer immediately and I realized suddenly I'd been tactless because Martha, whom he'd adored, had been working class. "Yes, I know." Larry, who is divorced, has a sheep place. Perhaps Margaret looks for the steadiness and stability in Larry which she lacks herself? And he, perhaps, admires her impetuosity which he lacks himself. Probably I'm too independent for marriage, as I warned Harry. I thought Larry pleasant and relaxed with a typical countryman look. He has a strong, tanned face with a beaky nose, a high forehead and short crinkled brown hair. All through lunch I kept thinking I'd met him before. Later I remembered he reminded me of that nice Scots game warden we met in Uganda. A compassionate man with a real feeling for everything alive from tiny insects to bulky elephants, which he occasionally has to kill when their numbers grow too large for the reserve. This is, of course, a bit rhapsodic—I'm sure Larry regarded most animals as competitors for grass.

Margaret seems anxious for Harry to approve her marriage. "Has Harry said anything about Larry?" she asked in the ladies—I'm quoting from the sign. "He used to check on my escorts when I was young. He was such a ram"—a bitchy smile for my benefit—"he suspected every man I went out with. With good reason." Another smile beneath hooded eyes. "I'm sure he approves," I said.

At lunch I steered the talk to Harry's central Australian quest. "Ask Harry to include you in his party," I urged when I sensed their interest.

"Why not?" Margaret said.

8

Just before I left for central Australia I tried cutting
down on smoking. As a substitute oral satisfaction I
took to chewing peppermints. I chewed them, one after
the other, crushing them with my molars; the amount
of aggression I displayed amused me. I'm ashamed to
tell you that this attempt to give up smoking failed. I
managed not to smoke until 4 p.m. and told myself that
one wouldn't matter. Then it was another. I told myself
I could try to stop tomorrow. I didn't. I'd got to rolling
my own cigarettes in a machine when I found manu-
factured ones too bland, just as I found most whiskies.
They were after the mass market—and the women's
market—and the cigarettes got milder and milder and
as characterless as most of the short stories the late
unlamented *Saturday Evening Post* used to publish.
I'd found Four Square Curlies Fine Cut tobacco and I
used to say that when I no longer enjoyed it I'd have
to give up smoking.

I always mean well but my weaknesses surprise me.
I can rarely resist making a pass at an attractive woman
—unless, of course, she's a friend's wife or a near child.
It's as though I have to prove something to myself, or it
could simply be the strength of my sexual drive. I'd
intended to be fatherly towards Elizabeth. One night we
worked late and I offered her a drink with no other
intention in mind. But she looked so enchanting with
her long legs coiled under her I was stirred. Only the
young human animal has much grace; we're an ugly lot
as we get older—even before middle age, I add hastily,
because few animals live past middle age. There's no
great harm in it, I told myself when I sensed some
response in her. And, again, she's not a child. Then,
suddenly, I got control of myself and was able to put on

77

once more my fatherly and ornithological role. I remember I was a long time getting off to sleep that night, lying in a half-dream with an erection so imperative that my penis ached. I recall I had an almost schoolboyish pride in such a phenomenon before I drifted off to sleep after repressing an impulse to seek some ease with one or other of the women I knew. Sadie, for instance. It would have been a bit poor.

The next evening we worked late again and I felt suddenly giddy—too much sitting—so I stretched out on the divan.

"You look flaked," Elizabeth said. "I'll bring you a whisky."

"I don't need one," I said. "Pour one for yourself if you wish."

"Sure?"

"Perfectly." My tone was a bit terse. I was trembling suddenly. I got up and left the room.

Once in an attempt to control my smoking I used to mount newspaper and magazine cuttings on a wall-board —SELF-CURE CLAIM FOR SMOKERS was one heading. And, CIGARETTE TAR LEVELS COULD SAVE LIVES. Then there was the Queensland Health Education Council pamphlet, SMOKING AND LUNG CANCER . . . "the cigarette, in particular, can be a suicidal weapon. Inevitably, time pulls the trigger."

The next morning I felt noble but also a little surprised at myself because my taste had been for older women. Lunching later with Rosemary, I found myself smiling. She'd be shocked if she knew. I was so old in her eyes and remote, too, because of the years of separation. I'd had access, of course, but the children had never been easy with me when they came at first for week-ends and after a time I'd given up. I couldn't compete with Jessica for their affection. Or so I decided then. I should, perhaps, have persisted.

78

Rosemary is a nice child but she was much on her guard with me. And immature, as I'd expected. After our marriage Jessica hadn't developed but stayed armoured in her upper-middle-class prejudices. That had been the trouble. But my daughter had a chance. She was majoring in sociology, and the discipline of that science would jolt her out of some of her Darling Point conditioning. For my part I was a little self-conscious—I could imagine Jessica's repeated warnings, "Your father has plenty of charm—when he wants to use it." With that in my ears, it was hard to be myself. Our conversation was unimportant. We exchanged clichés of communication, identifying each other and paving the way for the assumption of roles. Affection would come later. I was tenderly aware of how awkward it must be for her, recalling my own youth and its gaucheries. I almost wished she'd say something blunt—it might have cleared the air. Such as, "Why do I have to act this way just because you're my father? I owe you nothing. You're the kind of person who should never have been a father. You ran from a marriage when it looked a bit difficult—lucky you! Most other men are stuck with poor marriages and can't buy their way out."

And I could have said, "Lucky you, because you wouldn't be as sane as this if your mother and I had stayed together. You'd have been destroyed between the two of us. Your mother is a disappointed woman—she'd have been worse if she'd stayed bound to me."

I like young people. They're better than we were. More honest, better educated. And more desolate because there are no easy options such as those we had—socialism, communism. We had gods even if later we found they had clay feet.

So Rosemary and I got on fairly well and I restrained myself from asking about David, her brother. But she mentioned him. She had, I noted, the Vincent eyes and nose. Good-looking child.

"Mad on photography," she said. "Photographs birds all the time."

My heart jumped with pleasure. I tried not to make the flattering observation that David, in spite of Jessica, had taken me as his father image after all and taken up photography.

"He wants to leave *The Clarion* to be a professional photographer, but grandfather won't hear of it."

"I didn't know about the photography," I said.

Rosemary was looking steadily at me and I thought I could read something in her half-smile. Did he want to come to central Australia with me? But I wasn't going to intrude.

We parted soon afterwards and I was sad that my daughter was so dull and conformist. And I was to blame, for I'd left Rosemary in that cage. But she was young and intelligent and would, doubtless, get free. And, on a sudden resolution, I decided to get in touch with David before too long.

9

Dr S. continues his little daily chats with me—mostly in my own room but sometimes in his. His is lined with books which I suspect he's never read—they're there to impress the patients. Some are *Reader's Digest* Condensed Books. He seeks rapport and today encouraged me to talk about Red. I could not envisage him understanding so told him as little as I could. When Red

80

failed as a stimulus he tried to get me to talk about Jessica.

I wonder if my championing of Red was in the nature of a practical joke? I was very addicted to them early. In England Jessica and I drove to Piddletrenthide one day and, on impulse, I bought twenty-five postcards, scribbled greetings on them and shot them off to people all over the world. In Paris I bought cards showing allegedly alluring girls, wrote amorous messages on them concluding with *"Pense à toi"* and signed them "Marie", "Louise", etc. and addressed them to city fathers at their temples of finance and commerce (Jessica not quite approving but laughing).

In a fashion, my search for the night parrot was a practical joke on a large scale.

In the grounds of Chisholm there's a tall spotted gum with a long dead limb I'd been intending to get lopped. Last night I dreamt it fell during a storm. I looked up at the jagged ends protruding from the great trunk. "It will smash everything," I thought, but when I looked I couldn't find the limb.

Which fantastic dream landscape in the Mona Lisa will I choose for my afternoon walk? The left-hand one with the lower horizon has knife-edge outcrops like the rocks of the Centre. And a stream like the one I found.

Pseudemydura umbrina persisted in questioning me about that stranger I shot at Parramatta. I said "stranger" but, of course, I know his name now. It was in the paper with his photograph.

"Pure impulse," I said. "I'd never seen him before. Don't you believe, doctor, in uncontrollable impulses?"

"Sometimes." He plucked his bottom lip with a fore-leg. "Can you describe this man?"

"He was about forty," I said. "Fair with a high forehead. A thin nose."

I paused, trying to see the face again. "Sunburnt."

"What would you say if I told you they've arrested someone for the shooting?"

"Then they've got the wrong man," I said. "I've made my confession."

I was probably too easy-going with Jessica. I'm sure her second husband wasn't as long-suffering as I was. He, too, in time got the edge of her tongue. That thing she had about drink.

"My luck to pick a second alcoholic!" she would have greeted him one night. I knew the routine. With froggish lips searching for insults.

"But you're not a Cambridge gentleman like Harry with ten million dollars." (Oxford, but Jessica always got it wrong.) Golden hair undone and dressing gown open over short nightdress.

"No, I'm not," he said.

"Just a drunken butcher's son." Jessica had a skill in denigration. "Wholesale butchering business. Johnny-come-lately buying into sheep stations." Or such like. "Not a gentleman like Harry."

"I'm not a gentleman and that makes it easier," he said and slapped her face. "You're a termagant and a frigid bitch." And he pulled her across his knee and spanked her hard, reddening that still delectable bottom, nightdress up-riding. And Jessica tumbling on the floor, golden triangle between cozening legs and grabbing his ankles and pleading, "I'm not frigid with you, darling."

Living happily together thereafter. Something like that, anyway, must have happened between them.

"Do you remember that crap she used to hand out about her drunken father?" he asked, triumphantly. I nodded, remembering my compassion for Jessica. "And the story that he tried to rape her one night when she was fourteen?" Drunken and lurching round the

82

room with undone fly, knocking over the wooden chair, while the child pleaded, "Daddy, don't please!"

"Pure fantasy," he said. "She made the whole lot up. It's lucky her old man didn't get five years."

"She certainly fooled me, old chap," I said magnanimously, ordering him another whisky.

If it was really like that. But it's true I probably failed Jessica.

"You're self-sufficient," she reproached me once. It's not true, of course, but she meant this thing that drove me all my life—that searching for something that was, perhaps, never to be found, that could not be expressed in words but in striving, and work, and questing. And perhaps she'd got the left-over, the husk.

Something of me died in Spain. My generation lost our political innocence in Spain. We weren't driven from the Garden; instead, the Garden which Rousseau first invoked was suddenly revealed to be as barren as the Gibson. Some of my Oxford friends went off to fight while I hesitated. The Craddock caution? I don't think so. I was groping my way to a new faith, not wholly committed. I went finally, flaming with youthful idealism.

Another bit of me died with Martha. "You have a lovely voice," I said when I met her first. The high cheek bones, the haughty little nose so slightly aquiline, the gleaming brown hair, the fine hands. Twenty. Brilliance and warmth. And then after six months of marriage, the strange behaviour, the emotional shallowness, the withdrawal and depression. And the bloody fool of a psychiatrist who said there was no danger of suicide—as I'd feared. I relaxed my guard and she killed herself.

"Schizophrenia," the doctor said. "She'd have got worse." I suspected it was the panacea he handed bereaved young husbands. I couldn't accept it and I can't even now. My trouble is that sometimes I think

83

I'm omnipotent. I blamed myself for not preventing her suicide. Not now. They buried part of me with her. The others—and Joanna—got the left-overs.

"There's not much to be said," I told Dr S. when he asked again about Jessica. "I failed her just as I've failed most people." By each other we were undonne.

"Do you want to talk about it?"

"No," I said. "I take the responsibility. It's right that I am locked away now. I was capable of murdering her at times—therefore it is right that I should be here."

"You haven't always thought that."

"I see it differently now."

I wouldn't say any more but he went away well satisfied. He wanted me to say that. He wanted me to behave like a well-trained lion or bear when given its cue. Some time I may talk to him about Jessica but I won't discuss Martha.

Or Sarah. I never liked Sarah and it was reciprocal. I know she tried to turn Jessica against me. A slim brown girl with cold eyes that disapproved of me. Always in the house and staying with Jessica when I was away from home for any considerable length of time. "Good for Jessica to have company," I said early on. And then Jessica, "Sarah says she doesn't know how I put up with you!"

"She is an authority, no doubt," I agreed. One marriage to a husband who could barely raise it and was probably a homosexual and a second one with a chap who did all the washing and ironing at the week-end because, she said, she couldn't cope with two children.

I came home a day early and couldn't find Jessica at first and I went upstairs into the bedroom and they were entwined, naked, slim brown body and golden rich body plunging in their mindless passion. I did what they do in the bush with coupling dogs. I got a bucket of cold water and heaved it over them.

84

Delete that last sentence. I didn't do that. Delete all of this about Sarah and Jessica. I can't be sure it happened.

When I returned to Sydney from central Australia Swinburne wrote begging me to set him up in business.

"Outstanding record of success . . . built business from nothing . . ." etc. I threw the letter in the basket . . . no, I didn't. I framed it and set it up on Red's grave. I'd never subscribe to anything as anthropomorphic as burying a dingo, a free-living creature, let alone putting an offering on a non-existent grave. I threw the letter in the basket.

I'm writing all this by hand in the blue-ruled foolscap notebooks. I prefer artists' clutch pencils with 3B and 4B leads because then my handwriting slides smoothly over the paper—I must ask Joanna to see if there's not a better quality somewhere in Sydney—and, moreover, with these thick leads it's easy to cross out when I go wrong. I write on every second line and about seven words only to a line. There's a physical satisfaction in writing this way, as though I am sculpting my story—I cannot abide the typewriter. I'm hewing it out. I've just changed to a larger Staedtler Mars-Lumograph 4B— blue plastic handle and the word "handle" is about one and a half inches long—very different from the word "handle" you're reading now. I write up to two thousand words a day with many stops and starts as I try to recall not only what happened chronologically but what I thought and felt. I know things now I didn't know then. My method of writing on every second line only enables me to insert something I have overlooked. For instance I inserted "Mars" because I had overlooked it —constant use has worn the lettering. Looking at it again I notice the word "TECHNICO". The other clutch pencils are a small Staedtler Mars-Lumograph, also blue, and a Faber, green, both with 3B leads. Both are six-

sided. Sometimes when my hand tires—and my mind—I
use a biro, but the best of them dig into the paper.
Smoothness is what I seek. I should have told you the
leads are black. I've tried various colours—red, blue,
green, purple, orange—but although I like the patterns
of various colour, the leads aren't smooth or bold
enough. *Tara-diddle-deino; this is idle feino.*

> *Tee-hee, tee-hee, O sweet delight,*
> *He tickles this age who can*
> *Call Tullia's ape a marmosite,*
> *And Leda's goose a swan.*
> *Tara-diddle-deino; this is idle feino.*

IO

I recall that after I said good-bye to Rosemary, I walked
up Martin Place and into Macquarie Street. I'd decided
on impulse to make another random search in the
Mitchell Library. Somewhere I might find a reference to
the night parrot. It was like looking for a needle in a
haystack. I'd spent hours in this way in the past and
found little that was useful.

Somewhere buried in some dull account of the
interior might be a reference to a strange parrot which
flew little and fed and watered at night. But the
observers would not be trained ornithologists but lay-
men and probably unreliable. I'd gone through all the
more obvious works—Giles's accounts and those of other
explorers. Few had much knowledge or interest in
animals. They were stronger on geology and on botany.

I'd have given my right arm to have been in Ernest Giles's boots when he made those journeys in central Australia and Western Australia from 1872 and 1876.* He must often have camped near these wanderers in the night. There were many Aborigines, too, in his day. They could have guided him to the birds. Today there are only a few nomadic families. But conscience or whatever you call it was driving me to try once more. I was depressed at the thought of the task before me. The private detective had found nothing, either, about Laurence Jordan. "There must be something, somewhere," I'd told him. Our two tasks seemed suddenly equally dispiriting.

I'm allergic to libraries. After an hour or so my head aches dully as if a band were compressing it and I can scarcely copy out anything. I have to force my hand to write and my handwriting becomes increasingly ragged. I switch from a biro to a thick pencil to a fountain pen—anything to vary the agonizing monotony which eventually affects my belly. This goes back to my Oxford days. I was under pressure then.

Have you asked why didn't I send Elizabeth? I thought of it, but, competent as she is, I couldn't expect her to do this. I couldn't endow her with years of experience and knowledge that might make my mind trip over a seemingly innocent sentence and find a rich treasure. In this kind of research I am always guided by what could appear to be intuition or luck. For no apparent reason, something suddenly assumes obsession-

* EDITOR: Ernest Giles (1835-97) born at Bristol and educated at Christ's Hospital, was one of the greatest of Australian explorers. He was a fine bushman, skilled in horsecraft, and gifted with resource and great courage. The *Australian Encyclopaedia* observes: "His most notable expedition took place in 1875, when, starting from Beltana, he traversed the desert wards of Lake Torrens and reached Perth, then set off again (January 1876) to return to South Australia along a line just south of the Tropic of Capricorn—a total distance of more than 5000 miles, for the most part in completely arid country."

al importance. What has happened is that it has evoked a subconscious memory which in time usually emerges. I had to do it myself, whatever the nervous tension it caused.

Nothing of significance was produced by my labours on this occasion and I emerged in the freedom of the neon-splashed night. Walking down the broad steps, I found myself thinking of the Gibson Desert. I dismissed the idea almost instantly—in that arid waste of gravel and sand-ridges there'd be no night parrot but only the bones of poor Alfred Gibson, who'd been lost there on Giles's expedition and had his great graveyard named after him. "Poor" is pejorative, to some extent, for men have died as dreadfully and not been pitied a hundred years later.

The next day I heard that the British expedition had returned to Adelaide without a glimpse of the night parrot. I was petty enough to be relieved. None the less, if they had found the night parrot I'd have still gone. The real work would start with the discovery of the bird—the detailed study of *Geopsittacus occidentalis* in its habitat.

I remember that when Elizabeth first came to work for me gods and heroes stalked into her life—famous and not so famous Australian scientists, writers and painters who were my friends. The sweet naïvety of it amused me—all were without flaw and she was, at first, ready to worship them all. (I had expected more sophistication in a newspaper woman). Once when she asked me about X, a much-praised writer, I ventured, "I don't think he'll get much further." And, added, pompously it sounds now, "They fail as writers because they fail as people." I couldn't have supported it although I could have cited Tolstoy and Chekhov as great men and great writers and pointed out that X wasn't a generous man. "He's a malicious gossip by proxy," I said unkindly.

"And Y is a bitch—she holds parties where they indulge in brittle, catty remarks about everyone they know—including some of the guests who may be temporarily absent buying more grog. X doesn't join in but sits in the corner like a great tawny desexed tom-cat, enjoying it all." I realized I'd been almost as bad, but I'd wanted to get it off my chest; I'd been to one of Y's parties and been dismayed by what I'd seen. Was that my reason? Was I name-dropping to impress Elizabeth?

I like young people, of course. Sometimes I delude myself by thinking that at fifty I think and feel as passionately as when I was twenty-five. There is some truth in this—and much self-deception. Harry Craddock, the eternal adolescent, the prematurely mature juvenile, measuring his life with coffee spoons.

Elizabeth, of course, evoked my youth. She was like a friendly puppy, so enthusiastic and idealistic that I found myself sometimes smiling indulgently and disliked myself for doing so. Life is a series of defeats. When you're young you throw yourself into causes but later your anger or quixotism isn't so easily aroused. You tell yourself it is experience and maturity. Some of it may be, but it is also the toll of many defeats. Each defeat saps some of your courage. You die by inches. So I tried not to knock her. One Monday I noticed she limped slightly. I asked about it.

"A copper was a bit rough with me," she said, grinning.

"You were in the demonstration?"

"Yes." She looked questioningly. "You don't approve of demonstrations?"

I almost said, "I'm not sure that they achieve much. The newspapers can dismiss them as the activity of an exhibitionist minority." Instead, I said, "I'm too respectable and bourgeois to demonstrate."

"It would be good if the bourgeois did demonstrate."

89

She sat down, shoulder-length brown hair tossing. "It's fun."

"You shouldn't do it for fun," I said. The late-middle-aged moralist.

"I didn't mean fun that way. When you sit in, you are committing a form of disobedience. You are showing your resistance to something that is immoral and unjust."

I understood what she meant. The young had a peculiar freedom to express their anger and despair. I had no outlet—except the night parrot, I told myself wryly, and recalled that Elizabeth herself had suggested as much when she had interviewed me. I recall that I felt suddenly old and tired. I had had a trust once and I had run away from it.

She must have sensed some of my anguish for she said, gaily, "We're advised to wear stout slacks and brassières."

I caught on. I'd heard it from a student that large police fingers bruised breasts unless they were protected. I felt a sudden flush of anger flooding my temples and knew that I was acquiring what Joanna once called my "emotional face". I remember thinking that if one of my kids was a demonstrator and was badly hurt by the police I'd be so mad I'd be capable of shooting the man responsible. Little danger with Rosemary, I added. "If I was a student or even a bit older I'd demonstrate, I suppose," I said. Those middle-class reservations, shades of grey instead of the blacks and whites of the young. Age is not only a defeat but a betrayal, I thought with a kind of melancholy resignation. (I don't know that I really accept this.) This was the nearest I'd come to confronting myself. If I hadn't been committed to the search for the night parrot, I think I might have gone abroad. I had come to echo in my heart the despair over Australia that Edmund Wilson had expressed about

America: "I have finally come to feel that this country, whether I live in it or not, is no longer any country for me." I could not feel any pride in a country that from self-interest and cowardice supported the immoral commitment in Vietnam, which allowed illiterate Cabinet Ministers to censor books and films, and was racially intolerant. We were offering a blood sacrifice of our twenty-year-olds as an insurance that America would feel under an obligation to come to our aid *if* China tried anything. As a post-middle-aged man I was ashamed to try to save my skin in this way—even assuming it was in danger. The fear of China struck me as a form of national paranoia. I'm sick at heart because the Vietnam war has shown my countrymen to be basically intolerant and authoritarian. If I went abroad I could make no defence but merely smile wanly when friends in more civilized lands twitted me. I was like the father of a delinquent child. I couldn't disown the land I loved. I didn't care what other countries did, but I did about Australia and most of the time I was ashamed. I felt cut off from my fellow Australians. I remember sitting in a train going to Lindfield and, irrationally, hating everyone in it. "You smug, selfish, unthinking amoeba." You could call it my second loss of innocence.

About this time I rang Tom Drake and suggested dinner at the University Club.

"I'll come if the expedition is in our joint names," he said over the coffee, with a flash of large white teeth.

"That's all right with me." I was irritated because I'd agreed to this earlier.

"To be quite frank with you, I've been unhappy about this venture," he said, shrugging his wide shoulders. He stirred his coffee with his left hand. He had curious clumsiness in everything he did. He rarely smiled. "How can I put it? I don't want to give offence—"

91

"Too spectacular?" I said. "I'm not looking for publicity. The night parrot attracts me because it's elusive—" I was nearly floundering into mysticism.

"I'll come, Harry," he said. "It's only that you have to be careful. To hell with them."

"Then that's settled," I said.

About that time I was sliding into a depressive trough —I knew the signs by now. When it hit me fully I'd be unable to do much. Even to get dressed and shave would be an effort. When I was twenty doctors diagnosed it as "low blood pressure". It was a fashionable diagnosis like focal sepsis which led to the cutting out of millions of innocent tonsils (castration substitute?) Doctors are today's witch-doctors. When my "low blood pressure" struck, my days would be aimless, without purpose. I'd do nothing while nagged by my conscience to do what had to be done. In turn I'd consider all the various things clamouring for my attention. But I'd not summon the psychic energy to tackle any of them. And as the day, and days passed, I'd be in a black mood of self-hatred and contempt. Once, I remember, I put on a recording of Beethoven's *Grosse Fugue* and played it again and again for three days.

None the less, I forced myself to do some more digging at the Mitchell Library. I got tense after an hour or so and had to force myself to take the simplest notes. I finished finally and went back to Chisholm.

"You look tired," Elizabeth said.

"Pour me a whisky, please," I said. "I've got to go to a blasted party."

"I'll drive you there," she said.

She did, in her car, and I talked her into coming in with me. I didn't notice at the time, but, knowing myself fairly well, I can tell you how it happened. I started drinking double Scotch after double Scotch and was soon pretty high. I talked a lot, flirted with the women with hand-kissing and so on—all fairly circumspect. But later I did a barking dog act, wandering into the garden and cocking my leg on the shrubs. "I'm marking out my territory just like Red!" I remember crying out as I sprinkled a camellia amid cheers. I did it several times. I saw Elizabeth looking at me and I shouted, "Do you still think I'm beaut?" I don't remember much more until later when I was out in the street and trying to stake my territory on a lamp-post. I couldn't have bothered to unzip my fly because I was wet all down the legs. Then I saw Elizabeth's Hillman alongside me with the engine running and I heard her call, gently:

"Hop in, Harry. I'll drive you home."

That's how it started. I think now that I got drunk deliberately to protect Elizabeth—so that she would be disgusted with this elderly fool. But later that night we loved each other much as I described it earlier. Her skin, I remember thinking, was cool as my alabaster eggs.

A few pages back I said I'd get in touch with David. I went so far as to dial his number one night and then hung up. What *could* I say to him? And David—shall I tell you about that day when he was ten and I took him to the zoo? No, that won't do.

"Would you like to see the lions?" I asked.

"If you would like to." In neutral, clear, modulated tones.

"What do you want to see?"

"I'm indifferent."

I think he was preferable at twelve when he and his cousin played cricket on the front lawn and Stephen hurled himself into a bed of my best Kurume azaleas chasing the ball and I said, gently, "Stephen, will you

93

be careful? Those plants are very brittle."

"My father is obsessional about azaleas," David said.

David was twenty-two when I set out for the Centre. Boys grow into young men. But why should I coerce him into any relationship with me because of a casual congress I'd had for my pleasure—and, I hope, for Jessica's? Nor did I want immortality in my children, to live vicariously in them. I'd like a natural friendship with David, but it's unlikely. He's not been to see me. Rosemary has several times; our relationship is good, perhaps because our roles are somewhat reversed. She humours me quietly and I accept.

"I'm told you aren't co-operating with the doctor," she said gaily on her last visit.

"I see no reason why I should. Does he impress you?"

She hesitated. "There are other psychiatrists."

"The key to the matter is that there is nothing wrong with me. I've never felt better."

"Don't you want to get out?"

"On my terms."

"You'll have to make some concessions. You've always said that—" She mimicked my voice, "Don't fight battles you can't win."

"Did I sound like that?"

"Yes." And we both laughed.

"My God! And you want me to behave. It's too late." And so on.

I've reread what I wrote earlier about Jessica and am concerned that I might have been a trifle unfair. Most women want a cave so they can bear their cubs and you can't have cubs on a raft or trying to climb the Himalayas. A cave with all mod. cons, of course, and a husband to play the role she (Jessica) had cast for him. The catch was I wouldn't change, but Jessica can't be blamed for that miscalculation. After all her mother had told her I'd change—and, so, too, had my father.

94

They were much older, presumably sensible and mature people, and she was an inexperienced young girl. I think now Jessica started to worry when I bought my first alabaster egg. In Rome it was. She didn't say so but she thought I was mad. This was well before Victoriana became fashionable. You could almost say our marriage broke up on alabaster eggs—and food. The first summer when we were in Paris she was always wanting to eat our evening meal in the hotel, whereas I wanted to find the little restaurants where the French ate. She didn't say it straight out but:

"Darling, can we go back now? My feet are aching." Graceful, small feet, too.

"We can sit down here." "Here" was a park seat or a sidewalk café in the Boule Mich' or the Boulevard St Germain.

"I want to put my feet up, sweet." So we'd go back to the hotel and then by the time she recovered she'd say it was too late for anything but something on a tray if we were to get to the ballet or whatever. I didn't catch on at first.

That girl spoilt her life worrying about Salmonella, like those plumbing-obsessed Americans I've met in Europe. When Jessica dies they'll find Salmonella engraved on her heart. (I lost the chance of buying a wonderful Arab mare in Syria once because she wouldn't drink the coffee the sheikh offered. She did it nicely, but he knew.) She had some hygiene or purity bug, I suspect now. Perhaps something to do with an earlier man. I never knew, except that she wasn't a virgin when we married; it was no business of mine and it didn't worry me. The sex part was good at first. I slobbered over that rich golden body. She had full, round breasts—"Venetian globes," I used to call them—and a taut expanse of firm belly leading to that golden-haired pyramid and sumptuous thighs—not too much so. She wasn't a Rubens type, thank the Lord. They're too flabby for my taste.

I've no complaints about the first year or so. "You're as wanton as I am," I used to tell her. It was not until David was on the way that she started to change, and then after Rosemary she (figuratively) put a lock on the bedroom door.

And I? I wanted to use her for my own ends. She offered me affection—or so I thought.

We deceived each other. We were undonne. John Donne and Anne Donne. Undonne. Harry Craddock; Jessica Craddock. Barren paddock.

II

When you fall in love there begins for both a charming but indiscreet series of confessions. Elizabeth had been married.

"I'm divorced, very happily," she said. "A boy and girl thing. I was twenty-one and had just graduated. I thought he was marvellous." He was a classical guitarist. It seemed glamorous. But the boy, cosseted by his mother, wasn't ready for marriage. He drank too much and sometimes failed to keep professional engagements. "We needed the money. I worked and then I got pregnant. He preferred talking and drinking to work." Seven weeks before her baby was due, he walked out of the marriage, taking her books and records. The child was stillborn.

She told me much more in those first dewy days. I was less confessional, not from reticence, but because I'd been through this delightful practice a few times before and the part was a bit stale.

But in other ways—I'd never have believed it—I went in off the deep end over Elizabeth, waiting for her to arrive in the morning (she insisted on keeping her flat and not moving in), sending her flowers, presents, even trying to write verses about her. They were not good and were derivative, such as:

> *Upon the nipples of her breasts*
> *Which more slim than vintage grapes*
> *Do mock such clumsy shapes.*
>   *Such nipples do invite*
>   *A lover's teeth to bite*
> *Deep in the wax of her cool breasts,*
> *The love his foolish heart protests.*

Writing this out now I wrote "suck" instead of "such". I did a whole series such as:

> *Upon her hair*
> *Which blinds mine eyes*
>   *With its held light*
> *When to the sun it swift replies*
>   *With fire as bright.*

> *Upon her chin:*
> *Helen foolishly stole hearts;*
> *If she'd taken my love's chin,*
> *She'd have quickly found*
> *All her glories were therein.*

We had lovers' quarrels. "I'm jealous of your other women," she said once. I got jealous one night when she talked too long with a young man at a party and left me holding both drinks for five minutes.

"Admit you were jealous."

"I got fed up of hanging on to the glasses."

97

I mended it with writing and reading the following to her:

> *Li Po had*
> *a musical stone of jade.*
> *Its sound was sweeter*
> > *than*
> > *the knocking together*
> > *of ice crackle ware.*
> *Li Po lost the jade stone*
> *but yesterday I heard it again.*

Three times married was enough. I was grateful that Elizabeth had no notions that way. Scratch most so-called independent women and you'll find they're looking for that cave. And I was spared her having a conscience about Joanna—a lot of women don't like infringing on another woman's territory. She knew Joanna and I had separated and asked no questions.

"Let's keep it this way," she said one night in Sydney.

"Which way?"

"Like it is now. Affairs end, but promise you'll stay my friend."

But if she didn't want a lair for cubs she wanted to remake you. With her it was Ouspensky who, she said, had the key. She lent me his books but they meant nothing to me. My logical positivist mind rejected them and I never got past the first few sentences.

I tried to mutter the right things when I returned the books and said I wasn't in the best mood to concentrate on anything except the night parrot. She accepted this—or appeared to. Then one night in her flat in the darkness, except for the castrated glow of the street light through the curtains, I walked finger-tips up noble thighs, across gentler belly, to circle pearly glow of erectile nipples, while she talked Ouspensky.

Soon, darling, but I want to talk. Between my legs powerful, powerpole me.

She sat upright. "You don't want to listen!"

I tried to reassure her.

"You won't let anyone help you. No one can help you."

The whole time we were in Sydney she was lying in wait for me with salvation through Ouspensky and every now and then she'd bring it up. I'd explain it was all the fault of my rationalist and scientific training, but to no avail.

12

Dr S. had another session with me today. He is patient, but our rapport is nil. "Ours is a guilt culture," he explained today, and expatiated. It was supposed to put me at ease with such guilt feelings as he supposes me to have. Today he tried to get me to talk about my child-hood and my mother's divorce and death. While he talked I chose the right-hand Mona Lisa landscape for my afternoon walk because it was more tamed than the other. I've had my share of wild places. It would be nice to walk upon that bridge and eat a peach.

Not only was Ouspensky in ambush for me, as I also discovered in those last few hectic days before we left Sydney. In the evenings I began showing Elizabeth the Sydney I enjoyed, mainly the restaurants I knew. I took her one night to an Italian restaurant where they serve the most wonderful mussels, sweet as an orgasm, and where they put red-and-white check bibs round your neck so you feel just like kids and make corny jokes about regression. We dined there several nights. Walking along the street with its Victorian terraces to the restaurant I got the old familiar prickle on my chest. I hadn't experienced it for years but there was no mistaking it. Unless I was developing a fresh form of nervous dermatitis, someone was following us. (That's another of my troubles—I get a form of dermatitis on my chest and my skin specialist says it's because of conflict. "You scratch yourself when you're worried." One time he got fed up with treating me and he asked, "Whom do you hate? You scratch because you hate someone." "Not me," I said. "I don't hate anyone." "Think," he said.) Who could be following us? Not Joanna, I decided; she'd no need to put a private detective on my trail; and besides, it wasn't her style. She could have any settlement she liked but said she didn't want it. Robbery? Although the street was dark, it was rarely empty. I pretended to have a loose shoelace—though my shoes have no laces—and bent down, but my backward visibility wasn't extensive. I saw nothing. The gutter, I recall, was sour-smelling and nearly made me retch. My trousers were tight on my belly as I straightened up. 5BX was called for.

"What's the matter?" Elizabeth asked.

"Stone in my shoe," I said. I took it off and shook it. Cranes have more skill in balancing on one leg. I thought I could hear footfalls well back.

I walked on, screening Elizabeth's prattle with my brain, and straining to hear what might be behind me. The idea when you're followed is not to let him or them know because after a while they may grow too confident. I searched the street ahead for an open shop—I didn't expect to find one. I'd have a chance to go into the shop and get in a casual-seeming backward look. No shops, but then I saw the lit-up hotel, the Lion's Head, on the opposite corner to the Italian restaurant, a veritable chiaroscuro in the dark street, and I said, "I want to show you this place", and took her arm just above the elbow, firmly fleshed, and we crossed the street. As we entered I looked left down the street. I saw someone slip into a doorway of one of the three-storey terraces (late Victorian with urns on the pediments). Or thought I did. A young man with dark hair, my senses then reported.

The saloon bar was near empty. It was too early in the night.

"It's got character." Elizabeth appraised my choice. The old pub had white wooden floors, much sandsoaped and scrubbed over eighty years. (I almost thought I could sniff that sharp astringent smell I used to know in my grandmother's large kitchen.) The bar was cedar, red, rich, like a good burgundy. I ordered two whiskies and then leaning back against the bar I saw him pass outside, head and shoulders above the frosted window frame, a young pale face and black hair. I'd never seen him before until this night. I was sure of that. He went right past.

When we came out about ten minutes later I could catch no further sight of him. But later when I was enjoying the first half-dozen of yellow-and-black mussels, nose tingling with the joy they evoked, I saw him again. I'd taken the seat that enabled me to look out of the window.

I said to Elizabeth, "Don't look, but we've been followed tonight."

I described him.

"That's Leo," she said, not surprised but calmly.

"Who's Leo?"

"One of my exes," she said.

"Well, he can go home."

"He's harmless," she said. "He told me he'd do this if I ended it."

"An interesting fellow. How long has he been doing this?"

"I suppose for a year," she said.

She bit a mussel and golden juice squirted on to the bib. "I didn't know until tonight—I've never seen him." She smiled. "You're not angry? I don't think I believed him when he said he would, but I do now. Leo's very obstinate . . . if he says he'll do something he'll do it." Elizabeth half turned, trying to look out of the window. I found her calmness annoying. I felt myself getting tense in the throat. If the fellow had followed her every time she'd been with me what had he seen?

I asked, "Did he say why he'd follow you?"

"He said it would upset me." She began to laugh. "It didn't because I forgot."

My first impulse was to wait until he came past, rush out, and tell him to go home. But I decided against it, and the next time I saw that pale moon drifting past the window I waved gaily and then beckoned with my hand. I thought that would disconcert him. About a minute later I saw him gliding towards our table.

"Please join us," I said, pointing to a chair. "My name is Craddock."

He sat down. I saw for the first time his fierce yellow eyes and beaky nose.

"Do you know you are out with my girl?" he asked. His voice was not aggressive but almost rhetorical.

"Elizabeth has been telling me about you," I said. "Will you have some mussels?" He shook his head. "Anything else? Some wine?"

"You haven't answered my question."

"Good evening, Leo," Elizabeth said, pleasantly.

Leo gave her a curt nod and then looked expectantly at me.

"Look, Leo, be a sensible chap," I said. "Elizabeth isn't your girl now."

"How long have you been following me, Leo?" Elizabeth asked. "It's not very nice, is it?"

"Every night," he said.

"For a year?"

"Yes."

"It's not good for you, Leo," Elizabeth said, almost gently. "You'll get sick."

He stood up suddenly. "Good night." He nodded at me. "Good night, Elizabeth." He walked outside. I don't know if he went home but I didn't see him pass the window again. When we left later, we changed taxis twice and went finally to Chisholm. The place was big enough to lose him if he crouched outside in the grounds, and we used one of the other bedrooms.

After that he must have got a bit cleverer because I couldn't get a glimpse of him the next night. But the one after there he was on Farmer's Pitt Street corner, not trying to conceal himself at all.

"Do you know you've got my girl?" he called after me. I think I shed him later that night—I'd had a bit of practice in the past. He was, I think, harmless, but he began to worry me a little. I was never sure where he'd pop up and always with that one question—or complaint. You could never be sure which it was. The tone was so polite. One thing I was determined on was that I wouldn't lose my temper or threaten him. Or complain to the police.

"You won't do that, will you?" Elizabeth asked. "You could. I mean, you're entitled to."

"No," I said.

I think now she was worried less by him than I was. She could even have been flattered in some perverse way. I can't say I was. This was the rival songbird which had won her earlier and which was competing for her once more. It became a real battle between us. I had the greater resources in money—or so I thought—

103

and I'd change taxis three or four times.

That flawed window-pane is distracting when you're lost for a sentence and stare out into the garden. I lift myself slightly in my chair and the landscape adjusts satisfactorily.

This didn't always lose Leo, as I discovered. I remember admonishing myself in these terms, "You're slipping if you can't shake this young chap or at least discourage him. You'll have to sing a bit louder." I had twinges of guilt before I took my next step and bought a Lamborghini 400 GT 2 plus 2 with a 360 h.p.p. and capable of dawdling along, according to the agents, at 155 m.p.h. (I never drove so fast, of course.) Cost about $19,000. "Craddock you're a bastard," I told myself. "How can that kid match this?"

With this I shed him for a couple of nights. He tried to follow on the second in something or other, but the white Lamborghini could accelerate from nothing to sixty in four seconds.

Elizabeth thought it was fun and I admit to experiencing some myself. The only trouble was people. Wherever we went there'd be a crowd and a host of questions. "How fast can you go?" was a common one. "I don't know," I'd say. I got a supply of pamphlets and I'd hand these out whenever there was a crowd: four-litre, double overhead camshaft V12 motor, six double choke Weber carburettors, etc., etc. This satisfied the adolescent Australian preoccupation with motor-cars. Whenever I return to Australia this childish identification of my countrymen with their motor vehicles always startles and amuses me. (What will we get up to next? I was looking out the window today and I saw a large truck hurtling by with the sign RENOVATED COW MANURE. Another sign added that it was "weed free".)

On the fourth night Leo had something in silver enamel. I didn't know what it was—I'm not clued up on

104

cars—except that it wasn't a Lamborghini. And it took me an hour to lose him. I was beginning to wonder if he'd let me. I drove on to a motel in Windsor, half expecting to see him on our heels.

"How did he get it?" I asked, puzzled. The Lamborghini was supposed to be the fastest thing in Australia.

The look on Elizabeth's face was a mixture of resignation and, I thought, admiration.

"Leo always manages."

I admit I lost a little of my poise then. We'd pulled up outside a motel. "It's a wonder you kicked him out," I said. "If he's so good."

She embraced me. "I think you're beaut," she said. "I wouldn't be here if I didn't."

The next night I couldn't lose him. I tried at noon the next day and it was the same. I sent the Lamborghini back to the dealer.

Then one day I got some luggage delivered to a hotel and booked in ahead under another name. I was sure that time he'd never find our bedroom, but when we got out of the lift he was waiting for us. Only this time he didn't say a word. We went on into the bedroom. I couldn't think how he'd outsmarted me. I'd even used a public telephone, but there it was. Elizabeth looked really upset for the first time.

"I'm worried," she said. She hung in my arms.

"Leo doesn't do anything without reason," she said. "He never did. A lawyer."

I'd never wondered about what he did. I wondered what she'd done to him, although it was no business of mine.

"Tell me, why did you break up?"

"I found I didn't love him."

"Someone else?"

"No, not then. I didn't love him any more."

I went outside and he was still there, leaning against

the lift-well. I thought, "Well, he can't stay there all night."

It was too late to think of moving. We went to bed, but he'd won that night hands down. And he started to win a few others. He was good—I have to concede him that. Something like this happened to me in Spain when secret police tailed me. They were so clumsy I thought it was funny at first. But I think now they might have been very clever. I got to wondering when they'd arrest me. They searched my baggage twice—once openly when they said they were looking for contraband and another time when I was out of the hotel. (I knew about the last because I'd set a few little traps—I won't bore you with the details because you've seen some of these on the movies.) I started worrying whether I mightn't spend six months rotting in a Francoist jail and so I cut my visit short by two weeks.

Probably it was Leo as much as anything else made me decide about this time to throw up the night parrot quest. But I'm not really sure what influenced me to think of going to Mexico instead, with Elizabeth. I do know that I was acutely depressed for a couple of days. One day I did not get up until noon and couldn't get the energy to shave until about four o'clock in the afternoon. The next day was worse—but I've described my malaise in detail earlier. As I realize now, in such moments when everything is blackest I'm liable to do something outrageous, striking out as it were in panic. Deciding to go to Mexico, a country with which I've always had a love affair, was a form of panic. I suspect I was afraid, deep inside, to go to central Australia and, as it happened, it would have been better if I had cut and run.

Joanna didn't believe me at first when I told her I was going to Mexico. When I did convince her she got upset.

106

"But why, Harry? What ever for?"

"I've often talked of going to live there. Interesting birds, too. The quetzal, for instance. I'd like to study the hoatzin some time. And the hummingbirds." I won't bore you with the long list I recited, some with their generic and specific names—the "in-talk" of the professional.

I saw her looking steadily at me and I thought I could read the unspoken question in her mind: "Who has been getting at you?"

"No one," I said.

I couldn't tell her about Leo.

"It's my idea."

She said, "You can't give up this central Australian quest—not now."

I told her I could.

I could have saved my breath, I realize. I didn't know what was stacked up against me.

15th May 1967. Harry's sudden switch from the night parrot to Mexico worries me. I had a hunch that the girl reporter working for Harry might have the clue so I invited her to lunch. All very civilized, as it happened. I hadn't a mortgage on Harry and conveyed this to her, not by what I said, but by my manner. A nice child— perhaps a woman. How could I make her understand that Harry had to go to central Australia?

"It's Harry's idea to go to Mexico," she said and I believed her. "Not mine."

"But out of the blue like this!"

"He wants to get away from Sydney." I sensed she was holding something back.

"But why Sydney?"

"There's a young man I used to be in love with—" she broke off, looking embarrassed.

107

I tried to tell her that happiness for Harry lay in the night parrot quest. I think she accepted it.

16th May 1967. I feel like a puppet master. Margaret has agreed to ask Harry to take her and Larry to central Australia. Although Harry affects to be amused by Margaret, I don't think he'll refuse her.

17th May 1967. Harry rang today.
   "Call them off," he said, laughing. I pretended not to understand. "I'm still going to Mexico."
   "Even if I said I'll go to central Australia?" I asked. He said, "Now you've given the show away."

18th May 1967. Harry rang early today. "All right, central Australia," he said.

13

I've decided to interpolate some more entries from Joanna's diary here. In addition to the other reasons I've given earlier, Joanna with her painter's eye is better at descriptive writing than I am. Moreover, having to write about the geographical features of the Centre bores me and I'd certainly be tempted to skimp it. There's a more important reason. Joanna's journal should be more accurate than my version recollected much later. But before you start reading her journal, I've interposed a blank page—this is to substitute for the fifteen hundred words of rubbish I dashed off to placate Dr Sullivan. For the fifteen hundred words take any appropriate excerpt from the autobiographies of Nietzsche, Rousseau, George Moore, Frank Harris, Goethe, Benjamin Franklin, Havelock Ellis—the list is infinitely long and suitable for a psychiatrist who has never read anything in his life. If you think I'm being capricious or lazy, then I remind you that seventeenth-century composers frequently sketched only the outline of a piece of music and left it to the musicians to improvise the rest. I'm only asking you to do the same.

The excerpts I have been supplying sometimes contradict each other. If he notices—and he must—he makes no comment. His ambition, I suspect, is to remake me in his own image, to adapt me to his other-directed world.

Excerpt of fifteen hundred words from Jean-Jacques Rousseau's *Confessions*, or what you will:

28th June 1967. Circus Water, Rawlinson Ranges, central Australia. Evening. When I start painting again I'll have to give up this diary habit. I'm a stout believer in conservation of energy and keeping a diary in which I can talk to myself and catharsize my tensions—I hope there is such a verb—must channel away some of my creative energies, just as when I was living with Harry I was absorbed with his problems. Chekhov's "Darling" —that's me. Harry's tentacles are relaxing and now I'm restless. I want to be doing something—painting something—but I don't know what.

We've been in the Centre for over a month and haven't seen even a feather of *Geopsittacus occidentalis*. But we never thought it would be easy.

We're about three hundred and fifty miles south-west of Alice and camped near a spur of the Rawlinson Ranges at the Circus Rock Hole, where a party of surveyors saw what was presumably a pair of night parrots a few years ago. This was one of the camps of the heroic Ernest Giles. There's an engraving of it in his published journals and I doubt if this "rocky tarn" has changed at all in almost a hundred years. Several deep pools lie in the gorge and include the one in the large semicircular basin which inspired the name. The ramparts tower to a thousand feet, and on the Circus floor grow the same dark-trunked desert oaks (or their descendants). And descendants of the same pigeons coo among the rocks and trees. You could live on the pigeons for months, Giles thought. After mainly tinned food, I share his speculation but put it away resolutely. Of merely academic interest, we are in Western Australia—the border with the Northern Territory is about eighty miles east! It's just after dawn. The conviction that we're in a vast sea grows stronger daily. The first day we headed out from Alice I had the feeling that it was all very familiar but could not put a name to it. Mixed

111

with this was a haunting nostalgia. Where had I seen it before? Some of this feeling is intellectual, imposed by the mind. In the plane to Alice I'd read some of Laseron's *Ancient Australia* and his account of beds of conglomerate which had once been water-worn boulders, of masses of quartzite which had once been sand on the bottom of a great tropical sea, of red slates which had once been soft mud, of limestone built from the skeletons of countless billion upon billion of sea creatures. So many must have been needed to manufacture the 400-foot-deep strata that my mind reels trying to comprehend the infinity of time and the living and the dying. All these outrageously measureless beds of that ancient sea have been pounded together and twisted and folded and broken and thrust up, stood on edge or at angles and scoured by wind and water to make the grotesque convoluted mountains and hills of the Centre. But more important is the land itself, of red plains dotted with grey mulga and yellow spinifex stretching all around to infinity, so that you are made aware of being alone in all that featureless immensity of space—and time. So this morning just after dawn I looked out through the open flap of my tent, half asleep, and the long low range became suddenly a rocky shore broken with bays and inlets into which you might sail, a rugged spur became a headland and the sun-bleached grasses, rippling with the wind, were waves tumbling on the pebbly beaches. And the night parrot was metamorphosed into an elusive petrel. Our quest acquires an ambiguity.

The Rawlinsons—and other ranges—are giant sponges that trap the rains and feed them slowly to the rockpools and to the wide belts of bloodwoods (*Eucalyptus terminalis*) at their base. In some ravines they feed water to scattered clumps of tall river red gums (*E. camaldulensis*). Beyond the gums stretches the vast

112

ocean of petrified red combers, the sandhills, with their froth of spinifex, mulga (*Acacia aneura*), saltbush (*Atriplex nummularia*, mainly), mallees (*Eucalyptus* spp.), and scattered desert oaks (*Casuarina decaisneana*).*

The country is only slowly recovering from the long drought. Much of the mulga is dead and so are some of the desert oaks and eucalypts. I notice tallish trees in isolated clumps—fed from a stream that has gone underground, or perhaps they'd got their start during a stretch of good years.

I cannot understand why some people find the vegetation of the arid lands drab. I nearly pinched myself the first time I saw a brilliant green ironwood (*Acacia estrophiolata*). With its rounded top it looked like a topiarized English oak strayed from a Home County estate to stand on a cinnabar sandhill under an ultramarine sky.

It's a wildly beautiful land and the days are gentle, rising usually to the mid-seventies, with the odd days into the nineties. The only flaws in this Eden are the bush-flies. In darting clouds they home tirelessly on your eyes and mouth—seeking moisture, Harry says. They crawl inside your sleeves and down your neck. Sometimes you swallow one and gag. Although they're loathsome, they have a strangely sweet taste. I remarked on this. Margaret said I had a habit of insisting on unpleasant truths! When you walk about they settle thickly on your shoulders, perhaps a thousand or more. Repellants and veils (which I dislike) give you some freedom.

"You don't complain about the flies," said Ted Summers soon after we left Alice.

"You can't do much about them."

"Most city people complain." I know I'm in with Ted. The flies were in millions when we first arrived

---

* EDITOR: These generic and specific names appear to have been inserted by Harry Craddock.

113

about four weeks ago. There seemed to be tens of thousands to every cubic yard of air and Ted joked that they'd break the springs of the Land-Rovers when they settled underneath them at night. They were so bad we preferred to eat after dark when they had retired. They are less plentiful now. Too cold for breeding, says Harry.

Harry wants to persist here for a few days more. He says this area is more likely than most. There's first of all, an ocean of spinifex and the only water is in the pools on the cool deep ravines in the Rawlinson Range. Tomorrow the Cessna flies out from Alice with supplies. The drome the oil-search team made is in fair state and we have made a wind-sock to help Ken Turner with his landings. After the plane is unloaded Harry goes on a reconnaissance in it. He'll watch for birds winging to water at sunset—particularly for zebra finches, which drink every day—and plot where the water-holes may be. We're on the fringe of the Gibson Desert and westward the water-holes become fewer until there are none for a stretch of three hundred miles or so. But a road of sorts, thrust through with a bulldozer and grader, runs west for four hundred and fifty miles to Carnegie in Western Australia. This is the Gunbarrel Highway built by a National Mapping Team in 1958. The construction team called it the Gunbarrel Highway because they liked to make their roads as straight as possible. Their jocular name appears on official maps; the road I observed on Harry's Royal Australian Survey Corps maps is shown with double dotted lines and the legend declares "Road unimproved earth". Most of the few roads in the Centre are of this nature. We're told it's in poor condition with great holes and gutters washed out by storms, large enough to swallow one of the Land-Rovers.

We have set nets at the approaches to four waterholes in the Ranges and have installed blue lights to
114

mimic moonlight over one pool. Parrots are seed-eaters and a reasonable assumption is that they must water regularly, unlike some other desert birds which eat insects and get some of their water from them.

Harry and Tom Drake have been arguing about methods for a week. Tom ridicules the lights. His face shows little expression, as though it were somehow muscle-bound.

"You're arguing from analogy," he says. "We don't know if *Geopsittacus* will accept them like the kiwis—their eyesight is poor and they rely on smell mainly."

"Of course we don't," says Harry. "We don't know anything at all about *Geopsittacus*. We don't even know where to look—we think it eats the seeds of *Triodia* but we don't really know. We can try the lights."

Tom agrees finally. Harry has ordered a hundred additional nets from Sydney. He has a notion of setting a solid wall of them across the plain and beating through the spinifex in daylight. I know Tom thinks it a waste of effort. I don't think he cares whether we find the night parrot or not. He has other aims. Day after day he's observing other birds—the Bourke parrots, the little brilliant green Lincoln parrots, budgerigars, spinifex pigeons, even the great soaring wedge-tailed eagles. At this moment he's out in one of the hides we've built near the water-holes.

Harry and Ted Summers have spent the night moving about checking the mist nets, using their electric torches sparingly so as not to frighten the birds. Birds must not be left long in the cool desert night lest they die. Here on the Great Western Plateau we are over 1500 feet above sea level. The night before last Harry and Ted caught and released several hundred Bourke parrots and five owls. The dawn before a flock of about one thousand budgerigars crashed into one net before they'd had time to lower it. It took them half an hour to release them.

One night I sat with Harry near the nets set round the rock pool. Suddenly the dark silence was broken by a shrill whistling of wings and high-pitched musical chatter.

"Bourkes," Harry whispered.

Some of the invisible flock thumped! thumped! thumped! into the nets. I counted about a dozen thumps. We waited ten minutes. Then Harry flicked on his torch. Shining like pinkish-green opals with diamond eyes, some were momentarily fixed on the pool's edge. Then with short, stubby wings they soared and dipped, darting away.

Harry is in high spirits. He's absorbed in the quest and his romanticism has a role to play. He invents himself daily. He'd like to be Ernest Giles exploring this region for the first time and with death his companion. Not far from here Giles's companion Gibson died and Giles, too, narrowly escaped. But those, Harry recognizes, were other times and Giles, if he could, would have taken two-way radios.

Harry's cheerfulness is infectious. Even Tom thaws at times. Very little ruffles Harry—or appears to—not even the constant run of flat tyres on our sweeps in the orange-coloured Land-Rovers through the spinifex shallows or climbing the arrested rollers of the sandhills. But Tom and Larry swear, sweat and fume. I fume a little, too—I suppose because there's nothing much I can do.

Harry seems reconciled to Larry Jordan and talks to him without any apparent strain. Of course, this could be Harry in another of his roles—that of the civilized man of the world who never shows what he really thinks. "The trouble with the English upper classes is that you never know where you stand with them," he once said to me. "They'll never betray whether they

116

hate you—Australians nearly always do. You remember that Macaulay said that the Greeks in their decadence were like that and so were the Renaissance Italians. Why declare your hatred when you could quietly have an enemy stabbed in the back by a paid assassin or by a poisoned draught of wine? I've forgotten the exact wording."

The latter-day Greeks were the English, Harry went on, and the Americans were the Romans, rather naïve and still trying to cling to principles. I recall a conversation Harry had with a London drama critic. Harry thought him amoral. The Englishman said he wrote criticism first of all to sell newspapers and, secondly, he wanted to be remembered as a wit and have his books of criticism handed down to posterity. "What about your responsibilities?" Harry asked.

"You Australians!" the other exclaimed. "You're nearly as bad as the Americans."

Anyway, Larry and Margaret are here with us on Harry's invitation and everything goes amicably.

I suppose it's a measure of Harry's good leadership and generosity that we get along so well together. I don't think I could be as patient as he is with Tom, who is a constant complainer. The mist nets are faulty. The equipment the university supplied is no good. We're looking in the wrong place. Nothing good will come of the expedition. Etcetera. The complaints aren't stated as directly as I've put them, but that is what they amount to. A sentence ending in a preposition. My father would not have approved. The charitable thing is to assume that Tom has a pessimistic outlook—he expects to fail or he's preparing an excuse in case he does. Or if he does succeed, his success will be the greater for overcoming these difficulties. His life style is not an easy one! His lower-middle-class background accounts for some of it. People in our class expect to succeed. "A G.P.S. education is worth several thousands a year," Harry said once. "Even the most mediocre leave their schools believing they're an élite."

Last night before I fell asleep I heard a dingo howling and realized suddenly it hurt no longer the way it did. That first night out from Alice I heard a dingo howling and could not get to sleep for hours.

29th June 1967. The Rawlinson Range glows saffron yellow in the dawn. The thermometer registers 43°F. and the soles of my shoes are chilly. A hundred galahs lift off a dead bloodwood tree and it bursts suddenly into bloom with a mass of pink and grey blossoms—like an exotic magnolia. The pulsing noisy cloud wheels away and envelopes a ghost gum (white trunk gleaming) and it sheds its Palladian elegance and assumes a Rococo sumptuousness. I must leave this, make coffee and start breakfast.

The same evening. After his flight with Ken—landing with a flurry of billowing red sand—Harry says, yes, there are water-holes to the east along the northern flanks of the Rawlinsons. He points out that some are shown on the map—Tyndall Spring, Groener Spring, Luehman Spring, Sladen Water, and others. We have all pored over these names on the Royal Australian Army Survey Corps map and I have read about them in Giles's books. It's obvious we should try further to the east. Ted Summers, who has taken parties there, supports him. But Tom Drake wants to try the northern areas. The arguments he advances don't seem compelling, even to my uninformed unornithological mind. I suspect it is a ploy in the power game. Ted points out that the sandhills run east and west so the northern trip will be difficult. And he says there's no permanent water. You only find that where there are mountains to act as catchment areas. Harry produces the map. It

118

shows nothing to the north but sand-ridges and scattered scrub. He concedes there might be water in the low Gillespie Hills, about thirty-six miles north. "But I saw none and no finches feeding there at sunset." The argument continues, but in the end Harry, always too good-hearted, gives in to Tom. "What's another two hundred miles or so?" And Drake shrugs heavy shoulders.

I like Ted Summers more and more. He knows what's going on. He must be sixty but is as active as men half his age, bull-necked and wrinkled. There's a gentleness about him. He doesn't expect Harry or the others to be able to match him, and thank God these outback Australians don't indulge in that ceaseless aggressive banter of their coastal brothers.

"Okay, we'll give it a go," Ted says.

We agree to move in the morning and return here later to pick up the extra mist nets Harry has ordered. The Cessna 182 will freight them out when they arrive.

I sent a short piece about the Craddock and Drake Expedition on the transceiver to Alice today to be wired to *The Clarion* and *The Times*. I volunteered for the job before we left Sydney. And I suggested that Elizabeth should write the copy. This way I'll know what is sent. Tom Drake wasn't pleased.

2nd July 1967. Evening. No entries for yesterday because I was too tired. We all flopped into bed and fell asleep. It was a tough trip clambering through mile after mile of the red sandhills, with crests forty feet high, thrusting up like red ribs from the thick mulga scrub on their flanks. They were thirty to a hundred yards apart. Some we had to charge up to six times to make finally their crests, in swirling clouds of bulldust (as the locals call it), so that we were all soon coated with a pink powder, fine as talc, through which we gleamed at each other with white teeth and chatted grittily with pink

I

tongues. At intervals between the sandhills were great stony or gibber plains. Aeons of wind and water have smashed the once solid siliceous or flinty horizontal strata and winds have carried away the loose soil cover until only a gleaming stony rubble remains. Wind-blown sand has abraded the stones and small boulders into smooth shiny pebbles with sloping sides. Pick one up and you'll discover it is shaped like a low tent or a pyramid. They're polished, too, with a coating of "desert varnish"—a deposit of colloidal silica or oxide of iron. Back from one immense plain lay a table-topped low hill (mesa) crowned with a red crust of gibbers, its sloping flanks eroded by wind and water. Each vehicle in turn had several flat tyres—the mulga and mallee scrub was rough on tyres and body work as we smashed our way through. We suffered a smashed differential in our vehicle and the one Tom drove broke an axle. Such things are all in the day's work. In spite of the screens in front of the radiators, insects, spinifex husks and wild flowers lodge in the core of the radiators. Two vehicles became overheated and forced us to halt. The men cleaned out the radiators with pieces of bent copper wire. In the late afternoon we drove on to sand plains and the garish orange-coloured Land-Rovers left a wake through the spinifex sea. Then we came to the edge of a vast puce-coloured salt-pan and were tempted to cut across it. But Ted warned us not to try. "It could be soft after the rain," he said. There'd been a thunder-storm here a few weeks earlier he said, pointing to the clusters of mauve pussytails, bluebell bushes, yellow jack, white and yellow daisies, splotching the brown earth under the straight-limbed desert oaks and twisted hakeas on the plain. Here, too, the rain had brought an early flowering of the spinifex; fluffy seed-ears grew from the centre of the clumps and waved above the level of the radiator.

120

So we skirted the pan for six miles and then rode over a mulga and saltbush steppe with splotches of spinifex, and later on a claypan which Ted tested with a geological hammer. It rang like iron, and he pronounced it safe. We drove across it for three miles and with evening approaching made camp.

We are relatively sophisticated, but I notice that in the stillness of that night we huddle close together round the campfire. Soon after sunset we heard the primeval howling of a dingo. Sometimes in the morning Ted points out their tracks circling our camp. As for the night parrot, Harry says laconically, "It's as likely to be here as anywhere else."

The desert which is so silent and empty by day, except for the slow wheeling of a black-brown eagle or hawk and the prattling of finches at a water-hole or the complaint of a crow, comes to life at night. Marsupial mice, wombats, bandicoots and northern native cats emerge, and the alien rabbits. Their tracks print the dawn-viewed sands.

6th July 1967. Early morning. Thursday, too, though days of the week grow meaningless. We're back at the drome. The north was a flop. Harry proposes to search among the spinifex for tracks of the birds. He's nothing if not thorough. The museum has sent him casts of the feet of the night parrot specimens it has. Harry makes tracks in the sand and studies them with Ted while Tom stands watching amusedly. It's funny or touching, depending on your attitudes. Caught up in this new thought, Harry has asked Alice to fly out a black tracker. He despairs of running into any wild or near-wild Aborigines. Ted reassures him. "We may run into some any day," he says. "There's a few about—perhaps a family or two. They'll have seen our fires by now." Fortunately he knows a few words of the Pitjantjatjara tongue.

121

I give an impression of calm and stability and so I invite confidences. Also, it's probably because I don't seek intimate friendships—people have to talk, confess, to someone and I'm as impersonal as the confessional box. I'm that stranger on a long train journey whom you'll never see again. Thus Tom seeks me out and unburdens himself and I listen patiently. He reproaches himself. "I turn on people and abuse them," he said tonight.

"Why do you do it?"

"I don't know," he said. "Everyone gets abusive letters from me at some time or another."

"Harry, too?"

"He's had several."

"I didn't know. What did he do?"

"He ignored the first ones and then—" he leaned forward clicking his fingers—"he hit back at me. I was sorry because I owe him a lot."

"Harry doesn't see it that way. No one owes anyone anything, he says."

"But the money he's loaned—given me."

"For science."

"So he says."

"Can't you accept it for that reason? Harry's money is a happy accident."

I couldn't help him. I'd learnt that long ago; these people didn't want advice; they wanted an audience. I'm always telling myself I'll shed these people because of their emotional drain on me. Tom pressed my hand warmly when leaving. Like Larry, Tom is growing a beard. Shaving, they say, is too much trouble.

Elizabeth has become as absorbed in her reptiles as Harry is with his night parrot. She has overcome her maidenly fears of handling them. And she has taken to digging among the spinifex in search of sleeping and

122

hibernating creatures. "You be careful!" Ted warns. "You could flush a sleeping brown snake."

Harry gravely proceeded to tell her how to catch a western brown snake by grabbing its tail and snatching it clear of the ground. He explained it couldn't bite you provided you kept it off balance. "Its muscles are designed for going forward—not backward. I'll show you how to do it." Always the precisionist, Harry points out that a snake would be pretty sluggish at this time of the year. I don't think Elizabeth's keenness will go so far. None the less, she has to be called several times to meals and sometimes at table she does not hear when she's spoken to. Oddly, this intensity irritates Margaret though she has been helping Elizabeth and seemed to be enjoying it. In other respects Margaret has adapted herself well. Gossip has it that she once got Balenciaga to design some gardening slacks for her. If true, she's more like Harry than I suspect —turning a stately ballroom into a phytotron and *haute couture* gardening slacks are on a par. She has a fund of dirty/bawdy stories which she tells well. Good timing.

I can't quite see where Larry fits into the picture except that he seems devoted. He appears rather dull and dogged, but there's possibly more to him than that. He thinks Harry and I are very highbrow—his words.

"You really like that stuff?" he asked last night. I was playing Mozart's piano concerto in B Flat K. 456 on the transistor record player. Ingrid Haebler and the London Symphony Orchestra.

"Yes." What else could I say? He looked almost incredulous. I took the record off.

"Don't let me stop you."

"I'd sooner talk," I said.

"If I knew anything about cattle I wouldn't mind coming out here," he said presently.

123

"Once you've tasted the water," I said.

"You always come back," he finished.

In the main, conversation between Larry and myself is rather Pinterish. (My remark and his are, of course, Territory clichés.) Most of our conversation on this jaunt is Pinterish. We are a mixed lot bound together on a common quest about which we have varying degrees of intensity from Harry downwards. Larry is well up the scale.

"It's like a detective puzzle," he said. And I caught the same expression I'd seen on that game warden's face in Uganda when he'd spoken of some challenge he'd taken up.

Gossip item: Margaret and Larry were quarrelling about something this morning. I heard voices raised in their tent—hers mainly. I have too much interest in other people for the good of my soul. My excuse is that I'm concerned for the success of this expedition. Perhaps too much so, but I was the eldest of a large family. "Be careful you don't become an authoritarian," my father once warned jokingly when I was thirteen or so. Or a substitute mother, I think he nearly said, but was restrained by loyalty to my neglectful mother. My father had a keen sense of humour, a sceptical mind, and a rigorous love of his fellows. He saw them clearly but never lost his affection for them. I try to live as he did, but don't always succeed.

Tom was almost cheerful today and the chip was considerably smaller. I hope Harry hasn't made a mistake in including him. I have hunches and, unfortunately, they usually turn out to be correct.

Elizabeth is a choice I thoroughly approve. That's the end of my current catalogue of anxieties.

Social note: Keen competition among the amateur photographers—Elizabeth, Margaret and Larry—but only Elizabeth, I think, has those qualities which Harry has. Dedication, "feel", attention to detail.

7th July 1967. After lunch Harry, Ted and Larry went searching among the flax-coloured spinifex for tracks and tunnels of the night parrot. They came back to what we now call Base Camp at three o'clock, reporting that they had seen some possible tracks. Harry is disappointed that they can't send a tracker out immediately.

The spinifex grows out from a circular clump; the strands lean over, touch the ground, and take root. The old clumps die off so it grows outward, sometimes making complete circles like fairy mushrooms with clear ground in the centre; more frequently there are half-circles. These spinifex crescents and circles, up to four feet high, are the fortress homes of colonies of marsupial mice, skinks and insects. And of wallabies which make their squats in their centres. They must also provide the day shelters of the night parrots. A few mornings ago I got up just before dawn and threaded my way gingerly through the spinifex. The needle-sharp leaf-tips penetrate even the toughest clothing and cover your shins with a mass of tiny pinpricks. The coarsest of corduroy slacks—even canvas shin guards—offer little protection. I sat down in a clearing and waited. At the back of my mind was the extravagant hope I might see the night parrot. The adult marsupial mice were wary; they'd peer out with noses twitching, sometimes dart back, then creep along the spinifex wall before darting across the sand to another clump. The half-grown ones are more careless. One big-eared baby sat up and preened his coat in a shaft of sunlight for three minutes. Some day a hawk or a snake will swoop on him and, if he escapes, he'll be more cautious.

Only when the sun was well up and it was warmer did the small brown and reddish-coloured skinks, about a finger long, emerge, as suspicious as the marsupial mice and quicksilver fast in their erratic darting from clump to clump. These spiky clumps are the homes of snakes and goannas, but they're inactive now—and the snakes, Harry assures me, are nocturnal anyway. Occasionally you may come on a central netted dragon (*Amphibolurus reticulatus inermis*), up to a foot long, sunning itself on a rock. If you scare it, it scampers sluggishly into its burrow at the foot of the rock. A handsome fellow, this stocky lizard with its orange upper surface covered with a network of matt black. Its burrow is quite shallow, only six inches to a foot deep, sloping slightly backward from the entrance. Sometimes it digs its burrow into the side of a spinifex-capped sand mound.

Our reptile collecting will be restricted until the days get warmer. Harry thinks we may be able to track some down and excavate them rudely from their dream-filled(?) hibernation.

Harry worries the speculative bone, but sometimes I find myself not caring if we don't find the wretched bird. It's so peaceful here. My senses are sharper than they were in Sydney: the clean chaffy smell of spinifex is exciting; my ears hear the scamper of tiny marsupial mice and the soft slither of skinks; my eyes note the overlooked beauty of the mulga with its soft grey-blue leaves and black trunks and branches; the foliage is sparse and the tree projects a crossed-veined tracery of black twigs against a Della Robbia blue sky. I find a harsh, dramatic beauty in the gnarled hakeas (beef-woods). The sand-blasted terracotta rocks of the ranges, the red sands and the hard blue skies remind me, oddly, of the background landscapes in early Italian portrait paintings. Food has new intense flavours. I've

126

begun painting again. I've regained concentration.

I don't quite know why I came to the Centre. Sometimes I think I was drawn to it irresistibly, just as Harry was, but for a different reason or reasons. To get away from Sydney, which wearied me, and that criminally dishonest war in Vietnam? As though one can run away! Or a return to the freedom of childhood, to a lost paradise, casting away the chains of routine and trivial cares of adult life ("I must remember to get the vacuum cleaner repaired"). Return to nature? That's not my life style. The simple life normally doesn't appeal to me. It's too damned uncomfortable to seek it (I like my daily shower) but once there I enjoy myself. Did I come for Harry's sake? I don't know. Yet, recalling those last few weeks in Sydney, I was almost as keen as Harry was! We're a damnably self-conscious generation which tries to analyse everything we do—or don't do. Was Hamlet the first modern man revealed in literature?

8th July 1967. About noon today we saw several columns of smoke climbing into the far-off north-west metallic blue sky. "Pitjantjatjara," said Ted. "They're burning the spinifex to drive out the game."

"And incinerating the night parrots," Harry said. [*H.C.*: It is, perhaps, unimportant, but I did not say this. This is an instance where Joanna could confidently assume what I was in fact thinking—possibly by studying my face—but most emphatically I did not say it. It would have been fatuous to have done so.]

Jim Johnson, the Aboriginal tracker, and Ted have searched all afternoon for tracks of the night parrot. I think the tracker knows what to look for though he says he has never seen the bird. Soon after he was landed, Harry handed him the cast of the bird's feet and he studied them for ten minutes, turning them

127

about in his pale-yellow palms and peering at them, not speaking. One parrot foot looks like another to me, but if there is a difference he'll find it. Harry also showed him a colour photograph of a desert chat's nest with some night parrot feathers in it. This was found some years ago. Unfortunately, the slide isn't of high quality photographically. Jim is about forty-five, rather fat, with greying hair, and once was in the police force. I'd like to ask him his Aranda name but am inhibited. He has a typical great bulbous nose, full lips and wide mouth. His chocolate-brown skin gleams as though polished.

He and Harry have hit it off from the start. Both squat on their heels in the spinifex and peer at the sand. My interest aroused and eyes opened, I notice now there are plenty of tracks. "Spinifex pigeon!" says Jim, pointing. And again, "Crow." "Galah." "Mouse." But no night parrot in five hours. No tunnels either. Harry is not daunted. Jim's voice charms me: it is throaty, musical, rather like a magpie's call with the same dark tones. His English is good and no one insults him by speaking a bastard pidgin, as some tourists do in Alice. (No one except journalists and tourist publicity brochures call it "The Alice"—to the locals it is Alice.)

More confessions from Tom to which I listen without comment. My motives are probably not as pure as I'd claimed earlier. People fascinate me in the way animals excite Harry. (Animals are easier to understand.) Tom's childhood is almost a classic case of a rejected child. "I turned to animals. I kept guinea pigs and collected birds' eggs—I blush over that now . . ." And the unsuccessful marriage looking for a mother substitute. [H.C.: That dream he told me. He was somewhere in the East and dark-haired women siezed him, tore off his clothing and bound him to a

128

bed. They caressed his member and each had coitus with him. Another time, he said, he was on the top of the stairs with a girl cousin. On the landing. She is wearing a short nightdress and his only garment is a shirt. He is stimulated. The coy verb is his. He embraces the girl and he finds suddenly he is much shorter than she is. His member reaches half-way down her thighs. He ejaculates and he is suddenly worried his cousin will notice the stain. "You used to press yourself against your mother when you were a child!" I said. "That's a lie!" he cried indignantly.]

9th July 1967. The mist nets have arrived and we have laboured nobly all day to erect them in a gentle crescent six hundred feet wide—one hundred nets each sixty feet long and nine feet high—in the ripe wheat-yellow spinifex. Every spinifex blade has its questing needle point which penetrates even thick clothing. My ankles and shins are stinging.

10th July 1967. At nine o'clock in the morning the intrepid army formed a line and launched the attack across the spinifex-defended plain. Half a mile away lay our objective, the small white flags Harry had set on the line of nets to guide us through the head-high spinifex.

When our brave commander gave us the command to advance, we struck out into the spinifex shouting and beating our drums (kerosene tins). No band of conquistadors was bolder than we were. The cruel barricades of spinifex spears could not check our resolve or hold us back. Harry sometimes muttered an oath and plucked out the offending barb; Margaret uttered small cries of pain and was comforted by Larry; Tom strode along purposefully in a temper; Ted Summers said nothing though frequently injured,

129

for the spinifex clumps sometimes grew so closely together that we had to force our way between the defences; Elizabeth, young and dauntless, drummed louder than the rest; and, I, not to be disgraced in such gallant company, took as my model the stoical Aboriginal, Jim, who said nothing when wounded but grinned happily.

So we plunged on intrepidly, scaring out the grass wrens, spinifex pigeons, mice, but never a night parrot. If such were huddling in the spinifex fortresses, they were, no doubt, in quest of sleep after their night's foraging for food and not to be hustled out into the open by rude trespassers. Or, more likely, they crouched in fear and let the tide of the attackers roll pass them. We swept on to the mist nets, sweating, exhilarated, to find all empty except for grass wrens and spinifex pigeons to be released with hands unsteady from sudden exertion.

A second determined attack from the other direction was no more successful. The Grand Old Duke of York, etc. With our honourable wounds, caked in sweat-soaked dust and beating back armadas of bushflies, we retired to Base Camp. [H.C.: As we did on other occasions. You can repeat several times Joanna's imaginative description.]

Late this afternoon we saw our first semi-wild Pitjantjatjara. They revealed themselves first by lighting a fire about half a mile away, so we lit another. The men were away but we knew the protocol, having been put right by Ted. Twenty minutes afterwards two women, one young with a fat baby in her thin arms, and three children, walked shyly into the camp. Behind them stalked the husband, carrying spears and woomera—a tall handsome chap with one of his gleaming eye-teeth missing (tapped out in initiation rites). He seemed to flow over the ground with an

130

elegance of carriage that made us look clumsy and muscle-bound. He was lithe, alert, with an air of natural nobility. They wore clothing and the eldest lad, about twelve, used an old striped tie to hold up his trousers. Elizabeth, I saw, was denuding them with every look—they wouldn't photograph well in European cast-offs! Jim was away with the men so I attempted to talk to them.

"Have tea!" I urged and gestured towards the billy. They understood, but other attempts to speak brought laughter and giggles from broad mouths as they lost their shyness. We handed out staccato words and food; the eldest boy knew a little English; we were having a fine party when the men returned. The young lad had badly scarred hands and shoulders from rolling into a campfire when asleep one night. (They sleep between two or more fires.) The older woman, perhaps forty, was nearly blind from ophthalmia. They were, we learnt, on a walkabout from the Warburton Ranges to the Ernabella Mission in the Musgrave Ranges in South Australia—a four-hundred-mile trip —to attend a big corroboree.

Through Jim, Harry questioned the man and boys about *Geopsittacus* and showed them coloured photographs. They said they had no knowledge of it.

"That's more reliable than if they said they had," said Tom.

"Cynic," said Margaret.

Later the family moved over into the night, the women with their dilly bags, yam sticks, drinking vessels and a blackened billy, and the man carrying a fire stick with which he set fire to the spinifex clumps as they went to show them the way. The resinous clumps blazed pungently and brilliantly, hurling black smoke and a green light and red sparks into the darkness. (Spinifex, even when green, is as explosive as

131

though drenched in kerosene.) The family made a fire not far off and settled down to sleep. The desert nights are dark and silent; immensities of space and time encompass you. Some hours later I was wakened from sleep in the warm womb of my tent. I heard a frightening cry. A night bird or a dingo, I thought. I crossed to the flap and looked out. Against the dull red glow of their fire I saw the mother holding the baby and comforting him.

10th July 1967. Larry, bless him, has all the arrogance of the typical pragmatic Australian. Applied science he can appreciate, particularly if it assists those national benefactors, the men on the land. But Harry and Tom's brand of finding out, science for science's sake, is beyond him and he has contempt (well concealed) for their activities. Looking for an elusive bird is okay —that's a challenge—but studying birds generally without some aim of immediate profit is another matter. Larry's attitude to Harry is somewhat mixed. He respects Harry because he is a Craddock (money)! Accordingly, I was mildly surprised this morning when he came back from the kidney-shaped rock-pool with a large jar filled with water. He pointed to the four-inch layer of sand on the bottom.

"Ted's been telling me about them." He grinned. "I want to see it for myself."

Harry came over. "I'll get an aquarium sent up from Adelaide. That jar is a bit small."

"Thanks, but let me pay for it."

"Nonsense." Harry rushed off to the pool and returned with some pond weed.

[*H.C.*: Larry had gathered some sand from the shores of a shrunken pool which could be assumed to have the minute eggs of the shield shrimps—*Triops* (formerly *Apus*) *australiensis*—which often lie dormant for

132

months or even years until water fills the pools. In a remarkable adaptation to arid conditions these olive-green, shield-shaped crustacea with long multi-segmented abdomens, growing up to about three inches long, race through their complete life cycle in a few weeks. These creatures, among the most primitive of all crustacea, mature, breed, lay eggs and die in a life that, even more than man's, is solitary, poor, nasty, short and brutish!]

Ted and Jim are hard at work repairing tubes. Ted waves his tyre levers and points out that they're polished like silver from use on the trip north. Who said Aboriginals are lazy? They never saw someone like Jim with his chocolate-brown face gleaming with sweat as he struggled today with an obstinate tyre.

"Good worker," I said to Ted.

"They reckon that anything a white man can do they can do better," he said. No malice meant.

Ted has a birthday tomorrow. Sixty-five. He looks ten years younger. Harry winked at me.

11th July 1967. About 10 a.m. Jim heard a plane some-where in the west—at least five minutes before we could. Then we finally saw it over the Rawlinsons.

"Wonder where he's heading?" Elizabeth speculated.

It turned out he was heading for us—Ken landed with a couple of cases of beer, and some whisky and a rifle. Harry had ordered them last night as a birthday surprise for Ted.

We had a sudden storm today and half an inch of rain tumbled down in an hour, filling the claypan and scouring gutters in the sand. None of the tents leaked. We enjoyed the downpour but it puts a finish to our mist nets round the water-holes. There'll be water everywhere for several days and the night parrots need never venture near the holes.

14

Pseudemydura umbrina has a mirror in his office/ consulting rooms and I suspect it is cunningly placed so that you are caught unawares and encounter an image of yourself you'd rather not see. I was, I admit, flattered when someone I'd not seen for fifteen years phoned before I went to central Australia and said, "I saw you on television. You've got more hair than I have." That's the Vincent heritage, but it's a bit thin over the temples.

I told you I was a buffoon and Joanna in wifely loyalty underlines it with her description of our beating through the spinifex after ambiguities of petrel– night parrot and the meaning of existence.

Joanna has mentioned the flies; the ants were almost as troublesome—if you let them worry you. One tiny brown ant about the size of a grain of sugar seemed to have a radar device to home on anything living. Every time you stopped near one of their nests they formed a line and headed towards you. They sought out places that are moist with sweat and their sting was as sharp as a wasp's. In "ant country" the Aborigines kept the ants at bay with a circle of small fires—something we had to do twice. Generally we tried to avoid camping in ant country.

That native was a fine-looking chap but prickly as the rest of them where his women were concerned. When he challenged me to a duel with spears I had no course but to accept. He accused me of luring his younger woman away into the spinifex! I laid myself open to it, I suppose. I'd showed her some tracks of *Geopsittacus* I'd made with the cast and pointed. She made signs for me to follow. He came up a few min-

134

utes later, shouting in his own tongue at me and his wife. He thrust his sweating face near mine; I noticed for the first time a mole on his cheek with a single, very long hair. Jim came along, otherwise my story might never have got onto this page—although, no doubt, revenge is ritualized among the Pitjantjatjara. When Jim explained the husband wanted to fight a duel with spears, I said, "Okay! Tell him I accept. But I want a few trial throws." Dark heads wagged and voices lunged and riposted. In time it was agreed. I was to get some practice and then three throws each in turn—my challenger only had three spears—and he was to have first throw. Could you imagine anything more absurd? But what was I—a civilized man—to do? I couldn't insult him in his own country by refusing to abide by his customs. (It might have been settled another way but I doubt if Joanna would have agreed!) *

The spears were beautifully balanced, about nine feet long and weighing about five pounds, I judged. Two were fitted with two or three wooden barbs, hardened by fire, and carrying God knows how many millions of bacteria. Three others had steel barbs, equally unhygienic. (When Joseph Banks landed at Botany Bay he feared the Aborigines' "darts" were poisoned—he was closer to the truth than he knew.) I'd thrown Aboriginal spears before on an earlier trip and I soon recaptured the knack of engaging it in the woomera and hurling it with a full body swing. I'd no intention of trying to spear our friend, but I owed it to him to put on a good show. He was younger, about thirty-five, and fit, but I was taller and stronger. He saw the distance I got on my fifth throw and grew thoughtful.

* EDITOR: Aboriginal custom allows for disputes to be determined by an exchange of wives.

"About six throws on each side and honour will be satisfied!" I told myself aloud. I threw a few more and told Jim I was ready. We found a reasonably clear spot and, as I'd expected, our friend took himself off a good forty yards for the first throw. I wet a finger and estimated the wind. I seem to remember it was a steady four knots, blowing straight across the arena from my left. The knack when he hurled the spear was to wait as long as possible watching its flight, just as you do in the outfield at cricket, before moving to one side to let it fly harmlessly by. If it was coming at you, you could stand your ground because the wind would swing it away. The dangerous throw would probably be one a bit to my left.

He grinned, drew back his arm with the spear couched in the woomera, and hurled it towards me. I waited, resisting the urge to move too quickly. It was dead on. I stepped smartly to the left and it thudded into the ground behind me. I told myself sharply, "Step calmly, otherwise you'll trip." I should have had my mind on what was happening. His second spear was almost on me. I hadn't time to do anything except freeze where I was. It thumped into the ground. It seemed to me I could hear it humming in the wind. The third spear was launched almost instantly. I sighted it, waited, and skipped swiftly to the right.

"You thought you had me!" I said.

My turn came then. I didn't insult him with wide throws. I reasoned I couldn't hit him anyway and threw as straight as I could. The first was a foot to the left and he didn't bother to move. The second was right on. He dodged it with ease. The third was off.

Three more rounds followed. I remember asking myself what was the protocol and hoping he'd get tired soon of the silly game, as I prepared to hurl my last spear in the third return round.

A wind gust must have confused him. I thought the spear had curved well to the right of him. But then he seemed to side-step almost into its flight. The spear jangled past him safely, I thought. But he was staring down at his right calf and Jim called out something in Pitjantjatjara. I ran forward and saw the blood suddenly well out and afterwards spread in a sheet down the skinny brown leg. Fortunately it was only a nick and served its purpose—the game was getting dangerous. I was sorry for him.

"Tell him it was a lucky throw!" I urged Jim. Harold Piper Vincent Craddock, the Ajax of the Centre.

Birds were always a good pointer to the water-holes we sought. The zebra finch (*Taeniopygia castanotis*) wasn't an infallible guide because I knew it could tolerate a salt solution slightly stronger than sea water and I was reasonably sure the night parrot couldn't if it was like other members of the parrot family, such as the budgerigars.

In the desert grasslands where our search was concentrated birds were scarce except near water-holes— or after rain. We came to rely on them as reliable indicators. I remember that early one night we got to within ten miles or so of a rock-hole just on sunset and had to make camp.

"I hope there's water there," Ted said. In the morning he woke me, grinning, and pointing. A willy wagtail (*Rhipidura leucophrys*) was swooping up bush-flies within a few inches of our feet. And yellow-throated miners (*Myzantha flavigula*), spiny-cheeked honeyeaters (*Acanthagenys rufogularis*) and singing honeyeaters (*Meliphaga virescens*) were feeding among the isolated flowering bloodwoods. That morning we saw also two crows.

137

Earlier on Joanna made quite a bit about Margaret and her fiancé. I didn't attempt to correct the false impression she may have given, because no short interpolation would have served. I admit that at first I had had some prejudice about Larry, but I overcame it. If anything, I think Joanna was the one who had reservations about Larry by the time we'd got to Base Camp. Significantly, there are few entries about either Larry or Margaret in her journal and she'd been reserved with Larry. For my part, I'd accepted Larry by that time. He had money of his own—a good sheep property near Cootamundra, I'd discovered—was quite a pleasant fellow, and would make Margaret a good husband. At their time of life, age differences didn't matter a great deal.

In the Centre, Larry grew keen on finding the night parrot. "We could set up a few artificial waterholes—with polyurethane sheets," he suggested. It struck me as worth trying. We made eight artificial water-holes, each six feet by three, with sheets of polyurethane and set nets round them. Also he got curious about the shield shrimps, although I couldn't persuade him to do any field work. It's a pity because there's still much to be learnt about them and some of our greatest contributions in natural history have been made by amateurs.

As Joanna says, I delayed about going to the Centre —true enough—but I think Elizabeth was the major reason and not my sister's engagement. I wanted more time alone with Elizabeth. I wouldn't have that in the Centre. Earlier I'd tried to avert what had happened. I was, after all, fifty and I didn't want to live parasitically, as it were, renewing my youth in the affections of a young girl. But she had such tenderness and womanliness I surrendered. My depression fled overnight. When finally we went to the Centre my spirits

138

rose even higher; it was as though I'd escaped from my old life. I had an idea that I might even take up residence there. Most of all I enjoyed the cold nights under the clear cloudless skies when the stars crackled brilliantly and we'd build up the fire and carve our own warm pulsing circle. I remember one night watching for endless minutes the shadows scampering up and down the trunk of a large mulga, replete after a good meal, my work done for the day and tomorrow's well planned. Or walking round the nets at night I'd say absurd phrases to myself, and verses I'd remembered:

> "with an hoast of furious fancies
> whereof I am commaunder,
> with a burning speare, & a horse of aire,
> to the wildernesse I wander."

I'd sing this in what I hoped was a kind of early English. Or I'd start punning, what a site/sight for the night parrot. It'll be accidentalis if we sight *occidentalis*. *Geopsittacus* will opt to sit and laugh at us. I struggled hard with that last, trying to make a rhyme that made sense. The others would have got a shock if they could have listened in but, of course, I was able to keep it to myself then, even if some of the phrases became rather obsessional.

We were well out of the world though we could tune in to the news sessions and from time to time we got newspapers and mail. Some popular newspapers carried the usual beat-up stories about us with references to "the luxury air-conditioned expedition", etc. We didn't have air-conditioning, of course—we didn't need it with daily average temperatures ranging from 42°F. to 67°F. Several days it shot into the seventies, but the dry heat was pleasant. If anything, we needed heating with some mornings in the low thirties, frost on the ground and chill dry winds. It was winter, as I suppose the more intelligent readers have realized. But though it wasn't a luxury air-conditioned expedition, there was nothing particularly heroic about it. The once impassable deserts of Australia have become tourist jaunts for suburbanites and nothing is left sacred under the visiting moon.

Tom grew impatient much earlier than I'd hoped.

"We may be looking for a bird which no longer exists!" he said one evening.

"It's too early yet."

"Early?"

"The area to be searched is immense. The whole of the arid two-thirds of Australia, probably. We've barely started. And no one has ever looked for it systematically."

"It could take years." He frowned. I couldn't see why he worried, because we were busy—Tom particularly—gathering material on other birds. And Elizabeth and Joanna, enthusiastic amateurs, had started studying the skinks. When it got warmer there'd be other reptiles to study. They planned to use the blue lights to learn something about the two pythons (the carpet snake and the woma) and the western brown snake and the king brown (or mulga) snake, all of which were active at night.

For the main we were a harmonious team and respected each other's status and territory, as it were. This is meant only half seriously, but I am animal-oriented in my thinking. The territory thing extended to meals or even where we pitched our tents. We always took the same stools for meals. I remember observing to myself that, as leader of the expedition, I was much like the *alpha* animal which owed its dominance to seniority and strength (money in my

140

case!). A better analogy was probably with the lion-tamer who is accepted as the *alpha* animal by the lions and tigers in the troupe. And Tom was the young tiger who wanted to challenge my dominant position. As my consort, or ex-consort, Joanna took her status from me. My studies of work by Hediger, Tinbergen, Buytendrik, Schjelderup-Ebbe, Allee, Guhl and others, and the memoirs of the lion-tamer Court, helped to some understanding of the social hierarchy of the Craddock and Drake Expedition of 1967. As the *alpha* animal I had to preserve my moral superiority; I had to anticipate and forestall a revolt; and, I had, more-over, to protect the animals lower down the peck order —such as Jim, the Aboriginal, poor *omega* in the book of the well-fed city lions and tigers at first, but not later. Never in mine, I assure you! And Ted Summers was *beta* in my book, whatever he was in theirs.

I've often observed this territory business in other situations. Once in London I was on a bus that broke down near Piccadilly. We had to get out and wait fifteen minutes for a replacement bus—it was late at night. When we took our seats everyone resumed seats in the second bus exactly corresponding to those we had had in the old. Again, anyone who has given a series of lectures will observe that a very large proportion of his audiences sits night after night in the same seats. This is even true of ornithologists whom I've addressed and who ought to be more self-conscious about terri-tory than most people. And, of course, everyone has "his chair" at home and feels restless or uncomfortable if someone else takes it. Of course, he may deny it. You may laugh at all this and refuse to admit that territoriality permeates our life to an extraordinary extent. This is probably because you don't like to think you resemble animals so closely!

I have no such inhibitions. I sometimes speculate

on whether most of our quarrels aren't mainly over status. Could status contests have played a part in my marriages? Certainly territory came into it with Jessica, even if superficially. Early in our marriage I was often working on several projects at the one time —the blue wren study, a paper on the mating behaviour of eastern spinebills and a popular article for *Vogel-Kosmos* in Germany. As you can imagine, my quite large study was littered with reference material —books, notes, specimens—and my desk, a large one, was crowded. I recalled an English writer friend who'd solved this problem by having separate rooms and tables for each project. Half seriously I observed to Jessica, "Wolf has the right idea."

"You're always grizzling," she said. "You'll soon be able to take over the whole house."

This was a threat to leave me, but behind it lay the harsh truth that I am a solitary. Inherited wealth began it, my talent (modest) and my daemon perpetuated it. Just before I left Sydney for central Australia, a famous Australian writer said to me, "I'm having trouble with my new book. It's hard work!" Voice rising. "You've got to be monastic."

I sometimes ask myself if I have been a bad picker in my marriages. Certainly Jessica was a bad choice but I was only twenty-three and didn't know what I wanted—or, more correctly, I thought I knew and Jessica was able to assume the role I wanted her to play for the time being. For as long as it suited her. She was affectionate—or I thought she was. I was probably to blame as much as she was. And yet I know that no one remains friends with her for long. I don't want to be unkind, but nearly all her women friends—she has no men friends—are younger women, people she can dominate.

I'm not an easy person to live with so I don't want to

try to make a case against her. I didn't make a bad pick with Martha—that was just bad luck—but I don't want to talk about that; even now it can hurt. And I didn't make a bad pick with Joanna. To return to Jessica, the trouble was probably that I developed—not much, you may say—and she didn't at all. She stayed resolutely Ascham and Darling Point, with respect for money and little else—and I thought she was growing out of it. She, for her part, thought I would grow out of my socialism, my attempts to write, and my interest in zoology. Without illusions there'd probably be no unhappy marriages—or any marriages at all. Or anything else.

Joanna has described the melancholy beauty of the Centre. In a greater or lesser degree we all felt this—this haunting feeling of something familiar, of *déjà vu*, until Joanna put it into words for us, evoking for us the image of that ancient Cretaceous sea. And, oppressively there are regions where death has conquered, where it looked as though some malevolent hand had scalped and flayed the terrain to leave behind vast stony plains, warped and pitted mountains, and scalloped sandhills. I remember standing one day on a mountain that rose, like the four others linked to it, like a red whale from a vast ocean of scrub. The summit of this leviathan was covered with huge blocks and boulders of red granite, so riven and fissured, that for an instant the mind shrank before the ferocity.

This savage landscape, too, has often the stillness of death. We all experienced this when earlier we skirted that great travesty of a lake, Lake Amadeus, which Giles, in one of his wilder moments, named in honour of a king of Spain. Lake of the Love of God, indeed! A great ghost of a lake in a dead land where the trees are dead and the rivers are dead. On that vast glitter-

143

ing salty shroud nothing grows or moves. The silence is the deep silence of the tomb, broken only twice by the sudden splutter of a sally of zebra finches and the far-off plaint of a crow. Oppressed, even benumbed, we said little.

To balance this, there are, of course, those paradisal scenes that enchanted Ernest Giles.* But death, or perhaps more accurately nature's indifference, is what oppresses your spirit—or even invigorates it! Here you can have no comfortable illusions about divine purpose or man's overlordship. In these cruel immensities of space and time you see clearly that nature and the universe have no meaning or purpose.

Or could it have been because of this that Giles was always finding his paradises? After the dead lakes and trees and the still, waterless wastes he'd come on a cool, green oasis in the Rawlinsons where a creek "meandered through a piece of open plain, splendidly grassed and delightful to the gaze. How beautiful is the colour of green! . . . I could not resist calling it the Vale of Tempe."† Visions of the Eden he was seeking haunted Giles even in his dreams:

In my lonely sleep I had real dreams, sweet, fanciful, and bright, mostly connected with the enterprise upon which I had embarked—dreams that I had wandered into, and was passing through, tracts of fabulously lovely glades, with groves and grottos green, watered by never-failing streams of crystal, dotted with clusters of magnificent palm trees, and having groves, charming groves, of the fairest of pines, groves "whose rich trees wept odorous gums and balm".

If I were romantically minded I could think that

* EDITOR: *Australia Twice Traversed: The Romance of Exploration* (two volumes) by Ernest Giles, published 1889, and compiled from his journals.

† EDITOR: The Vale of Tempe, renowned from ancient times, lies between Mt Olympus and Mt Ossa in Thessaly. It was sacred to Apollo.

144

in Giles's dreams a race-memory stirred. Where he suffered and Gibson died was in the Tertiary period and early Pleistocene epoch a paradise of lush, spilling vegetation, of broad-leafed trees (oak, beech and magnolia), deep lakes and broad, perennial rivers. Along their shores lived now extinct creatures, kangaroos which stood ten feet high, diprotodons, which browsed on the rich herbage and were as large as rhinoceroses, emus seven feet tall, and monitor lizards twenty feet long. A pristine Eden indeed to creep into the slumbers of imaginative Ernest Giles, who had delighted in the narratives of voyages and discoveries, from Robinson Crusoe to Anson and Cook! Then came the Kosciusko Uplift; the new highlands on the east coast were thrust up to 10,000 feet to shut off the moisture-laden winds from the Pacific and started a slow progress to aridity; the once prodigal rainfall shrank sharply; rivers stopped flowing; the rich vegetation died and with it many creatures it had supported.

Or perhaps Giles was thinking of Dante's account of the lost Paradise. Or of the Greek legend that put it presumably in the centre of what is now known to be Australia. There, said the legend, in a palm grove —perhaps it was Giles's Glen of Palms * —our first ancestors lived. A large continent, which once occupied a great part of the Southern Ocean, had in its centre the earthly Paradise; during a great flood most of the continent sank under the sea, while in other parts of the world great land masses were pushed out of the sea. The earthly Paradise, however, was not reached by the flood-waters but remained on a large island which rose in a series of terraces to a giant, arid central plain. In the middle of the island was a

* EDITOR: Now called Palm Valley and remarkable for its palm-like ancient cycads (*Macrozamia macdonnelli*) and rare palms (*Livistona mariae*) , both relics from the time when they grew along humid seas.

145

beautiful palm grove, watered by the rivers of Paradise.

Giles's boyhood heroes were explorers, but mine were people like Father Damien, who lived among lepers and with them, comforting them to the last, and those who freed nations, such as Garibaldi and Bolivar. And Victor Trumper and Les Darcy. (On the walls of my father's garage—converted stables—were photographs reproduced in *The Referee* of Trumper leaping out to drive and Darcy shaping up to an invisible opponent, both put there probably by some past groom. Trumper was a hero to my father but he would never have created an icon in this way.)

If this analyst seeks to rewrite my biography in terms of his values, and to persuade me to accept it, then I constantly do it myself. As a boy I enthusiastically stalked and shot animals and birds—something I wouldn't do now. Our friend would say it was aggression—he hinted as much—but I have a simpler explanation. My father was a crack shot with rifle and shot-gun and I sought to emulate him. Learning to shoot was a challenge I met and a skill I acquired. My father and I crouched among the rushes at dawn. A chilly dewdrop fell on my neck. White mists rose and swayed over the surface of the billabong. I was twelve. My first duck shoot. "Follow them and sweep ahead," he whispered. "They'll be along any minute." A minute later he whispered, "Now." Eight or nine black ducks in the form of a harpoon, one leading and two on the barb on the left and the others making the shaft, were hurtling towards us, fifteen feet above the water. I waited, gun held horizontally, looking along the silver barrel to the bead. I got the bead on the top of the harpoon and kept it there as the birds drew level and went away. I swung ahead. "Ten feet," my father had said earlier. I remember my right foot was freezing—I'd stepped into a puddle. I pulled the first

146

trigger, then the second. The noise exploded in my head driving out thought; the shock jarred my shoulder. Something like a giant wind hit the duck harpoon. Three dropped, shedding feathers, into the billabong. The others, squawking in terror, veered to the right. One suddenly climbed the air. "You've hit him!" The bird clawed almost vertically. His wings slowed to feeble flappings. He fell from one hundred and fifty feet, flailing futilely. There are other sports that were passions once with me—cricket, football, tennis, golf. None interests me today. I'll still shoot an animal if I need it for my work—or if I want it for the pot. Trying to be honest, I don't think I ever killed a bird for the so-called blood lust. I'm aware of this now, of a frightening feeling of power and omnipotence when I hold a rifle and sight on some creature. Like God, I can snuff it out if I so will. That, magnified a thousand times, must have been the emotion experienced by the pilots who dropped the bombs on Hiroshima and Nagasaki. And the temptation today.

I think now that my wanting to go to Mexico—or even central Australia—was a form of fugue. As a child at the English prep school I'd sometimes break out into uncontrollable laughter during classes. Once a chalk drawing of a rooster set me off. Everyone looked at me. The master observed quietly, "He often does this." I gave up the habit after that.

Our plan of action was to establish a comfortable base camp near rock-holes. From there we made short sorties, usually in one vehicle, to likely places. For my own trips I naturally preferred Ted. This country (nature) was like Thomas Henry Huxley's chess player —perfectly fair but would take full toll of any mistakes you made. * Giles made some and nearly died. Gibson

*EDITOR: T. H. Huxley in *A Liberal Education* used his famous simile of the chess player.

147

made more grievous ones. We had a bigger margin for error than they had, but in 1876 or in 1967 a dehydrated man was still a dehydrated man. Ted respected the chess player.

Our early short expeditions were uneventful except on one occasion when Ted and I shot off to look at a rock-hole in a spur of the Rawlinsons. We went out wide of the ranges to skirt the deep water-worn creeks and gullies. We drove through parched spinifex and had gone about half a mile when we saw black smoke swishing behind us. The spinifex was alight, exploding with billowing, pungent fury. Some clumps flared up only yards behind.

I realized that I'd been driving with the brake half on. The drums had got hot and had fired the spinifex. I released the brake and pulled up, then saw my mistake. I stepped on the accelerator and we shot off.

I set the Rover at a sand-ridge and bullocked it over and down to the bottom where we stopped in the clearest spot I could find. I knew the wall of flames would have to slow up down the slope.

The next ten minutes were strenuous. We got mattocks and cleared as much of the spinifex as we could. A small clump under the Rover got alight. Ted crawled under and smothered it with sand. We stood the fire extinguisher by the radiator—our last line of defence. The fire, now on a hundred-yard front, topped the ridge and came on quite slowly. We hacked away at the spinifex, sweating and caked in pink mud, and dragged the heavy clumps well to the side. My hands throbbed from a million pricks. I saw minute blood splodges all over my forearms. The fire came on steadily to within a few yards of our small clearing.

"Under the Rover!" Ted yelled. We crawled under, burying our faces in the hot sand and pulling our

148

coats over our heads and shoulders. The crackle of the fire grew to a storm. The spinifex was popping all around us, set alight by wind-borne sparks. I felt a hot puff of heat on my legs. I stayed down.

"You all right?" I asked Ted.

"Don't worry about me."

Cautiously, I peered out. The fire had passed on with a swift rush. I scrambled out and raced to the extinguisher to play on the Rover. The hood was smouldering. A few handfuls of sand took care of that. We had a lucky let-off. Only a few yellow bubbles on the bonnet.

As I wrote earlier, you had to take this country seriously. We were only a few miles from camp, but if we'd been two hundred miles away and lost the Rover we could have paid for my momentary forget-fulness with our lives.

12th July 1967. Harry's good taste extends to concealing his infatuation from the vulgar gaze. With Elizabeth his public role is avuncular, but I wonder if Elizabeth wouldn't like a more public display of his affection? Tom is paying some attention to Elizabeth, but Harry doesn't notice—or affects not to.

14th July 1967. We've moved to a grassy valley be-tween two rocky shoulders—one of Ernest Giles's "little paradises". My bedside book is *Australia Twice Traversed* which Harry passed on to me with the injunction, "Look through it in case I've missed a reference to the night parrot. I couldn't find any." Giles delights me. We are following in his footsteps and his book is the only detailed account of this region. Moreover, he is the finest writer among our explorers—even if he drowns in purple passages from time to time. He has a poet's eye. He was the first

149

white man to see and name the red domes of Mt Olga, rising in unearthly splendour out of the great plains: "I think this is one of the most extraordinary mountains on the face of the earth. It is composed of several monstrous kneeling pink elephants . . . a heap of worn-out suns . . . the highest point of all . . . a Chinese gong."

A Blue-coat boy from the same school that fostered Hazlitt, Lamb and Coleridge, Giles even peopled one of his "paradisal glens" with Arthurian knights! The tragedy of Alfred Gibson as told by Giles haunts my mind. I conjure up the picture of that poor young Englishman, not very intelligent and a poor bushman, losing his way on his splendid horse, the Fair Maid of Perth, and dying alone and full of regret, believing erroneously that his error had cost Giles's life as well. No knight of Arthur's court.

As Harry observes, "Giles was bloody deficient in ornithology!" For instance, he's content to write: "dull-coloured small birds, that exist entirely without water, are found in the scrubs; and in the morning they are sometimes noisy, but not melodious, when there is a likelihood of rain". That wouldn't do for Harry and Tom, who identify the birds as probably western grass wrens *(Amytornis textilis)*. It's too much to hope he'd note the night parrot.

The days are spring-like and mild, except when the rather chill dry winds get up, and it would be idyllic but for the bush-flies ceaselessly trying to creep into your mouth and nostrils. Harry, the ever-seeking, speculates on whether we could divert them. "If they're seeking moisture—or food—from us, it ought to be possible to supply it," he says.

This is a land of illusions. Not only am I constantly reminded of a phantom sea, but other phenomena combine to deceive you. Mirages continually. Today

I saw a large expanse of blue, cool water stretching ahead but kept silent alongside Ted in the Land-Rover. Out of the corner of my eye I saw him stealing a look at me and smiling slightly. I'd not seen it before but guessed rightly—the dried-up bed of a salt lake reflecting the cloud-free hard blue sky.

We've all become interested in Larry's shield shrimps and peer many times a day into the jar—the aquarium is due tomorrow. We counted fourteen minute shield shrimps today. They're the larval form, according to Harry, and after several moults will grow into the adult form we've seen in the rock-pools—tiny olive-green plates with long, ringed abdomens, bearing at their ends two slender tails like those of a silverfish. Harry, who is a grab-bag of odd pieces of information, says the eggs sometimes hatch in eastern coastal areas, blown there a thousand miles by strong westerly dust storms. He says that much remains to be discovered about them and enthusiastically urges Larry to note down anything he observes. He adds there's always the chance of finding species of other creatures, such as water-fleas, unknown to science. Larry greeted the suggestion somewhat suspiciously.

"I just want to see them grow," he said. "It wouldn't be feasible." A favourite word. Another is "workable", and "viable".

15th July 1967. Some excitement today. Jim found two small tunnels about five inches in diameter going into the spinifex. But only mice tracks, he said, not birds. Perhaps mice had taken over an old parrot tunnel, Harry speculated. The men got mattocks and followed the tunnels in, looking for night parrot tracks and feathers. Nothing. What creature made the tunnels? Not the night parrot or the western ground parrot, else there would have been tracks and feathers. Mice?

151

But no known ones do. We have set nets round a large rock pool at the foot of red walls. The strata are horizontal, as though masons had built level upon level. Close to the walls, which go up for three hundred feet, our faces and arms glow salmon pink from reflected light. "I haven't the right make-up," complains Margaret. Native fig-trees with deep-green foliage cling to ledges and send questing roots like so many multi-fingered limbs down to the foot of the wall.

Chattering clouds of budgerigars swoop in at dusk —sometimes so many that they're forced to drink off the surface, hovering above the water like a gleaming green carpet. Last night a little black hawk sabred into the cloud and knocked three into the water. He swooped again and carried one away. When he returned later I had an impulse to frighten him away, but repressed it—Harry has trained me well. The hawk has to live. (Harry has trained me so well that I'm now wondering if the hawk was a "she" and not a "he". And what kind of hawk?) Harry and his colleagues can even prove that hawks benefit budgerigars collectively by preying on the sickly or weak and thus maintaining the vigour of the race! So I'll not play God here by this water-lily-clad pool. Not even with Elizabeth if it comes to that, short of rape. I came unexpectedly on Tom and Elizabeth today in a glen near the pool—I've caught Ernest Giles's habit of nomenclature. He was trying to kiss her and she was having to struggle quite hard. I don't think they saw me. I withdrew.

Our routine is much the same as it was at Base Camp. The men watch the nets and track through the spinifex. Sometimes we make small trips in the Land-Rovers to likely (?) places.

A warm day and mirages danced on the claypans; the light kneaded the familiar shapes of mulga and bloodwoods to assume those of chimeras, of giants and monsters.

16th July 1967. I woke some time in the middle of the night with the strange feeling that someone or something was outside in the darkness. I got up, groped for my torch and threw open the flap. A white animal— I suppose it was a dingo but it looked like a large lamb—was tiptoeing on the other side of the almost dead fire. Larry must have heard it, too, for he fired a rifle at it. The dingo fled, squealing and howling, and I hope only badly frightened.

"What did you do that for?" I demanded, angrily. Mansion Road and Cootamundra grazier, they're all the same.

"We don't want him nosing round here," he said, laughing excitedly. He was breathing quickly and heavily and his words came jerkily. "Did you hear him squeal? I must have hit him! I bet he doesn't come back."

"Why try to kill him?" I asked, still furious. "He wouldn't hurt you."

"I don't like them slinking around."

Everyone was awakened. Elizabeth appeared last and, oddly, fully dressed. Harry was irate. At such times he grows so quiet you can almost feel it. (Sometimes I wish he'd explode.) "An extraordinary performance," he said and went back to his tent. I was a long time getting off to sleep. Something tiptoed on the fringes of my mind; I couldn't bring it into the light but it troubled me. Something to do with, I think, Elizabeth.

Elizabeth brought up the Drake episode later today. If I were a man those brilliant eyes could be exciting. They shone intently on me and I could guess what was coming and shrank inside.

"You saw what happened yesterday? I want you to know I haven't encouraged Tom in any way."

153

"Why do you tell me this?"

"There's Harry—he'd be hurt."

"I won't tell him," I said. "It's not important. Or won't be if Tom behaves himself."

"I wish he would!" She put her hand on my arm. "Could you speak to Tom? No . . . of course you can't."

She went off assuring me she'd make sure never to be alone with Tom.

Took a trip with Ken Turner in the Cessna today. Quite hot. From the air, and even from the ground, many of the ranges are spectacular. Sedimentary strata have been metamorphosed and subjected to slow folding so that they dip vertically in long wave-like formation. It's as though you're looking down on a series of great arches. Equally impressive are the pedestal or mushroom rocks caused by corrasion—that's a new word I've learnt. Winds over countless centuries have sand-blasted the bases of the rocks and undercut them. Sometimes they have even gouged out natural bridges. The winds, of course, bear their greatest load close to the ground. Ted remembers that corrasion (I like using the word) cut through the wooden telegraph poles in the first days of the overland telegraph cable. This is a comforting titbit of information. There's so much timelessness here that it's good to know the wind did something within our near memory. The wind is king here. Chill in winter and furnace-hot in summer. It penetrates everything. Everything has to be packed in several layers of plastic when we move. Sometimes in the morning you wake up covered with a thin coating of pink sand—bed, floor, tent walls.

Jim has brought his own cooking gear and prepares his own meals. At first he used to make his own fire in obedience to the Centre's laws of segregation. Harry has persuaded him tactfully to join us. But he lets Jim

154

do his own cooking. "He may prefer it. In any case, we mustn't patronize him." I wonder what is Jim's real attitude to white people. His defence is a kind of grave clowning.

Our reptile collecting has speeded up since he joined us. He inspects a hole or burrow and informs us whether the creature is at home or gone for a walk. Today Elizabeth saw a large brown snake disappearing down a hole. The warm days we've had must have brought him out. We got mattocks and gingerly pursued. The hole was shallow and ran alongside a fallen log. Our caution was triggered by not wishing either to injure the snake, a western brown, or to be bitten. When a gentle probe of the mattock revealed a few inches of thin thrashing tail, Harry grabbed it and tugged back. He flung his hand high and there was the six-foot olive-brown snake clear of the ground and twisting and coiling. Its belly was yellow with greyish spots. When it tried to coil up Harry jerked his wrist downwards. A sharp ripple ran the length of the snake. Other attempts he thwarted in the same way. The glistening head with, I observed, a few scattered black scales, swung about from side to side, jaws opening and shutting rapidly. The snake suddenly urinated and then vomited a marsupial mouse.

Tom's university wanted a specimen of a large western brown snake so this one was photographed and then killed painlessly by an injection of Nembutal. Later it was injected with formalin and preserved in alcohol. It was six feet two inches long.

Harry has done his homework with Eric Worrell* and said there was nothing to it. I am not persuaded. He offered once more to coach Elizabeth and myself. "You've got to catch snakes with your hands," he

* EDITOR: Eric Worrell, Australian naturalist, author and expert snake-catcher.

155

insists. "They've got fragile bodies and you damage them otherwise." Elizabeth has accepted the offer and I can't be shamed. And Larry, too, wants to try.

As Ted puts it, you talk about acres of budgerigars here. Last night, with a clamour of wing-beats, a vast green cloud wheeled and turned, sheered away and swung back, swooped and soared over the rock pool with such synchronization you'd have thought it one vast iridescent green organism. The hawks later broke the pulsing concomitance.

Ornithologists can be as territory-minded as the creatures they study. Today Harry became interested in desert chats (*Ashbya lovensis*) which we saw hopping about on a gibber plain in pursuit of insects. Harry didn't notice that Tom was furious. Harry shot off several rolls of colour and black and white and made notes. Finally Tom burst out with, "I'm doing some work on them myself."

"Good!" Harry said. "You can have my notes and pictures, if they're any use."

One of the golden-breasted little birds suddenly mounted into the air, rather like a skylark, calling, "Whit, whit, whit!" I laughed at the sound.

This afternoon the wind got up suddenly to about twenty-five knots and drove us to shelter. Visibility nil. Fine pink sand everywhere. We breathed sand, ate sand, drank sand, and later we doubtless defecated sand. Only the creases in our eyelids and our teeth stayed white in pink faces. The sand came in under the sides of the tent and probably through the plastic itself! Ted tells us we can expect more storms in spring when winds get stronger.

17th July 1967. Watching the shield shrimps has become a major interest. About ten are now adult and swim about on their backs propelling themselves with their many large gills. It's as though they're rowing with feathers. They have these large gills, says Harry, because they need a tremendous amount of oxygen for their rapid growth. They're over an inch long and have prominent black eyes. There's speculation about their sex. We watch to see if they mate. Other creatures have hatched—gastropod snails and water-fleas and some we can't identify.

Harry makes notes, having failed to inspire Larry.

Elizabeth confided today that she was a renegade Roman Catholic—her words—which may explain her interest in Ouspensky and Gurdjieff. She lent me *The Fourth Way* today, saying she couldn't persuade Harry to read it. She seems hurt that he wouldn't. I promised her I'd read it. People continually surprise. She's brought to central Australia a whole library of this Russian mystic: *A New Model of the Universe, Tertium Organum, The Psychology of Man's Possible Evolution, In Search of the Miraculous*. She told me a little about a persistent young man in Sydney. "He follows me everywhere."

She asked me suddenly, "Did you hear something last night? Like another Land-Rover?"

I said, "No. I slept like a log. Did you hear one?"

"I don't know. That's why I asked."

18th July 1967. Last night I woke from a nightmare with my heart racing so fast I fancied I could hear it. In the dream Larry fired again at the dingo, which fled howling into the night. Then suddenly Tom was holding the rifle and aiming it at Elizabeth. I grew terribly afraid, not able to move to stop him. My mouth was wide open with no breath coming from it. Then I woke, trembling. What had I seen that earlier night which prowled on the edges of consciousness?

It's probably fortunate we are all busy in our separate ways. Our small talk is as ritualized as the average club. Religion and politics are taboo after a flare-up tonight between Larry and Elizabeth. Larry is all for the Vietnam commitment, even to uttering the paranoic absurdity that it's better to fight them there than here.

"Do you really mean we have to fight all Communists?" asked Elizabeth, passionately.

Ted didn't say anything but seemed to support Larry. It's depressing.

Nothing is to be gained; Larry, I fear, can't be re-educated. Elizabeth is reluctant to admit this but agrees to avoid the subject in future.

How much of our "conversation" consists of amiable noises like the contented chatter of Harry's Bourke parrots when they're feeding together? Or the mutual social grooming of primates? With us, Harry says, smiling and talk about weather replaces grooming.

"How are you?"

"No complaints," is Larry's answer. Harry has stylized his to "Things are reasonably under control" or "I make no extravagant claims." How insufferable it is when someone does tell you how he is! Sick or troubled people engage our attention more in fiction than they do in real life. Many characters in fiction would be intolerable bores in real life.

During the night the aquarium sprang a leak and the shield shrimps are dead. Harry mended the leak and filled the aquarium with water.

"On with the masquerade," he said. "Motley's the only wear." The eggs will hatch and the cycle will begin all over again and continue to the end of time.

The days are warming and today was spent mainly in snake-catching. I'm gaining courage and practice on the smaller ones. Larry captured a western brown snake which looked even longer than Harry's and so it, too, was dispatched for the Sydney collection—six feet eight inches. Elizabeth is counting the number of its scales—body scales, ventrals, sub-caudals—and checking their shapes in Eric Worrell's *Reptiles of Australia*. Harry thinks it may have more body scales and not be a western brown snake but the closely related dugite whose range is the southern parts of Western Australia.

We've all caught the snake-catching fever and were kept busy and happy today. If I didn't know Harry's talent for being enthusiastic about all and everything, I'd suspect him of introducing us to the new occupation on purpose.

Tonight I did, in fact, make a half-accusation.

"I didn't do it deliberately," he said, grinning. "I admit that I sometimes say 'Prrr' at times—or should it be 'Ooo, ah, ah'?"

"You're not sure whether we're tigers or lions?"

"Some of each," he said, "but all are well fed." He paused, waiting for my attention. "We could be well-fed dairy cows."*

* EDITOR: This was a reference to a scientific paper written by Harry Craddock and well known to Joanna Craddock. The paper discusses the tamer Court, who used to calm his tigers by imitating the "Prrr" sound they made when contented. "Ooo, ah, ah" was his approximation of the sound of a calm lion. Status contests are less frequent among well-fed Jersey cows; at best the contests between cows consist of more bluff than fight.

The following note on the secrets of lion taming are abridged from some of Harry Craddock's writings in this field:

Lion and tiger "taming" is based on an intuitive rather than an intellectual knowledge of territory and its code by the trainer. The trainer's whip is not used to intimidate the animal but is used as an extension of the trainer's body. Most animals, including lions and tigers, are cautious and usually give other animals a wide berth. Most have an escape or flight distance; should you barely infringe it, the animal will move away. But should you come too close, you touch off another reaction. The animal becomes afraid, and if cornered, may attack or make a pseudo-attack. By thrusting out his whip, the trainer can force a lion, say, to retreat to a place where it feels secure. Again, by moving the whip closer towards it he can provoke it into an aggressive display which will cause it to come forward—usually to climb on a stool or such. By such simple but dangerous means the trainer puts his fellow animals through their routine.

159

15

As you've probably gathered from Joanna's journal, our search for the night parrot wasn't exciting. It was mainly hard work, struggling with mist nets and searching the ground for tracks. Sometimes when you were tired there was an all too human impulse to skimp something—not to search a spinifex clump thoroughly or visit a spot that might be promising. I was more resolute than the others but tried to make allowances—it was my obsession. Any place was "likely".

I try to be truthful. My training as a scientist helps, but I am only too aware that we all, or nearly all, want the approval of our fellows—in my case the approval of you, the reader. As I write this I try to imagine who you are. Are you, for instance, a man or a woman? Young or old? Do you share my concern for the wild creatures with whom we share this earth? Or are you indifferent? Do you like or dislike me?

Recent happenings have probably made me more tolerant and benign. I have reproduced entries from Joanna's journal, for instance, which show her, I think, in a rather too favourable light and represent me as a bit of a fool. It's true I've called myself one. My fault is over-enthusiasm. But generally I try to act well even if I sometimes trust people too much. I think I'd prefer to give people the benefit of the doubt than be as clear-sighted as Joanna claims she is. I still have considerable affection for Joanna—so much so that I have probably depicted her rather too favourably except for my remarks about her neglect of the azaleas. I had to be prised from them, just as I had to be prised from my other obsessions—and from my friends. One by one they dropped off after we married. Joanna

160

didn't want to entertain them, as I realized after a time, though the excuses she offered varied. I bear her no grudge for these things. I have found a peace of a kind—in a mental home.

Some pages back I wrote about ambivalence of the landscape—of the opposed images of life and death it evoked: of that lost ancient life-giving sea and of its present purposeless malignity. These two moods alternated throughout my whole stay in the Centre—not obsessionally, of course, but whenever I was relaxed and my mind was switched off from everyday tasks. You may think that my reactions were subjective and that I reacted to one or other of these stimuli according to my mood. I should be inclined to agree.

Even when you're not emotionally involved, there's a danger of what someone called "pseudo-memories"— I forget the author's name, but I think the book was called *The Anatomy of Judgement.** The author said that we tend when recalling an incident or object to fill in the blanks in our memory with "pseudo-memories" so verisimilar that it is impossible for us to distinguish between those details in the recalled scene which are authentic and those supplied by imagination or by suggestion or by other memories or by wishful thinking. Was there now a single long hair on that mole on the Pitjantjatjara's cheek? Or even a mole?

Our search developed into a slow, methodical checking of area after area. A couple of days after we returned to Base Camp an Aboriginal came in with a story about a parrot belong night. He looked a cunning old humbug—good luck to him if he could fool some of the usurpers!—but I couldn't afford to pass it up. I started up one of the Land-Rovers and told the old chap to guide me there. Elizabeth got in the back. This was the first time I'd been alone with her for

*Editor: By Minnie L. Abercrombie (Hutchison, London: 1960).

161

more than a few minutes—I'm not forgetting our black friend—but words weren't necessary. I could look at Elizabeth and she could look at me. We probably wouldn't have said any more if he hadn't been there.

"Happy?" I asked once, looking back over my shoulder.

Elizabeth nodded and I was wishing I could stop the Land-Rover and kiss her and close those brilliant green-blue eyes and caress those silky firm soft legs. In my exhilaration I accelerated the Land-Rover to fifty, wrenching the wheel sharply to steer it round the bigger spinifex clumps while my mind raced, too, jerking to right and left with flashes of words and some that were wordless, but coherent for all that and meaning that I was happy and loved her and that she was gentle and warm and loved me, too, and downy and soft yet firm were her breasts and dazzling her eyes. And I was happy and she, too.

There was no night parrot, of course, and we dropped the old man off later. And made love. Then, masked, we drove back.

"When did it happen—us?" I asked.

"The time I interviewed you."

"Perhaps with me, too," I said. "I think so, but I didn't want it to happen."

I think that was how it was but I didn't know it until that afternoon.

I assure you the difference in our ages didn't worry me from the moment of that first night in Sydney. I wasn't really aware of it most of the time except when once she said, impishly, "You know, you're old enough to be my father." And waited, laughing, to add, "Perhaps you are my father." And giggled for a minute. "You don't know my mother!"

I recall that in central Australia I gave up the critical self-examination of every action and thought. I was

162

relaxed and tried to live by my sense. This, as I've said earlier, is how I imagine birds live all the time, at a joyous fever-heat of emotion. So most of my days were full and happy and, tired by the exertion, I slept deeply. I no longer questioned whether I was in love with Elizabeth or she with me or whether I should be. You may argue that I was indulging in a form of escapism. I'm indifferent. I wanted little part of the world we have created for ourselves. My infatuation with Elizabeth—if you must call it that—enriched my life. I felt thirty years old.

I continued to write verses for Elizabeth and leave them where I was sure she—and no one else—would find them. As I write I am living again those blissful, one-with-nature days in the Centre. Unhappily, they were not to last long.

While searching for the night parrot I managed to make some studies of the other birds. Tom, of course, outstripped me here. He devoted so much time and energy that he sometimes seemed to have little enthusiasm for our main objective, but I managed to curb my irritation by telling myself, "He's a career ornithologist and I'm not—I'm a bloody amateur!" On several occasions I suspected him of wanting to go to a place, not to search for the night parrot, but to study some particular bird such as the desert chat of the gibber plains.

Joanna credited me with too much skill—or calculation—in social relations. I'm not really good at them. But sometimes I can apply the things I've learnt from studying animals. For instance, soon after Jim joined us there was some trouble between Larry and him.

"Give a hand with this tent," said Larry to what he considered *omega* Jim. (Larry was *gamma* or thereabouts.) He struggled with the poles and ropes.

"In a minute." Jim was unpacking his own gear

some yards off. He looked not at Larry but at me. In his own eyes a *beta* animal, Jim was going to take his orders from me only—from the *alpha* animal.

"Cheeky bastard," Larry muttered.

His face, reddening, mirrored the central Australian cliché—give 'em an inch, etc.

I said quite loudly—it was the best I could devise on the spot—"Larry, will you take charge of the pitching of the tents tonight?"

God bless Thorleif Schjelderup-Ebbe who did that pioneering work in the twenties on the peck order of fowls and helped restore harmony in the Gibson Desert fifty years later!

I wonder, though, whether my preoccupation with animals and their behaviour alienates me from too much art. I remember an otherwise good French film was spoilt for me because they'd dubbed the wrong bird-calls on the sound-track. And I always trip momentarily over lines such as Eliot's in *The Waste Land*:

> . . . *yet there the nightingale*
> *Filled all the desert with inviolable voice*
> *And still she cried, and still the world pursues,*
> *"Jug Jug" to dirty ears.*

I know this is Philomela whom the gods changed into a nightingale to rescue her from Tereus; none the less the ornithologist intrudes with the observation that the male bird is the song bird.

I puzzle over myself and others—recent events and Dr S. encourage this introspection—and find myself complex and other people simple. This is because I see only the actions of others and cannot know their inner hesitancies.

Dr S. has a number of questionnaires and objective test batteries—the Rorschach ink blots, the Minnesota Multiphasic Inventory, Sixteen Personality Factor Questionnaire, Objective-Analytic Personality Battery,

164

the Humour Test of Personality, Neuroticism Scale Questionnaire, Maudsley Personality Inventory, Multiple Abstract Variance Analysis, the Anxiety Battery, Motivation Analysis Test, Two Hand Co-ordination Test, Culture Fair Intelligence Test—I shan't bore you by repeating all their names though I enjoy collecting them and write them down meticulously in a notebook, as evidence of man's folly. They are toys which delight him. For this reason I co-operate with him, or, rather, pretend to do so. Sometimes he seems puzzled by my conflicting answers though I cannot for the life of me see why he should be. He claims that you cannot cheat. Infallibility. Wouldn't we all like to find it?

About this time he questioned me about my collection of alabaster eggs. He evidently thought he saw some symbol or significance in them so I improvised on a lecture I'd once given to a group in New York and provided half an hour of fact and nonsense for his delight—and mine!

It must have been about the time that Larry clashed with Jim that I had a remarkable dream when I was alone on a sand-ridge after sunset. Ted had left me at a a rock-hole where I proposed to rig the mist nets and driven on to reconnoitre another one he suspected would be dry. He was overdue but I was not worried. I felt tired suddenly and coiled myself up under a bush which protected me from the suddenly chill winds— the waterless sands retain little heat—and shortly fell into one of those extraordinary dreams when, although we know we are alive, we yet think we are dead. At such times the fact of our death evokes no pain and is accepted without wonderment. I seemed to be looking down on my own body, which was approached by my mother dressed in black. She looked at me sorrowfully and sighed, and was followed by my sister and father. Then they were gone and Martha approached with her youthful grace, her oval face pearly white and she, too, looked down on me sadly before she went her way. Jessica came but stood off and would not approach. Other figures waited on the edge, merging in the darkness. Their shapes were familiar and I accepted them as such and did not strain to identify them. Then it seemed that I was walking through a series of linked green valleys, fed by crystal-clear streams. I trod beneath the shade of clusters of stately palm-trees and groves of oaks, pines, cedars and eucalypts while rich odours stole into my nostrils.

I heard music, so distant and ethereal that I could scarcely be sure it was music. (I remember a trip in a sulky with Grandfather Vincent and hearing faintly what I was almost sure was band music. For an hour I did not mention it because I thought he'd laugh, shaking that black beard.) I listened without conscious thought or feeling. Then the music grew louder, became discordant, and I awoke to hear Ted's Land-Rover somewhere on the right. Strangely, I waited almost an hour before I saw the flash of his headlights brushing the tips of the mulga.

I can recall vividly my sense of bereavement on waking from my dream. Those hot, wild mountains and measureless sand plains seemed so harsh and alien.

16

Excerpt of fifteen hundred words from Jean-Jacques Rousseau's *Confessions*, or what you will, for Dr Sullivan:

M

I have my troubles concealing this memoir from Dr Sullivan but they're not insuperable. He's kept busy with the other patients and, moreover, he knows I am writing up some of my notes from central Australia for scientific journals. This activity provides me with a reasonable cloak. Every day he contrives to drop in for a chat. I manage to dissemble my hostility and to tell him as little as possible. Today he asked about my mother's death.

"How old were you when she died?" he asked.

"Eight," I said. "No, thirteen."

"And your sister?"

"Sixteen." I caught a glint in his reptilian eye. I recalled I'd said "eight" when he asked me to think of a number. I added, impishly, "Mr Dedman blamed me at the time. He said I'd upset my mother and brought on her heart attack."

I paused and he was forced to ask, "Mr Dedman?"

"My mother's lover. We were told he was a step-father but he wasn't. I didn't like him. He whipped me once and I bit his thumb—no, index finger."

Sadistically, I stopped. Could the fool really swallow this rubbish? "He beat me unmercifully after that crying, 'David, you're a wicked child!'" He appeared to consider it seriously. I continued with the game, wishing I knew my Copperfield better.

After he'd gone I sat remembering when she died. We were asleep—Margaret and I—in our villa in Venice when he woke us. It was about one o'clock.

"Get up! Your mother is seriously ill."

We put on dressing gowns and followed Mr Hodder, dark and slim, walking on his toes. My mother lay on her back in her bed and breathing heavily. The Italian doctor with a round white face and big black eyebrows was giving her cardiac massage. As he bent over her, I saw a hole, large as a shilling, in the sole of his right

168

shoe. "She's unconscious," he said. "Take the children out." On the carpet under my slippers was a rabbit-shaped stain. The ignominy of death. My mother, her forehead damp with sweat, was breathing stertorously. "Like a coffee percolator," I thought. And it was. Today, sights, sounds, smells (of medicine and urine) of the room are still recorded indelibly on my mind.

"You shouldn't have brought them in!" the doctor cried at Mr Hodder as we left the bedroom. They had a row about it afterwards. The doctor came to us not long afterwards. His eyes were wet. We knew before he spoke. That was one of the times when I remember the uneasy feeling I've told you about.

He was a kindly man. The next day he drew me aside. "A tired heart," he said. "It was liable to give out at any time." The carnelian on his watch-chain was swaying from left to right, right to left, on his green velvet waistcoat. "Your mother had no pain. She lapsed into unconsciousness during sleep. I could do little." Then as he went on I knew Hodder had been talking to him. "You have nothing to reproach yourself about. Your mother was cross with you last night but that didn't bring on her heart attack." I think he wanted to say more but didn't.

Funny about my "weak" stomach of childhood. I can eat anything now. Admit yourself that you were cheated and deceived in your own childhood. And don't believe me when I claim I'm always truthful. Are you always truthful when you review yourself? What roles did you play today—with your wife, with your children, with your superiors, with your subordinates? Didn't you act a bit? Have you always been faithful to your spouse? A good double-barrelled word that. That touched you. Teddy Roosevelt had this posterity business sewn up. He used to write letters to posterity, paint the lily in letters he wrote about

169

the events in which he was engaged.

Back to central Australia! But first I must tell you my dream of last night. I was at a masked ball in Venice dancing under the arches. (Fornication from Latin *fornicare*, from *fornix*, an arch, because the prostitutes of ancient Rome gathered under the arches. So *fornix* by association became the word for brothel!) She was like Elizabeth but also unlike. I swung her round in a waltz, Mephistopheles-Craddock with a Spanish senorita—Donna Elvira with the torchlights scampering across the Venetian lagoon. A man with two faces tried to take her away. The back face was a woman's with a beard. He said, "You're old enough to be her father." But a dwarf drew his sword and said, "There's only one way to deal with Turks." The two-faced man ran off. The whole time I could do nothing except laugh immoderately. What fun Dr Sullivan would have with that!

COMMENT BY DR S.: In fairness to the reader I'm impelled to interpolate here that I did see this "dream". My patient gave me a handwritten version which is almost the same. At first I did not intend to comment on the "dream". On the surface, it is only too obviously a heavy-handed Freudian parody. Any layman can penetrate the symbolism. The disapproving androgynous figure is patently the patient's parents –note the implied word play of Janus and Janet (his mother's name). The beard is clearly a substitute for the mons veneris and the dwarf with the sword is too patently the child confronting the bad mother–need I go on? None the less, this piece of invention is not without interest to the professional psychiatrist. Even in apparent free choice the repressed subconscious of the patient breaks through; the ethics of my profession prevent me from elaborating.

170

17

I know what you're thinking! It's hard to tell when he's telling the truth. Perhaps he doesn't know himself —or else he's a practical joker. For instance, he told us how he made love to that girl Elizabeth with so much detail you thought it must have happened and then he nonchalantly says it was just a day-dream. I admit the truth of your accusation but don't say I didn't warn you! I've just told you my Janus dream. No doubt the doctor has one interpretation as to the identity of Janus but I've another! I suspect the trouble with you is that you are literal-minded. Wherein lies the greater truth, in the reality or in the dream? Was my dream of fucking Elizabeth any less real than the reality of some days later? The transcendental truth lies probably in the blending of both as the plumage colour of some birds. Thus in many green feathers the outer layers of the barbs contain a yellow pigment that filters some of the short-wave rays out of the incident white light. Below this filter are box cells containing minute air spaces that scatter the remainder of the short-wave rays. Thus the feather appears green. Or peer closely at an olive-green feather. No filter this time of, say, a yellow filter over a layer of box cells with a backing of melanin, but the juxtaposition of tiny spots of black and yellow pigments which create the sensation of olive-green.

What is the transcendental truth of my talk today with Dr S., who asked questions about Dedman-Hodder?

An omniscient recorder (eavesdropper?) might have reported some of it like this:

The thick-set balding (*Time* influence) doctor, lean-

171

ing forward at the table, asked:

"Do you want to talk about Dedman?"

The patient paused and said (how did he say it, reluctantly or calmly?):

"Yes, if you wish. He was my mother's lover, you know."

A pause. The patient, a tall, dark man in his fifties, tapping the table with restless fingers, added, "I didn't know it at the time." A nervous laugh. "I quite liked him."

"But you bit his hand."

"His thumb. He was giving me a hiding."

"Why his thumb?" The doctor's voice is calm but has an undertone of alertness.

"I suppose it was handiest."

"You said earlier you bit his index finger."

"Then it was his index finger."

Etc. Etc. Now the olive-green combination might have been something like this—remember you must read all three texts simultaneously:

Dr S.:	Omniscient Observer:	Harry Craddock:
Self confident as ever. Amoral. Almost psychopathic disregard for feelings of others. Alienation. My father . . . "Cut it off if you play with yourself."	"Do you want to talk about Dedman?" The patient paused and said (how did he say it, reluctantly or calmly?)	Pseudemydura umbrina Siebenrock. A small population of short-necked western swamp tortoises lives in two swamps near Perth. First collected by schoolboy.
The trauma's here—that nonsense he fed me only revealed the truth. He doesn't know it but he's relaxing with me; taking that sedative was a good sign. Some day he'll start talking. I know more than he realizes	"Yes, if you wish. He was my mother's lover, you know." A pause. The patient, a tall, dark man in his fifties tapping the table with restless fingers, added, "I didn't know it at	Admit it. He was my mother's lover. Arrogant in the carapace (length to less than six inches) of his technician's conceit. Short neck with pronounced conical

172

Dr S.:	Omniscient Observer:	Harry Craddock:
but he's got to do most of it himself . . .	the time." A nervous laugh. "I quite liked him."	tubercles; barbels present; intergular dilated, plastron flat, almost as wide as carapace; short tail; nuchal free on . . .
Index finger! Scissors. But the mistake is revealing. Patrician. Thought little girls had lost theirs. Smooth. Hated that "stepfather".	"But you bit his hand." "His thumb. He was giving me a hiding." "Why his thumb?" The doctor's voice is calm but has an undertone of alertness. "I suppose it was handiest." "You said earlier you bit his index finger." "Then it was his index finger."	Hodder rodder hugger mugger. He screamed. Finger stinking of tobacco. Bone grated. Short neck with pronounced conical tubercles. Colour brown above, buff-olive ventrally.
And mother's death in Venice. I wished baby sister . . .		Thomas Mann.

Stand back from the black spots of his version and the yellow pigment of mine and you'd get your olive-green. Or would you? You'd soon get tired of having to read all versions simultaneously. It's better I tell it my own way.

Back to central Australia. This time I won't digress, but what's life if you can't be diverted? To move back and forth in time is, perhaps, the only freedom there is. I, Harold Piper Vincent Craddock, inhabit an infinity of worlds . . . including that of Alfred Gibson just as in that certainly "paradisal" spot in the Rawlinsons he came to inhabit our world, as it were, because we spoke of him frequently and lived again some of his agony. By this time we had, of course, read Giles's story of his second expedition in 1873-4 into these regions when Gibson died. (You are probably thinking that this is another of my tedious digressions, but it's an important background to the events that followed.) Gibson assumed the identity of someone we'd known intimately. He was, as Joanna says, not very intelligent—his stupidity, indeed, cost him his life—and he wasn't engaging. He was obstinate and he was sulky, too, sometimes for days on end. His obstinacy contributed to his death. He was ill-educated. But, none the less, I warm to him. Exploration was in his blood. His brother died with Sir John Franklin in the polar deserts. Gibson, a short young man, sought out Giles at the Peake after Giles had begun his expedition with William Tietkens and young Jimmy Andrews, ex-sailor.

"My name is Alf Gibson and I want to go with you."

Giles asked, "Well, can you shoe? Can you ride? Can you starve? Can you go without water? And how would you like to be speared by the blacks outside?"

Gibson said, "I can do everything you've mentioned. I'm not afraid of the blacks."

He was not, said Giles, a man he would have picked out of a mob, but men were scarce and he seemed anxious to come. So Giles accepted him.

"That bloody Gibson," Jimmy Andrews called him once. They didn't get on, mainly because Gibson didn't like washing. Jimmy noted that Gibson went for eighteen weeks without washing or bathing, whereas the others washed regularly and bathed whenever they could. Gibson had his reasons. He said to Giles, "I can't think what you and Tietkens and Jimmy are always washing yourselves for." "Why," Giles said, "for health and cleanliness, to be sure." "Oh," said he, "if I was to bath like you do, it would give me the 'ives." In Giles's journal a picture of Gibson builds up. He could cook a Christmas pudding, he sang quite well ("two or three love songs"), and started and tended industriously a garden at one of the

174

base camps. Was he a farm boy? He was useful with his hands and made an axe handle when one broke. He built a gunyah to shelter the horses from the heat at one camp.

"He need not have died," Ted said one night when we were sitting round the fire. "As Jimmy Andrews said to Giles after Gibson was lost, Gibson was no bushman."

"That's true," Tom said. "He had only to follow the tracks made by their four horses. Or, if he lost them, to use the compass."

"If he could use it!"

EDITOR: Members of the Craddock and Drake Expedition were, of course, familar with the circumstances of Gibson's death. In January 1874 Giles and Gibson set out west on horseback and with two pack-horses carrying food and water from the Rawlinsons in search of water, leaving the other two of the party behind. They penetrated sixty miles through spinifex-clothed red sandhills and released two of the horses to find their way back. Two five-gallon kegs of water were cached here; Giles and Gibson pressed on for a further thirty miles without finding water. With their supplies of both water and food running out, they started back. Gibson's horse died and Giles sent him on ahead on his own lively mount, the Fair Maid of Perth—"as merry and gay, as is possible for any of her sex, to be", wrote Giles. (Giles refers elsewhere to "her lively, troublesome and wanton vagaries".) He was to keep due east, following their own tracks. As a guide he had the prominent landmark of the Rawlinsons due east. His task was to reach the base camp and return with fresh horses and water. Giles waved him off into the night and followed on foot.

At a spot about twenty-five miles from the Rawlinsons, the two horses they'd released earlier had left the tracks of the outward journey and headed south-east. Gibson followed the tracks they made. He was never seen again. Giles heroically made the ninety miles to water and the one hundred and ten to the base camp, resting during the searing heat of the day with temperatures over the hundred. He was unconscious for forty-eight hours during one part of the nightmare journey, which he made burdened with a keg of water on a stick across his shoulders. The keg weighed fifteen pounds and initially contained about two gallons of water weighing twenty pounds. Back at base, he set out with the others to search unsuccessfully for Gibson. They found the tracks of the released horses heading south-east, and those of Giles following them. The Rawlinsons, due east, jutted into the desert and would have been clearly visible during the next day when Gibson should have corrected his error. But instead he headed due south. And he had Giles's compass. Let Giles speak:

> He then said if he had a compass he thought he could go better at night. I knew he didn't understand anything about compasses, as I had often tried to explain them to him. The one I had was a Gregory's Patent,* of a totally different construction from ordinary instruments of the kind, and I was very loth to part with it, as it was the only one I had. However, he was so anxious for it that I gave it him, and he departed. I sent one final shout after him to stick to the tracks, to which he replied, "All right," and the mare carried him out of sight almost immediately.

*The Gregory's Patent compass was developed by the explorer Augustus Gregory, whom Giles acclaimed as "a great mechanical as well as a geographical discoverer". He devised horse pack-saddles to replace the "dreadful old English sumpter furniture" in addition to this compass, which Giles said was unequalled for steering on horseback through dense scrubs where an ordinary compass would be almost useless.

So stupidity, for which he can't really be blamed, cost him his life. And obstinacy, too, contributed because Giles didn't want him to ride the big cob which collapsed, but one of the other horses. (I think Giles subconsciously had realized the cob's imminent failure.) And, even Giles's kindness of heart helped to weigh the scale, because he hadn't wanted to take him on this reconnaissance:

> When I made known my intention, Gibson immediately volunteered to accompany me, and complained of having previously been left so often and so long in the camp. I much preferred Mr Tietkens, as I felt sure the task we were about to undertake was no ordinary one, and I knew Mr Tietkens was to be depended upon to the last under any circumstances, but, to please Gibson, he waived his right, and though I said nothing, I was not at all pleased.

> On such chances can a man's life hinge.

18

"Giles was a bit of a fool, too," said Tom. "He shouldn't have given his horse to Gibson."

"I'd call it generosity," I said. "Or unselfishness."

"Call it what you like. It nearly cost him his life."

"If you were the leader, you couldn't have taken the safest choice," I said.

"True leadership demands ruthlessness."

I remember we had several debates of this nature.

Looking south-west from our camp I'd often found myself picturing Gibson lost in the mulga among the sand-ridges. His lively young bay mare probably carried him a hundred miles or more until she fell with dried tongue protruding from lips bared to an extraordinary extent and her hide shrivelled and wrinkled.

It's difficult to convey what Gibson meant to me—and doubtless, to the others. If you press me I'd say he had *mana,* which is something both the dead and the living in Polynesia can possess. In Fiordland, New Zealand, I was shown a dead Maori chieftainess in a feathered cloak seated in a cave and looking out over a lake. She was of high rank and her people had done her full honour three hundred years ago before sorrowfully moving on. They were being thrust inland by powerful neighbouring tribes. I'm pretty hardheaded, but she had *mana* and I felt it the whole time I was there in the cave and for days afterwards. It was almost as though she was reproaching me for something I'd not done to help her. Whom did she love and who grieved for her? Who grieved for Gibson and whom did he love? Perhaps he loved most of all the quiet secret lands of the world as did his leader. On Giles's tomb at Coolgardie is the inscription, *"Ob terras reclusas."*

Martha wrote, "Harry dear, if this works keep it as quiet as possible and please keep the family away." I couldn't, sweet. These people know that. They came and they were sad you hadn't been found sooner because they said if you'd been just a little bit warm the priest could have given you extreme unction. I was glad he couldn't because you'd have hated it.

I think we all had that impulse to search for Gibson's remains. When I voiced it first, Margaret suggested, romantically, that Gibson could have met Aborigines and lived the remainder of his life with them, perhaps siring and founding a desert civilization!

So, in an attempt to follow in Gibson's footsteps,

we moved a hundred miles or so along the Gunbarrel Highway. The country lived up only too well to Carnegie's description after his crossing in 1896 of "a great undulating desert of gravel", with occasional sand-ridges.

We skirted Giles Weather Station with its tall radio masts and the large deep-blue dish of the radar aimed skyward and took the track that ran south-west through undulating sand-ridges and plains of yellow seeding spinifex. Some hours and some seventy-five miles later I was watching the side of the road intently. A few minutes later something on a dead tree glinted in the sun. "There it is," I said. Ted Summers slowed up and stopped. The two other vehicles did the same.

He pointed at a large aluminium plaque on the tree. We read:

Len Beadell, Surveyor
Doug Stoneham, Bulldozer
Scotty Boord, Grader
Rex Flatman, Fitter
Cyril Rock, Driver
Bill Lloyd, Fuel Supply
Bill Schapel, Cook
10th April 1958

I'd expected to find this plaque. I'd had several long talks with Len Beadell of the Department of Supply about the conditions we might expect in this area. And he'd repeated to me the opinion expressed in his book *Too Long in the Bush** that this spot was very near where Gibson must have died. "From a study of Giles's journal, I would guess it is within a few miles at the most, but it might be only a few yards," he said.

You may have been wondering why Gibson had

* EDITOR: Rigby Ltd. Adelaide, 1965.

headed south after he had left the tracks made by the two released horses. The Rawlinsons must have been to the north-east and clearly visible. The explanation lay before my eyes. From the crest of a sand-ridge I could see a couple of stony hills and behind them the Bedford Range, 1800 feet high, which Gibson must have mistaken for the western end of the Rawlinsons. They were less than ten miles away from us. Just beyond the marked tree was a wide belt of thirty-foot desert oaks evoking, paradoxically, water until I realized why: their shawl-like, drooping foliage reminded me of weeping willows. We drove the Land-Rovers over the crackling carpet of fallen needles, suddenly pungent, and made camp.

As we unpacked, we debated half-heartedly whether we'd look for Gibson's remains. It was a ludicrous notion, of course, in that limitless sea of confused sandridges with no particular patterns and of mulga scrub, to think you could happen on a few bones, a rusting revolver, field-glasses and a compass, a few metal (brass?) parts of harness. Just before sunset I took a short walk alone. I wanted to do some thinking about our search. Whenever I run into a tough problem I recall Charles Darwin's marvellous words: "You would be surprised at the number of years it took me to see clearly what some of the problems were which had to be solved. Looking back, I think it was more difficult to see what the problems were than to solve them."

I sat on a fallen log, rolled myself a cigarette, lit it and asked myself, "Have I been asking the right questions about the night parrot?" As is my habit, I tried to cut out conscious thought, to relax, and wait for any bubble of insight that might well up. I remember that the falling sun was flood-lighting the humped Bedford Range; it turned deep pink, then crimson, and, finally, molten red as though forced by a great

180

furnace, before the immensely swollen and throbbing sun. A desert chat somewhere called sharply and almost querulously—to my ears. It was suddenly still: or it could have been my mind. I do not know how long I sat there, merged in the desert and the on-rushing night. When I finally stood up I was a little stiff and felt chilled. I sneezed suddenly. While I'd been sitting nothing had floated into my mind that seemed of consequence. I walked back to the Land-Rover, guided by the fire they'd lit, relatively assured that we were on the right lines. I was about two hundred yards from the camp and found the going hard, stumbling into thick mulga scrub and bristling spinifex. I remembered Ted's story of a man who'd gone a hundred yards from his camp to look at a dingo trap one dark night. As he started back, his torch failed. He couldn't find his camp during the next hour so bedded down in the sand until morning when he followed his tracks back. He'd missed his camp by ten yards the night before.

When I got back, thankful that I'd had a fire to guide me, I found them discussing Alf Gibson.

"We could look for him tomorrow," said Margaret. She didn't say it with much assurance. I stretched my hands over the fire to warm them, flexing my fingers.

"There's just one chance of finding him," said Ted. "And an outside one. If he did mistake these hills or the Bedford Range for the Rawlinsons, then he would have kept bearing around their northern flanks. He'd be looking for the water-holes he knew were in the Rawlinsons, such as the Circus. He probably died in one of those gullies on the northern flanks. That is, if he got so far."

The argument seemed sound.

"Let's try them," said Margaret. As a child my sister was always optimistic. She called it her "Father Christmas complex"—always expecting the best and most unlikely things to happen. She was standing up to the strains of the trip better than I had expected. It wasn't a heroic or dangerous adventure—or so we thought —but it was often strenuous. A friend had once described Margaret as "inutile", but under the socialite was the toughness of our pioneer grandmothers and great-grandmothers.

"Since we've come so far—" Tom laughed.

I realized they were all looking at me—the *alpha* animal. I grinned. "Why not?" And so precipitated the most hazardous of my adventures.

I've reread that last sentence with some concern but I don't overstate. When I am writing this I am physically and mentally back in central Australia, two thousand miles in space and another age away in time from these shrunken walls.

19

I asked Dr Sullivan today to post a letter to Ted Summers.

"I want some sand from the fringe of the Circus Water," I explained.

He smiled, humouring me.

"I want to play God," I said.

And I'd half a mind to try. *Triops* had once a life expectation of months or even years. With the increasing desiccation of the Centre it had adapted itself successfully. With enough shield shrimps to provide sufficient mutations you could slowly increase the

182

desiccation and shorten its life cycle. Once when I'd expressed such an idea to Larry, he'd said: "It'll be like that bloody bird—I forget its name—and disappear up its arse—I mean, it'll no sooner start than it finishes."

"A fitting end for any species," I said. "If *homo boobiens* would only do the same—"

On the whole, I like Huizinga's *Homo ludens* better than Mencken.

If that *Triops* idea sounds crazy to you, consider what they've done with *Drosophila* (fruit-flies). In a special "population" cage an experimenter placed two populations of fruit-flies differing by a certain mutation; one population had vestigial wings and the other had long wings. The insects were given a relatively small amount of food to ensure that the larvae had to compete for it. After a few generations, the *Drosophila* handicapped with vestigial wings had died out.

I wrote out another confession today and the doctor promised he'd send it to the police.

"They've got the wrong man," I said. I was concerned because the police had arrested him. There was no excuse because they knew why I was in the mental home. I got worked up and only felt better when the doctor said he'd do everything possible to avert this miscarriage of justice.

N

The youngest policewoman in history was Anna Pichant of the town of Le Chartre, France. She was made Inspector of Police in that town in 1751 at the tender age of ten, in succession to her father who died.

Long excerpt from Nietzsche, Rousseau or anyone else you may care to suggest for Dr Pseudemydura umbrina—nice Italianate ring to that!

My undergraduate jape with the psychiatrist is wearing a bit thin and I no longer get much enjoyment from feeding him with other people's confessions or concocted rubbish. Moreover, I am finding it a painful distraction from the other life I am leading in central Australia. Most of my days and a lot of my nights are spent there. Remember that what you may read in an hour may sometimes take me several hours to shape first in my mind and then on paper. I said to him finally yesterday, "Look here, I have a confession to make. I have been writing a lot more which I haven't shown you yet. Let me finish my story and then I'll give it to you."

"Okay."

He sat himself across a chair leaning his elbows on the back. Order Testudines. *Pseudemydura umbrina* Siebenrock. Food is mainly tadpoles. Appropriately has its main habitat at Bullsbrook Swamp, twenty-four miles north of Perth, Western Australia. Mates in the missionary position, belly to belly. As you'd expect.

"Do you want to tell me anything about your trip?"

"It's in my memoir—you can read it there later."

"What was Gibson to you?"

"You've been talking to Joanna."

He nodded.

"Well, you know then."

"Not all of it. Do you want to tell me?"

"No," I said. "Wait until I finish." I'd no intention of letting him see the memoir, of course.

"As you wish. Do you want to talk about anything?"

"Do you know Tinbergen's work?"

"An ornithologist?"

"Animal behaviour."

"Not in my field."

"We can't talk about him then."

"No, we can't."

Nicolas Tinbergen went to Spitzbergen in defence of Konrad Lorenz alas and alack cried David Lack and I wish I'd never been borney said Karen Horney. My tortoisey friend would have liked to have listened in to my mind. I knew it was one of my turns on the way—only mild hypomania as yet with these nonsense rhymes. I wished he'd leave me so I could get back to central Australia.

"I think you'd like a tranquillizer, wouldn't you?" he asked.

"I don't need the damned thing!" I shouted. I was annoyed with myself for losing my temper.

"Just as you wish," he said. "We don't force anyone here to do anything they don't want to." He stood up. "Don't work too hard on that autobiography."

By way of apology, as it were, I did swallow his pill. After all, I'd taken them before they put me here— even in the Centre I took one occasionally. I'd nearly burst out with the statement that Alfred Gibson had been my saviour but, fortunately, I hadn't. He's a persistent man—even if he is a fool—and that would have started him going, just as now he often pops in a question about my sister. And lately an occasional one about Elizabeth.

Although he has sometimes stalked the subject in what he considers is an obliquely cunning manner, I have, so far as I am aware, no sexual peculiarities, not even a minor fetish. Sex is simply the most delightful of all sports and the greatest pleasure a man or a woman can experience. Nothing else remotely approaches this. I said this once, years ago, to a girl

187

and she looked incredulously at me. We were both very young.

Dr Sullivan has undoubtedly questioned Joanna and Elizabeth, so why does he persist? I am tempted to invent some nonsense for him such as a preference for girls in riding boots or for Negresses. That would be a kraffty touch of ebbony to stekel him in his own reich.

Pseudemydura umbrina is no doubt a decent chap in his own lights and objectively considered. I see him in his *alpha* role in the hospital. Our empathy is nil except for a mutual admiration of that lemon-scented gum.

Today he tried to persuade me to join in group therapy. No thanks. *Homo boobiens* ganging up to discipline a deviant. I recall that a sociologist voluntarily entered a mental home and found himself being "brainwashed" by group therapy. After all, we're gregarious animals and want the respect of our fellows. How could I, without a sociologist's professional training for an armour, resist?

21

I resume my memoir after a break of over three weaks —weeks—during which I was not able to write a word.

Soon after I got back to the camp and agreed to the romantic prompting of Margaret (mainly) to look for Gibson's remains, large but scattered drops of rain fell, some with a hiss in the fire. The smoke spun in a half-circle. The overhead sky was ebony. We didn't

188

move. What looked like storms in the desert often developed no further than a few drops. So it happened this night.

Elizabeth got up shortly and went to her tent to work on the reptile specimens she'd gathered that day. Margaret looked after her, frowning. Tom, too, went to his tent to work and I to mine. I had some field notes to write up. Ted rigged a light and began repairing punctured tyres—a nightly routine along with the servicing of the Land-Rovers. Larry and Jim gave him a hand.

Joanna began sending a news story and some telegrams to Alice. Margaret washed the dishes—we took turns at this.

It was in every way a typical busy evening, except that we had rigged no mist nets (this was, of course, an improbable place). I give these details because you may be curious and also because they're pertinent to what happened. We usually had tea or coffee before turning in about 9 p.m.—or 10 p.m. if there was a lot to do. About 9 p.m. Margaret made coffee—it was her turn—and called, "Come and get it."

I was busy with some field notes and kept working until Margaret called me again. "It's getting cold." Joanna brought me a cup soon afterwards and set it down on a corner she'd cleared among the jumble of papers.

"Come and drink it at the fire, Harry," she said in a warning tone. I carried the cup to the fire where everyone had gathered except Elizabeth. When she came finally, Margaret said, "I'll have to heat it up. It's cold."

"I'm sorry," Elizabeth said. "I'll do it."

I saw suddenly what I should, perhaps, have observed before, that Margaret resented our preoccupation with our own interests. I recall that as a diversion

189

I began talking about our quest for Gibson and the even wilder possibility that we might go one better and find Leichhardt!

"Or Lasseter's reef?" suggested Tom. "Why not go the whole hog?" His voice had a sarcastic edge to which I was more sensitive than I might normally have been.

"Why not?" I laughed. This was a pseudo-attack or even the real thing. The curved eye-teeth gleamed in the firelight. I recall noticing how heavy the dew was. The paper on which Margaret had set the cups was wet and the bodywork and windscreens on the Land-Rovers were covered with large drops which wriggled like tadpoles and linked up.

"Indeed!" Tom said. "This whole expedition is about on a par with the search for Lasseter's ephemeral reef—with gold as thick as raisins in a plum pudding." He was quoting from Ion L. Idriess's book,* which I'd read only a few weeks ago, as he had, in our search of everything written about this region. The tail was twitching from side to side. I retreated from the young tiger's territory and, essaying the equivalent of Court's "Prrr!", poured the whiskies—we generally had a nightcap—and resolved to take him aside in the morning and ask him if he wanted to withdraw and return to Sydney.

As was, perhaps, inevitable, tensions had developed.

I did not get off to sleep easily, partly because of the fraying tempers, and also because of the mulga ants. We'd picked a spot where they were particularly troublesome. I recalled with melancholy sympathy that Giles was plagued with them and reproached Dante with not having a region full of these wicked wretches. Some nights they gave Giles no sleep at all while his coarser companions were untroubled.

* EDITOR: *Lasseter's Last Ride* (Angus and Robertson Ltd.)

190

Steeped in self-pity, I thought of Tom Drake and Larry snoring contentedly while I was kept awake until two o'clock. I tossed about, wishing that at the least I could talk to Elizabeth, and told myself I was paying too big a price for the quest of this elusive night parrot, which was probably snuggled down close to its mate in the spinifex and sleeping soundly. I was finally forced to move my sleeping bag into the back of one of the Land-Rovers. Oddly the ants never climbed into the vehicles. I should have got up the energy to move earlier.

I woke later to find the others had had breakfast. Tom greeted me quite cheerfully and I decided not to ask him if he wanted to pull out. But I contrived to be alone with him for some minutes so that he had an opportunity to suggest it, if he wished. He didn't take it. What followed next is most truthfully recorded in Joanna's Journal.

27th July 1967. Writing on knees before take-off for the search for Gibson. "If we find him will we take the remains to Alice for Christian burial?" Larry asks with a throw-away grin. Elizabeth, not catching on, says earnestly, "It would have to be the Rawlinsons— he'd want that."

The same evening. Some of the heaviest bush-bashing we've done to date. Charging repeatedly at sand-ridges —ten attempts before we breasted one. Many flat tyres. The ridges seem to follow no pattern, which probably helped to confuse Gibson. (He's the sort of man who'd never be Alf—Alf Gibson, yes.) Welcome belts of desert oaks where the wheels crunched through fallen needles. The twelve miles in four hours. No Gibson, of course. Searched round Diorite Hill and now camped at foot of Bedfords. Found some puddles of water but no rock-holes. So Gibson might not have

191

died immediately if he got so far and if there'd been rain. Harry, indefatigable, has set mist nets round four of the puddles. Tom and Elizabeth discovered an Aboriginal gallery with red and yellow ochre, white pipe-clay and charcoal paintings of kangaroos, wallabies, emus, serpents, tracks of animals, stencilled hands, concentric circles, diamonds, squares and ancestral figures. One cult hero I think I recognized as a Figtree ancestor with the conventional head replaced by a large circle with projecting lines from the upper edge.* I'd seen him earlier in the Musgrave Ranges.

Ted pointed out that some of the figures were repainted. "They must still come here regularly," he said. That afternoon we'd seen in the west long plumes of smoke climbing slowly into the air.

28th July 1967. Noon. Speculation because we found a bloodwood tree with a large square of bark cut out years ago and some scratches on it. Some claim they make A.G., but not confidently. Harry suggests that Gibson could have blazoned the tree and other trees to show possible rescuers the way he took. "But the piece is too big," he says. "A notch would have served. Aborigines probably did it." We've searched for other marked trees and found two more, but they don't appear to have any pattern.

Same evening. The horse's skull we found this morning is the big talking point. Larry says it was six years old, which could fit the Fair Maid of Perth. No metal harness or even the rest of the skeleton. We reason that dingoes could have dragged away the head of some horse (or donkey?), not necessarily Gibson's, that died. The parched white skull is to go to Sydney.†

* EDITOR: This was a *nuiti* or headdress worn by the Fig-men in the Dreaming.

† EDITOR: Experts later confirmed it as the skull of a six-year-old mare.

If it is the Fair Maid of Perth, we've had a wild share of luck to find it in this wilderness of scrub and drifting sand.

30th July 1967. Searched all day along the Bedfords, exploring ravines, overhangs, without success. Some more imaginative members thought red ochre marks in one overhang could be a message from Alf Gibson. Our more sceptical members fail to decipher the message.

Tom suddenly cheerful and persistent in search for Gibson. I am puzzled by the dramatic change. More fires in west and getting nearer. Tom up early and reported that some wild donkeys walked through the mist nets last night and knocked them flat. One net is torn badly. Ted is surprised they'd be in this desolate area. No night parrots, but no one really expected to catch one here. We've not seen a wallaby, for instance, for over six weeks. We're almost ready to leave Alf Gibson here. I don't think he'd approve of us, but then he might.

31st July 1967. Got back to Gunbarrel Highway late today, dust-coated and eating dust with every mouthful of food. Don't know what I've done to Elizabeth. She spends as little time with me as she's obliged with our reptile collecting.

1st August 1967. Tom and Ted have gone to Giles to pick up more supplies. Uneventful day. I think I have a touch of flu. Turning in early.

4th August 1967. It was flu or something like it. No entries for two days. Item on the A.B.C. news session last night heard in stunned silence with sharp inhalations of breath and varied grunts. We heard something to this effect:

193

"A compass carried by the explorer Alfred Gibson has been discovered in the Bedford Ranges in the Gibson Desert. The explorer Alfred Gibson became separated from the Giles expedition in 1876. He perished somewhere in the desert which now bears his name.

"The compass was found this week by Mr Thomas Drake, the co-leader of the Drake and Craddock scientific expedition which is in central Australia searching for the rare night parrot. . . .

"Mr Drake said he had every reason to believe that the compass called a Gregory Patent was the one carried by Alfred Gibson when he disappeared. He said the expedition hoped to recover other relics of the explorer Alfred Gibson.

"Mr Drake said he thought that the night parrot for which the expedition had been searching no longer existed. An intensive search of likely areas for several months had failed to find any trace of the bird. An earlier search by another expedition had been equally fruitless."

The broadcast went on to give Tom's reasons for the extinction of the night parrot. It had been on the way out before man's coming. Introduced cats and rats and grazing had merely speeded up the inevitable extinction.

Tom gave us an explanation with apologies. At Giles he had telephoned a friend at the university on private business and the clot must have passed on the information—and misinformation. "I said we *were* looking for a Gregory Patent compass."

Harry accepted the explanation. I don't know that I do. But what is Tom's purpose? Does he want to leave the expedition?

"You're a sly one," Margaret teased him. "Keeping that compass to yourself!"

"They'll have us finding Leichhardt's remains before they finish," Tom offered with a smile and, I think now, in an attempt to put the blame on the A.B.C.

Later same day. More fires in the spinifex. We've lit our own fire.

"Why don't they come in?" Harry wants to know. He consults with Ted, who says he thinks it is a small family hunting party. I swear I saw Harry fingering the septum of his nose! (My sense of humour will land me in trouble yet.)

The reptile collecting seems to have become my responsibility—not that I mind, but there was more fun working with Elizabeth. For a moment today I thought I might set the scientific world alight. I fancied I might have found a new species of skink which would be named after me. Something-or-other *Macleayi* would sound nice. (I think I'd revert to my maiden name, the more particularly as Harry already has a bird named after him, I believe . . . something *craddocki*.) I'd miscounted the scales.

22

Dr Pseudemydura today asked me if I wanted any more books. I gave him the following list:

Francis Kirkman, *The Unlucky Citizen Experimentally described in the various Misfortunes of an Unlucky Londoner, Calculated for the Meridian of this City but may serve by way of Advice to all the Cominalty of England, but more perticularly to Parents and Chil-*

dren / Masters and Servants / Husbands and Wives / Intermixed with severall Choice Novels. Stored with variety of Examples and advice / President and Precept (1673); John Dunton, *A Voyage Round the World: or, a Pocket-Library, Divided into several Volumes. The First of which contains the Rare Adventures of Don Kainophilus, From his Cradle to his 15th Year. The Like Discoveries in such a Method never made by any Rambler before. The whole Work intermixt with Essays, Historical, Moral and Divine; and all other kinds of Learning. Done into English by a Lover of Travels. Recommended by the Wits of both Universities* (1691). *Vitulus Aureus: The Golden Calf; or, A Supplement to Apuleius's Golden Ass. An Enquirey Physico-Critico-Patheologico-Moral into the Nature and Efficacy of Gold . . . With the Wonders of the Psychoptic Looking-Glass, Lately Invented by the Author —Joakim Philander, M.A.* (1749); [Thomas D'Urfey?], *An Essay Towards the Theory of the Intelligible World. Intuitively Considered. Designed for Forty-nine Parts. Part III. Consisting of a Preface, a Post-script, and a little something between. By Gabriel John. Enriched with a Faithful Account of his Ideal Voyage, and Illustrated with Poems by several Hands, as Likewise with other strange things not insufferably Clever, nor furiously to the Purpose. The Archetypally Second Edition. . . . Printed in the Year One Thousand Seven Hundred, &c.* (n.d.); *Like will to Like, as the Scabby Squire Said to the Mangy Viscount . . .* (1728); [Francis Gentleman], *A Trip to the Moon. . . . By Sir Humphrey Lunatic, Bart.* (York, 1764-65); *Sentimental Lucubrations, by Peter Pennyless* (1770); [Richard Griffith], *The Koran: or, the Life, Character, and Sentiments of Tria. Juncta in Uno, M.N.A. or Master of No Arts. The Posthumous Works of a late Celebrated Genius, Deceased* (1770).

I should, perhaps, have mentioned that Joanna comes to visit me regularly in the mental home. Our relationship to each other remains good even if our roles have changed slightly. I am not the Harry Craddock who, a few pages ago, was in central Australia or earlier planned an expedition to search for a rare bird. In my life there have been multiple Harry Craddocks, some co-existing together. Today I play the part of Harry Craddock, mental patient. We all conspire to create this part—society, the doctor, nurses, Joanna, myself.

Joanna and I have little to talk about; my life is within these pages with occasional excursions into the so-called real world; and Joanna's life is lived now with brushes and paints. If I question her she will talk about her work, but we're both aware that no real communication can be achieved with words. I can sense her struggles to find the shapes and colours to express what she wants to say, but you cannot make a conversation about it.

"Chisholm is being well looked after," she said today. "The Bourkes are doing well." I resolve that they should be freed but say nothing.

And the bulletin continues of the things she thinks I want to learn . . . that David has set himself up as a professional photographer, that Rosemary is engaged, and that the sons of an Arab stallion I once owned are siring good stock. And briefly I assume the various identities, Harry Craddock the ornithologist, Harry Craddock the father (not very successful), Harry Craddock the breeder of Arabs, Harry Craddock the amateur gardener.

I have little to offer in return. Joanna has desisted from trying to persuade me to "co-operate" with Dr Sullivan. Today she did ask how things were going.

"They're not," I said. "He, no doubt, wants to create a new identity for me and rewrite my biography. All will be *explained*, forgiven and made meaningful.

197

He wants to show me that I've been re-enacting solar myths—Oedipus or Hamlet in Venice. I'd sooner become a Roman Catholic and accept some pimply-faced priest's picture of Harry Craddock."

I said this without any heat. I'd said it before to Joanna and I knew that she hadn't much respect for psycho-analysis. Her earlier attempts to persuade me to co-operate with the psychiatrist had come from a well-meaning if slothful nature.

I want to see her paintings and she agrees.

"I'm enjoying myself," she said. "I don't know if they're any good. I may have more dedication than I thought."

Rosemary, too, comes to see me regularly, as I've mentioned. Margaret comes infrequently and I pretend to accept her excuse that now that she's married and living at Cootamundra it's a bit difficult, but she knows the real reason, and so do I. Margaret avoids anything that can cause her pain. Death frightens yet fascinates her.

23

In the Centre I clean forgot about Leo and shed him along with my other worries. After all, I told myself, we'd be hard to track down in the immensities of the Rawlinsons and the Gibson. Then, just after we'd got back to our camp on the Gunbarrel Highway from that wild-goose chase to the Bedfords, I got a shock.

Elizabeth drew me aside and asked me if I'd heard the sound of a Land-Rover during the night. I'd slept heavily and told her I'd heard nothing.

"I'm sure I heard one," she said. "In the south-west."

"Leo?"

"Perhaps."

Then I remembered that night with Ted when I thought I heard his Land-Rover long before I could have heard it. I'd thought little of it at the time but now it had to be taken into consideration. I asked the others and Tom said he thought he'd heard one. "About one o'clock."

It could have been anyone, of course. But then soon afterwards Jim disturbed me by saying that on a couple of occasions in the last week he'd seen the fresh—"very new"—tracks of another Land-Rover. "Bin follow us, maybe."

The Pitjantjatjara who had been lighting fires while we looked for Gibson did come in finally late one afternoon. Altogether there were about twenty, men, women and children, and nearly as many lean mongrel dogs, dingo and domestic crosses, with conspicuously large heads. (There was such a uniformity of huge heads and small bodies that I speculated, half-heartedly, whether they were regressing back to *Tomarctus*, the now extinct small, civet-like ancestor of both wolves and domestic dogs.) The Pitjantjatjara were on walkabout from the Warburton Mission some forty miles south. Some wore unromantic cast-off European clothing, but I, anyway, responded to the unleashed "primitiveness" of their quest, as it were, for a rebirth in the ways of their ancestors. On this walkabout they would perform their initiation and increase rites. I showed them the photographs of the night parrot and they talked excitedly amongst themselves. Jim talked with them and we learnt that they had seen birds like that last year—not many, but two or three—in the Docker Creek and the Lake Hopkins

199

o

area north of the Petermann Ranges. I cross-examined them through Jim and they nodded their heads vigorously. Some young girls giggled, pointing at the photographs and talking together. It was the nearest we'd come to a clue to the night parrot. We set off, *Triops* and all, for the Docker Creek area next day and reached it finally, following the Sandy Blight Junction Road which was no better than the legend on our maps in which a dotted road equalled "road unimproved earth". One of the Pitjantjatjara, a grey-haired man, agreed to go with us. Our route ran first across Giles Creek, a broad expanse of wind-rippled sand, past the rock needle of Gill Pinnacle (which Giles named for his brother-in-law) and the blue humped backs of the Schwerin Mural Crescent, and along Rebecca Creek to the Banggalbiri Rock-hole in the Walter James Range. Here in a bright-green gully where cool water trickled from the rocks to make first a creek with a string of pools and finally a large oval pool, a hundred and fifty feet long, we made another base camp and resumed our search for the night parrot.

I was still infatuated with Elizabeth and thought we might to to Mexico later. When the age gap obtruded, I'd tell myself that it was in the blood. John Piper had been twenty years older than his Mary Ann, the daughter of a convict, who'd borne him two sons before marriage and nine children afterwards–a programme I'd no intention of following. My weakness has been an inordinate hunger for affection. Joanna couldn't offer me enough. Elizabeth gave me warmth. But, I realize, I was too dependent on her, as I had been on others. I demanded too much.

About this time Larry and Margaret talked of returning to Sydney. "We'll try Docker Creek and then call it a day," Margaret said.

In addition to Banggalbiri Rock-hole in the Walter

200

James Range, there were four others and we rigged the mist nets round them that first evening and visited them at first eagerly and then with diminishing enthusiasm. We caught no night parrots, but just before dawn something happened that set my blood racing. The net I was inspecting at the Banggalbiri hole was empty except for a boobook owl, which I freed with only a minor scratch from its talons. On impulse I flashed my torch on the far edge of the pool and two birds, parrots, larger than Bourkes, beyond the nets which glistened like spider-webs, rose clumsily and flew off into the darkness. I couldn't swear to what I'd seen. My sight of them was momentary and, after months of finding nothing, I wasn't alert, but reason told me they must be night parrots. I ran back to the camp to awaken the others. By this time I was regretting I'd used the torch—they might have come in to drink and been netted.

"I rarely use the torch and I had to use it at that moment!" I said. But then, on reflection, I realized that if the birds were night parrots—and I was fairly positive they were—they would come again to the pool and would be caught.

That day passed quickly as we set nets in position round every pool and trickle of water for a couple of miles. We left the nets collapsed, of course, during the day. Jim and I searched acres of spinifex for tracks. By this time, my senses had sharpened under his coaching and I knew what to look for. Some of the others joined us—Elizabeth and Tom, and, I think, Larry. We found nothing and the night's harvest was the usual one of nocturnal birds.

The next afternoon at about one o'clock—it was unusually warm, almost 90°F., and I was sweating in spite of the strong south-east breeze—I found unmistakable tracks leading into a tunnel in a large spinifex clump.

I called out to Jim to join me. My voice shook slightly.

"Him night parrot!" he said. "Him home."

I'd worked out what we'd do: this was to throw one or more mist nets over the clump to trap the bird or birds. So, watching the entrance to the tunnel and ordering Jim to keep watch at the back, I called out to Tom to bring three mist nets.

"I think we've got one," I told him.

"Go on!" he said. I heard him set off at a run. He had about three hundred yards to go to one of the Land-Rovers. I sat down to wait. The hole was on the eastern side of the clump and the tunnel was dim. I remembered that earlier I had used a small torch on these searches. But I hadn't one with me.

"Lend me your compact mirror," I said to Elizabeth.

I knelt and guided the shaft of sunlight into the tunnel. I saw about two feet in a gleaming eye and the sheen of green feathers. The bird, frightened, moved deeper into the tunnel.

"It's one, all right," I said. "You look." My hands shook, handing her the compact. She guided the light into the tunnel.

"I can't see anything," she said. "It's gone—no, wait." She drew in her breath sharply. "Harry, it is! I saw it!"

"We'll find out soon," I said. "It may be another species of parrot." My innate caution was intervening to guard me against disappointment. After all, all I'd seen was a momentary flash of a sapphire eye and a green glint—was it green?"

Tom was a long time bringing the nets, or it seemed a long time. Keeping our eyes on the tunnel entrance, we got the nets spread, and then suddenly the whole clump seemed to be spitting flames and heat and pouring out columns of black smoke. We broke off branches of mulga and tried to beat out the flames.

202

We hadn't a hope. I don't know if you've seen a spini-fex clump fuelled with resinous oil on fire. The clump was gutted in about half a minute. And it threw sparks like a Roman candle. Within minutes the clumps for yards around were going up in flames. We had to run to windward.

At the time we thought it must have been a ciga-rette—Tom admitted to having been smoking one. Today I'm not sure. With that cigarette butt or match some of my life died there and then. There had been two night parrots in that tunnel. Later we found two small charred lumps. And with the fire died our hopes of the Docker Creek area—as you'll see. The spinifex fire, ever expanding in an advancing crescent fifty miles wide, swept north-west to die finally on the salty shores of Lake Hopkins thirty miles to the north.

I don't think I consciously blamed Tom at the time. I only felt he'd been careless. But subconsciously I think I may have recognized the truth—that he had deliberately lit the fire. There's no other explanation for the surge of hatred I suddenly felt. Everyone makes mistakes and though they are annoying—or worse, as this one was—they don't evoke hatred in me. At the time I had to do something so I wouldn't say some-thing I'd regret afterwards. I got into the Land-Rover with the idea of getting to the side of the fire to see if any night parrots were driven out by the flames. I started up the engine and saw Joanna climbing in alongside me.

"I want to see if any night parrots are being driven out," I explained, taking off.

"There was one, wasn't there, Harry?" she asked, quietly. Her tone told me she accepted there had been one. And, I think now, she half suspected Tom. As her journal shows, she knew him much better than I did.

I nodded. I worked the Land-Rover round to the periphery of the fire. It was travelling at about five miles an hour, crackling and billowing. At times the wind died and then the flames climbed into the crown of the mulga and the smoke increased so you could see for a few yards only. Then the wind rose to twenty knots and the smoke died and the flames, now low, flew ahead. They licked through the tops of the spinifex clumps and there was little smoke. I've noticed this phenomenon of grass fires before: they do not burn evenly but pulse in this way. Eight brown hawks (*Falco berigora*) darted and sliced through the air ahead of the fire front to prey upon the birds, skinks, lizards and other creatures routed by the fire. A harsh smell tickled my nose and made my eyes water.

"Wind up the windscreen," I cautioned Joanna when I was forced to drive through a small front about twenty yards wide. We felt only a momentary puff of heat. Contrary to popular belief, there's little danger of petrol tanks exploding in a bushfire—only if they're almost empty, and mine weren't. Some years ago before my first outback trip I'd studied my bushfire drill as enjoined by the Commonwealth Scientific and Industrial Research Organization's Bushfire Research Section and, although I might have appeared to be taking risks in racing to the front of the fire, we were in no danger while we stayed in the Land-Rover—even if it stalled in the fire's path. The closed cabin would protect us from the few minutes of intense heat while the fire swept past us. As I got to the fire's front I remember regretting I hadn't plunged my hand in and tried to grab the bird I'd seen—but I expect it would only have retreated farther into the tunnel. Scrub wrens flew jerkily before the front, blinded by smoke and dehydrated by the heat. I swerved suddenly to avoid a singed hare-wallaby. It doubled back into the front

204

and toppled suddenly as though it had been brained. I watched the flames overtake a skink. It moved with chilling slowness—reptiles haven't the lungs for a sustained effort. The fire closed on it and the skink stopped. It curled up in a single swift galvanic movement. Rat-kangaroos, jumping wildly, emerged from the smoke; nail-tailed wallabies, too, leapt and wove between the spinifex clumps. Marsupial and native mice, bandicoots, rabbits, goannas—all the many hidden creatures of the desert were being driven out by the fire. But no night parrots. The fur smouldered on a nail-tailed wallaby that moved up on the offside of the Land-Rover. Joanna saw and seized my arm.

Here was one factor that had contributed to the rarity of the night parrots. For centuries the Aborigines had been firing the spinifex and destroying them—and other ground-dwelling birds. In that instant a hawk plunged on a scrub wren. It struck and feathers exploded.

Then I saw it. A night parrot flew drunkenly only thirty yards before the front.

"Look! Look!" I shouted to Joanna and pointed with my left hand. "A night parrot! Keep your eye on it."

Although tiring, the bird was doing about twenty miles an hour and I had my work cut out to keep up with it, smashing through the belts of mulga and dodging the clumps of eucalypts. Then it went to ground about sixty yards ahead. I took a sight, lining up the spot with a rock outcrop, and raced up to where it had gone into the spinifex, revving the engine loudly. I was hoping to flush it again—I'd heard that the Aborigines in the past had run them down.

It didn't take wing. On impulse, I clambered out of the vehicle, yelling to Joanna to keep the motor running. I hurried ahead hoping I might see it but scarcely expecting that I would in all that spinifex. I must have nearly walked on it because with a clatter of wings it erupted almost from under my feet, flew about twenty yards only, and lobbed on a small sand-hill. On the wing I heard unmistakably its call—that "double note, loud and harsh". I ran towards it. Behind me the air was suddenly filled with dense black smoke as the wind dropped. It was a bloody silly thing to do. I had an idea I might throw my hat over the exhausted bird. As I ran I was wishing I had one of the mist nets. Ten yards short of the bird I slowed up. I began to advance on it slowly. It lifted its head and cocked it to the right and I froze. When it straightened I moved forward slowly, advancing one foot and drawing my body up to it. A rabbit shot past me and the night parrot fluttered its wings, lifted itself a foot above the sand and then landed heavily. I got to ten feet from it. Its wings were fanned out and its bill opened and shut convulsively. "It'll die any moment from fright or exhaustion," I thought. I slid forward another foot. A few more feet, a sudden lunge, and the bird would be mine. Then suddenly it exploded into ragged flight. Simultaneously, the horn of the Land-Rover roared. I half turned and saw the fire rushing towards me, borne by the wind, only fifty yards away, sweeping past the Rover. I raced to a fallen log and threw myself down on the far side. The log was about a foot high and I knew would offer some protection from the radiated heat. I set my hat on the back of my head and jammed my face into the sand, wishing I had my coat to put over my shoulders. I pulled up my shirt collar, clasped my hands over my ears and cheeks and waited. Hot embers showered on and around me. I felt a quick searing pain in my hands as the fire went over me. Some of my hair caught alight. I beat out the burning hair but kept my head buried until the fire passed. My trousers were smouldering from sparks in half a dozen places. I beat them out, too, and then saw my hands were red and beginning to show blisters. But I wasn't too badly burnt, for all the abominable smell of singed hair.

"The bird?" I asked Joanna when she drove up.

"Are you hurt?"

"What happened to the bird?"

"I couldn't follow it after the fire got to you."

We drove to the flank of the fire and got ahead of the front, though Joanna insisted I should treat my burns. We didn't see the bird. We stopped briefly and I got the first-aid kit from the back. While Joanna drove, I treated myself. If there was one night parrot, there could be another, I told myself.

I realized suddenly I'd made a most serious and mortifying error. I should have set a line of mist nets well ahead of the fire front. There was still time—or so I thought. We went back, gathered the others, and together we set about twenty nets ten miles ahead of the fire. We had to work frantically to do this. At the pace the fire was travelling, we had a bare hour only to watch the nets and salvage them, if possible. I was prepared to sacrifice some nets for the chance of snaring a night parrot. I won't bore you with details of what happened. We didn't catch a night parrot. Afterwards we—*Homo ludens*—were able to laugh. We caught everything else. I don't think the Pitjantjatjara with their waddies and spears were ever as successful when they fired the spinifex.

I think now Joanna had much the worst time during the fire. She wrote in her journal a couple of days later:

"I live and relive those moments of the fire when Harry stalked the exhausted night parrot and I wanted to blow the Rover's horn and warn him and could not because I knew he'd never forgive me if he lost his chance of capturing the bird because of me. So, sweating, fingers trembling on the button, wanting to scream, I waited, waited. Mechanically, I have gone over the scene again and again, each time experiencing its pain, until it is beginning to ease."

Compared to that kind of ordeal, the physical pain of my burns was unimportant, though they laid me up for three weeks and involved a dash in the Cessna to Alice for treatment.

I got over my disappointment fairly quickly, or so I thought. The big thing was that the night parrot was not extinct. At the same time I experienced a feeling of unease, of disquiet which I find difficult to describe. As a child I called it "the uneasy feeling". I suppose it's an illogical fear that something dreadful is about to happen. It is almost like a feeling of guilt, of having done something wrong for which I would be punished. As a child I had this often when I could not think of anything wrong I'd done. A master at King's School had only to say, for instance: "Stand up the boy who broke that window!" and, although I had nothing to do with it, I'd feel guilty. This, oddly, was what I experienced now. With hindsight I wonder whether subconsciously I thought I was guilty of something and had been shown that I wasn't worthy to find the night parrot. I had sometimes asked myself whether my quest initially had not come from vanity.

This could have been precipitated by my suspicions of Tom, which I repressed.

"Stop reproaching yourself," I told Tom the first night. "It could have been the exhaust of the Rover—anything. The thing is, what do we do tomorrow?"

And I went on to talk of plans to set mist nets round the rock-holes on the eastern slope of the Walter James Range, and to search the spinifex on the periphery of the fire. I said that some night parrots might have escaped into there. Moreover, the search could be extended to the Sir Frederick Range without too much trouble because the Sandy Blight Junction Road ran there.

The arrival of the Pitjantjatjara, too, cheered us all. Spurred by promises of tobacco, they would search the broad bosom of the spinifex. My enthusiasm for the quest was greater than ever. But Joanna observed a change in me of which I was not aware. She wrote about this time:

7th August 1967. Bank Holiday. Harry is still infectiously happy but I think only when he is in company. It's almost as though he puts on a mask. Alone, he does not smile and twice today he blew up when something went wrong. He drinks more—not seriously, but four or five whiskies in the evening when once he made do with two. Tonight he sat staring at the fire. I think he half suspects Tom of lighting the fire. But why? It's a joint expedition. Such glory as there is will be shared. Tom may turn on those who help him, write them abusive letters. But to prevent us catching the night parrot would be a self-inflicted wound. And, ostensibly, Harry is magnanimity itself.

Soon after the fire Margaret and Larry decided they'd leave us—Margaret rather reluctantly because she'd like to be in on the kill. But Larry was fretting for that sheep-station. As a consequence, I inherited the aquarium with its tiny world of *Triops* which I could observe during the days when my burns kept me from the active search for the night parrot.

Our near capture of the night parrot was not reported at the time. I was in favour of a discreet press release to the effect that the expedition had established that the night parrot still persisted. But Tom and some of the others thought it better to wait until we had captured and photographed one or more birds.

"If we announce it, then we'll have other people rushing here and beating us to the punch," he said.

It carried weight with some of the party, though I couldn't see anyone mounting an expedition without a good deal of preparation.

About a week later Tom brought out his surprise. He was leaving the expedition to lead his own for the night parrot. He supported his action by arguing that I would be out of the search for some weeks because of my burns. He added that this separation was necessary because we disagreed on the areas of search. He said he had just received a grant from a university.

At the time, I saw no point in arguing with him and, to be truthful, experienced a certain relief. He departed the next day with Ted in one of the Land-Rovers to pick up his own vehicle and driver at Giles. I resumed the search in the Walter James Range area, directing it from my stretcher, and urging the Pitjantjatjara to new prodigies of tracking with rewards of tobacco—not without twinges of conscience.

About a month later when we had moved to the Petermann Ranges we tuned into the A.B.C. news and learnt that Tom had found a night parrot on the Bedfords. He had one bird which, unfortunately had died soon after being netted. He proposed to continue the search, particularly since, he was quoted, this was the first time the bird had been seen alive for fifty years. There was a lot more—several months' intensive search of much of central Australia had finally been successful.

I was pleased, though disappointed that I had not shared in the discovery. Here was something tangible for our work even if the bird was dead. The bird was definitely far from extinct. We'd seen two at least in the Docker Creek area and now one had been captured in the Bedfords. I rang him on the radio telephone and congratulated him.

"What did he say?" Joanna asked, after I hung up.

"He said something about not expecting a call."

"Where did he catch it?"

"At a rock-hole. He says it died of fright when he was releasing it from the net."

I went on with my search. As I saw it the major task was still before us—myself and Tom—to study the living bird. So we worked through the rock-holes of the Petermanns and debated whether to move from there to Eyre's Peninsula where a reliable observer had seen a night parrot a few years earlier.

It was about two weeks after Tom's capture that I chanced to say to Ted after a rather tiring day—the temperatures were rising and so were the winds:

"Pity we missed that rock-hole in the Bedfords." I realized he didn't understand. I added, "Tom caught his bird there."

"A rock-hole in the Bedfords?"

"Yes."

I think it must have troubled Ted—I failed to notice it at the time—because it was not until next day he said, "You know what you said about the Bedfords? A rock-hole." He looked straight at me. "I'm pretty certain there are no rock-holes in the Bedfords. I've been there several times."

"Are you sure?" You get a mental blackout at such times and speak aimlessly.

"Positive."

"I thought he said rock-hole . . . it could have been 'pool'."

I said to him later, "There could be a rock-hole or some more or less permanent water. Remember the donkeys? They'd need it."

"I suppose so, though they could have been moving

211

through after a storm. There are no pools in the Bedfords."

I don't think that I was consciously suspicious at that time. I was more puzzled than anything else and concluded that Tom had possibly meant a pool of water left after rain.

"That water we saw at the Bedfords?" I asked. "How long would it have lasted?"

"About a week."

I should have left it there. Man differs from an animal in being aware of himself and, as Broad* points out, in having a great store of memories. Perhaps the greater "happiness" of birds happens because of this lack of self-consciousness and the possession of few memories? Perhaps our trouble is that we're too much like Paul Bunyan's Goofus bird on the Big Onion River which always flew backwards. "It doesn't give a darn where it's going, it only wants to know where it's been."

That night when I talked with Joanna the jigsaw bits began to assume a more definite shape—the suspicion that Tom had found the night parrot, not when he claimed he did, but when we'd been at the Bedfords. Wishing to keep the triumph for himself, he'd killed the bird when he'd discovered it in one of the mist nets and put it in his kerosene refrigerator. This hypothesis would explain the fire in the spinifex and his leaving the joint expedition. And it would explain, too, that curious A.B.C. news release about Gibson's compass. He just had to tell the world something—not that he'd found the night parrot because he'd have to share the glory—but something substitutary! A displacement activity.

* EDITOR: Professor C. D. Broad, *The Mind and its Place in Nature* (Routledge and Kegan Paul, 1925).

212

At the time the whole hypothesis appeared so tenuous that I wanted to dismiss it.

"Let's forget it," I said.

"It fits," said Joanna. "I wonder?" Excitedly she began turning the pages of her journal. "See!" I followed her finger, reading, "Tom suddenly cheerful and persistent in search for Gibson."

She put the journal down slowly. "He was suddenly very cheerful . . . excited."

"I'd sooner forget it," I said. I wasn't being generous so much as self-protective. I couldn't bear to think he'd cheat me like this. And more unbearable, horrifying, was the thought that Tom, a trained zoologist, had robbed science of a chance to study the living bird. I thrust it away from me. I didn't sleep well that night. Those absurd jingles: what Scotch should you watch out for and "what?" asked Mrs Appel also apelled Apple. "Which Watt?" pealed Mr Appel and elevated his el. And, levitating, Mr Appel yelled to Mrs Appel. The introverted Goofus bird, *Retrovolornis?*—my Latin is now rudimentary—met inverted William Rufus . . . or something like that. There was another: a beard in the bush was worth two in the Strand. I thought it was very funny—and sometimes do now.

I recall they went on for hours and I couldn't stop them. That was when I started to be afraid.

The next morning I rang Tom in the Bedfords (at least, that's where I thought he was) and after some questions about what had been in the bird's stomach—"spinifex seeds and some I can't identify"—I asked him where the rock-hole had been which we'd missed.

"Easy enough to miss," he said. "On the southern flank." He laughed. "Remember those donkeys? They smashed a couple of my nets one night."

He sounded convincing and I think I almost accepted it at the time, arguing to myself that Ted

213

must have missed the rock-hole. Tom was friendly. He told me he had not found any sign of other night parrots but intended to persist with the Bedfords for a little longer. He promised to let me know what the other seeds in the bird's stomach were when they had been identified in Sydney.

That day Elizabeth got a telegram from Sydney saying that her mother was seriously ill. She had to leave, of course, but it upset me to lose her. I could only snatch a few minutes with her.

"Come back as soon as you can," I urged.

"I don't know how long she'll be ill," she said. I was holding her and kissing her in my tent.

"I'll always think you're beaut, Harry," she said. She pushed me away gently. "I must go."

I thought she must be worried about her mother. "Off you go and—some time Mexico," I said. "Or anywhere."

"Anywhere." I saw suddenly she was crying. "Look after yourself, Harry. Take care of yourself."

She walked out of the tent. My white oryx, I thought, of grace and warmth. She left the same afternoon with Larry and Margaret in one of the Land-Rovers with Ted driving. Their destination was Alice. Our party had suddenly diminished and to that I attributed my sudden gloom that evening as I began my vigil among the mist nets, a melancholy Alonso Quijano of doubtful goodness, deprived of his Dulcinea.

My moodiness persisted for about a week. At such times I try to spare others, but it was apparent to Joanna, who noticed I rejected food. She said suddenly:

"You'll have to go to the Bedfords and see for yourself."

She was right. I left the same day and insisted on going alone. Ted wanted to accompany me and normally I'd have welcomed having him. But if there was

214

any scientific dirty linen to be washed it was to be done privately. I gave as a pretext that Tom wanted to consult me. Ted, I'm sure, had his own thoughts but kept them to himself.

I won't bore you with many of the mechanized details of my preparations. The thirty-six gallons in the two tanks was enough fuel, at five miles to the gallon, for one hundred and eighty miles. I carried also two gallons of oil, twenty gallons of water (in a tank and jerry cans), six spare tubes and two tyres, engine spares and tools, a radio transmitter and three sleeping bags. I threw in a few tins of meat, jam, honey, fruit juices, some flour, bread and cheese.

I chose one of Ted's two station-wagon Land-Rovers.

"You're sure you want her?" he asked. "She's got a lively engine but she can be cantankerous."

But I was set on my choice. I reached the Bedfords, retracing our earlier journey along the Gunbarrel Highway in two days and, as I'd half expected, there was no rock-hole there. And, I'll swear, no low-lying water for months. And no Tom, either, although I found the remains—necrotic word—of his camp. I called Giles Weather Station asking about his movements.

"They went through about a week ago."

I heard myself ask, "They?"

"Him and the girl from your party."

"Miss Trumbull?"

"That's the name."

I thanked them and hung up. I don't know what I intended but I started up the Land-Rover and headed back for the Gunbarrel Highway. When I struck it I kept heading north-west, bush-bashing through the mulga scrub and up and down the brutes of sand-ridges. I was hurt and wanted to run. I don't remember what happened in much detail as I was living in a kind of waking dream. I think I had several punctures in the first two hours—I must have had them. (Punctures were usually in the near front tyre and punctured by large mulga stakes.) I did sixty miles that day, going on after sunset and using the headlights. I was so exhausted I fell asleep over the wheel and woke four hours later with a kinked neck.

I realized then I was retracing Gibson's route. It made me laugh. I remember I found myself scratching my chest and I asked myself, "Whom do you hate?" And, answered, "Tom. And perhaps Elizabeth." I started off again before dawn and saw a long pillar of smoke out in the spinifex void on my left. I'd seen Aboriginal fires yesterday, I recalled. All that day I kept charging at those red hells of sandhills, the wheels slipping and the motor roaring. Sometimes I had to make up to six runs to get over but kept hurling the Land-Rover, lively and troublesome, at them. Half a mile away a black finger of smoke probed the harsh blue sky. Other fingers grew, keeping level with me, as I moved that day. By late afternoon I was, I knew suddenly, somewhere near where Gibson had turned off the tracks that would have led him to water and life. On my right, due east, about fifty miles away, lay the convoluted Rawlinsons. I turned the switch and the stillness roared in my ears. I got out of the Land-Rover and went for a short walk along the crest of a ridge. The black finger was closer, I observed.

Whoever smashed up the Land-Rover did it expertly. (Leo? The Pitjantjatjara with whom I'd fought a duel?) Axe-blows had gashed the petrol and water tanks and smashed the radio telephone. The canned food had been battered open and spilled. Petrol fumes flooded into my brain and made me vomit.

I came to then and took stock. I had the choice of staying where I was until I was found or I could start out for the Rawlinsons. I chose the last, reasoning it might be several days before Ted started searching for me. The August temperatures were usually mild. Fifty miles didn't seem much of a walk, even without water. Nor would it have been if I hadn't sprained my right ankle in the first hour when I trod on a stone that shifted with my weight. I kept going, however, and rested up during the heat of the day, while my ankle swelled. I broke off a sapling and used it as a crutch—it soon chafed my armpit raw. I kept going until midnight, making only about a mile an hour. By this time my mouth was dry and I was choking for water. (I found this amusing at the time. I have active saliva glands and my dentist has a drainage problem when filling my teeth.) I was chilled to the bone, chattering with the cold so that I slept badly.

As soon as it was light I set off again. My ankle shot fiery pains with every step; my tongue was cracked and swollen; and the spinifex, almost as high as I was, made every step an agony. My arms and legs were punctured with spines. With every step more spines thrust through at me and broke off in my flesh and clothing. Around each puncture in my flesh grew minute red pustules, continually growing and bursting. With lack of both water and food I was by now light-headed. I had an almost overpowering desire to lie down. At midday I crawled under the shade of some mulga. My late afternoon and night were a pain-racked replica of what I've described, and the next morning my position was desperate. I think I was probably unconscious for almost twenty-four hours, because I dozed at midday and woke to see the sun in the east.

I struggled to my feet. As soberly and accurately as I can I shall report what appeared to happen next. I had gone painfully only a few yards when I saw the small bay mare trotting towards me with flirting tosses of her finely moulded head. I could scarcely believe my eyes as she continued to approach me until she was only a few feet away. There she stopped, waiting. She bore a saddle and the wild hope sprang up: "If I could get into the saddle, she'd bear me to safety."

I approached her cautiously and the beautiful bay mare waited rock-still, neck arched and watching me with a large, wonderful, brown eye. I reached her side, gathered up the reins which were tied to the saddle, put my good left foot in the stirrup and swung into the saddle. Immediately I was settled in the seat, swaying slightly, she set off at a gentle but swift walking pace, due east for the Rawlinsons, as I later could verify from the curious compass set in the pommel. After perhaps an hour I must have dozed or half fainted because when I awoke she was entering a narrow, rocky defile which, astonishingly, opened out into a green valley through which ran a wide stream. We went along its banks in the cool shelter of tall palms and oaks, pines, cedars and eucalypts and, as faint music seeped into my mind, I realized with a shock that this was the same valley I had visited in my dreams some weeks before when I'd waited for Ted.

I checked the mare and dismounted—rather painfully because I had to take my weight on my swollen ankle—and made for the stream's edge where I drank deeply and then fell asleep. Then in a half-conscious state I became aware of strong arms lifting me and heard the soft voices of women, as I was carried into a cool building. I assume that it was such from the change of temperature on my face and arms and the sound of feet on a stone(?) floor. In my delirium I saw nothing but retained my other senses. Presently a man was lifting my shoulders while a girl fed me with an odorous soup, a spoonful at a time. Meanwhile others gently dressed my spinifex-pricked hands and legs. Before they finished I lapsed into unconsciousness again and, presumably, spent several days alternating between deep sleep and near consciousness.

I do not know how I came to be again in the rocky defile in the Rawlinsons where Jim and Ted found me in a deep sleep. The rational explanation is that I had experienced an intense hallucination brought on by my ordeal. With part of my mind I accept this. My own doctor (not Dr Sullivan) informed me on my return to Sydney that not only genuine hallucinations, but delusional interpretations of real perceptions, were possible in my mental state after the shock I'd experienced. None the less, there are puzzling aspects. If it was a hallucination, how did I survive for eight days without water or food? The tracks of a horse did lead into the defile.*

I was some time recovering in Alice.

That was the end of the quest for the night parrot. We went back to Chisholm and I was suddenly exhausted, mentally and physically. I blamed myself bitterly for everything that had happened, including the death of the night parrot.

"I can't be sure I didn't destroy the few remaining birds there were."

"That's nonsense," Joanna argued. "You, yourself, were pleased we'd found the birds because it showed they existed."

"One killed by Tom and others destroyed in the fire!"

My self-reproaches were endless; I couldn't even work up a healthy hatred against Tom, who'd had

---

* EDITOR: This was confirmed by Ted Summers later in Alice Springs: "We nearly didn't search the defile because Jim said only horse tracks led in there. But we did luckily. We lost Harry's tracks about thirty miles east of the Rawlinsons and, though we made several circles, we couldn't pick them up again—only the tracks of a horse."

enough sense not to make too much of his find. I didn't want to eat and I lost weight. I slept badly—I'd go off to sleep all right but wake up about two or three o'clock and lie awake until dawn blaming myself for everything, including that man's death. I remember I was often constipated and this worried me a great deal.

To be frank with you, I was so depressed that my doctor feared I'd attempt suicide—as I'd done earlier but botched in true Piper style because Joanna found me, unconscious. The upshot was I was committed by my doctor and a colleague to this place. I didn't argue with them. I was too sick and exhausted to dispute anything and, importantly, I knew I deserved to be put away for shooting that man at Parramatta.

I don't believe that any longer and told the doctor so yesterday. "I recognize that it was a delusion," I told him. "I didn't shoot him." As I spoke I looked over Dr Sullivan's head and realized I could choose either landscape in the Mona Lisa for my walk—the arid left-hand one where Gibson died or the mannered one with the bridge. I wanted neither of them. We went on talking and I tried to be helpful. He could rewrite the story of my life in his terms and I could pretend to accept it, and to relate to others, as he put it.

As I said earlier, it all started with Red's death and the search for the night parrot in the wastes of central Australia. The power of what I've called my obsession has worried me but it does so no longer. With the insight I've acquired while writing this account I have come to accept myself for what I am and not to seek to justify my every action. Or, to question myself continually. I accept my common humanity. And I'm resolved to continue my search for the night parrot—with as much dedication as before but with less desperation. Joanna, I think, will accompany me.

220

I'm still a clown, but then I'm like the chimpanzees I mentioned earlier which wanted to know what was happening in the laboratory. I accept this.

For the present I prefer to look at the lemon-scented gum. Its trunk, straight and slender as a flagpole, runs up seventy feet to the plumy crown. When I leave here I'll have to plant some at Chisholm.

EPILOGUE

Harry Craddock's account ends here. He handed me the MS. shortly before leaving for the Centre.

"Make any use you like of it. You might be able to work up a straight story of the expedition or a few articles, at least. I'm off to the Flinders Ranges—I'm a dog that only knows one trick."

I saw him by chance two months later when my work took me to Adelaide. He had flown down from the Flinders Ranges to collect some mist nets. Over a drink in a North Terrace hotel he said, smiling, that he hadn't even a feather to show for two months' search of the Flinders Ranges, but that there were other places.

I'd never seen him look better.

"I've given up smoking," he said. He patted his belly—it looked slim enough in spite of his consistent concern.

Joanna had joined him in the Flinders, he said. He made no reference to the MS. I mentioned it and he laughed, but said nothing. I sensed he was enjoying a quiet private joke—a kind of detached ironic amusement at himself. We had a few more drinks.

"Time pulls the trigger," he said when leaving. We were standing on the footpath. I didn't at first catch the echo of the anti-smoking pamphlet until he said: "I didn't think the Queensland Health Department had so much poetry in its soul."

He stepped out on the road. I don't think he saw the truck that hit and killed him.

SO-BDL-201

VILROS

Raspberry PI
User's Guide

Raspberry PI User's Guide

Copyright © 2014 Vilros. All rights reserved.
www.vilros.com
1-855-207-9254
ISBN: 978-0-692-31936-9

No part of this publication may be reproduced, distributed, or transmitted in any form or by any means, including photocopying, recording, or other electronic or mechanical methods, without the prior written permission of the publisher, except in the case of brief quotations embodied in critical reviews and certain other non-commercial uses permitted by copyright law.

Trademarked names, logos, and images may appear in this book. Rather than use a trademark symbol with every occurrence of a trademarked name, logo, or image, the names, logos, and images are used only in an editorial fashion and to the benefit of the trademark owner, with no intention of infringement of the trademark.

The information in this publication is provided on an "AS IS" basis. Vilros makes no warranties, express or implied, regarding use of the information alone or in combination with your products. Neither the author nor the publisher can accept any legal responsibility for any errors or omissions that may be made.

Conventions Used in this Book

The following table describes the text conventions used in this book.

Convention	Meaning
Italic	Text that appears in italics refers to file names, variable and function names, or other code. Within the context of giving instruction, italic text should be typed exactly as shown.
Bold	Within the context of giving instruction, items in bold text are user interface elements, such as key strokes, menu items, or button labels.
Monospace font	A monospace font is used for shell commands and Python code that should be typed in on the keyboard.

Contents

1 – Getting Started

1.1 Introduction

The Raspberry Pi is a small computer, a *very* small computer.

It consists of mostly the same parts as a standard desktop computer or laptop. A central processing unit (CPU) acts as a brain, random access memory (RAM) and long-term storage devices are used to hold data, a video display shows you what is happening, and you interact with all of this using mice, keyboards, joysticks, and other universal serial bus (USB) devices. The Pi may be less powerful than your Windows PC or Macintosh, but it is still impressive that it fits all of this on a board only slightly larger than a credit card.

The original goal of the UK-based Raspberry Pi Foundation was to create a device that would address their perception of falling standards in the teaching of computer science. As computers have evolved, they have become more difficult to write software for at a "low-level" – with close interaction between hardware and software. And as they have become more integrated in our daily lives, the consequences of breaking your computer by experimenting have become more severe…and expensive.

So, unlike conventional systems, the Pi is a machine that is designed to be played with and used for experiments. Its diminutive form factor and relatively low cost mean that you can do what you want with it, and this attracts far more diverse groups of users than just students and teachers.

It is suitable for a wide range of applications, including:

Using the Pi for General Computing
You can install a variety of operating systems on the Pi, and many of these have full desktop environments. With support for external hardware devices, Internet connections, and downloading and installing software, you can use the Raspberry

Pi as a regular computer. It can do just about everything your main system can do...only a little slower.

Playing Games

The range of games available on the Raspberry Pi's operating systems is extensive. But you can also install "emulators", which are pieces of software that allow programs from other machines to be run on the Pi. This gives you access to titles on classic machines such as the Atari 2600, Nintendo Entertainment System, Sega Genesis, Sharp X1, MSX, Panasonic 3DO, and many more. All Raspberry Pi models support HDMI video output and USB game controllers, making the Pi a popular choice for fans of retro computing and retro video games.

Playing Movie Files and Music on Your TV

Put the Pi in a case, connect it to a television using an HDMI cable, and install XBMC. Then you have a capable media center that can load movie files from the SD card, USB hard drives, or across your local network.

Providing Network Services

As a small, standalone device that connects to the Internet and local networks, the Raspberry Pi makes an excellent server. You can use it to serve files and webpages, answer domain name system (DNS) requests, share hardware devices (for example, printers) across a network, and almost anything else you might need a server for.

Setting up Development Environments

The simple nature of the Pi, and its support for many different programming languages, make it an ideal system to use when learning how to program. The Pi contains an ARM processor, and these are popularly used in cellphones, tablets, games consoles, and in the computer-controlled equipment used in manufacturing. The ability to program one is a skill that is in high demand.

Building Controller Boards and Interaction with Electronics

Its small size, low cost, and ease of programming make the Raspberry Pi very useful in "embedded" applications. In these types of project, the Pi is used along with other electronics circuits to create everything from 3D printers, to home automation systems and robots.

1.2 Technical Specifications

The Model B+ is a revised version of the Model B that will eventually replace the earlier model. It has more general purpose input/output (GPIO) pins than earlier models, and twice as many USB sockets.

	Model B+
CPU	Broadcom microprocessor running at 700 MHz (ARMv6 architecture)
GPU	Broadcom VideoCore IV, 250 MHz OpenGL ES 2.0 MPEG-2 and VC-1, 1080p h.264/MPEG-4 AVC decoder
Memory	512 MB
Video Output	HDMI, composite video (PAL and NTSC) through 4-pole 3.5 mm jack, LCD panels through DSI.
Audio Output	4-pole 3.5 mm jack, HDMI, I2S
USB Ports	4 (2 dual sockets)
Input/Output	17 x GPIO, UART, I2C, SPI
Networking	10/100 Mb/s Ethernet, USB devices
Storage	microSD card slot
Power	5V through micro-USB socket or GPIO header

The following diagram shows the available connectors on the Raspberry Pi Model B+.

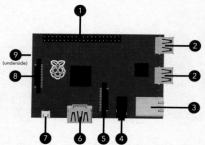

Figure 1. The Raspberry Pi and its connectors

1	General purpose input/output (GPIO) header – these pins can be controlled from software.
2	Universal serial bus (USB) socket for attaching peripheral devices such as mice, keyboards, or memory sticks. This is a dual socket and two USB devices can be connected at the same time.
3	10/100 Mb/s Ethernet (RJ45) socket for connecting to a network router.
4	4-pole 3.5 mm output jack for audio and video.
5	Camera serial interface (CSI).
6	High-definition multimedia interface (HDMI) video output.
7	Power in via micro-USB socket.
8	Display serial interface (DSI) flexible flat cable connector for liquid crystal displays (LCDs).
9	microSD socket. The card socket is attached to the underside of the board.

1.3 Basic Setup

To start using your Pi, you need to connect it to:

1. Power
2. An SD card with an operating system or "bootable" program installed

Without these, the Pi will do nothing, not even output a video signal. For the initial configuration, you may also need to connect:

1. A display (using HDMI or composite video)
2. A USB keyboard
3. An Ethernet cable or USB Wi-Fi "dongle"

The display, and any USB devices you may connect, can be removed when they are not in use. For example, a Pi acting as a file/print server may only accept input from computers on the network and does not always need a keyboard or screen.

Fitting a Heat Sink

When the components in a computer system work hard, they generate heat. And above a certain level, this heat can reduce the lifespan of the components or even break them altogether. A *heat sink* is a carefully designed block of metal that takes the heat away from the electronic component and then passes it into the air surrounding the device.

There are three chips on a Raspberry Pi that can get very hot if the device is working hard: the central processing unit (1), the chip that controls the Ethernet and USB ports (2), and the power regulator (3).

To install a heat sink:

1. Unplug the Pi and leave it to cool before attempting to handle the device.
2. On the bottom of the heat sink, peel away the plastic backing that covers the adhesive.
3. Press the heat sink down firmly and directly onto the chip. Hold the pressure for a few seconds to allow the adhesive to work.

If you buy heat sinks for your Pi, only use the thermal adhesive that they arrive with; never use any other type of adhesive or sticky plastic to install a heat sink on a Raspberry Pi. The adhesive must be a special compound so that it effectively transfers heat from the chip on the Pi to the metal of the heat sink.

Figure 2. The three heat-out points on a Pi (left); and installing a heat sink on the CPU (right)

Connecting Power

The Raspberry Pi requires a power supply of 5 V that can provide at least 700 mA of current. Before connecting the Pi and turning it on, you should check the rating of the power supply carefully.

Many cellphone chargers will work, but some supply less current than the Pi needs. Using inadequate power supplies, or even powering the Pi from the USB port of another computer, is not recommended as the lack of current may make the Pi unstable. You should certainly avoid doing this if you need to connect any other devices to the Pi.

Power can be fed in to the Pi through the micro-USB socket or, if you have a suitable connector, through the general purpose input output pins. However, you should be aware that providing power through the GPIO header pins bypasses the on-board protection circuitry that is designed to prevent damage to the device. For this reason, it should only be attempted by people who are experienced in building electronic circuits.

It is worth noting that the Raspberry Pi does not have an on/off switch. Some operating systems can power down the device or put it into standby mode but when you want to turn it off, you will often have to remove the power supply or switch it off at the wall socket.

 There are two holes on the printed circuit board (PCB) of the Model B+. These holes are labelled "RUN" and you can solder a switch across these two connections to create a reset button.

Connecting a Display

HDMI offers a high-quality video and audio signal, and is the preferred way of connecting all models of Raspberry Pi to a modern television. To connect a high-definition television:

- Plug one end of an HDMI cable into the Raspberry Pi's HDMI socket, and the other end into an HDMI input on your TV.

If your display does not support HDMI, you can connect the composite video and audio outputs to the auxiliary A/V input of most televisions. These connections are colored yellow, red, and white. With Model B+ devices, you need a cable that has a 4-pole jack on one end, and three RCA plugs on the other (one yellow, one red, and one white). To use these cables:

1. Plug the 4-pole 3.5 mm jack plug into the 3.5 mm jack socket on the Raspberry Pi Model B+.

2. Connect the yellow composite video plug to the yellow video input socket on your TV.

3. Connect the red RCA plug to the red audio socket on your TV.

4. Connect the white RCA plug to the white audio socket on your TV.

If your TV does not have the yellow, red, and white auxiliary inputs, you can plug the composite outputs into a SCART adapter and connect that to your TV instead.

When using the composite video, you always have the option of connecting the video to a television and the audio output (the red and white connectors) to other devices, such as headphones, powered speakers, or amplifiers.

To use a computer monitor as the Pi's display, you will need an HDMI to VGA, or HDMI to DVI adaptor. However, when connecting to a monitor using an HDMI to VGA/DVI adapter, you will initially be unable to connect speakers to the audio connector. When the HDMI cable is connected, the composite video and audio output ports are turned off. This can be changed once you have an operating system running on the Pi.

 Although not covered in this book, all Raspberry Pi models support DSI for connecting LCD panels.

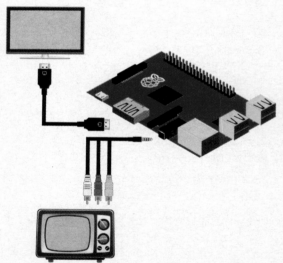

Figure 3. Connecting a display to the Model B+

Connecting USB Devices

With most operating systems that you run on the Pi, human interface devices (HIDs) that connect using USB (such as mice, keyboards, and game controllers), and storage devices (such as USB memory sticks and hard drives) will work without any problems or installation processes. You may need to install *drivers* – pieces of software written to pass messages between the operating system and the hardware device – to use more complicated peripherals like soundcards.

To connect a USB device, insert its USB connector into an available socket on the Raspberry Pi. You can usually do this safely whether or not the Pi is turned on and running.

The Raspberry Pi can only supply a limited amount of power to USB devices. It is recommended that you do not connect any devices that draw over 100 mA. To use more power-hungry devices, you can use a powered USB *hub* – a device that allows multiple USB peripherals to be connected to a single port, and that has its own power supply. This also allows you attach more devices to the Pi.

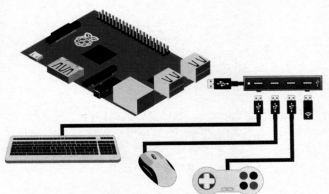

Figure 4. Connecting the Pi to a 4-port USB hub

Connecting to a Network

To make a wired network connection between the Pi and a network router:

1. Plug one end of a CAT5 or CAT6 Ethernet cable with RJ45 connectors into the Ethernet socket on the Raspberry Pi.
2. Plug the other end of the cable into your network router.

The actual network connection is made by the software or operating system running on the Pi.

In theory, Wi-Fi is a faster technology than the 10/100 Mb/s Ethernet circuit that is built-in to Model B+. In practice, however, this is not always the case. As the Pi cannot process data as quickly as a brand new desktop computer, the difference in speed between Ethernet and Wi-Fi is less noticeable and you should use whichever is most convenient for you.

 Not all Wi-Fi and Ethernet adaptors are compatible with the Raspberry Pi. Before buying, check that the adaptor is known to be working by looking at the list at http://elinux.org/RPi_USB_Wi-Fi_Adapters

1.4 SD Cards

In the next chapter, you will learn about Raspberry Pi operating systems (in particularly, Raspbian Linux) and how to install them onto a secure digital (SD) card. This will complete the set-up of the Pi.

Unlike conventional desktop computer systems, the Pi does not have a hard drive from which to load an operating system. Instead, it uses the card socket to load files from a memory card.

When the Pi is first turned on:

1. The main ARM processor and SDRAM (memory) are disabled.

2. The graphics processing unit (GPU) loads the "first-stage bootloader" that is built-in to the Pi, and this contains all of the code necessary to work with memory cards.

3. The first-stage bootloader enables SDRAM, detects the presence of a memory card, and loads the "second-stage bootloader" from it.

4. The second-stage bootloader loads the operating system or bootable program from the card.

Classifying Memory Cards

There are three main types of SD card, with three physical-size variations and several speed classes of each.

- Standard SD cards are available in capacities ranging from 4 MB to 2 GB.
- Secure digital high capacity (SDHC) cards are available in capacities up to 32 GB.
- Secure digital extended capacity (SDXC) cards are available in capacities up to 2 TB.

Full-size cards are approximately 24 mm wide and 32 mm long. miniSD cards are slightly smaller, only 20 mm wide and 21.5 mm long; and microSD cards are slightly smaller again – 11 mm wide and 15 mm long.

Model B+ Raspberry Pi devices have a single microSD socket on the underside of the board. You cannot use full-size SD cards with this model, but microSD cards are often packaged with adapters that allow the microSD card to be used in a PC's card reader.

| full-size card | microSD card | microSD + adaptor |

Figure 5. Full-size and microSD cards

As memory cards are made by many different manufacturers (over 400), deviations from the standard can occur and prevent the Pi from working with a specific card. If you are intending to buy a new memory card for use with your Raspberry Pi, you can check the compatibility list at *http://elinux.org/RPi_SD_cards* to ensure that you purchase one which is known to work.

Inserting and Removing SD Cards

It is likely that you will need a memory card with at least 4 GB capacity if you are intending to run an operating system on the Pi. 4 GB SDHC microSD cards are widely available and generally very cost-effective.

To insert an SD card:

1. Ensure the Pi is unplugged.
2. Locate the SD card socket on the underside of the Pi's board.
3. When looking from above, the SD card's contacts should be facing up.
4. Gently, but firmly, push the SD card into the socket until it clicks into place.

Figure 6. Inserting SD cards into the Raspberry Pi

To remove the SD card:

- First push the microSD further into the device until it clicks. Then pull the card out.

When inserting and removing SD cards in other computers, it is not always necessary to turn off the device. However, as the memory card contains its operating system, the Pi may access it at any time. Removing the card while the Pi is accessing it can corrupt data and, in extreme cases, may stop the card working at all.

2 – Introducing Raspbian

2.1 Raspbian and Linux

An operating system (OS) is a unique type of application that you run on your computer. It is an environment in which many other applications can run at the same time, with a consistent user interface and sharing the same resources. Microsoft Windows and Apple's Mac OS X are probably the two most well-known operating systems, but there are others.

Linux is one of a small group of operating systems that are "free". It usually doesn't cost anything to use and people can modify the OS, repackage it with other software, distribute their version, and generally do what they want with it. Because of this, you can find Linux running on most types of computer – from large servers used by corporations such as Google, to small devices like the Raspberry Pi. A bundle of the Linux core with other applications (such as desktop environments, file managers, and web browsers) is called a "distribution" (or "distro").

Raspbian is a Linux distribution that is based on Debian, another popular version of Linux. It is designed for the Raspberry Pi and is the OS recommended by the Raspberry Pi Foundation. Although different Linux distributions can usually all run the same applications, this book is focused on using Raspbian and it may be helpful for you to run this OS while you are learning. Once you are familiar with Raspbian, you will find that you are able to use other varieties of Linux without much help.

2.2 Installation of Raspbian with NOOBS

New out of Box Software (NOOBS) is a tool that you can run on your Raspberry Pi and it will help you install an OS. It stays on the SD card, even after the OS installed, and can also be used to edit the Pi's main configuration file or replace the installed OS if problems occur. The SD card supplied with your Pi already contains NOOBS.

Installing NOOBS to an SD Card

There are two versions of NOOBS available: NOOBS and NOOBS Lite. NOOBS Lite is quicker to download, but does not come with the installation files for Raspbian. Instead, your Pi connects to the Internet to download the relevant files when you start the installation process. It does not support USB Wi-Fi adapters, and this means that you will need an Ethernet cable plugged in to your Raspberry Pi to use NOOBS Lite.

The full version of the latest version of NOOBS only comes with the files needed to install Raspbian. To install a different OS, you need an Internet connection.

The space that NOOBS occupies on the SD card is not available for use by the OS that you are installing. Even a 4 GB SD card will sometimes not be large enough to hold NOOBS and an OS, and still have adequate space for your files and programs.

If you cannot use NOOBS, you can install an OS "disk image" to your SD card. This is described in section 2.3 Installation of Raspbian using a Disk Image on page 21.

The process for installing NOOBS to an SD card is the same whether you are using the full NOOBS package, or NOOBS Lite.

On Windows (8/7/Vista/XP):

1. Insert the SD card into a suitable card socket or USB card reader.
2. Press the **Windows logo key + R**. Type *explorer* and press **Enter**.
3. In the **Windows File Explorer** window, right-click the card device (usually labelled "SDHC" or "Removable Disk") and then click **Format**.
4. In the **File system** list, click **FAT32**.
5. In the **Allocation unit size** list, click **Default allocation size**.
6. Click **Start**.

7. Download one of the NOOBS packages from *http:/ /www.raspberrypi.org/downloads/*

8. Find the *.zip* file you downloaded and right-click it. Point to **Open with** and then click **Windows Explorer**.

9. Press **Ctrl + A**, to select all of the files in the *.zip* archive.

10. Press **Ctrl + C**, to copy the selected files into memory.

11. In the **Windows File Explorer** window, right-click the card device.

12. Click **Paste** to copy the files to the SD card.

13. In the **Windows File Explorer** window, right-click the card device.

14. Click **Eject**.

On Mac OS X:

1. Insert the SD card into a suitable card socket or USB card reader.

2. On the dock, click **Finder**.

3. On the sidebar, click **Applications**.

4. Click **Utilities**, and then double-click **Disk Utility**.

5. In the left panel, click the SD card (usually labelled "NO NAME" if the card was not formatted with a volume name).

6. On the **Erase** tab, from the **Volume Format** list, click **MS-DOS File System**.

7. Click **Erase**.

8. Download one of the NOOBS packages from *http:/ /www.raspberrypi.org/downloads/*

9. In **Finder**, locate the .zip file you downloaded.

10. Double-click the NOOBS zip file and it will unzip to a new folder. For example, a folder named *NOOBS_lite_v1_3_9.*[1]

11. Double-click the folder to open it.

12. Press **Cmd + A** to select all of the files.

13. Press **Cmd + C** to copy the files into memory.

14. In the left panel, click the SD card (usually labelled "NO NAME" if the card was not formatted with a volume name).

15. Press **Cmd + V** to copy the files to the SD card.

16. In the left panel, click the **Eject** icon next to the name of the SD card.

Installing Raspbian

To install Raspbian, you will need to connect a keyboard, mouse, and display to your Pi.

First, ensure the Pi is completely off and unplugged, and then insert the SD card into the Pi's card socket. Reconnect the power to your Pi. The Pi will start and will load the NOOBS tool. When everything is ready, you should see a window similar to Figure 1.

Figure 1. NOOBS on a Raspberry Pi

The window shows a list of the operating systems that you can install.

---

1. If you have archiving software installed on your Mac, the NOOBS file might open with this instead..

To install Raspbian:

1. In the list, click the box next to **Raspbian**.
2. On the toolbar, click **Install**.

When the installation is complete, the Raspberry Pi restarts and loads the raspi-config tool. This helps you to change certain important settings. For more information, see section 2.4 Raspi-config on page 23.

 If you put the SD card back into a Windows PC then the card will appear to have shrunk in capacity. If you want to wipe the card, you can use the command-line tool *diskpart* to destroy the partitions and create a new "primary" partition using all of the available space.

2.3 Installation of Raspbian using a Disk Image

A *disk image* is a special type of file for making a copy of storage devices, such as floppy disks, CDs, hard drives, and memory cards. It not only contains all of the files from the device, it also stores all of the information necessary to recreate the same file structure and physical layout on another device.

Many operating systems that have already been made to work on the Raspberry Pi are available for download as disk images. To write the image to an SD card, you can use a Windows PC, Mac or Linux computer.[1]

Download the Raspbian disk image from *http://www.raspberrypi.org/downloads/* – it is a .zip archive that you need to unzip before it can be used.

To unzip the file on Windows (8/7/Vista/XP):

1. Find the *.zip* file you downloaded and right-click it. Point to **Open with** and then click **Windows Explorer**.

---

1. Only instructions for Windows and Mac OS X are covered in this guide.

2. Click the *.img* file, and then press **Ctrl + C**.
3. In the left panel, click **Desktop**.
4. Press **Ctrl + V** to copy the *.img* file to your Desktop.

To unzip the file on Mac OS X:

1. On the dock, click **Finder**.
2. Find the *.zip* file you downloaded.
3. Double-click the *.zip* file to unzip it to a new folder.

Users of Windows will need to download and install Win32DiskImager from *http://sourceforge.net/projects/win32diskimager/* before continuing. Users of Mac OS X should install ApplePi-Baker from *http://www.tweaking4all.com/hardware/raspberry-pi/macosx-apple-pi-baker/*

To write the Raspbian disk image to an SD card on Windows (8/7/Vista/XP):

1. Insert the SD card into a suitable card socket or USB card reader.
2. If you are running Windows XP: on the **Start** menu, under a group named **Image Writer**, click **Win32DiskImager**.
3. If you are running a later version of Windows: on the **Start** menu, under a group named **Image Writer**, right-click **Win32DiskImager**. Then click **Run as administrator**. You may be asked to confirm this by a window titled "User Access Control". Click **Yes**.
4. In Win32DiskImager, under **Image File**, click the folder icon. In the left-hand side of the Window titled "Select a disk image", click **Desktop**, and then double-click the *.img* file that you unzipped.
5. Under **Device**, ensure that the drive letter shown matches the one that is displayed in Windows Explorer next to your SD card.
6. Click **Write**.

7.   When the process is complete, click **Exit**.

8.   Press the **Windows logo key + R**. Type *explorer* and press **Enter**.

9.   In the Windows File Explorer window, right-click the card device (usually labelled "SDHC" or "Removable Disk") and then click **Eject**.

On Mac OS X:

1.   Insert the SD card into a suitable card socket or USB card reader.

2.   On the dock, click **Finder**.

3.   On the sidebar, click **Applications**.

4.   In the right panel, double-click **ApplePi-Baker**.

5.   If multiple SD cards are listed under **Pi-Crust: Possible SD-Cards**, click the one you want to write to.

6.   Under **Pi-Ingredients: IMG Recipe**, click **IMG to SD-Card**.

7.   Locate the *.img* file that you unzipped, then click **Open**.

8.   Enter the administrator password for your Mac.

9.   When the process is complete, click the **Close** button. Then in **Finder**, click the **Eject** button next to the SD card.

Ensure the Pi is completely off, and then insert the SD card into the Pi's memory card socket. Reconnect the power to your Pi.

2.4 Raspi-config

When Raspbian starts for the first time, it runs a tool called raspi-config. You can use this to change several configuration options that affect how Raspbian operates. Raspi-config is a command-line application and is controlled using the keyboard:

- Use the **Up** and **Down Arrow** keys to highlight menu items.
- Press **Enter** to activate the highlighted item.
- Press the **Tab** key to move the highlight down to the two options at the bottom of the window – **<Select>** and **<Finish>** – and then use the **Left** and **Right Arrow** keys to choose between those two options.
- To move back to the main menu, press the **Tab** key again.

When you have finished editing the settings, highlight the option **<Finish>** and press **Enter**.

 When Raspbian's graphical desktop is running, you can access the raspi-config tool at any time by double-clicking LXTerminal on your desktop. Then enter the following command and press Enter: sudo raspi-config

Exploring the Settings in Raspi-config

The table below summarizes the options available from the main menu in raspi-config:

Menu Option	Description
Expand Filesystem	Make the full capacity of the SD card available to the operating system – if is not already available.
Change User Password	Change the password for the default user (*pi*).
Enable Boot to Desktop/Scratch	Raspbian can automatically load different applications when it starts. This setting changes that.
Internationalisation Options	Configure language, keyboard and culture settings (such as date format and time zone).
Enable Camera	If you have a Raspberry Pi Camera module, you need to enable it using this menu option.

Menu Option	Description
Add to Rastrack	Rastrack (rastrack.co.uk) shows the location of Raspberry Pi devices around the world. Use this option to add your Pi to the map.
Overclock	Overclocking your Pi makes it run faster than the manufacturer designed it to. However, this can also cause the system to overheat or become less stable.
Advanced Options	See below.
About 'raspi-config'	Display information about the raspi-config tool.

Selecting **Advanced Options** from the menu takes you to another menu:

Menu Option	Description
Overscan	The display in many older televisions is slightly larger than the visible area. If your Pi's display runs off the edge of the screen, you can enable black borders (overscan) to ensure that you can see all of the picture.
Hostname	Change the name given to the Pi when it is connected to a local network. This can be useful when searching for the device, or when you have several Raspberry Pi devices.
Memory Split	The Pi's memory is shared between the CPU and GPU. You can change how much memory is allocated to the GPU using this setting.
SSH	Enable or disable SSH access.
SPI	When connecting certain SPI devices, it can be useful to load the SPI kernel module when the Pi starts. Use this setting to change whether the module is loaded automatically.
Audio	Used to send the audio signal to the audio output connector, even when using an HDMI cable for video.

Menu Option	Description
Update	Connects to the Internet and updates the raspi-config tool to the latest version.

For some users, the default settings are ok. However, there are three settings in particular that many users might want to change at this stage:

Changing the Default Password

When Raspbian is installed, it creates a new user called *pi*. The default password for this user is *raspberry*.

To change this:

1. Press the **Down Arrow** key to highlight **Change User Password**, and then press **Enter**.
2. Press **Enter** again to select **<OK>**.
3. Type a new password and press **Enter**.
4. To confirm the password, type it again and press **Enter**.
5. Press **Enter** to select **<OK>**.

If you connect your Pi to the Internet and are unsure whether your network router allows incoming connections then it is a good idea to change this password so that other people cannot login to your device.

Expanding the File System

If you installed Raspbian to the SD card using a disk image, it is possible that the OS cannot use the full capacity of your SD card.

To fix this:

1. Use the **Up** and **Down Arrow** keys to highlight **Expand Filesystem** and then press Enter.
2. When the process is complete, press **Enter** to select **<OK>**.

3. Press the **Tab** key and then the **Right Arrow** key to highlight **<Finish>**. Press **Enter**, and when you are prompted to reboot the Pi, select **<Yes>**.

Changing the Default Boot Sequence

The default setting is for Raspbian to finish loading and place you at the command line.

From the raspi-config tool, you can instruct Raspbian to load the graphical environment every time the Raspberry Pi starts up. To do this:

1. Use the **Up** and **Down Arrow** keys to highlight **Enable Boot to Desktop/Scratch**, and then press **Enter**.

2. Press the **Down Arrow** key to highlight **Desktop Log in as user 'pi' at the graphical desktop**, and then press **Enter**.

2.5 Raspbian's Desktop Environment

If you have not changed the setting in raspi-config, the Raspberry Pi will boot into Raspbian's command line.

To start the desktop environment:

1. Type *pi* as the username, then press **Enter**.
2. Type your password, then press **Enter**.[1]
3. Type the following command and press **Enter**:

    ```
    startx
    ```

After a short period of loading, you will see a screen similar to Figure 2.

---

1. If you have not changed the default password, it is raspberry.

Figure 2. Raspbian's desktop environment

Raspbian's desktop is a customized version of LXDE, which stands for lightweight X11 desktop environment. It is similar to Microsoft Windows and many of the ways that you use it are the same.

The screen is divided into two distinct areas: the desktop, and the LXDE panel.

Figure 3. Elements of the Raspbian desktop environment

1	Desktop area. Here you can find files and links (shortcuts) to applications. Double-click the icons to open the file or application that it links to.
2	LXDE panel. Contains the main menu, shortcuts to commonly-used applications, the desktop pager, and the system tray.
3	Menu. The LXDE main menu provides access to many of the system settings, tools, and any applications that you have installed.
4	Desktop Pager. For more information, see Switching the Desktop on page 30.
5	Taskbar. Open applications are shown as an icon and description in this area. If you minimize an application window, you can click the icon in the LXDE panel to restore the window to full view.
6	System Tray. This is usually used by system processes and applications that run in the background, so that the user has some way of interacting with them. By default, the system tray contains the CPU monitor (which shows how busy is the CPU is), the current time, and the application launch bar (another place you can store icons to open commonly-used applications). You can usually double-click the icons in this area to open their window, or right-click the icon to access the application's menu.

Opening and Closing Applications

On the desktop, and in the menu that you access from the LXDE panel, you can see that many applications are already installed on your system.

There are several ways of running applications in Raspbian, but the three most common are: clicking icons on the desktop, using the menu, and opening an application from the command line.

For example, to open the web browser Midori:

- On the desktop, double-click **Midori**.
- On the **LXDE panel**, click the **Menu** button. Point to **Internet**, and then click **Midori**.
- From a command-line terminal running in the desktop environment, type *midori* and then press **Enter**.

If you run applications from the command line, you will return to the prompt when they are finished. With applications that open a window in the graphical environment, you can close them in three ways:

- Press **Alt + F4** on the keyboard.
- Click the **Close** button in the top-right of the window. It looks like an x.
- Click the icon in the top-left of the window, and then click **Close**.

Switching the Desktop

On most Linux desktop environments, you can have two (or more) *workspaces*. A workspace is collection of the windows and files that are currently open. Switching to another workspace hides all of the windows that are currently visible, and displays all of the windows from the other workspace. In Raspbian, workspaces are also called "desktops".

You can switch between these using the two desktop buttons that make up the Desktop Pager.

For example:

1. On the desktop, double-click **Midori**.
2. Drag the window to the top-right corner of the display.
3. On the desktop, double-click **LXTerminal**.
4. On the **LXDE panel**, point to the light gray square. After a few moments, the text "Desktop 2" will appear. Click the button.
5. On the desktop, double-click **Pi Store**.
6. Click the "Desktop 1" button (to the left of the "Desktop 2" button) to switch back to the first desktop.
7. Click the "Desktop 2" button to switch to the second desktop again.

To move a window to another desktop: click the icon in the top-left of a window, point to **Send to desktop**, and then click the name of the desktop.

To increase the number of desktops that you can use:

1. On the **LXDE panel**, right-click the **Desktop Pager**.
2. Click **"Desktop Pager" Settings**.
3. On the **Desktops** tab, type a number into the **Number of desktops** box, or use the up and down arrow buttons to increase and decrease the number of desktops.
4. Click **Close**.

Using the File Manager

You can use the File Manager to copy, rename, delete, and change the properties of files that are stored on the SD card or any USB storage devices that you have attached.

To open the file manager:

- On the **LXDE panel**, click the **File Manager** button – the second button from the left; or
- On the **LXDE panel**, click the **Menu** button, point to **Accessories**, and then click **File Manager**.

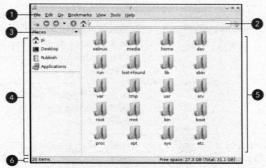

Figure 4. The File Manager

1	Application menu.
2	Toolbar – navigation buttons and address bar.
3	Tab bar.
4	Left panel – for selecting places, devices, and file trees.
5	Right panel – for selecting files and folders.
6	Status bar.

Like a web browser, the File Manager window can open multiple folders at the same time by using tabs. To open a new tab:

- On the toolbar, click the first button from the left.

This will create a new tab in the same folder, and will show the tab bar. You can use the tab bar to switch between the tabs that are currently open.

If you have used the Windows Explorer in Microsoft Windows or the Finder in Mac OS X, you already know how to complete many of the most common tasks. However, the table below is a brief summary of how to use the Raspbian File Manager.

To	Do This
Switch between the "Places" view and the full directory tree	In the left panel, click **Places** and then click **Directory Tree**.
Change the way icons files and folders are displayed in the right panel	On the application menu, click **View**, and then click on one of the four view options – **Icon View**, **Thumbnail View**, **Compact View** or **Detailed List View**.
Open a folder	In the left panel, click the name of a folder. In the right panel, double-click folder's icon.
Open a folder using a file path	In the address bar, type the full file path and then press **Enter**.

To	Do This
Open the current user's home directory	On the application menu, click **Go**, and then click **Home Folder**; or on the toolbar, click the **Home** button.
Open the desktop folder	On the application menu, click **Go**, and then click **Desktop**.
Open the current folder in the command line	On the application menu, click **Tools**, and then click **Open Current Folder in Terminal**.
Select a file or folder	In the right panel, click an icon.
Select multiple files or folders	In the right panel, hold **Ctrl** and click the icons of the files and folders that you want to select.
Delete a file or folder	Right-click an icon and then click **Delete**.
Rename a file or folder	Right-click an icon and then click **Rename**.
View the properties of a file or folder	Right-click an icon and then click **Properties**.
Open a file in its default application	Double-click a file's icon.
Move a file or folder to a new location	Right-click an icon and then click **Cut**. Browse to the folder that you want to move the item to, right-click in the right panel, and then click **Paste**.
Copy a file	Right-click an icon and then click **Copy**. Browse to the folder where you want a copy to be created, right-click in the right panel, and then click **Paste**.
Create a new folder	Right-click in the right panel, point to **Create New...**, and then click **Folder**.

If you are used to Microsoft Windows, the Linux file system might seem a little strange at first. It contains a large number of folders, and many of these have specific purposes. The key ones are:

Folder	Description
home	Contains a folder for each user account on the system. For example, /home/pi is the home folder for the default user on Raspbian installations. This is where you should store all of your personal files.
etc	Contains most of the configuration files for the operating system.
dev	Linux creates file system entries in this folder for hardware devices that are attached to the system. Media devices (for example, DVD drives) are placed in /mnt or /media instead.
media	When storage devices such as CDs, memory cards, and USB flash drives, are inserted, the system creates a "mount point" for them in this folder. Mount points provide access to the file system on the device.
root	This is the home folder for the system administrator account.
tmp	Temporary files used by the system. The contents of this folder are deleted when the Pi starts.
boot	Contains files needed to start Raspbian.
var	Stores variable and temporary files that are created by the user or applications running as the user.
bin	Contains applications that are used by all user accounts, the system, and the system administrator.
usr	Contains applications and documentation for all user applications.
sbin	Contains applications that are only available to the system and the system administrator.

Folder	Description
lib	Contains libraries – collections of code and information – that must be shared among all applications.
mnt	Similar to /media, this folder contains mount points for non-removable media.

In general, try to keep all of your data in the /home/pi folder. When installing new software and hardware devices, they will use the special folders if they need to.

Accessing the Command Line

While most tasks can be completed using the desktop environment, there are still some things that you will have to do from the command line.

To access the command line from the graphical environment:

- On the desktop, double-click **LXTerminal**.
- On the **LXDE panel**, click the **Menu** button, point to **Accessories**, and then click **LXTerminal**.

In the command line, files and folders have file names and file paths. The file path includes the names of the folders and subfolders that the file is stored in. For example, a file ocr_pi.png in the pi user's home folder has the full file path: /home/pi/ocr_pi.png

File paths that begin with a forward slash start from the top-level folder. So the example above tells the system: start at the top-level and move into the home folder, then move into the pi subfolder, and then find the file ocr_pi.png.

If you are already in the home folder, you can refer to the same file as: pi/ocr_pi.png

And if you are in a subfolder of /home/pi, you can refer to the file using two dots that symbolize moving to the parent directory: ../ocr_pi.png

To run commands: type the command using the keyboard and then press **Enter**. There are a large number of commands available (too many to list here), but these are some of the most common:

To	Do This
List the contents of the current folder	Type *ls* and then press **Enter**.
List the contents of a specific folder	Type *ls* followed by a space and then the name of the folder. Then press **Enter**.
Move into a subfolder	Type *cd* followed by a space and then the name of the folder, and then press **Enter**.
Move to a parent folder	Type *cd ..* and then press **Enter**.
Create a subfolder	Type *mkdir* followed by a space and then the name of the folder, and then press **Enter**.
Delete a folder	Type *rmdir* followed by a space and then the name of the folder, and then press **Enter**.
Delete a file	Type *rm* followed by a space and then the name of the file, and then press **Enter**.
Copy a file or folder	Type *cp* followed by a space and then the name (or full file path) of the file to be copied. Type another space and then the name (or full file path) to call the copy. Press **Enter**.
Rename or move a file or folder	Type *mv* followed by a space and then the name (or full file path) of the file to be copied. Type another space and then the name (or full file path) to call the copy. Press **Enter**.
Clear the command line window	Type *clear* and then press **Enter**.

To close the command line, do one of the following:

- Press **Alt + F4** on the keyboard.
- Click the **Close** button in the top-right of the window.
- Click the icon in the top-left of the window, and then click **Close**.
- On the application menu, click **File** and then click **Quit**.
- Type the following command and then press **Enter**:

  ```
  exit
  ```

In the *Accessories* group of the LXDE panel menu, there is another terminal. This one is called "Root Terminal". When you open the command line using this application, you are automatically granted system administrator privileges.

 If you only want to run a single command, you can do this from the Raspbian menu. On the LXDE panel, click the Menu button and then click Run. Type your command and then press Enter.

Understanding Linux Users and Superusers

If you have used more recent versions of Microsoft Windows then you may be used to running certain applications as an administrator. This concept is also in Linux.

Superusers (often called "root") have full access to the system. Any applications you run as a superuser will also have full access to the system. To protect the system from accidental or malicious damage, you rarely login to Raspbian as a superuser.

Normal users have less access to the core files needed by the OS, and this means that any applications that they run also have less access to the system. In Raspbian, *pi* is the user that logs into the desktop environment, and it is a normal user.

When you do need to change part of the system, or accomplish a task that only superuser can do, you can:

- On the **LXDE panel**, click the **Menu** button, point to **Accessories**, and then click **Root Terminal**; or

- From the normal command line, type *sudo* followed by a space before the command that requires superuser access privileges.

2.6 Common Tasks

In this section, you can find instructions for some of most common tasks that people perform after installing Raspbian. These instructions continue into the next section, 2.7 Network Connections and Remote Access on page 41.

Restarting and Shutting Down the Raspberry Pi

To restart the Pi:

1. On the **LXDE panel**, click the **Menu** button and then click **Run**.
2. Type the following command and then press **Enter**:

   sudo shutdown -r now

To shut down the Pi from the desktop:

1. On the desktop, double-click **Shutdown**.
2. Click **Yes**.

To shut down the Pi from the command line:

- Type the following command and then press **Enter**:

   sudo shutdown -h now

Configuring the TV Service

If you connect your Pi to a television using an HDMI cable, Raspbian automatically selects a screen size that it decides will be the best for your setup. However, this is not always the highest resolution.

The configuration setting that controls how Raspbian selects the screen size is in the file */boot/config.txt* and you can adjust this setting with a text editor:

1. On the **LXDE panel**, click the **Menu** button, point to **Accessories**, and then click **Root Terminal**.

2. Type the following command and then press **Enter**:
```
tvservice —d edid
```

3. Type the following command and then press **Enter**:
```
edidparser edid
```

4. Find the video mode that you want to use, and make note of the mode number and whether it says "DMT mode" or "CEA mode".

5. Type the following command and press **Enter**:
```
nano /boot/config.txt
```

6. Press the **Down Arrow** key until you find the lines that begin with
#hdmi_group=
#hdmi_mode=

7. Remove the # from the start of both of those lines.

8. If the video mode is DMT, change the hdmi_group to 2:
```
hdmi_group=2
```

9. If the video mode is CEA, change the hdmi_group to 1:
```
hdmi_group=1
```

10. Type the mode number after *hdmi_mode=*, for example:
```
hdmi_mode=16
```

11. Press **Ctrl + X**.

12. Press **Y**, and then press **Enter**.

13. Restart the Raspberry Pi.

Installing a Graphical Package Manager

When installing new applications, there are a few steps that need to be taken:

1. Find out whether the application is compatible with the OS.

2. Install any other pieces of software that this new application requires.

3. Download the application from the Internet.

4. Install the application to the correct folders.

In Linux, the *package manager* handles all of this for you. You can also use it to uninstall applications that you do not want anymore. Package managers connect to *repositories* – online libraries of software. And since Linux is open-source, most of the software in these repositories is also open-source (and free).

The package manager that is built-in to Raspbian is accessed from the command line. However, you can also install one that runs in the graphical desktop environment.

One such tool is Synaptic. To install it, use the command-line package manager:

1. On the **LXDE panel**, click the **Menu** button, point to **Accessories**, and then click **Root Terminal**.

2. Type the following command and then press **Enter**:
   ```
   apt-get install synaptic
   ```

3. When the process is complete, type the following command and then press **Enter**:
   ```
   exit
   ```

To run the Synaptic package manager:

- On the **LXDE panel**, click the **Menu** button, point to **Preferences**, and then click **Synaptic Package Manager**.

2.7 Network Connections and Remote Access

Setting up Wi-Fi

Before buying a USB Wi-Fi adapter for use with the Raspberry Pi, check that the adaptor is known to be working by looking at the list at *http://elinux.org/RPi_USB_Wi-Fi_Adapters*

To install a USB Wi-Fi adapter on your Pi and connect to your network:

1. Insert the USB device into an available USB socket on the Pi, or on a USB hub.
2. On the desktop, double-click **WiFi Config**.
3. In the **Adapter** list, click **wlan0**. If you have no adapters in the list, your USB device is not compatible with the Raspberry Pi.
4. Click **Scan** to open the "Scan results" window.
5. Click **Scan**.
6. Double-click the name of your Wi-Fi network.
7. Check that the **Authentication** and **Encryption** settings match how your other computers connect to your router.
8. Type your network password into the **PSK** box.
9. Click **Add**, and then click **Close**.

Finding the IP Address

To connect to the Pi from another computer on your network, you will need to know its *IP address*. To find this:

1. On the desktop, double-click **LXTerminal**.
2. Type the following command and then press **Enter**:
    ```
    ifconfig
    ```

The address you need is called "inet addr" and consists of four numbers separated by dots. If you are connected to your network using an Ethernet cable, you can find the address in the

42

section labelled "eth0". If you are connected to your network using a wireless adaptor, you can find the address in the section labelled "wlan0".

Using a Static IP Address

When the Pi restarts, or reconnects to the network, your network router will give the Pi an IP address. However, this can change every time.

You can configure the Pi so that it always uses the same IP address. You need a few pieces of information and you will need to edit a configuration file in a text editor.

To do this:

1. On the desktop, double-click **LXTerminal**.
2. Type the following command and then press **Enter**:
   `ifconfig`
3. If you are using an Ethernet cable, in the section labelled "eth0", make a note of the values "inet addr", "Bcast" and "Mask".
4. If you are using Wi-Fi, in the section labelled "wlan0", make a note of the values "inet addr", "Bcast" and "Mask".
5. Type the following command then press **Enter**:
   `netstat -nr`
6. Make a note of the values in "Gateway" and "Destination". If you can see two entries in the table, ignore the values 0.0.0.0 and use the value from the other line.
7. Type the following command and then press **Enter**:
   `sudo nano /etc/network/interfaces`
8. If you are using Wi-Fi, skip to step 12.
9. If you are using an Ethernet cable: change the line that reads *iface eth0 inet dhcp* to
   `iface eth0 inet static`

10. Add the following lines, starting on a new line after the word "static". Replace the values in angled brackets with the values from the previous steps:

```
address <inet addr>
netmask <mask>
network <destination>
broadcast <bcast>
gateway <gateway>
```

11. Skip to step 14.

12. If you are using Wi-Fi: change the line that reads *iface wlan0 inet dhcp* to

```
iface wlan0 inet static
```

13. Add the following lines, starting on a new line after the word "static".

```
address <inet addr>
netmask <mask>
gateway <gateway>
```

14. Press **Ctrl + X**.

15. Press **Y**, and then press **Enter**.

16. Restart the Raspberry Pi.

Transferring Files to and from the Raspberry Pi

You can use secure copy (SCP) to transfer files from your computer to a Pi, or to copy files from the Pi to another computer. Raspbian already supports this, and so you only need to install a client on your main computer.

On Windows, WinSCP is very popular application for transferring files. You can download it for free at *http://winscp.net*

On Mac OS X, you can use an application called Cyberduck. This is a free download from *http://cyberduck.io/* or you can download it from the Mac App Store.

The details you need to make a connection to the Pi are largely the same regardless of which SCP client you use:

Server/Hostname: the IP address of your Pi
Username: *pi*
Password: this is *raspberry* if you have not yet changed it.
Protocol: *SCP*

To download files from the Pi, drag the icons from the SCP client's window to a Windows Explorer or Finder window. To upload files to the Pi, drag files from a Windows Explorer or Finder window and drop them onto the SCP client's window.

Connecting to the Pi with SSH

Secure shell (SSH) is a way of talking to your Pi over an encrypted transmission. It is typically used when you want to access the Raspberry Pi's command line from another computer. As long as your Pi has a network connection, you can connect to it remotely and type commands.

On Windows, you will need an application that understands the SSH protocol. There are many of these available, but PuTTY is one of the more popular ones. Download it from *http:// www.chiark.greenend.org.uk/~sgtatham/putty/*

You do not need an additional SSH client to connect to the Pi on Mac OS X.

To connect to your Pi over SSH on Windows (8/7/Vista/XP):

1. Locate the file *putty.exe* that you downloaded, and then double-click it.
2. In the **Host Name (or IP address)** box, type the IP address of your Pi.
3. Click **Open**.
4. At the login prompt, type *pi*.
5. At the password prompt, type your password and press **Enter**. This is *raspberry* if you have not changed it.

To connect to your Pi over SSH on Mac OS X:

1. On the dock, click **Finder**.

2. On the sidebar, click **Applications**.

3. Click **Utilities**, and then double-click **Terminal**.

4. Type the following command, replacing <IP> with the IP address of your Raspberry Pi:

   ```
   ssh pi@<IP>
   ```

5. Press **Enter**.

6. At the password prompt, type your password and press **Enter**. The default password is *raspberry* if you have not changed it.

Connecting to the Pi with Remote Desktop

Microsoft Windows comes with an application called "Remote Desktop". You can use this to connect to your Raspberry Pi and use the desktop environment from a Windows computer. Mac OS X users need to download "Microsoft Remote Desktop" from the Mac App Store.

You also need to install a small software application on the Pi before you can connect using Remote Desktop.

To install the software from the command line:

1. On the **LXDE panel**, click the **Menu** button, point to **Accessories**, and then click **Root Terminal**.

2. Type the following command and then press **Enter**:

   ```
   apt-get install xrdp
   ```

To start a Remote Desktop connection from Windows (8/7/Vista/XP):

1. Press the **Windows logo key + R**. Then type *mstsc* and press **Enter**.

2. In the **Computer** box, type the IP address of your Raspberry Pi, and then press **Enter**.

3. In the "Login to xrdp" window, in the **username** box, type *pi*.

4. In the **password** box, type your password.[1]

5. Click **OK**.

Browsing the Web

If you are using the latest version of Raspbian, the web browser is called Epiphany and it is installed when you install the OS. In other versions, the web browser is Midori.

To open a web browser:

- On the **LXDE panel**, click the **Menu** button, point to **Internet**, and then click **Midori** or **Epiphany Web Browser**.

2.8 Other Operating Systems

Raspbian Linux is not the only OS that you can run on a Raspberry Pi. Many varieties of Linux have been repackaged so that you can use them, and there are several non-Linux operating systems that also work.

Arch Linux

Arch Linux is an extremely lightweight version of Linux that is ideal for servers or devices with unusual purposes – where many of the packages that are normally installed to create a usable desktop environment are not needed.

You can download a disk image of Arch Linux from *http://www.raspberrypi.org/downloads/*, or it can be installed using NOOBS.

RISC OS

RISC OS is available at *http://www.raspberrypi.org/downloads/* or you can install it using NOOBS. It has been in use since 1987, and was designed for Archimedes line of computers made by

---

1. If you have not changed the default password, it is raspberry.

Acorn Computers Ltd. These machines used the first ARM
processors.

RetroPie

RetroPie is a customized version of Raspbian that repackages the
OS with a variety of emulators for classic computers and video
games consoles. Find out more at *http://
blog.petrockblock.com/retropie/*

Plan 9

Plan 9 is developed by Bell Labs, and has its origins in an OS that
was released in the 1980s. It is very light on system resources,
and quite different from the operating systems that people are
used to today. You can download a disk image of Plan 9 from
http://plan9.bell-labs.com/wiki/plan9/download/

AEROS

AROS is designed to be a successor to the operating system
AmigaOS, which is itself based on the operating system used by
the Commodore Amiga range of 16-bit computers. The
Raspberry Pi version is called AEROS. The current version is only
available to registered users, but older versions are available at
http://www.aeros-os.org/styled-11/index.html

Android

Android is an operating system for tablets and smartphones, but
it is not yet fully usable on the Raspberry Pi. The webpage for this
project is *http://androidpi.wikia.com/wiki/Android_Pi_Wiki*

No Operating System

If you are an experienced software developer and you do not
need to run any other applications, then you might be able to
run your code without installing an operating system. This is
called "bare-metal" programming and there are various tutorials
and samples available on the web to help you.

3 – Building a Media Center with XBMC

3.1 XBMC

XBMC is a media player that is developed by the XBMC Foundation. As a multi-platform, highly-customizable, and open-source software package, it is extremely popular and is used on a wide variety of devices.

XBMC can play audio and video files in many formats, including: 3GP, AAC, APE, AVI, CDDA, FLV, MIDI, MKV, MP3, MP4, M4A, MPEG, OGG, WAV, WMA, WMV, and many more.[1] It can even play DVDs from ISO disc images.

Many people have a Raspberry Pi specifically for the purpose of running XBMC. The Pi's compact size, low cost, support for USB devices and networking, and built-in HDMI output make it an excellent choice for a media player that sits next to the TV and does not take up a lot of space.

 The current version of XBMC for the Raspberry Pi is 13.2 "Gotham". When the XBMC Foundation release version 14 of the software, they will rename XBMC to "Kodi".

In this chapter, you can see how to install XBMC on your Pi. You will also learn the basics of how to work with the user interface, and how to add media files to the system.

To complete this tutorial, you need:

- A Raspberry Pi (any model) connected to your local network and with access to the Internet.
- A keyboard and mouse.
- A USB storage device, such as a memory stick or hard drive.

---

1. For the complete list of container formats and codecs that XBMC supports, see http://wiki.xbmc.org/index.php?title=Features_and_supported_formats

3.2 Installation

If you have a blank SD card that you will be using for your media center then you can install the operating system and XBMC together. RaspBMC and OpenELEC are two Linux distributions that already contain XBMC, and you can install these from NOOBS. For more information about installing operating systems using NOOBS, see section 2.2 Installation of Raspbian with NOOBS on page 17.

To start NOOBS when an existing OS is already on the SD card: turn off the Pi, and then hold the Shift key as you turn the Pi back on and until you see the NOOBS window.

 NOOBS can either remove your existing OS, or add RaspBMC or OpenELEC as an additional option. To remove an OS, uncheck the box next to it before you click Install. If you leave your existing OS on the SD card, you will be asked to choose which one you want to load when the Raspberry Pi starts up.

If you cannot use NOOBS, you can also download disk images of the distributions from *http://www.raspberrypi.org/ downloads/* and then refer to section 2.3 Installation of Raspbian using a Disk Image on page 21 for more information about how to write the file to an SD card.

If Raspbian is already installed on your card and you want to add XBMC to it, installing XBMC usually only takes a few minutes. To begin, you need to add Michael Gorven's repository to the list of application sources in Linux:

1. On the **LXDE panel**, click the **Menu** button, point to **Accessories**, and then click **Root Terminal**.

2. Type the following command and then press **Enter**:

    ```
    nano /etc/apt/sources.list.d/mene.list
    ```

3. Type the following text as the first line in the file:

    ```
    deb http://archive.mene.za.net/raspbian wheezy
    contrib
    ```

4. Press **Ctrl + O**, and then press **Enter**.

5. Press **Ctrl + X**.

6. Type the following command on one line, and then press **Enter**:

    ```
    apt-key adv --keyserver keyserver.ubuntu.com --recv-key 5243CDED
    ```

7. Type the following command and then press **Enter**:

    ```
    apt-get update
    ```

To install XBMC from the command line:

* Type the following command and then press **Enter**:

    ```
    apt-get install xbmc
    ```

XBMC does not work correctly if 64 MB or less memory is allocated to the GPU. As this is the default setting for Raspbian installations, you need to change it in raspi-config:

* In the **Root Terminal**, type the following command and then press **Enter**:

    ```
    raspi-config
    ```

* or, on the **LXDE panel**, click the **Menu** button, and click **Run**. Type the following command and then press **Enter**:

    ```
    sudo raspi-config
    ```

When the Raspberry Pi Software Configuration Tool appears:

1. Press the **Down Arrow** key repeatedly until **Advanced Options** is highlighted, and then press **Enter**.

2. Press the **Down Arrow** key twice to select **A3 Memory Split**. Press **Enter**.

3. Change the value to *128* and then press **Enter**.

4. Press the **Right Arrow** key twice to select **<Finish>**. Then press **Enter**.

5. Press **Enter** to select **<Yes>** and reboot the Pi.

Running XBMC

XBMC is a standalone application and does not run the desktop environment. To run it, you must drop back to the command line: press **Ctrl + Alt + F1**. To return to the desktop environment, press **Alt + F7**.

To start XBMC:

- Type the following command and then press **Enter**:

  `xbmc-standalone`

However, starting XBMC this way reduces the amount of memory and system resources available to it. If you want to use your Raspberry Pi as a dedicated media player and automatically run XBMC when it starts up:

1. On a command line or **LXTerminal**, enter the following command and press **Enter**:

   `sudo nano /etc/default/xbmc`

2. Change *ENABLED=0* to

   `ENABLED=1`

3. Change *USER=xbmc* to

   `USER=pi`

4. Press **Ctrl + X**, then press **Y**, and then press **Enter**.

5. Type the following command and then press **Enter**:

   `sudo raspi-config`

6. Press the **Down Arrow** key twice to highlight **Enable boot to Desktop/Scratch** and then press **Enter**.

7. Highlight **Console Text console, requiring login (default)** and then press **Enter**.

8. Press the **Right Arrow** key twice to highlight **<Finish>**, and then press **Enter**.

9. Press **Enter** to select **<Yes>**.

3.3 First Steps

Once XBMC is finished loaded, you should see a screen similar to Figure 1 below.

Figure 1. The XBMC home screen

1	Recent videos. When the **Movies** or **TV Shows** menu option is highlighted, XBMC will show the files that have most recently been added to your library. You can click one of these items to start playing.
2	Main menu.
3	Favorites. Click this button for quick access to items that you have placed in your favorites list. To add an item to your favorites, right-click it to open its context menu.
4	Exit. To close XBMC and return to the Linux command line, click the **Exit** button, and then click **Exit**.

All of XBMC's features can be accessed using its mouse-driven menu system, you generally only need to use the keyboard for typing in configuration settings.

To control the home screen menu:

- Move the mouse pointer to the far left and far right sides of the menu to scroll it.
- Point to a menu item to bring up any options that are available in that category.
- Click a menu item (or option underneath) to open it.

Most menu items open a different screen when you click them. To control these screens:

- Click with the left mouse button to activate menu items and buttons.

- Right-click an area of the screen that does not contain a menu item or button to move to the previous screen.

- Right-click a media file or folder to bring up a context menu which has additional options that affect the selected item.

- To open the sidebar, move the mouse pointer over to the tab on the left side of the screen. To close the sidebar, move the mouse pointer away to the right.

- Click the **Back** button to return to the previous screen.

- Click the **Home** button to return to the home screen.

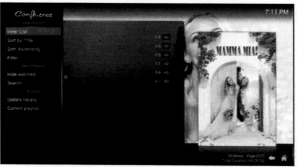

Figure 2. The Movies browser and the sidebar

XBMC divides media files into categories depending on whether they are a movie file, an episode of a TV show, a music file, a picture or photo, or a program. The different types of file are accessed using different menu items on the home screen menu.

Changing the XBMC Skin

The Raspberry Pi version of XBMC uses an interface theme (or "skin") called "Confluence". If you want to change this, you can download new skins directly from the XBMC system settings.

To download and enable a new skin:

1. On the XBMC **Home** screen, click **System**.
2. Click **Appearance**, and then click the first item in the right panel. This item has the word "Skin" on one side, and "Confluence" on the order.
3. Click **Get More...**
4. Point to each skin to load a preview and description.
5. To download a skin, click it, and then click **Install**.
6. When asked if you want to switch to this skin, click **Yes**.

To change the skin back to Confluence:

1. On the XBMC **Home** screen, click **System**.
2. Click **Appearance**, and then click the first item in the right panel.
3. Click the Confluence skin.

The basic controls for using XBMC do not change with different skins. However, the layout, colors, and the way media files are displayed and previewed can change.

3.4 Media Files and the Library

Using XBMC, you can view files from USB devices (such as memory sticks and hard drives) or over your local network.

In addition to browsing for files each time you want to play something, you can add devices and network folders to your XBMC *library*. The library is a list of all of the files that you have available, and usually contains extra information such as preview images and descriptions.

Note that even if you add a file to your library, it is still stored on the original device and will not be available if that device is unplugged or turned off.

Playing Media Files from USB Devices

Keeping your media files on USB storage devices means that you are not taking up space on the SD card used to run XBMC. And you can remove USB devices at any time – making this a convenient way of transferring files from your PC to be played on your media box.

To play a file without adding it to your library:

1. Insert the USB device into a free USB slot on the Pi or USB hub. You can do this when the Pi is on and running XBMC.
2. On the XBMC **Home** screen, point to **Videos** and then click **Files**.
3. Click the USB device that contains the file you want to play.
4. Browse to the file and then click it.

Adding Files to your Library

Your XBMC library is made up of a list of *sources*, and information about the media files that you have on your system.

A source is XBMC's term for a file path that it remembers between sessions, and that it associates with a particular type of content (for example, a movie). When XBMC updates your library, it opens each source folder and examines all of the compatible media files inside.

During this process, XBMC runs special programs called "scrapers". These add-ons find the information about the files in your library and for this to work, the file names of movies and TV shows that you want to add must follow a set pattern. If the scraper cannot identify the file from the file name, XBMC will not add the file to your library.

The instructions below are an example to get you started; for more detailed information, see *http://wiki.xbmc.org/ index.php?title=Naming_video_files*

If your USB device contains movie files and TV shows, create two subfolders on the device and use one for movies, and the other for the TV show episodes.

When naming movie files, use the pattern: *Title (Year).ext*
For example: *House On Haunted Hill (1999).mp4*

To add the movies folder on the USB device as a source, and load the files into your library:

1. Insert the USB device into a free USB slot on the Pi or USB hub. You can do this when the Pi is on and running XBMC.

2. On the XBMC **Home** screen, point to **Videos** and then click **Files**.

3. Click **Add Videos...** and then click **Browse**.

4. Click **Root filesystem**.

5. Click **media**, and then click the "name" of the USB device.

6. Click the movies folder, and then click **OK**.

7. Click **OK**.

8. From the **This directory contains** list, select **(Movies)**.

9. Under **Choose a Scraper**, click **The Movie Database** (or another scraper if you have already installed one).

10. Click **OK**.

11. If you are asked whether you want to refresh info for all items, click **Yes**.

> ▼ If **The Movie Database scraper cannot find your movie in its listings, XBMC will not add the file to your library. There are other scrapers available and you can install them in section 3.6 Add-ons on page 66.**

To add TV shows to your library, it is advisable to create a directory structure inside the TV show folder on the USB device.

Create a folder for each TV series. For example, create a folder called *The Addams Family*. Then create subfolders inside that for each season. For example, *The Addams Family/Season 1* and *The Addams Family/Season 2*.

Place the video files for each season in the correct subfolder, and name each file with the pattern: *Anything Including Spaces_sXXeYY.ext*. Replace XX with the season number, and YY with the episode number. For example: *The Addams Family_s01e01.mp4*

To add the TV shows folder on the USB device as a source, and load the files into your library:

1. Insert the USB device into a free USB slot on the Pi or USB hub. You can do this when the Pi is on and running XBMC.

2. On the XBMC **Home** screen, point to **Videos** and then click **Files**.

3. Click **Add Videos…** and then click **Browse**.

4. Click **Root filesystem**.

5. Click **media**, and then click the "name" of the USB device.

6. Click the TV shows folder, and then click **OK**.

7. Click **OK**.

8. From the **This directory contains** list, select **(TV Shows)**.

9. Under **Choose a Scraper**, click **The TVDB** (or another scraper if you have already installed one).

10. Click **OK**.

11. If you are asked whether you want to refresh info for all items, click **Yes**.

 If the scraper cannot find your file in its listings, XBMC will not add the file to your library. There are other scrapers available and you can install these using the Add-ons menu.

Playing and adding music files to your library works in the same way. On the **Home** screen, point to **Music** and then click **Files**.

Removing USB Devices

Make sure that you properly eject USB devices from the system. This process stops XBMC from reading or writing to the device while you unplug it, and ensures that all of the changes that need to be made to the file system are completed.

To safely remove a USB device:

1. On the XBMC **Home** screen, point to **Videos** and then click **Files**.

2. Right-click the device, and then click **Remove safely**.

3. Remove the USB device from the USB socket.

If the USB device contains the files for items in your library, those items will be unavailable until you plug the device back in to your Pi.

Playing Videos from Your Library

Once you have added some videos to your library, you can access them from the XBMC home screen. To play a movie, either:

• On the XBMC **Home** screen, point to **Movies**, and then click the preview of the file that you want to play; or

- On the XBMC **Home** screen, click **Movies** to load the movie browser.

If you use the movie browser, click the name of a movie to start playing, or right-click the movie and then click **Movie information** to bring up a window containing all the information that the scraper could find out about that file.

Figure 3. The movie information display

To play a TV show, either:

- On the XBMC **Home** screen, point to **TV Shows**, and then click the preview of the file that you want to play; or

- On the XBMC **Home** screen, click **TV Shows** to load the show browser.

If you use the TV show browser, click the name of a series to load the episodes or right-click it and then click **TV show information** to view the details of that series. Click an episode to start playing, or right-click the episode and then click **Episode information** to bring up a window containing all the information that the scraper could find out about that particular episode.

3.5 Network Devices and Other Computers

Connecting to SMB Shares

Server message block (SMB) is a networking protocol for sharing printers, files, and folders between devices on a local network. It is a well-established system, and support for it is built-in on most popular operating systems. Using SMB, XBMC can access folders on your Windows, Mac OS X, or Linux PCs as if they were local devices.

SMB shares must be added to XBMC as sources, and so it is usually useful to have your movies, TV shows, music, and pictures separated into different folders.

To create a new shared folder on Windows (8/7/Vista/XP):

1. Press the **Windows logo key + R**. Type *explorer* and then press **Enter**.

2. Browse to a location on your PC that either all users can access (such as an extra hard drive partition) or that belongs to the user that is currently logged in.

3. Right-click in the right panel, point to **New**, and then click **Folder**.

4. Type a name (for example, *Videos*) and then press **Enter**.

5. Right-click the folder, and then click **Properties**.

6. On the **Sharing** tab, under **Network File and Folder Sharing**, click **Share**.

7. In the **File Sharing** window, click **Share**.

8. Click **Close**.

9. In **Windows Explorer,** double-click the folder. Right-click in the right panel, point to **New** and then click **Folder**. Type a name (for example, *Movies*) and then press **Enter**.

10. Right-click in the right panel, point to **New** and then click **Folder**. Type a name (for example, *TV Shows*) and then press **Enter**.

11. Copy or move your movie files into the movies folder, and TV show episodes into the TV shows folder.

To create a new shared folder on Mac OS X (10.5 or later) using *Guest Sharing*:

1.   On the dock, click **Finder**.

2.   Browse to your home folder.

3.   On the **File** menu, click **New Folder**. Type a name (for example, *Videos*) and press **Enter**.

4.   Click this folder.

5.   On the **File** menu, click **New Folder**. Type a name (for example, *Movies*) and press **Enter**.

6.   On the **File** menu, click **New Folder**. Type a name (for example, *TV Shows*) and press **Enter**.

7.   Copy or move your movie files into the movies folder, and TV show episodes into the TV shows folder.

8.   On the **Apple** menu, click **System Preferences**.

9.   Click **Sharing**.

10. Click the box next to **File Sharing**.

11. Below the **Shared Folders** list, click the **+** button.

12. Browse to your videos folder, double-click it, and then click **Add**.

13. Next to **Everyone**, click **Read Only**, and then click **Read & Write**.

14. Click **Options**.

15. Click the box next to **Share files and folders using SMB**.

16. Click **Done**.

Now that sharing is enabled and you have folders that you want XBMC to look at, add the SMB share as an XBMC video source:

1. On the XBMC **Home** screen, click **Videos**.

2. Click **Add Videos...** and then click **Browse**.

3. Click **Add network location...**[1]

4. In the **Protocol** list, click **Windows network (SMB)**.

5. Next to **Server**, click **Browse**.

6. Click the name of your workgroup, and then click the name of the Windows PC or Mac.

7. In the **Username** box, type your Windows username (or the name of a user account that has access to the shared folder.) Do not enter a username if you are using Guest Sharing on Mac OS X 10.5 or later.

8. In the **Password** box, type the password for that user.

9. Click **OK**.

10. Click the new network location. This is *smb://*, followed by the name of your PC or Mac.

11. Browse to your movies folder and then click it.

12. Click **OK**.

13. Click **OK**.

14. From the **This directory contains** list, select **(Movies)**.

15. Under **Choose a Scraper**, click **The Movie Database** (or another scraper if you have already installed one).

16. Click **OK**.

17. If you are asked whether you want to refresh info for all items, click **Yes**.

To add the TV shows folder, repeat this process but select **(TV Shows)** from the **This directory contains** list and **The TVDB** scraper from the **Choose a Scraper** list.

---

1. The "Add network location..." option allows for more control over the username and password than the "Windows network (SMB)" option.

XBMC's scrapers will attempt to add the files from your sources to your library. This means that the files in your shared folder must follow the naming conventions described in Adding Files to your Library on page 55.

If the scraper cannot find information about the file, XBMC does not add the file to your library. However, you can still use the *Videos* file browser to access any files that were not added.

The most common cause of problems when creating SMB shares and adding them to XBMC is user permissions. If you cannot connect to your share, or cannot see the files inside it, then check the user account permissions on your PC or Mac. If necessary, you can delete a source and start over.

To delete a source:

1. On the XBMC **Home** screen, point to **Videos**, and then click **Files**.
2. Right-click a source, and then click **Remove source**.

Connecting to UPnP Devices

Universal plug and play (UPnP) is a collection of networking protocols that allows devices on a local network to find each other, to find out what type of services and files other devices offer, and to share those files.

You can setup your PC or Mac so that XBMC on the Raspberry Pi can play the media files from it. On Mac OS X and Linux machines, you will need to install and configure a UPnP media server, such as MediaTomb (*http://www.mediatomb.cc*). Microsoft Windows has a built-in UPnP server, but this is usually disabled when the operating system is installed.

To enable the UPnP server on Windows (8/7/Vista):

1. Press the **Windows logo key + R**. Type *control.exe /name Microsoft.NetworkAndSharingCenter* and then press **Enter**.

2. On Windows 8/7: click **Change advanced sharing settings**. On Windows Vista: click the arrow to the right of **Network Discovery**.

3. Click the box next to **Turn on network discovery**, and then click **Save changes** (or **Apply** on Vista).

To enable the UPnP server on Windows XP:

1. Press the **Windows logo key + R**. Type *appwiz.cpl* and then press **Enter**.

2. Click **Add/Remove Windows Components**.

3. Click **Networking Services**, then click **Details**.

4. If it is not selected, click the box next to **Internet Gateway Device Discovery and Control Client**.

5. If it is not selected, click the box next to **UPnP User Interface**.

6. Click **OK**.

7. Click **Next**.

8. Press the **Windows logo key + R**. Type *services.msc* and then press **Enter**.

9. Double-click **SSDP Discovery Service**.

10. On the **General** tab, in the **Startup type** list, click **Automatic**.

11. Click **OK**.

12. Restart your PC.

UPnP devices and their folders should be added to XBMC as sources. Although files stored on these types of devices cannot be added to the XBMC library, they can still be accessed using the videos and music file browsers.

To add a video source:

1. On the XBMC **Home** screen, click **Videos**.

2. Click **Add Videos...** and then click **Browse**.

3. Click **UPnP Devices**, and then click the name of your device.

4. Browse into a folder, if you want to add it and its subfolders only.

5. Click **OK**.

6. Click **OK**.

To add a music source:

1. On the XBMC **Home** screen, click **Music**.

2. Click **Add Music...** and then click **Browse**.

3. Click **UPnP Devices**, and then click the name of your device.

4. Browse into a folder, if you want to add it and its subfolders only.

5. Click **OK**.

6. Click **OK**.

If your UPnP device appears in the UPnP Devices list but you cannot open it to browse its content, there are a few things to check:

- If you are running a firewall on a Windows PC with UPnP enabled, you may need to create an exception for the Windows Media Player Network Sharing Service or UPnP Framework.

- On Windows, place your video and music files in the *Videos* and *Music* folders of the user that is currently logged-in. Check that the Windows user *Everyone* is able to read from those folders.

- Check that your network router allows devices on your network to talk to each other.

- Update your operating system to the latest version.

- Update XBMC to the latest version.

3.6 Add-ons

Add-ons extend the functionality of XBMC in unique ways, and there are many add-ons available. These vary from making small changes to the interface, to letting you watch live TV and stream videos over the Internet.

To download and install an add-on:

1. On the XBMC **Home** screen, point to **System**, and then click **Settings**.
2. Click **Add-ons**.
3. Click **Get Add-ons**, and then click **XBMC.org Add-ons**.
4. Click the type of add-on that you want to install. For example, "Video Add-ons" add new ways of watching videos.
5. In the list of available add-ons, click one to bring up a description.
6. Click **Install** to download and install the add-on.

Installing Movie Information Add-ons

Movie information add-ons are a type of extension for finding information about the video files in your library.

By default, the scraper that finds information about your movie files uses The Movie Database website. To install a different movie scraper, and configure a video source to use it:

1. On the XBMC **Home** screen, point to **System**, and then click **Settings**.
2. Click **Add-ons**.
3. Click **Get Add-ons**, and then click **XBMC.org Add-ons**.
4. Click **Movie information**, and then click **Universal Movie Scraper**.
5. Click **Install**.

6. On the XBMC **Home** screen, point to **Videos**, and then click **Files**.

7. Right-click your video source, and then click **Change content**.

8. Under **Choose a Scraper**, click **Universal Movie Scraper**.

9. Click **OK**.

10. If you are asked whether you want to refresh info for all items, click **Yes**.

Installing Program Add-ons

Program add-ons are powerful extensions that include programs for accessing the web and social media sites, clients for file sharing and file hosting services, backup utilities, and even torrent clients.

To open the list of program add-ons:

1. On the XBMC **Home** screen, point to **System**, and then click **Settings**.

2. Click **Add-ons**.

3. Click **Get Add-ons**, and then click **XBMC.org Add-ons**.

4. Click **Program Add-ons**.

3.7 Remote Controls

XBMC has a built-in web server that you can use to control it. This turns any device with a web browser into a remote control for XBMC.

There are also several remote control apps available for smartphones and tablets. These apps usually talk to XBMC using the web server.

To enable the web server:

1. On the XBMC **Home** screen, click **System**.

2. Click **Services**.

3. Click **Webserver**.

4. Ensure **Allow control of XBMC over HTTP** is selected.

5. In the **Port** box, type a port number. This number must be over 1024.

6. In the **Username** box, type *xbmc*.

7. In the **Password** box, type a password that you want to use.

8. Press the **Back** or **Home** buttons to leave the system settings.

To connect to XBMC, you need to know its IP address on your local network. The IP address is shown in the **Summary** and **Network** tabs of the System info screen. To find this:

- On the XBMC **Home** screen, point to **System**, and then click **System info**.

Test the remote control feature by opening a web browser on a device on your local network. In the address bar, type *http://* followed by the IP address of the Raspberry Pi, then a colon, and then the port number that is set in the XBMC settings.

For example, to access the remote control web interface over port 8080 on a Pi with the IP address 192.168.0.9, type http://192.168.0.9:8080

Login with the username *xbmc*, and the password that you set in the XBMC settings.

If you cannot connect to XBMC, first check that the Raspberry Pi has an active network connection and then verify that the connection settings you are using match those that you entered in the XBMC settings. If you still cannot connect, try a different port number.

Figure 4. The XBMC web interface

To use a smartphone or tablet app, you will need the same details that you used to access the remote control with a web browser. Apps are available for iOS, Android, and Windows Phone. However, the Official XBMC Remote app is only available for iOS and Android devices.

At the time of writing, the current version of the Official XBMC Remote has a few problems. But developers update apps extremely frequently, and the issues may be fixed by the time you read this. If you cannot get the official app working, search your device's app store and you will find many others to try.

4 – Programming with Scratch

Scratch is a visual programming language that helps teach the concepts of programming to people who have never worked with traditional programming languages. It is aimed primarily at people who want to learn to build small games. However, the combination of its simple interface and rich feature set also make it useful for presentations, simulations, and prototypes of software that will be implemented in other languages.

 The current version of Scratch for the Raspberry Pi is 1.4. Version 2.0 of Scratch is available on many platforms. However, it is not compatible with the Pi.

4.1 The User Interface

To start Scratch on Raspbian:

- On the desktop, double-click **Scratch**; or
- On the **LXDE panel**, click the **Menu** button, point to **Programming**, and then click **Scratch**.

The Scratch window is divided into several distinct areas:

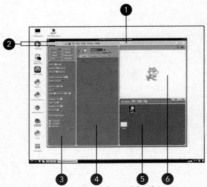

Figure 1. Scratch on Raspbian

1	Cursor Tools. These buttons are for duplicating, deleting, growing, and shrinking the sprites on the stage. Click the cursor tool, and then click a sprite to activate the function.
2	Menu.
3	Blocks Palette.
4	Scripts Area. This is where you combine blocks to control the sprite that is selected in the Sprite List.
5	Sprite List. All of the sprites in your project are shown here. Click a sprite to show the scripts that you have added for a particular sprite.
6	Stage. This is where your sprites move and interact with each other.

The key concept behind Scratch is that everything you need to move, animate, or control is a *sprite*. Each sprite is a collection of images and scripts, and is independent of all of the others. You combine the colored blocks from the Blocks Palette to set the behavior of a specific sprite.

Opening and Saving Projects

Scratch projects are saved in a special file format that uses the extension *.sb*. These files contain all of the graphics and sound files that you import into Scratch, and all of the scripts that you create.

To save a project to a new file:

1. On the **Menu** bar, click **File**, and then click **Save As...**
2. In the **New Filename** box, type a name for your project and then click **OK**.

If you have previously saved your project and you want to save it again:

- On the **Menu** bar, click the **Save this project** button (it looks like a floppy disk); or
- On the **Menu** bar, click **File**, and then click **Save**.

To close the current project and open another:

1. On the **Menu** bar, click **File**, and then click **Open...**
2. Browse to the file that you want to open, click it, and then click **OK**.

Using the Stage

All of the sprites in your project appear on the *Stage*, and this is where all of your actions and scripts take place. A sprite cannot completely leave the Stage, however, you can hide sprites that are not needed at specific parts of your project.

In Scratch, the Stage is always 480 steps wide and 360 steps tall. It never changes size, it never moves, and it never resets. For example, once a sprite moves it remains at that position on the stage until another script moves it. The position of each sprite is described with a coordinate – two numbers, one that represents the horizontal position (x) and one that represents the vertical position (y). The top-left of the Stage is -240,180, the bottom-right of the Stage is 240,-180, and this makes the center of the Stage 0,0.

In the Sprite List, there is an image for the Stage. If you click this, you can add blocks to the Stage itself. When the Stage is selected, the tabs at the top of the Scripts Area change.

You can change the background of the Stage from the Backgrounds tab. You can either use the *Paint Editor* to draw a new background (The Paint Editor is described in section 4.9 The Paint Editor on page 91), or import graphic files. Imported graphics should be 480 pixels wide and 360 pixels tall, or Scratch will position them in the center of the Stage surrounded by borders of the current background color.

You can have multiple backgrounds in a Scratch project, but only one can be visible at a time.

 You cannot move backgrounds in Scratch, so if you want areas of the background to move then you have to create them as sprites.

Building and Running Scripts

This section describes how to work with blocks from the Blocks Palette to create *scripts* – sequences of blocks. Each sprite (and the Stage itself) can contain many scripts.

To attach a block, select an item in the Sprite List and then drag blocks from the Blocks Palette to the Scripts Area. For example:

1. In the **Sprite List**, click **Stage**.

2. In the **Blocks Palette**, click **Control**.

3. Click the block **when <green flag> clicked** and, while holding the mouse button, drag the block over to the **Scripts Area**. Release the mouse button.

4. In the **Blocks Palette**, click **Looks**.

5. Drag the block **change color effect by 25** to the **Scripts Area** and below the other block. The white line shows where the block will go. Release the mouse button.

6. In the **Scripts Area**, on the block **change color effect by 25**, click **color**, and then click **brightness**.

7. On the block **change brightness effect by 25** click the white box that contains *25*. Change this to *-25*.

8. In the **Blocks Palette**, click **Control**.

9. Drag the block **wait 1 secs** to the **Scripts Area** and to the bottom of the block **change brightness effect by -25**.

10. On the block **wait 1 secs**, click the white box that contains *1*. Change this to *0.5*.

11. In the **Blocks Palette**, click **Looks**.

12. Drag the block **change color effect by 25** to the scripts area and snap it to the bottom of the **wait** block.

13. On the block **change color effect by 25**, click **color** and then click **brightness**.

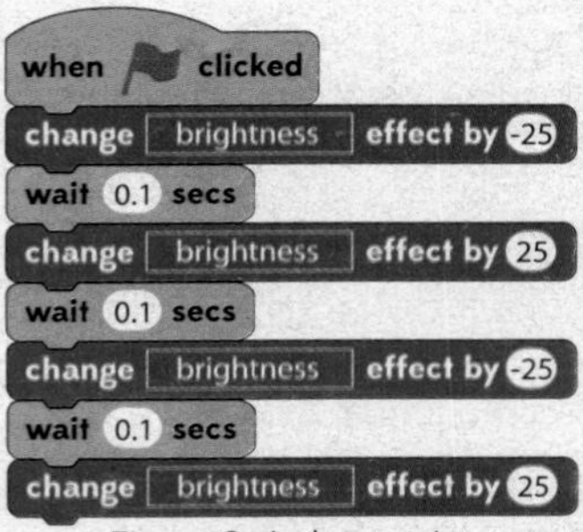

Figure 2. A short script

Above the Stage, there are two buttons: the green flag button starts all scripts in the project, and the red octagon stops all of the scripts.

The first block that is in the script, *when <green flag> clicked*, states that the script should run when the green flag button above the Stage is clicked. Click the green flag button now and you should see that the background briefly changes color.

To	Do This
Run a script (for testing)	In the **Scripts Area**, double-click any of the blocks in the script.
Insert a block above an existing block	In the **Blocks Palette**, drag a block over to the **Scripts Area** and over the top of an existing block. The white line indicates where the block will be inserted.
Detach a block (and any blocks that follow it) from a script	In the **Scripts Area**, click the block and drag it away from the block above it. All of the blocks below the selected block will move with it.
Remove a block, a series of connected blocks, or a script from the project	In the **Scripts Area**, click the first block that you want to remove and drag it over to the **Blocks Palette**.

To	Do This
Duplicate a block, a series of connected blocks, or a script	In the **Scripts Area**, right-click the first block in the series that you want to copy, click **duplicate**, and then click in the **Scripts Area** to position the new blocks.

Fitting the Blocks Together

Scratch uses the color and shape of blocks to indicate how they can be connected to each other. Blocks with a curved top, such as the *when <green flag> clicked* block, are the start of a script and can only have blocks connected underneath them.

Figure 3. You can only snap in blocks below this one, not above.

A notch in the top of a block indicates that it can be attached to blocks above it. A tab on the bottom indicates that you can snap other blocks into position below it.

Figure 4. A block that allows other blocks to be connected on top, or underneath.

An eight-sided white box in the block means that you can type numbers in there, but also that you can add variables and blocks from the Operators section of the Blocks Palette.

To use an operator or variable block instead of a number:

- Drag an eight-sided block from the **Blocks Palette**, into the **Scripts Area**, and over the white box.

Some blocks have square boxes that you can type in. These accept numbers, strings (sequences of characters), variables, and eight-sided operator blocks.

Blocks like *if* in the Control section of the Blocks Palette have spaces for six-sided blocks. Six-sided blocks represent the values

Yes or *No*, or *True* or *False*. These are described in more detail in section 4.4 Decisions on page 84.

4.2 Sprites

In Scratch, you will spend the majority of your time moving and changing the appearance of sprites in response to key presses.

Adding and Removing a Sprite

To add a sprite to the current project and make it appear on the Stage:

1. Above the **Sprite List**, next to **New Sprite**, click the **Choose new sprite from file** button. This is the second button in that area.
2. In the **New Sprite** window, browse to a sprite that you want to add, click it and then click **OK**.
3. On the **Stage**, click and drag the sprite to a new location.

If a sprite is the wrong size, click on the **Shrink sprite** or **Grow sprite** button in the Cursor Tools area and then click on the sprite:

To delete a sprite:

*   In the **Sprite List**, right-click a sprite and then click **delete**.

Creating a New Sprite

There are two ways of creating new sprites in Scratch: you can use the built-in drawing tools to paint a new sprite, or you can import graphic files from other tools like Adobe Photoshop and KolourPaint.

In either case:

- Above the **Sprites List**, next to **New Sprite**, click the **Paint new sprite** button. This is the first button in that area.

If you want to import a graphic file, click **Import** in the Paint Editor. The editor is described in section 4.9 The Paint Editor on page 91.

Importing and Exporting Your Sprites

You can export your sprites to a single file (including all of their costumes and sounds). You can share these files with other Scratch users, or simply re-use the sprite in another project.

To export a sprite:

1. In the **Sprite List**, right-click a sprite, and then click **export this sprite**.
2. Browse to the location where you want to save the file. Then in the **New Filename** box type a name for this sprite.
3. Click **OK**.

To import a sprite:

1. In the **Sprite List**, next to **New sprite**, click **Choose new sprite from file**.
2. Browse to the location where the sprite file is saved, and then click the sprite.
3. Click **OK**.

Understanding Costumes

In most projects, and especially in games, you will need to change the appearance of your sprites as the project is running. These can be frames of an animation, as is the case when the sprite is "walking". Or these can be alternative versions of the sprite that use different colors or hold different weapons.

In Scratch, variations of a sprite are known as "costumes". If you create a new sprite, it will only have one costume. To add another costume to the selected sprite:

1. In the **Scripts Area**, click **Costumes**.
2. To draw a new sprite using the built-in editor, click **Paint**.
3. To import a graphic to use as a costume, click **Import**.

To	Do This
Set the current costume of a sprite from the Scripts Area (not from a script)	In the **Scripts Area**, click **Costumes**, and then click the image of the costume.
Rename a costume	In the **Scripts Area**, click **Costumes**. Click the textbox that contains the name (for example, *costume1*) and then type a new name.
Duplicate a costume	In the **Scripts Area**, click **Costumes**. Next to the costume that you want to duplicate, click **Copy**.
Delete a costume	In the **Scripts Area**, click **Costumes**. Next to the costume that you want to remove, click **x**.
Edit a costume using the built-in Paint Editor	In the **Scripts Area**, click **Costumes**. Next to the costume that you want to change, click **Edit**.

Scripting Your Sprites

Motion blocks set the position of sprites. On the Stage you can click and drag sprites where you want them, but to move them from scripts (for example, in response to the user pressing an arrow key) you need to use one of the motion blocks.

These are:

Block	Description
move ? steps	Moves a sprite a number of steps in the direction it is currently pointing.
turn (clockwise) ? degrees	Rotates a sprite a number of degrees in a clockwise direction.
turn (counter-clockwise) ? degrees	Rotates a sprite a number of degrees in an counter-clockwise direction.
point in direction ?	Rotates or flips a sprite to face the specified direction.
point towards ?	Rotates or flips a sprite to face the mouse pointer or another sprite.
go to x: ? y: ?	Sets the position of a sprite.
go to ?	Moves a sprite to the location of the mouse pointer or another sprite.
glide ? secs to x: ? y: ?	Animates the movement of a sprite to the specified location.
change x by ?	Moves a sprite horizontally by the number of steps specified. This number can be negative.
set x to ?	Moves a sprite horizontally to the specified position.
change y by ?	Moves a sprite vertically by the number of steps specified. This number can be negative.
set y to ?	Moves a sprite vertically to the specified position.
if on edge, bounce	Changes the direction of a sprite when it reaches the edge of the Stage.

Each sprite also has three variables that are changed by the motion blocks. These can be used in decision-making and arithmetic blocks.

Variable	Description
x position	The horizontal position of the sprite on the Stage.
y position	The vertical position of the sprite on the Stage.

Variable	Description
direction	The direction that the sprite is currently facing.

When sprites are added to the Stage, Scratch assumes that they face to the right. When you change the direction that a sprite faces, Scratch rotates the sprite. To tell Scratch that it should flip a sprite and not rotate it:

1. In the **Sprite List**, click a sprite.
2. At the top of the **Scripts Area**, next to the picture of the sprite, click the **only face left-right** button. This is the second button of the three that are arranged vertically.

The Looks blocks in the Blocks Palette change the appearance of sprites on the Stage. Some of these blocks change a sprite's costume, and some of them apply effects (such as fades).

Block	Description
switch to costume ?	Sets the costume displayed for this sprite.
next costume	Changes to the next costume. If the current costume is the last one, the first costume will be used instead.
say ? for ? secs	Displays a speech bubble next to the sprite.
say ?	Displays a speech bubble next to the sprite. This bubble remains until you use a **say** block with no text.
think ? for ? secs	Displays a thought bubble next to the sprite.
think ?	Displays a thought bubble next to the sprite. This bubble remains until you use a **think** block with no text.
change ? effect by ?	See below.
set ? effect to ?	See below.
clear graphic effects	See below.

Block	Description
change size by ?	Grows or shrinks a sprite by the amount specified.
set size to ? %	Grows or shrinks a sprite by setting its size. This is a percentage of the size of the graphic used to create the sprite, and it can be greater than 100%.
show	Shows the sprite on the Stage if it is currently hidden.
hide	Hides a sprite if it is currently shown.
go to front	Moves a sprite in front of all others.
go back ? layers	Moves a sprite behind other sprites.

There are seven different effects that you can add to sprites:

Effect	Description
color	Changes the color (hue) of a sprite.
fisheye	Distorts the sprite.
whirl	Distorts the sprite into a swirl around its center.
pixelate	Makes the sprite appear to be made up of larger pixels.
mosaic	Makes the sprite appear to be made up smaller clones of itself.
brightness	When used with positive numbers, this increases the brightness (how close the colors are to white). When used with negative numbers, this decreases the brightness (how close the colors are to black).
ghost	Makes the sprite translucent (so that other sprites can be seen through it) or completely transparent (the sprite is invisible).

You control these effects using three blocks:

- To set an effect to a specific value, use the **set ? effect to ?** block.

- To increase or decrease the amount of an effect that is applied to a sprite, use the **change ? effect by ?** block.
- To remove all active effects from a sprite, use the **clear graphics effects** block.

All sprites have two variables related to their appearance:

Variable	Description
costume #	The number of the costume that is currently displayed for this sprite.
size	The size of a sprite on the Stage. This is a percentage of the size of the graphic used to create the sprite, and it can be greater than 100%.

You can choose whether Scratch should display these variables on the Stage. To show the value of a variable:

- In the **Blocks Palette**, click the box next to the variable name.

Click the box again to remove the variable from the Stage.

4.3 Arithmetic and Variables

In the Operators section of Blocks Palette, there are eight blocks that you can use to perform basic math operations, such as adding two numbers together. These blocks are eight-sided, green blocks and they fit into any other block that accepts a number.

Block	Description
? + ?	Adds two numbers together.
? - ?	Subtracts the second number from the first.
? * ?	Multiplies two numbers together.
? / ?	Divides the first number by the second.

Block	Description
pick random ? to ?	Picks a random number between the first number and the second number.
? mod ?	Performs modular arithmetic – the first number "wraps around" if it reaches the value of the second number.
round ?	Rounds the specified number to the nearest whole number.
? of ?	Select from a range of additional math functions.

You can use arithmetic operator blocks as inputs to other arithmetic blocks. For example, the expression *1 + ((14 / 3) x 3.14)* can be created with three blocks:

Figure 5. Nested operator blocks

Creating and Using Variables

A variable is a named area of the computer's memory in which you can store pieces of data.

To create a variable in Scratch:

1. In the **Blocks Palette**, click **Variables**.
2. Click **Make a Variable**.
3. Type a name for your variable.
4. If you want all sprites to be able to access the variable, click the circle next to **For all sprites**.
5. If you only want this sprite to be able to access the variable, click the circle next to **For this sprite only**.
6. Click **OK**.

When you create a variable, Scratch adds a block for it in the Variables section of the Blocks Palette. These orange variable blocks will fit into blocks that accept a number. There are four blocks in the Variables section of the Blocks Palette for working with variables:

Block	Description
set ? to ?	Sets the value of a variable.
change ? by ?	Increments or decrements a variable.
show variable	Adds the specified variable to the Stage.
hide variable	Removes the selected variable from the Stage.

4.4 Decisions

There are six blocks that you use to compare numbers and make decisions. The result of these blocks is a "Boolean" value – either *true* or *false*..

Block	Description
? < ?	Is *true* if the first number is smaller than the second, or *false* if it is not.
? = ?	Is *true* if the two numbers are the same, or *false* if they are not.
? > ?	Is *true* if the first number is larger than the second, or *false* if it is not.
? and ?	Is *true* if the both of the attached blocks are *true*, or *false* if either (or both) of them is *false*.
? or ?	Is *true* if either of the two attached blocks is *true*. If neither are *true*, then it returns *false*.
not ?	Is *true* if the attached block is *false*, and *false* if the attached block is *true*.

Two blocks in the Control section of the Blocks Palette are used with the Boolean operator blocks to make decisions.

Block	Description
if ?	Runs the blocks inside it, if the attached Boolean operator is *true*.
if ? else	Runs the blocks in the top section if the attached Boolean operator is *true*, and the blocks in the bottom section if the attached operator is *false*.

You can snap any number of blocks into the middle of the *if* and *if...else* blocks. This includes adding other *if* blocks to create highly-complicated decision-making.

Controlling Your Scripts with a Keyboard and Mouse

Users play Scratch games and interact with projects using the mouse and keyboard.

There are two blocks in the Controls section of the Blocks Palette that you can use to start a script when a key is pressed, or when the user clicks with the left mouse button. These blocks have curved tops and so you cannot place them in an existing script, they must always start a new script.

Block	Description
when ? key pressed	Runs the blocks snapped below when the user presses a key on the keyboard.
when sprite clicked	Runs the blocks snapped below when the user clicks on a sprite.

In games, the *when key pressed* block is used many times to move a sprite when the player presses one of the arrow keys.

Figure 6. Multiple scripts to control a sprite

All sprites can listen and react to the same key presses.

There is a special set of operators in the Sensing section of the Blocks Palette that you can use for making decisions based on keyboard or mouse input from the user. Unlike the control blocks, these blocks must be used as part of an *if* decision or with a Boolean operator block.

Block	Description
mouse down?	A Boolean value that is *true* if the user is currently holding the left mouse button down.
key ? is pressed?	A Boolean value that is *true* if the user is currently pressing the specified key on the keyboard.

You can use them in combination with the control blocks. For example, to create two different actions depending on whether the user clicks a sprite normally or holds the up arrow key when they click a sprite.

Detecting a Collision between Sprites

A *collision* is when two sprites overlap each other on the screen. The blocks that you need are in the Sensing section of the Blocks Palette, and there are two ways you can detect a collision in Scratch:

- Use **touching** to check if sprites are touching; or
- Use the **touching color** and **color touching color** blocks.

Checking if two colors touch is useful in games when you need to know if a specific part of a sprite is making contact with a specific part of another. But because Scratch is programmed to ignore transparent areas of your sprites, the *touching* block is all you need for many games.

 The *touching* block does not detect collisions when sprites are hidden with the *hide* block. However, it does detect collisions when sprites are made invisible using the *ghost* effect.

4.5 Loops

Loops have space in the middle for you to snap in other blocks, and you can use them to pieces of a script repeatedly. There are three types of loop in Scratch: infinite loops, which run until the script is stopped; definite loops, which run a set number of times; and indefinite loops, which run repeatedly until a certain condition is met.

Block	Description
wait ? secs	This is a special kind of loop that repeatedly does nothing until the specified number of seconds has elapsed.
forever	Repeatedly runs the blocks until the script is stopped.
repeat ?	Repeatedly runs the blocks a set number times.
forever if ?	Checks the Boolean operation and if it is *true* then Scratch runs the blocks that are in the middle of the loop. Then it checks the condition again. If the Boolean operation is *false*, the looping ends.
wait until ?	This is a special loop that repeatedly does nothing until the Boolean operation is *true*.
repeat until ?	Checks the Boolean operation. If it is *false* then Scratch runs the blocks that are in the middle of the loop. Then the loop checks the condition again. If the Boolean operation is *true*, the looping ends and Scratch runs the block below the **repeat until** block.

The *forever if* and *repeat until* blocks seem very similar. However, there are two important differences:

1. *Forever if* runs blocks while the Boolean operation is *true* – it ends when the operation is *false*. *Repeat until* runs blocks while the Boolean operation is *false* – it ends when the operation is *true*.

2. You cannot snap other blocks to the bottom of a *forever if* block.

4.6 Strings

A *string* is a sequence of characters, like a name, word, or sentence. Many of the blocks that you can use to work with strings are introduced earlier in this chapter:

Block	Section	Description
set ? to ?	Variables	Sets the value of the specified variable to a string.
say ? for ? secs	Looks	Displays a speech bubble next to the sprite for the number of seconds specified.
say ?	Looks	Displays a speech bubble next to the sprite.
think ? for ? secs	Looks	Displays a thought bubble next to the sprite for the number of seconds specified.
think ?	Looks	Displays a thought bubble next to the sprite.
ask ? and wait	Sensing	Shows the specified string and a text input box to the user. When the user presses **Enter** or clicks the button, their answer is stored in the variable **answer**.

But in the Operators section of the Blocks Palette, there are three operator blocks that only work with strings:

Block	Description
join ? ?	Joins two strings together.
letter ? of ?	Extracts the character at the specified position of the string.
length of ?	Calculates the number of characters in the string.

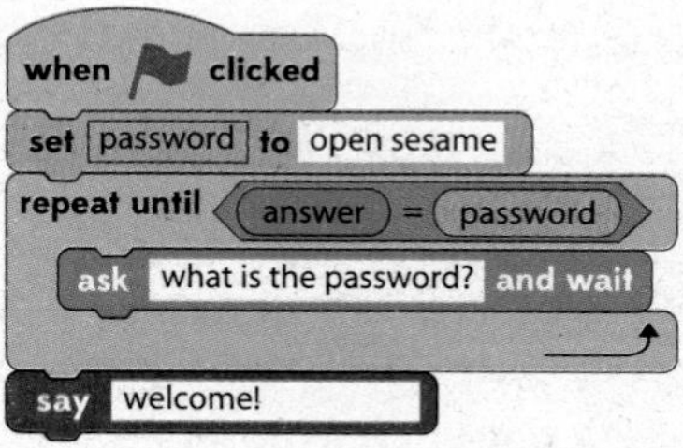

Figure 7. A basic login prompt using strings

4.7 Messages

In Scratch, all scripts are associated with an individual sprite and run independently of any other scripts. *Messages* allow the different sprites on the Stage to communicate and synchronize with each other. These messages are never shown to the user.

In the Controls section of the Blocks Palette, there are two blocks for sending messages, and one for receiving them:

Block	Description
broadcast ?	Sends the specified message to all sprites in the project.
broadcast ? and wait	Sends the specified message to all sprites in the project and then waits. When all of the sprites that listen for that message have finished their work, Scratch runs the blocks that are snapped onto the bottom of the **broadcast and wait** block.
when I receive ?	Starts a new script when a sprite receives the specified message.

To send a message from a sprite:

1. In the **Blocks Palette**, drag a **broadcast** block over to the **Scripts Area** and into position.
2. On the block, click the down arrow, and then either click the name of the message that you want to send, or click **new** to create a new message.

3. To create a new message: in the **Message name** box, type a unique name for the message, and then click **OK**.

To receive a specific message when it occurs:

1. In the **Blocks Palette**, drag a **when I receive block** into free space in the **Scripts Area**.
2. Click the down arrow, and then click the message.
3. Snap blocks onto the bottom of the **when I receive** block. When the message is received, Scratch runs these blocks.

4.8 Sound and Music

There are two ways to add sound effects and music to your project: import .*wav* and MP3 files into Scratch, or create music by playing notes.

Sound files are attached to individual sprites, and only the sprite that the sound is attached to can play it. To import a sound file:

• In the **Scripts Area**, click **Sounds**, and then click **Import**.

There are five blocks in the Sound section of the Blocks Palette for working with imported sound files:

Block	Description
play sound ?	Starts playing the specified sound.
play sound ? until done	Plays the specified sound and until the end.
stop all sounds	Stops all sounds that a sprite is playing.
change volume by ?	Increases or decreases how loud a sound plays.
set volume to ? %	Sets how loud the sound plays, as a percentage of how loud that sound is when imported.

Play sound and *play sound until done* appear to do the same thing, but there is an important difference between them. If you snap two *play sound* blocks together then Scratch plays both sounds at the same time. But with a *play sound until done* block, Scratch will play the sound file all the way to the end before running the blocks below.

4.9 The Paint Editor

Although it cannot compete with the features of dedicated software packages such as Adobe Photoshop, Scratch's Paint Editor has all of the tools that you need to draw sprites from within Scratch.

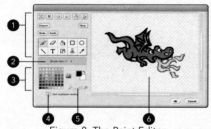

Figure 8. The Paint Editor

1	Tools.
2	Options. This area changes depending on the tool you select.
3	Color palettes. Use these to change the color that you draw with.
4	Sets the center point of the picture. You can use this for controlling how sprites rotate and where on the picture the location variables of the sprite refer to.
5	Zoom. Click the - button to look at your picture from further away, or the + button to view your picture close up.
6	Drawing area.

The tools area contains tools for painting and drawing your sprites and backgrounds..

To	Do This
Make the picture bigger	In the **Tools** area, click the **Grow** button.
Make the picture smaller	In the **Tools** area, click the **Shrink** button.
Rotate the picture counter-clockwise	In the **Tools** area, click the **Rotate counter-clock-wise** button.
Rotate the picture clockwise	In the **Tools** area, click the **Rotate clock-wise** button.
Flip the picture so that it faces in the opposite direction	In the **Tools** area, click the **Flip horizontally** button.
Flip the picture so that it faces the same direction, but is the other way up	In the **Tools** area, click the **Flip vertically** button.
Import a graphic file	See below.
Clear the drawing area	In the **Tools** area, click **Clear**.
Reverse the last change you made	In the **Tools** area, click **Undo**.
Remake the last change that you undid	In the **Tools** area, click **Redo**.
Close the editor without saving the changes you made to the picture	Click **Cancel**.

The ten larger buttons in the tools area are selected by clicking them, but only activate when you do something in the drawing area.

Tool	Description
Paintbrush	Draw freehand shapes in the drawing area.
Eraser	Click and hold the left mouse button in the drawing area to erase parts of the picture under the mouse pointer.
Fill	Fills an area with a color or gradient.

Tool	Description
Rectangle	Draws rectangles and squares when you click and drag the mouse pointer in the drawing area.
Ellipse	Draws ellipses and circles when you click and drag the mouse pointer around in the drawing area.
Line	Draws a straight line between two points.
Text	Type text onto the picture.
Selection	Click and drag out a rectangle to select a part of the picture. You can then move, rotate or change this selection without affecting the rest.
Stamp	Click and drag out a rectangle to select a part of the picture and copy it into memory. You can then paste it down onto the picture repeatedly. To stop stamping, select another tool.
Eyedropper	Click anywhere in the drawing area. The eyedropper sets the current color in the color palette area to match whatever is under the mouse pointer.

Using Transparencies

The background of the drawing area is a grey and white checkerboard pattern. This indicates that the area is transparent. Sprites and backgrounds that are underneath the sprite on the Stage will show through these transparent areas.

When using the Paint Editor to draw or change sprites, anything in the drawing area that is not transparent is part of the sprite.

Importing Your Graphics

If you have a graphic file that you want to use as a sprite, costume, or background then you can import it into the Paint Editor.

To import a *.jpg* or *.png* file:

1.   In the **Paint Editor**, click **Import**.

2. Browse to the file, click it, and then click **OK**.

If you are importing graphic files for use as sprites, you may need to remove the solid-color background in the Paint Editor. In the color palettes area, click the transparent color (the grey and white checkerboard pattern) and then use the *Fill* tool to clear the sprite's background.

4.10 Automatic Startup of Scratch Projects

Scratch has a full-screen option that it calls "presentation mode", where only the Stage and three buttons are shown on the screen. By editing a few configuration files in Raspbian, you can open a project in presentation mode when the Pi starts.

There are two steps you should take before you do this. First, save your project in a folder that does not contain spaces. For example, */home/pi/MyGame.sb*. Next, you will need to disable remote sensor connections for your project. Open the file in Scratch, and then:

1. In the **Blocks Palette**, click **Sensing**.
2. Right-click one of the two sensor value blocks at the bottom of the **Blocks Palette**, and then click **disable remote sensor connections**.
3. On the **Menu**, click **File** and then click **Save**.

Now, use the raspi-config tool to change the boot order:

1. On the desktop, click **LXTerminal**.
2. Type the following command and then press **Enter**:
   ```
   sudo raspi-config
   ```
3. Use the **Down Arrow** key to highlight **Enable Boot to Desktop/Scratch**, and then press **Enter**.
4. Press the **Down Arrow** key to highlight **Scratch Start the Scratch programming environment upon boot**, and then press **Enter**.

5. Press the **Right Arrow** key twice to highlight **<Finish>**, and then press **Enter**.

6. Press **Enter**.

7. When Scratch appears, press **Ctrl + Alt + F1**.

8. Press **Ctrl + C**.

9. When prompted, press **Ctrl + C**.

10. Type the following command and then press **Enter**:

    ```
    sudo nano /etc/profile.d/boottoscratch.sh
    ```

11. On the line that ends with *xinit dev/stdin*, change it to *scratch presentation* followed by the path to your Scratch project. For example:

    ```
    scratch presentation /home/pi/MyGame.sb
    ```

12. Press **Ctrl + O**.

13. Press **Enter**.

14. Press **Ctrl + X**.

15. Type the following command and then press **Enter**:

    ```
    sudo shutdown -r now
    ```

4.11 Sharing Your Finished Projects

When you are finished with a Scratch project, you can share it with the world. However, the *.sb* files that Scratch uses can only be opened in the Scratch environment.

There are two other ways that you can distribute your projects:

Putting Your Project on the Scratch Website

The official Scratch website is at *http://scratch.mit.edu* and if you are a registered user then you can upload your Scratch projects. Visitors to the site can then play your games in any web browser that supports Adobe Flash.

To publish a game on the Scratch site:

1. In a web browser, open *http://scratch.mid.edu*

2. On the top menu, click **Join Scratch**.

3. Complete the registration process and make a note of your username and password.

4. In Scratch on the Raspberry Pi, on the **Menu**, click **Share** and then click **Share This Project Online...**

5. In the **Your Scratch website login name** box, type your scratch.mid.edu username.

6. In the **Password** box, type your scratch.mid.edu password.

7. In the **Project name** box, type a name for your project.

8. In the **Project notes** box, type a description of your project (for example, how to use it).

9. Under **Tags**, click the boxes next to any keywords that describe the type of project you are uploading.

10. Click **OK**.

Converting Your Scratch Project Files to Executables

Aside from their website, the developers of Scratch do not currently offer a way to run Scratch projects on machines that do not have Scratch installed. However, several Scratch users ("Scratchers") have written software to convert .sb files into standalone executables.

You can find an up to date list of all of these types of conversion tools on the Scratch wiki at
http://wiki.scratch.mit.edu/wiki/Porting_Scratch_Projects

5 – Building an Arcade Game in Scratch

In this tutorial, you can see how to build a very basic version of the arcade game Double Dragon®[1]. Double Dragon® is a side-scrolling action game in which the player takes control of a character and must walk from the left-hand side of the level, to the right. In the way are numerous enemies that the player must defeat by punching and kicking. If you are not familiar with this game, it might be useful to watch a few videos of it on YouTube.

 This project pushes Scratch on the Raspberry Pi to its limits. If Scratch struggles to run the game when you click the green flag, try Scratch in "presentation mode".

Compared to many of the example games that you find on the Scratch website, the game you are building may seem complicated. It is intended to help you learn Scratch, having a working game at the end is a bonus.

5.1 The Title Screen

Even simple games usually start by showing some kind of title screen to the player. When the game ends, the title screen appears again so that the player can have another go.

To begin, start Scratch on Raspbian and delete the cat:

1. On the desktop, double-click **Scratch**.
2. In the **Sprite List**, right-click **Sprite1**, and then click **delete**.

The Stage's background color should match the background color of the logos and graphics that you use. To change it:

1. In the **Sprite List**, click **Stage**.
2. In the **Scripts Area**, click **Backgrounds**, and then click the **Edit** button next to **background1**.

---

1. Double Dragon is a registered trademark of Bally Gaming, Inc.

3. In the **Paint Editor**, in the **Color Palettes** area, click the black square in the grid of colors.

4. In the **Tools** area, click the **Fill** tool, and then click in the drawing area.

5. Click **OK**.

To create a line of text that tells the player to press the Space key:

1. In the **Sprite List**, click **Paint new sprite**.

2. In the **Tools** area, click the **Zoom out** button so that you can see the entire drawing area.

3. In the **Tools** area, click the **Text** tool, and then click the white square in the grid of colors in the **Color Palettes** area.

4. Type *Press Space*, and then click **OK**.

5. On the **Stage**, drag the text into position.

6. In the **Scripts Area**, click the box that contains **Sprite1** and change the name of the sprite to *PressSpace*.

You need a logo graphic for your title screen. Click **Paint a new sprite** and either draw a logo in the Paint Editor, or import one. Rename this sprite *TitleLogo* using the box in the Scripts Area.

To tell the two sprites on the title screen to fade in when the Scratch project begins, you might normally use the *when <green flag> clicked* block. However, the title screen needs to re-appear at the end of the game and the green flag is not clicked then.

To create a new start point for the title screen, you can use a *broadcast* block attached to the Stage:

1. In the **Sprite List**, click **Stage**.

2. In the **Blocks Palette**, click **Control**, and then drag a *when <green flag> clicked* block to the **Scripts Area**.

3. From the **Blocks Palette**, drag a **broadcast** block over to the **Scripts Area** and snap it into position underneath the **when <green flag> clicked** block.

4. On the **broadcast** block, click the **down arrow**, and then click **new...**

5. In the **Message name** box, type *StartGame* and then click **OK**.

You can use the *brightness* effect to create a simple fade-in animation. You can see this script in Figure 1, in the *when I receive StartGame* scripts.

The *when <green flag> clicked* block is currently the only place where the game is started. But later, other sprites can broadcast "StartGame" to reset the project.

To finish the title screen, you need to detect when the user presses the Space key and then broadcast a message to tell the first level to start. You could also make the "Press Space" sprite flash and play a sound effect when this happens.

To detect the key press:

1. In the **Sprite List**, click **PressSpace**.

2. In the **Blocks Palette**, click **Control**, and then drag a **wait until** block over to the **Scripts Area** and snap it into position below the **repeat** block.

3. In the **Blocks Palette**, click **Sensing**, and then drag a **key space pressed** block over to the **Scripts Area** and drop it onto the six-sided slot on the **wait until** block.

4. In the **Blocks Palette**, click **Control**, and then drag a **broadcast** block over to the **Scripts Area**. Snap it into position below the previous block.

5. On the **broadcast** block, click **StartGame** and then click **new...**

6. In the **Message name** box, type *Level1* and then click **OK**.

If you have a sound effect in *.wav* or *.mp3* format that you want to play when the user presses the Space key on the title screen:

1. In the **Sprite List**, click **PressSpace**.

2. Import the sound file.

3. In the **Scripts Area**, click **Scripts**.

4. In the **Blocks Palette**, click **Sound** and then drag a **play sound** block over to the **Scripts Area** and underneath the **wait until key space pressed** block.

5. Make sure the correct sound file is shown in the **play sound** block.

To hide the *TitleLogo* when *PressSpace* broadcasts "Level1".

1. In the **Sprite List**, click **TitleLogo**.

2. From the **Blocks Palette**, drag a **when I receive** block over to the **Scripts Area**. Click the **down arrow** and then click **Level1**.

3. In the **Blocks Palette**, click **Looks**, and then drag a **hide** block over to the **Scripts Area** and snap it into underneath the previous block.

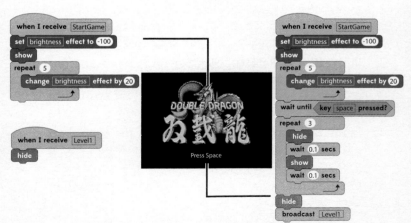

Figure 1. Original artwork ©1987 Technos Japan Corp.

5.2 The Level Backgrounds

Scrolling is an effect where the background of a game moves in the opposite direction to the player. This makes it look like the player's character is moving when they are actually standing still.

However, Scratch cannot move the project background so your scrolling has to be created using sprites. But it has two further restrictions that make this complicated:

- Sprites cannot move completely off the Stage; and
- The maximum size of a sprite is 480 steps x 360 steps. You cannot use one sprite for the entire background.

Preparing the Background Sprites

You can find an image of the NES version of Double Dragon® on The Spriters Resource (*http://www.spriters-resource.com*). To use this background, you need to make it twice as large – 2030 pixels wide and 384 pixels tall. Then you will have to trim off 24 pixels from the top.

Scratch's Paint Editor is not ideal for working with large files, so you should use a different paint editor, such as Adobe Photoshop, Microsoft Paint, or KolourPaint.

> ▼ **If you are using Adobe Photoshop: when resizing the image, next to *Resample Image* click *Bicubic* and then click *Nearest Neighbor*.**

Next, you need to divide the background into four images that measure 480px by 360px and one image that measures 110px by 360px. Save each piece to its own file in portable network graphics (PNG) format.

Figure 2. The five background sprites. Original artwork ©1987 Technos Japan Corp.

If you prefer to draw your own background then you can do this in Scratch's Paint Editor instead of importing your graphics in the next section. Try to make the overall shape and design similar to the image above, as this will help in later sections of the tutorial.

Importing the Background Graphics

To import each background sprite:

1. In the **Sprite List**, click **Paint new sprite**, and then click **Import**.
2. Browse to your background file, click it, and then click **OK**.
3. Click **OK**.
4. In the **Sprite List**, click your new sprite and then in the **Scripts Area**, rename the sprite. For example: *L1M1* for the first sprite, *L1M2* for the second, and so on.

Hiding the Background on the Title Screen

The furthest position that a sprite of this size can move to the left is -462. This means that a 480px wide background sprite cannot move far enough to the left to hide the last 18 pixels. The furthest position that a sprite of this size can be positioned to the right is 462. This means that the first 18 pixels of the image are always visible.

These two 18-pixel-wide areas at the edge of the Stage cause visible errors in the appearance of the scrolling and are hidden later.

When the game starts, the title screen broadcasts the message "StartGame". At this point, the background sprites should not be visible on the screen. You need to add a script to each background sprite so that it hides when that message is received. Make sure that when the background sprites are made visible, that they are on the lowest layer. Do this by bringing each sprite to the front, and then sending it back six layers.

To do all of this, add the following script to the *L1M1* sprite:

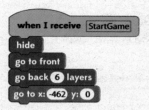

Now copy this script into the other four background sprites:

1. Right-click the **when I receive StartGame** block, and then click **duplicate**.

2. Move the mouse pointer to the **Sprite List**, and click **L1M2**.

Repeat this process for the remaining background sprites.

Scrolling the Background

The scrolling in this project works like this:

1. There is a variable called *scrollX* that controls the position of the background.

2. When *scrollX* is zero, all of the background sprites are in their default position.

3. Each background sprite calculates its position slightly differently, so that they appear one by one.

4. If *scrollX* is changed, the background sprites recalculate their position. For example, if *scrollX* is changed to 10, then all of the background sprites will move 10 pixels to the left.

5. Sprites that have an x position of greater than 462 will stay in the area on the right side of the Stage.

6. Sprites that have an x position of less than -462 will all be in the unusable area on the left-hand side of the Stage.

Add the variable *scrollX* to the project:

1. In the **Sprite List**, click **Stage**.

2. In the **Blocks Palette**, click **Variables**, and then click **Make a variable**.

3. In the **Variable name** box, type *scrollX* and then click **OK**.

4. In the **Blocks Palette**, click the box next to *scrollX*.

When the title screen broadcasts the message "Level1" to start the game, the first background sprite should make itself visible. Add the following script to the *L1M1* sprite:

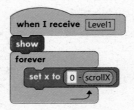

Since the first background sprite starts in the center of the Stage, its x position is *0 - scrollX*. So if *scrollX* is 10, then the x position is -10. This is how increasing the value of *scrollX* causes the background sprites to move to the left.

Copy that script into *L1M2*. Since *L1M1* starts at coordinate 0,0 and is 480 steps wide, *L1M2* starts at 480,0. So you need to change the value in the *set x to* block to *480 - scrollX*.

Copy that script into *L1M3*. Since *L1M2* starts at 480,0 and is 480 steps wide, *L1M3* starts at 960,0. So change the *set x to* block to *960 - scrollX*.

Copy the script into the next background sprite, *L1M4*. This starts at 1440,0. So change the *set x to* block to *1440 - scrollX*.

The last background sprite is different. Because it is less wide than the others, its start point is 1735,0. And when this sprite is at coordinate 195,0 it is fully on-screen. As the last sprite in the chain, *L1M5* must stop any more scrolling from happening. To do this, create a variable called *CanScroll*:

1. In the **Blocks Palette**, click **Variables** and then click **Make a variable**.

2. In the **Variable name** box, type *CanScroll*.

3. Click the box next to **For all sprites**.

4. Click **OK**.

5. In the **Blocks Palette**, click the box next to **CanScroll** to remove it from the Stage.

To make *L1M5* scroll with the others and set *CanScroll* to zero, add this script to *L1M5*:

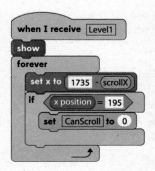

Before continuing, it is important that these two variables are set to default values when the game begins:

1. In the **Sprite List**, click **Stage**.

2. In the **Blocks Palette**, click **Variables**.

3. Drag a **set ? to 0** block over to the **Scripts Area** and position it above the **broadcast StartGame** block.

4. On the **set ? to 0** block, click the **down arrow** and then click **scrollX**.

5. Drag a **set ? to 0** block over to the **Scripts Area** and snap it below the previous block.

6. On the **set ? to 0** block, click the **down arrow** and then click **CanScroll**.

7. On the **set CanScroll to 0** block, click the white box and change the value to *1*.

Masking the Awkward Areas

To hide the two areas at the far left and far right of the Stage where the scrolling does not work properly, create a new sprite that adds 20 step (or pixel) thick black borders around the Stage. Name this sprite *Border*, and add the following script:

Adding the Background Music

Arcade games from the time period when Double Dragon® was released have background music that plays in a loop. You can use any *.wav* or *.mp3* file for this.

To import a file to use as background music in Scratch:

1. In the **Sprite List**, click **Stage**.
2. In the **Scripts Area**, click **Sounds**, and then click **Import**.
3. Browse to the file, click it, and then click **OK**.

To play the sound when Level 1 starts:

1. In the **Scripts Area**, click **Scripts**.
2. In the **Blocks Palette**, click **Control**. Then drag a **when I receive** block over to the **Scripts Area**.
3. On the **when I receive** block, click the **down arrow** and then click **Level1**.
4. Drag a **forever** block over to the **Scripts Area** and attach it underneath the previous block.
5. In the **Blocks Palette**, click **Sound**. Then drag a **play sound until done** block over to the **Scripts Area** and snap it in the middle of the **forever** block.
6. On the **play sound until done** block, click the **down arrow** and then click the name of the background music.

5.3 The Player Sprite

For the main sprite, you need 10 costumes:

- Four "walking" sprites.
- One costume for when the character throws a punch.
- Two costumes for when the character kicks.
- One costume for when the character is hit.
- Two costumes for when the player is knocked over.

Figure 3. Ten costumes for the main sprite. Original artwork ©1989 Technos Japan Corp.

You can use Scratch's Paint Editor to create your costumes. However, it is often easier to use an external editor. On The Spriters Resource, you can download images of the main sprite from the NES game. However, many of the enemies are not available. Instead, use the sprites from Double Dragon 2.

When preparing the costumes, keep them on a solid-color background and make each graphic file the same size. Save each costume to a new file in portable network graphic (PNG) format.

Create a new sprite in Scratch by importing the first costume. Name this sprite *Billy*, and then import the other costumes. This tutorial assumes that the costumes are named *Billy-1*, *Billy-2*, *Billy-3*, and so on. You may need to rename the first costume.

When you have imported all of the costumes, you can remove the solid-color background using the *Fill* tool in the Paint Editor, without Scratch moving the sprites.

Finally, drag the *Billy* sprite into its starting position on the Stage. And then in the Scripts Area, click the *only face left-right* button.

Hiding the Sprite on the Title Screen

The main sprite should not be visible until the title screen broadcasts the message "Level1". Add these scripts to *Billy*:

 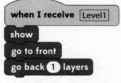

Controlling and Moving the Main Sprite

The player will control an invisible "ghost" sprite which tells the *Billy* sprite to move by broadcasting messages. Add these blocks:

The *if* block and costume changes cycle the sprite through the four frames of animation that show the character walking.

The ghost sprite broadcasts two other messages: *FakeWalk* and *MoveToGBilly*. These are used later, so add these two scripts to the *Billy* sprite:

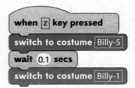 

> ⋁ **The ghost sprite is not created until section 5.4 Collision Detection on page 111. If you want to test the movement with the keyboard, add scripts that broadcast and wait the move messages when the arrow keys are pressed.**

When the player presses the Z key to punch or the X key to kick, the *Billy* sprite changes costume. It then waits, so the player has time to see the attack and enemies have a chance to be hit, before changing the costume again. Note that kicking has an extra costume (an extra frame of animation).

Add these scripts to *Billy*:

```
when z key pressed
switch to costume Billy-5
wait 0.1 secs
switch to costume Billy-1
```

```
when x key pressed
switch to costume Billy-6
wait 0.1 secs
switch to costume Billy-7
wait 0.1 secs
switch to costume Billy-1
```

At this point, the player sprite can move across the Stage. But it can move anywhere on the screen (including up into the air and through walls) and the movement of the sprite does not cause the background to scroll. These limitations are addressed in section 5.4 Collision Detection on page 111.

Adding Variables for Health, Lives Remaining, and the Player's Score

Since the *Billy* sprite represents the player in the game, now is a good time to create three variables that are needed for the game to work: *Health*, *Lives*, and *Score*.

Add these three variables and select the *For all sprites* option so that all sprites can see and modify the variables.

Health should never be displayed on the Stage. *Lives* and *Score* should be displayed on the Stage when the level starts, but not on the title screen. So:

1. In the **Sprite List**, click **Stage**.

2. In the **Blocks Palette**, click **Variables**, and then drag a **hide variable** block over to the **Scripts Area** and snap it into position underneath the **stop all sounds** block.[1]

3. On the **hide variable** block, click the **down arrow** and then click **Lives**.

4. From the **Blocks Palette**, drag a **hide variable** block over to the **Scripts Area** and snap it into position underneath the previous block.

5. On the **hide variable** block, click the **down arrow** and then click **Score**.

Then add three *set variable to* blocks below the *hide variable* blocks that you have created. Use the first to set *CanScroll* to 1, the second to set *Health* to 5, and the third to set *Lives* to 3. Then

1. From the **Blocks Palette**, drag a **show variable** block over to the **Scripts Area** and snap it into

---

1. If you do not have a "stop all sounds" block because you did not add background music, snap it to the bottom of the "broadcast StartGame" block.

position before the **forever** block in the **when I receive Level1** script.

2. On the **show variable** block, click the **down arrow** and then click **Score**.

3. From the **Blocks Palette**, drag a **show variable** block over to the **Scripts Area** and snap it into position underneath the previous block.

4. On the **show variable** block, click the **down arrow** and then click **Lives**.

5.4 Collision Detection

To prevent the player sprite from moving through walls and into areas that it is not supposed to move, you can use what Scratchers call a "wall-sensing sprite".

This "ghost" sprite is invisible and moves ahead of the player sprite. When the player presses an arrow key on the keyboard, the ghost sprite moves. If it collides with a wall, or an area that the player sprite is not supposed to go, then it moves back to its previous position. If it does not collide with a wall, it tells the player sprite to move to the same location.

To make this work, create five new sprites ("masks") – one for each of the five backgrounds. These new sprites are also invisible, but their costume shows the areas that the player sprite cannot move. The areas in which the player sprite can move are transparent.

You can create these masks in any image editor, but you can also do this using Scratch's built-in tools.

To create the mask for the first background sprite, *L1M1*:

1. In the **Sprite List**, right-click **L1M1** and then click **duplicate**.

2. Click the new sprite and then rename it *ML1M1*.

3. In the **Scripts Area**, remove the **go to front** and **go back 6 layers** blocks from the **when I receive StartGame** script.

4. In the **Scripts Area**, click **Costumes**, and then click **Edit**.

5. Using a single, solid color (for example, bright green), draw shapes over the areas that the player sprite cannot walk.

6. Using the **Eraser** tool and **Selection** tool, delete the parts of the image where the player can walk. These areas must be transparent.

Repeat this process for the other background sprites – for the second mask, copy the second the background; for the third mask, copy the third background, and so on. Name the masks *ML1M2*, *ML1M3*, *ML1M4*, *ML1M5* respectively.

 Make sure all of the areas in your mask are joined. Do not have two separate pieces of green – it will work, but causes the collision detection to run much too slowly for this project.

Because you copied most of the blocks from the background sprites, these masks will scroll with the background. It does not matter what layer they appear on as you will not see them. Scratch cannot detect collisions between hidden objects, and so use the *ghost* effect to make the masks invisible.

In the *when I receive Level1* scripts on each of the masks:

1. In the **Blocks Palette**, click **Looks**.

2. Drag a **set color effect to** block over to the **Scripts Area**, and snap it into position above the **show** block.

3. On the **set color effect to** block, click **color** and then click **ghost**.

4. Click the white box, and change the value to *100*.

Then create the wall-sensing sprite:

1. Above the **Stage**, click the **green flag** to start the game.

2. Press the **Space** key at the title screen.

3. When the main sprite appears, stop all of the scripts.

4. In the **Sprite List**, click **Paint new sprite**.

5. Click **Import**.

6. Browse to the graphic file for the first costume of the main sprite, click it, and then click **OK**.

7. Draw a solid color rectangle (any color) around the feet of the main sprite.

8. Using the **Eraser** and **Selection** tools, delete the rest of the sprite.

9. Click **OK**.

10. In the **Sprite List**, click the new sprite.

11. In the **Scripts Area**, rename the sprite *GBilly*.

12. Add the following scripts to the **Scripts Area**:

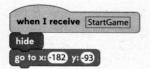 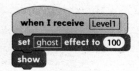

Scratch will put the current sprite coordinates into the *go to x: y:* block. You do not need to change them. The rectangle should be positioned correctly over the feet of the *Billy* sprite. If it is not, you may have to move it in the Paint Editor.

Make a note of the difference between the y position of the ghost sprite and that of the *Billy* sprite. Then go back to the *Billy* sprite and change the number in the *when I receive MoveToGBilly* script from *34* to this value.

Moving the Ghost Sprite

To move the wall-sensing sprite, first:

1. In the **Sprite List**, click **GBilly**.

2. In the **Blocks Palette**, click **Control**.

3. Drag a **forever** block over to the **Scripts Area**, and snap it into position below the **show** block.

The player should not be able to control their movement when they are attacking, or when they have been hit.

1. Drag an **if** block over to the **Scripts Area**, and snap it into position inside the **forever** block.

2. In the **Blocks Palette**, click **Operators**.

3. Drag a **? < ?** block to the **Scripts Area** and snap it into the **if** block.

4. On the **? < ?** block, click the second white box and type the value **5**.

5. In the **Blocks Palette**, click **Sensing**.

6. Drag a **x position of ?** block to the **Scripts Area** and snap it into the first white box on the **? < 5** block.

7. Click **x position** and then click **costume #**.

8. Click the **down arrow** in the box, then click **Billy**.

9. Add the blocks on the following page into the middle of the **if costume # of Billy < 5** block:

Where it says "See Above" on the diagram, you need to create an operator block that reads: touching ML1M1 *or* touching ML1M2 *or* touching ML1M3 *or* touching ML1M4 *or* touching ML1M5.

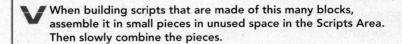

> When building scripts that are made of this many blocks, assemble it in small pieces in unused space in the Scripts Area. Then slowly combine the pieces.

If the right arrow key is pressed then the script checks that the *GBilly* sprite is in the far right of the Stage. If it is, and scrolling is enabled, then there is a block to increment *scrollX* (which in turn causes the background sprites to move to the left). If scrolling the background causes a wall to come in contact with the wall-sensing sprite then one of the touching blocks will be *true*. In response, the script pushes the ghost sprite and the *Billy* sprite to the left.

If the player is not at the far right of the Stage, then the *change x by 10* block moves the ghost sprite to the right. It then checks whether it collides with a wall. If it does, it moves back to its previous position. If not, it tells the *Billy* sprite to walk to the right.

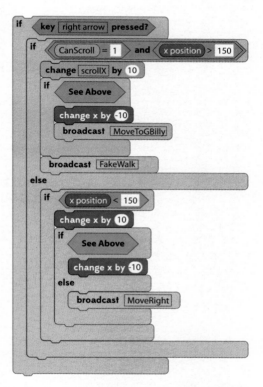

To move left or up, add the following blocks underneath the entire *if key right arrow pressed?* block. Duplicate the long operator block, and all of the *touching* blocks, and insert them where the diagram says "See Above".

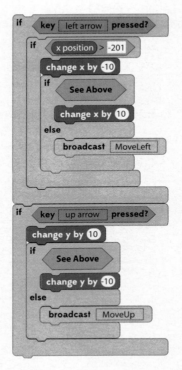

When moving up, this script relies on the background masks to stop the player sprite. But the script to move down uses the *y* position to restrict the player's movement. Add these blocks underneath the *if key up arrow pressed?* block:

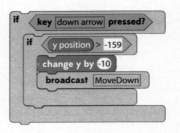

When you move the Billy sprite, your walking sprites may not line up with *GBilly*. To fix this, edit the costumes in the Paint Editor and "nudge" the costumes to the left or right.

5.5 Enemies

When the player reaches set points in the level, the scrolling stops and the game "spawns" enemies that the player must defeat. Only having two enemies on screen at once (like the NES game) is a sensible limitation for this project.

Prepare the graphics for an enemy sprite in a similar way as described in section 5.3 The Player Sprite on page 107. Enemies only need nine costumes, as shown in Figure 4 below.

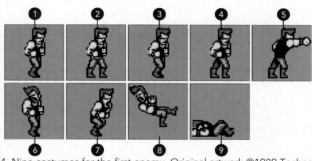

Figure 4. Nine costumes for the first enemy. Original artwork ©1989 Technos Japan Corp.

Name the sprite "Williams1" in Scratch and set it to only face left and right. Drag the sprite where you want it to appear on the Stage.

Add the following script to this sprite:

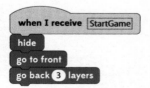

The enemy needs two variables: *Defeated* and *Hits*. *Defeated* is used to ensure that the sprite only moves and attacks until the player defeats it. *Hits* is the health of the enemy and is reduced when the player hits the sprite. Add these variables to the *Williams1* sprite only by selecting the *For this sprite only* option.

You already have the variable *CanScroll* which is used to stop the player scrolling the background when enemies appear or when the end of the level is reached. But you need one that holds how many enemies must be defeated before scrolling is re-enabled. Call this *EnemiesRemaining*, and make it visible to all sprites.

To detect when the player reaches a point when enemies appear, create another invisible sprite. This is sometimes called a "spawn point".

1. Start the game and then stop it on the first screen.
2. In the **Sprite List**, click **Paint new sprite**.
3. Draw a solid-color rectangle and then click **OK**.
4. This sprite must be tall enough to block the player's path. Drag the sprite into position on the **Stage**, and edit the costume if it is not large enough.
5. In the **Scripts Area**, rename the sprite *Spawn1*.
6. Make a note of the **x position** of the sprite.
7. Add the following scripts to the spawn point:

The position of the spawn point is calculated using *scrollX*, in the same way as the background sprites and masks are positioned.

Assuming the x position of the spawn sprite is 88 and the first screen starts at coordinate 0,0 then the position of the spawn sprite can be calculated as *88 - scrollX*.

When the spawn point touches the *Billy* sprite, it:

1. Sets *CanScroll* to 0 to stop the background scrolling.
2. Sets *EnemiesRemaining* to 1.
3. Broadcasts the message "Spawn1".
4. Hides itself so that no further collisions between it and the *Billy* sprite are detected.

Now you need to make *Williams1* respond to this message. Add these two scripts to it:

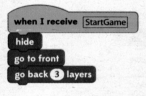
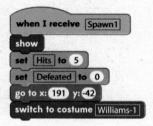

To create a new spawn point for the second screen, calculate the position of the new sprite with the second background sprite fully in view. The second background sprite starts at 480,0, so the position of the second spawn point is the x value (from the Scripts Area) plus 480 and then minus *scrollX*.

Making Williams Attack

To make the *Williams1* sprite attack the player, you need to add a loop that runs until the sprite is defeated. This loop:

1. Points the sprite in the direction of the *Billy* sprite.
2. Calculates if it is in striking range and if so, punches.

3. Walks a few steps if it is not in striking range.

Add the following blocks underneath the *go to x: y:* block:

```
repeat until  ( Defeated = 1 )
    point towards [Billy]
    if < distance to [Billy] < 25 >
        broadcast [HitBilly]
        switch to costume [Williams-5]
        wait 0.1 secs
        switch to costume [Williams-1]
        wait 0.1 secs
    else
        point in direction ( direction - ( pick random -65 to 65 ) )
        repeat 4
            move 5 steps
            if < costume # < 4 >
                next costume
            else
                switch to costume [Williams-1]
```

Eventually, there will be two copies of this sprite on the screen at the same time. To avoid them moving identically, notice how the script picks its direction by looking at *Billy* and then changing the direction by a random number of degrees. And the sprite intentionally moves slower than the player's character – otherwise it would be impossible to escape and the game would be very difficult.

Updating the Order of Layers

Because of the perspective used in the background graphics, when the sprites move up the screen they are actually moving into the distance. When the sprites move down the screen, they are coming closer. However, Scratch does not know that sprites with a greater y position should be behind other sprites.

The solution is to check the y position of sprites, and use the *go back ? layers* block to re-order the sprite layers. You also need to allow for sprites disappearing when they are defeated, and bear in mind that the names of enemy sprites may change.

One way to do this is to make a "list" of the sprites that are on the screen. Lists store strings and numbers, and give each item in the list a number. The first item is number 1. The second is number 2, and so on. Where this becomes useful, is that you can use an item in a list with many of the blocks in Scratch; in particular, the *? of ?* block in the Sensing section of the Blocks Palette.

First, make a list called *Mobs* (short for "mobiles") on the Stage (so that it is accessible by all sprites).

To add *Billy* to the *Mobs* list:

1. In the **Sprite List**, click **Billy**.
2. In the **Blocks Palette**, click **Variables**.
3. Drag an **insert ? at ? of ?** block over to the **Scripts Area** and snap it into position between the **when I receive Level1** block and the **show** block.
4. On the **insert ? at ? of ?** block, click the first box and then type *Billy*.
5. Click the second box and then type *1*.
6. Click the third box and then click **Mobs**.

Do the same for the *Williams1* sprite:

1. In the **Sprite List**, click **Williams1**.
2. In the **Blocks Palette**, click **Variables**.
3. Drag an **insert ? at ? of ?** block over to the **Scripts Area** and snap it into position between the **when I receive Spawn1** block and the **show** block.

4. On the **insert ? at ? of ?** block, click the first box and then type *Williams1*.

5. Click the second box and then click **last**.

6. Click the third box and then click **Mobs**.

The script that looks at the *Mobs* list and determines the order in which sprites are placed on layers will be on the Stage. For it to work, you need two other lists: *ZSprites* and *OZSprites*. Create these two lists in the same way that you created the *Mobs* list.

You also need to clear *Mobs* at the start of the game:

1. In the **Sprite List**, click **Stage**.

2. In the **Blocks Palette**, click **Control**.

3. Drag a **when I receive** block to the **Scripts Area**, and change it to be *when I receive StartGame*.

4. In the **Blocks Palette**, click **Variables**.

5. Drag a **delete ? of ?** block over to the **Scripts Area** and snap it into position underneath the previous block.

6. Click the **down arrow** on the first box and then click **all**.

7. Click the **down arrow** on the second box and then click **Mobs**.

Create the script to order the player sprite and active enemies:

1. In the **Blocks Palette**, click **Control**, and then drag a **when I receive** block to the **Scripts Area**.

2. Change the selection to **Level1**.

3. Drag a **forever** block over to the **Scripts Area** and snap it into position underneath the previous block.

4. Add the following blocks to the middle of the **forever** block:

```
delete all of ZSprites
insert Billy at 1 of ZSprites
if < (y position of ( item 2 of Mobs )) < (y position of ( item 1 of Mobs )) >
    insert ( item 2 of Mobs ) at 1 of ZSprites
else
    insert ( item 2 of Mobs ) at 2 of ZSprites

if < (y position of ( item 3 of Mobs )) < (y position of ( item 1 of ZSprites )) >
    insert ( item 3 of Mobs ) at 1 of ZSprites
else
    if < (y position of ( item 3 of Mobs )) < (y position of ( item 2 of ZSprites )) >
        insert ( item 3 of Mobs ) at 2 of ZSprites
    else
        insert ( item 3 of Mobs ) at 3 of ZSprites
```

ZSprites is used to store the sprite names in the order that they should be displayed on the Stage.

The *if* block checks to see whether the sprite that is second in the *Mobs* list has a y position that is less than the item in position one of the *ZSprites* list.[1] If it does, then the sprite is lower down on the Stage and should be displayed in the front, so the script inserts the second item from *Mobs* into the first position of *ZSprites*. This pushes *Billy* into second position in *ZSprites*. If it does not have a lower y position, the script puts the item in *ZSprites* after *Billy*.

The next *if* block checks whether the sprite that is third in the *Mobs* list has a y position that is less than the first item in *ZSprites*. If it does, the script puts this item first. If it does not, the script checks whether it has a lower y position than the second item – if it does, the script adds the item to *ZSprites* as the

---

1. The item in position one is always the Billy sprite.

second item; otherwise the item is added to the end of the list. It does not matter if there is only two (or one) items in the list.

Add the next half of the script inside the *forever* block, but below the previous blocks. Where the diagram says "See Above", create an operator block that reads:
not (item[1] of ZSprites = item[1] of OZSprites and item[2] of ZSprites = item[2] of OZSprites and item[3] of ZSprites = item[3] of OZSprites)

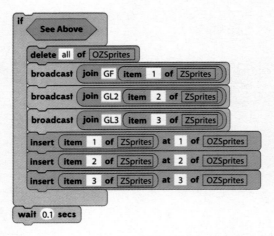

This reduces the number of times that Scratch re-orders the layers. The *OZSprites* list contains a copy of the *ZSprites* list from the last time the script was run. If *ZSprites* has changed, then two things happen: the script copies the items from *ZSprites* into *OZSprites*, and then broadcasts three messages to tell the sprites which layers to move to.

It builds a message by combining the name of the sprite with the strings "GF", "GL2", or "GL3", depending on which layer the sprite should move to. You need to add three scripts to *Billy*:

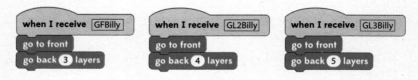

Copy these into *Williams1*, and then change the *when I receive* blocks to "GFWilliams1", "GL2Williams1", and "GL3Williams1".

Layer re-ordering is not instantaneous as the Raspberry Pi is not powerful enough. The approach may work very quickly in other projects, but if it slows this game down too much then remove it.

Hitting Williams

Enemies can have any name, so it is easier for them to detect the collisions than to have the player sprite do it. They need to listen to the player's attack keys, so add these blocks to *Williams1*:

There are also two changes that you need to make to the *when I receive Spawn1* script. This will reduce how frequently the enemy attacks:

1. Create an **if** block that reads *if costume # < 5.* Then duplicate it.

2. Drag one of the **if** blocks directly underneath the **repeat until Defeated = 1** block, so that it is inside the loop and surrounds the other blocks in the loop.

3. Drag the other **if** block directly underneath the **repeat 4** block, so that it is inside the loop and surrounds all of the other blocks in the loop.

4. Add a *wait 0.1 secs* to the bottom – inside the **repeat until Defeated = 1** block but underneath the **if costume # < 5** block.

To detect when the enemy is defeated and reactivate scrolling, create these blocks underneath the *switch costume to Williams-1* block in the *when Z key pressed* script.

The final block moves the sprite to a known location off the Stage – this is to allow the script that re-orders the sprite layers to remove "dead" sprites from the *Mobs* list. You need to add a few blocks for this to happen. Select the Stage in the Sprite List, and then add the following blocks as the first blocks inside the *forever* loop:

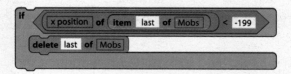

To finish the scripts for the *Williams1* sprite, click it on the Stage. Then, duplicate the whole script that begins with *when Z key pressed* and make the following changes:

1. Change *when Z key pressed* to *when X key pressed*.
2. Change the *switch to costume Williams-6* blocks to *switch to costume Williams-7*.
3. Change the *change by Hits by -1* blocks to *change by Hits by -2*.
4. Change the *if costume # = 6* block to *7*.
5. Add a *wait 0.1 secs* block to the top of the script.

Hitting the Player

When the *Billy* sprite is hit, the variable *Health* must be decremented. When it reaches zero, the sprite is knocked back 50 steps. However, this could cause the player to be knocked off the screen, and the ghost sprite would be in the wrong position. To fix this, the spawn point that triggers the enemies declares an x and y position on the Stage that is safe for the player. When they lose a life, a script tells the ghost sprite to move to this safe location. The ghost sprite then tells the *Billy* sprite to update its position.

Two new variables are needed for this: *RespawnX* and *RespawnY*. Create them on the Stage so that all sprites can see the values. The spawn points must set these variables:

1. In the **Sprite List**, click **Spawn1**.

2. Under the **Broadcast Spawn1** block, create a *set RespawnX to* block and enter the x position where the player sprite will reappear.

3. Create a *set RespawnY to* block and enter the y position where the player sprite will reappear.

Now, add the following script to the *Billy* sprite:

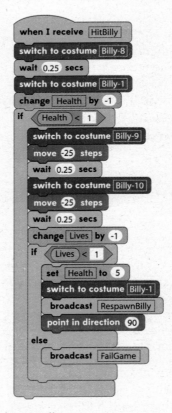

And this script to the *GBilly* sprite:

```
when I receive RespawnBilly
go to x: RespawnX y: RespawnY
broadcast MoveToGBilly
```

5.6 More Enemies

By duplicating the spawn point and *Williams1* sprites, you can fill up the rest of the level with enemies:

1. In **Spawn1**, change **set EnemiesRemaining to 1** to *set EnemiesRemaining to 2*.

2. In the **Sprite List**, right-click **Williams1** and then click **duplicate**.

3. Click the new sprite and rename it to *Williams2*.

4. In the **when I receive Spawn1** script, change **insert Williams1 at last of Mobs** to *insert Williams2 at last of Mobs*.

5. Change the block **when I receive GFWilliams1** to *GFWilliams2*.

6. Change the block **when I receive GL2Williams1** to *GL2Williams2*.

7. Change the block **when I receive GL3Williams1** to *GL3Williams2*.

8. If you want this sprite to spawn at a different location: change the values in the **go to x: y:** block under **when I receive Spawn1**.

9. If you want to give this sprite a slightly different random movement, change the values in **pick random -65 to 65**.

To complete this project, you need to add at least one more enemy – the end of level "boss". The process is largely the same:

1. In the **Sprite List**, right-click **Spawn1** and then click **duplicate**.

2. Click the new sprite, and then rename it *SpawnE*.

3. Change the block **set x to 88 - scrollX** to *set x to 1700 - scrollX*. This moves the spawn point to the far right of the fourth background sprite.

4. Change the block **set EnemiesRemaining to 2** to *set EnemiesRemaining to 1.*

5. Change the **broadcast** block to send *SpawnE.*

Following the previous instructions, make another copy of *Williams1.* Name this sprite *Williams3* and change the *when I receive Spawn1* block to *when I receive SpawnE.*

In the *when Z key pressed* and *when X key pressed* blocks, replace the *set CanScroll to 1* blocks with *broadcast WinGame* blocks.

5.7 Game Over

The game broadcasts two messages that are not yet received by any sprites: "FailGame" is sent when the player loses all their lives, and "WinGame" is sent when the player defeats the enemy in the last part of the level. You can use these to return to the title screen.

If you are converting your Scratch project to an *.exe*, *.app*, or *.jar* file, then it will run a lot quicker and you may be able to add more into the game. There are a lot of areas in this project that you can extend. For example:

To	Do This
Stop the enemies from walking through walls	Use a wall-sensing sprite for each enemy.
Add another level	Change the final enemy so that it broadcasts "Level2".
Add weapons	Include an extra set of costumes for the player and enemy sprites that shows them holding a weapon.
Make the animation smoother	Use more costumes, reduce the number of steps in the movements, and the amount of seconds in *wait* blocks.

6 – Programming in Python

Python is a widely-used programming language that is available on most modern operating systems and computers. On the Pi, Python is a great way to write software and games, and to control the GPIO pins.

Unlike programming languages such as C++ or Objective-C, Python is an *interpreted* language. This means that special software reads your code files and runs them. You do not have to *compile* Python files to executables or .app files before you can use them.

When programmers write code, they usually do it in a piece of software called an integrated development environment (IDE). An IDE is a text editor that is packaged with other tools to make writing code a little easier. On Raspbian, there are two Python IDEs on the desktop – IDLE and IDLE3. This is because there are two versions of Python, and they are incompatible with each other. In this chapter, you will learn Python 3 using the IDLE3 IDE.

6.1 Your First Python Program

"Hello, World!" is a short program that people often write as their first program in a new environment or language. It is a test, and only displays the message "Hello, World!" to the user.

In Python, you can write this program with one line of code, and it is a good way of introducing you to the IDE and how to run Python programs.

To start:

1. On the Raspbian desktop, double-click **IDLE3**.
2. Type *print("Hello, World!")* and then press **Enter**.

The first thing to note is that the window opened by IDLE3 is titled "Python Shell". The Python Shell works like the Linux terminal – it runs commands that you type here when you press the Enter key.

Python programs (or "scripts") are text files that contain all of the commands that you want to run. You can use any text editor to create these files, but there is one built-in to IDLE3:

1. In the **Python Shell**, on the **Menu**, click **File** and then click **New Window**.

2. Type *print("Hello, World")*

3. On the **Menu**, click **File** and then click **Save As**. Save your file with the extension *.py*.

4. On the **Menu**, click **Run** and then click **Run Module**.

The results of your program are shown in the Python Shell.

To run your program from a Linux terminal:

1. On the Raspbian desktop, double-click **LXTerminal**.

2. Type *python3* followed by a space, and then the full file name (including the file path) of your *.py* file.

If you want to run your program by clicking it on the desktop then you need to create a *desktop shortcut*. These are short text files that create additional icons on your desktop and describe what happens when the user clicks them.

To create a desktop shortcut for a Python script:

1. On the **LXDE panel**, click the **Menu** button, point to **Accessories**, and then click **Leafpad**.

2. Type the following text into the document. Replace *My Test Script* with what you want to call the icon, and the file name after *python3* with the location of your *.py* program.

```
[Desktop Entry]
Type=Application
Name=My Test Script
Exec=lxterminal --command "python3 /home/pi/
```

```
Desktop/test.py"
Terminal=False
Categories=None
```

3. On the Leafpad **Menu**, click **File**, and then click **Save As**.

4. Save the file to your desktop with the extension *.desktop*.

If you double-click the icon on the desktop, you should see a terminal window open and display the text "Hello, World!" However, the terminal window closes as soon as the program completes.

While you are developing your programs, it can be useful to keep the program running (and keep the terminal window open) until the user presses a key. In IDLE3, add the following command to your *.py* file. Put it on a new line underneath *print("Hello, World!")*.

```
input("Press any key to close this window.")
```

6.2 Python

In the following sections of this chapter, you will learn about the features of the Python 3 language.

Adding Comments to Python Programs

As your Python scripts become more complicated, you can put in explanations of what parts of your code do. This is to help you in case you need to a change a program that you wrote a long time ago.

To add a comment to a *.py* file:

• On a new line, type a # symbol and then any text.

Performing Basic Arithmetic

You have seen the function *print()* that displays information to the user. From a Python *.py* file, you need to use this to show the result of arithmetic calculations. But from the Python Shell, you can type the expression and the result is automatically shown.

For example:

- In the **Python Shell**, type the following expression and then press **Enter**:

```
5 + 5
```

To	Do This
Add two numbers together	Type one number followed by a + symbol and then another number.
Subtract the second number from the first	Type the first number followed by a - symbol and then the second number.
Multiply two numbers together	Type one number followed by a * symbol and then another number.
Divide the first number by the second	Type the first number followed by a / symbol and then the second number.
Divide the first number by the second, and return a whole number	Type the first number followed by // and then the second number.

Using Variables

In programming terms, a *variable* is an area of the computer's memory that you give a name to. You can store information in these variables and access it later.

To create a variable: specify a name, followed by an equals sign, and then the value it should contain. For example:

```
result = 5 + 5
print(result)
```

Variable names must start with a letter (a–z, or A–Z). The remaining characters in the name can be letters, numbers, or an underscore (_). You cannot use punctuation marks or other special characters in the names of variables, and there are several words (such as "print") that you cannot use as a variable name because they are already used for something else.

In Python, variables can hold any type of information. To extend the example above, you could assign a string (a sequence of characters) to the variable result, even when it currently contains a number.

```
result = "Hello"
```

You can use variables wherever you would otherwise type a value. For example, in math expressions such as x + 5 and x / y.

 Python is a "weakly typed" language. This means that you do not have to declare what type of data a variable holds. For example, if result contains "Hello" then result+5 is "Hello5". However, 5+result causes an error when the program is run because Python tries to use result as a number.

There are many types of data in Python, but these are some of the most common:

Type	Description
Boolean	Can either be *True* or *False*.
Number	A number or fraction of any size. However, you can specify the type (and size) of number when you need to be specific.
String	A sequence of characters (letters). For example, "Hello, World!" is a string.
List	An ordered sequence of items. Each item can be any type of data (including other lists). See Using Lists and Dictionaries.
ByteArray	A list of bytes (small, 8-bit numbers). This is mainly used for writing binary files (see section 6.8) and when working with the Pi's GPIO pins.
Tuple	Like a list, except that the contents of tuples cannot be changed while the program is running.
Set	An unordered list where each item is unique.

Type	Description
Dictionary	A collection of key-value pairs. See Using Lists and Dictionaries below.

However, most things in Python are *objects*. You will learn more about these in section 6.6 Classes and Objects on page 144.

Using Lists and Dictionaries

Lists collect items together into a single variable. They are ordered – each slot in the list is given a number starting at zero.

To create a list, use square brackets. And then each item in the list is accessed using square brackets and the item number:

```
Beatles = ["John", "Paul", "Pete", "George"]
print(Beatles[0])
```

The items in a list can be changed:

```
Beatles[2] = "Ringo"
```

Lists are useful when you do not want to give each item a separate variable name, or when the amount of data that you have changes when the program is running.

You can find the length of a list using the function *len()*. For example, *len(Beatles)* gives the result *4*.

To delete an item from a list, use *del()*. When an item is deleted, all of the items that follow it move up one position. So, in this example, deleting the first item makes "Paul" the new first item. "Ringo" would then be second item, and "George" third.

There are also several useful "methods" that you access using a dot after the variable name. For example:

```
Beatles.reverse()
```

Method	Description
append(obj)	Adds the specified item to the end of the list.
count(obj)	Counts how many times the specified item appears in the list.
index(obj)	Searches the list for the specified item and returns its position in the list.
insert(position, obj)	Adds an item to the list in the specified position. All list items that follow are moved down a position.
remove(obj)	Removes the specified item from the list. For example: Beatles.remove("John").
reverse()	Reverses the order of items in the list.

A dictionary is a special type of list. Instead of accessing the item by its position in the list, you use a name. You create a dictionary using curly braces. For example:

```
Beatles =
{"Lead":"John","Bass":"Paul","Drums":"Pete","Guitar:","Ge
orge"}
```

Each item is now made up of a pair of values – a *key* (the name), and a *value*. To access the items in a dictionary, use the key inside square brackets. For example:

```
Beatles["Drums"] = "Ringo"
```

The *len()* and *del()* functions work the same way for dictionaries as they do for lists. And there are also several useful "methods" that you access using a dot after the variable name.

Method	Description
clear()	Removes all items from the dictionary.
copy()	Returns a copy of the dictionary.
has_key(key)	Returns *True* if the specified key is in the dictionary, or *False* if it is not.

Method	Description
keys()	Returns a list of the keys in the dictionary.
update(dic)	Adds the items from the specified dictionary to the current dictionary.
values()	Returns a list of the values in the dictionary.

6.3 Decisions

In Python, making a decision involves calculating whether an expression is *True*, or whether it is *False*. Depending on the result of that calculation, you can run different blocks of code.

The basic decision-making command in Python is the *if* statement.

```
if variable == value:
    doThis()
    andThis()
```

The == operator compares the two values and returns *True* if they are the same, or *False* if they are not. If the result is *True* then Python runs the commands below the *if* statement.

It is very important that you pay attention to the white space that you use around the commands under an *if* statement. Use the Tab key to indent lines that you want to run if the result of the comparison is *True*.

You can extend the *if* statement with another block of code that runs if the two values are not the same:

```
if variable == value:
    doThisIfTrue()
else:
    doThisIfFalse()
```

There are several other operators that you can use in Python:

Operator	Description
!=	Returns *True* if two values are not equal, and *False* if they are.
>	Returns *True* if the first number is greater than the second, and *False* if it is not.
<	Returns *True* if the first number is less than the second, and *False* if it is not.
>=	Returns *True* if the first number is greater than or equal to the second, and *False* if it is not.
<=	Returns *True* if the first number is less than or equal to the second, and *False* if it is not.

You can combine two (or more) expressions by surrounding each with parenthesis and then using one of the logical operators below.

For example:

```
if (variable1 == value) or (variable2 == value):
    doThis()
```

Operator	Description
and	Returns *True* if both expressions are *True*, and *False* if either one is *False*.
or	Returns *True* if either of the expressions is *True*. Returns *False* if they are both *False*.

You can use *not()* to reverse the result of an expression, turning *True* to *False* and *False* to *True*. For example:

```
if not(variable == value):
    doThis()
```

By using correct spacing, you can also put *if* statements inside the code that runs if an earlier *if* statement is *True*. However, using *elif* is often a little easier to read.

The example below runs *doThis1()* if the value of variable is *1*. If it is not, it checks whether the value is *2* and runs *doThis2()*. If it is not *2* either, it checks whether the value is *3* and runs *doThis3()*. If the value is not *1*, *2*, or *3* then it runs *doThisInAllOtherCases()*.

```
if variable == 1:
    doThis1()
elif variable == 2:
    doThis2()
elif variable == 3:
    doThis3()
else:
    doThisInAllOtherCases()
```

6.4 Loops

Loops are blocks of code that repeat a sequence of Python commands a set number times, or continually until a certain condition is met.

There are two types of loop in Python:

Loop	Description
while	Checks a condition in the same way as the *if* statement, and then runs the code underneath if the condition is *True*. Then it checks the condition again and if it is still *True*, it runs the code underneath again, and so on. The loop ends when the condition is *False*.
for	Runs the block of code for each item in a list or sequence. The loop ends when there are no more items.

There are two main ways to use a *while* loop.

To run something a set number of times, use a variable to keep track of how many times the loop is run. For example:

```
count = 0
while (count < 5):
    print("Hello")
    count = count + 1
```

This sends the message "Hello" to the terminal while the variable *count* contains a number that is less than 5. In effect, it prints "Hello" five times.

You can also use a *while* loop to run code until something happens. The example below continually prompts the user to type some text and echoes what they type back to them, until they press the Enter key without typing anything.

```
text = "?"
while not(text == ""):
    text = input("Type something (or nothing to quit). >")
    print(text)
```

The *for* loop is for "iterating" over a list or sequence. It runs as many times as there are items in the list, and assigns each one to a variable so that you can access it. For example, using the *Beatles* list that you saw earlier, you can print each item using a *for* loop.

```
Beatles = ["John", "Paul", "Ringo", "George"]
for beatle in Beatles:
    print(beatle)
```

 It is easy to write a loop that never ends. To stop a program that is running in the Python Shell or Linux terminal, press Ctrl + C.

There are two Python commands that you can use inside *while* and *for* loops, and that affect how a loop runs.

Command	Description
break	Immediately exits the loop.
continue	Restarts the loop, ignoring any other commands that are underneath the continue command.

6.5 Functions

Functions are one of the ways that you break a Python program into smaller chunks. This can help you manage projects, and it makes it easier for you to reuse parts of one project in another.

You have already seen a few examples of functions built-in to Python, but you can also create your own. When writing a function, you can choose whether it should accept arguments (values that are passed into the function), and whether it should return a value.

To create a function in Python:

1. Type the keyword *def* followed by the function's name.

2. Type opening and closing parenthesis – ().

3. If you want to accept arguments: type them between the parentheses and separate each one with a comma.

4. End the line with a colon.

5. (Optional) Add a string on the next line that describes the function.

6. Place any lines of code you want to include in the function on following lines, and use the Tab key to indent them.

7. If you want to return a value, use the command *return*.

For example:

```
def myFunction():
    "A function that prints a message. This line is
ignored."
    print("My first function")

def myFunction2(val1, val2):
    "A function that adds two numbers and returns the
result."
    return val1 + val2
```

Function names follow the same rules as variable names. They must start a letter (a–z, or A–Z), and the remaining characters in the name can be letters, numbers, or an underscore (_).

To call one of your functions from other parts of your code, use the function name and then parentheses. For example:

```
myFunction()
z = myFunction2(x, y)
```

To specify the arguments in a different order, you can use *keyword arguments*. As shown below, keyword arguments specify the parameter name before the argument.

```
myFunction2(val2=y, val1=x)
```

 An argument is a variable or value that you pass into a function. In the examples above, *x* and *y* are arguments. Parameters are part of the function's definition and refer to the names given to the data when it is passed to the function. For example, *val1* and *val2* are parameters.

It is important to realize that when you change an argument inside a function, the value of it also changes outside of the function. This is because Python actually passes a reference to the argument, not a copy of it.

For example:

```
def Inc(val):
    val = val + 1

x = 1
print(x)
Inc(x)
print(x)
```

Making Parameters Optional

Sometimes it can be useful to call a function without including all of the arguments. You can do this by specifying the default value that a parameter should have if an argument is not passed into the function.

```
def PrintAndMultiply(val1, val2 = 1):
    print(val1 * val2)
```

You can call this function with *PrintAndMultiply(5,2)* to see the value *10*, or just *PrintAndMultiply(5)*. If you do not pass the second argument, then Python assigns the value *1* to *val2* because that is the default specified in the function's definition.

6.6 Classes and Objects

Python is an object-oriented language. Object-oriented programming (OOP) is a way of writing code that treats data and concepts as standalone *objects*. These objects can contain multiple items of data ("fields"), and even functions that operate on that data ("methods").

There are several benefits to OOP:

- It is easier to reuse code in other projects.
- It breaks large projects down into smaller, more-manageable chunks.
- Certain types of information are well-suited to being represented as objects.
- Objects can "inherit" fields and methods from other objects.

As a simple example, consider an entry in your phone's address book or contact list. You can think of each entry as an object, and inside each object there are numerous fields. "First name" is one field, "Last name" is another, and so on.

Introducing Classes

In Python, a *class* is like a blueprint. It describes the structure of objects and defines their methods. To use an object, you need to create an *instance* of the class that describes it.

You create your own classes in Python by using the *class* keyword. For example:

```
class AddressBookEntry:
    firstname = ""
    lastname = ""
    telephone = ""
```

To create an instance of that class and get a usable object:

```
Alice = AddressBookEntry()
```

To access to the fields and methods that is inside an object, use the dot syntax.

```
Alice.firstname
Alice.lastname
```

You can add methods to the class by indenting them. To refer to fields inside the object from methods, use the keyword *self*.

```
class AddressBookEntry:
    firstname = ""
    lastname = ""
    telephone = ""

    def printName(self):
        print(self.firstname + " " + self.lastname)
```

To call the *printName()* method from other parts of your code, specify the variable name, then a dot, and then the method name. For example:

```
Alice.printName()
```

__init__ is a special method that Python runs when an instance of the class is created. You can write your own and use this to ensure that the correct arguments are passed into the code when you try to create an instance of the class. For example:

```
class AddressBookEntry:
    firstname = ""
    lastname = ""
    telephone = ""

    def __init__ (self, firstname, lastname):
        self.firstname = firstname
        self.lastname = lastname
```

```
Mark = AddressBookEntry(firstname="Mark",lastname="White")
```

Inheriting Fields and Methods

Inheritance is where objects that are similar share parts of their structure. Using the address book example again, you could have a separate object for business contacts. Since this object contains the same basic information (name, phone number, and so on), it can inherit those fields from the standard entry object. But then you can add other fields that are specific to business contacts (such as company name and website).

```
class AddressBookEntry:
    firstname = ""
    lastname = ""
    telephone = ""

    def __init__ (self, firstname, lastname):
        self.firstname = firstname
        self.lastname = lastname

    def printName(self):
        print(self.firstname + " " + self.lastname)

class BusinessContactEntry(AddressBookEntry):
    company = ""
```

Create an instance of *BusinessContactEntry* using the syntax:

```
Bob =
BusinessContactEntry(firstname="Bob",lastname="Smith")
```

Even though the *BusinessContactEntry* class only defines the field *company*, the fields *firstname*, *lastname*, and *telephone* are also usable. It inherits these fields from *AddressBookEntry*.

```
Bob.firstname = "Bob"
Bob.company = "Bob's Widgets, Inc."
Bob.printName()
```

This relationship does not work the other way. Since *AddressBookEntry* does not inherit from *BusinessContactEntry*,

you cannot access the *company* field from an instance of
AddressBookEntry.

Overriding Inherited Methods

In the example above, the *BusinessContactEntry* class inherits
the *printName()* method from *AddressBookEntry*. However, if
you include a new definition of *__init__* and *printName()* in
BusinessContactEntry then you can override the inherited
versions.

```
class BusinessContactEntry(AddressBookEntry):
    company = ""

    def __init__(self, firstname, lastname, company):
        self.firstname = firstname
        self.lastname = lastname
        self.company = company

    def printName(self):
        print(self.firstname+" "+self.lastname+" (" +
self.company + ")")
```

Where this gets interesting, is if you have a function like the
example below:

```
def printEntry(entry):
    entry.printName()
```

This function accepts either type of object, and does not know
the difference. It simply calls the method *printName()* and the
two different types of object respond slightly differently.

Hiding Fields and Methods

In Python, you can stop other parts of your code accessing fields
and methods in an object by defining them with a name that
starts with two underscore characters.

```
class HiddenData:
    __vat = ""

    def __setVat(self, value):
        self.__vat = value
```

The field __*vat* and the method __*setVat* can only be accessed by code in the *HiddenData* object. You cannot access them from other parts of your program.

6.7 Modules and Packages

A module is a collection of functions and classes that are related to a specific purpose. You can download modules that are written by other programmers and use them in your projects.

Raspbian already has a large number of Python modules pre-installed. To see a list of all the modules that are installed on your Pi:

1. On the desktop, double-click **IDLE3**.
2. In the **Python Shell**, type the following command and then press **Enter**:

    ```
    help("modules")
    ```

Some of the most useful ones, particularly for Pi owners, are:

Module	Description
base64	Functions for encoding and decoding in Base16, Base32, and Base64 formats.
curses	Functions for creating text-based terminal-style windows with advanced features.
http	Modules for making and receiving hypertext transfer protocol (HTTP) requests over the web.
math	Advanced math functions.
picamera	Provides access to the Raspberry Pi camera from Python scripts.
PIL	Python Imaging Library. Adds the ability to edit and convert image files from your Python scripts.
RPi.GPIO	Functions to control the Pi's GPIO pins from Python.

Module	Description
xml	Contains classes for working with extensible markup language (XML) files in Python.

Installing a Module

You can find many additional Python modules that you can download and install with the Package Manager in Raspbian.

If you download a module without using the Package Manager, you will have to install it yourself. Modules usually come with an installation script (*setup.py*) that copies the module(s) to the correct location on your system. To run it:

1. On the desktop, double-click **LXTerminal**.
2. Move into the folder that contains the module that you want to install. Use the **cd** command.
3. Type the following command and then press **Enter**:

   ```
   python3 setup.py install
   ```

Using a Module

Before you can use a class or function from a module, you need to *import* it into your project.

To import the entire module, put an import statement at the top of your .py script. For example, to import the *math* module use the statement:

```
import math
```

Then access items from a module using the dot syntax, as you do when working with objects. For example, to call the *floor()* function in the *math* module:

```
math.floor(10.3)
```

If you only want to import a specific item from a module, rather than everything that the module contains, you can use the *from…import* syntax. In the following example, only the *floor()*

function is imported and so the call to the *ceil()* function generates an error.

```
from math import floor
print(floor(10.3))
print(ceil(10.7))
```

Learning about Packages

Packages group modules together in *namespaces* – organized and hierarchical trees of modules. Working with namespaces is a little like working with the file system, except that you use dots instead of slashes.

 You use package names when importing modules and reading their documentation. So you will become familiar with how this works without having to make a special effort.

6.8 File I/O

Working with files and folders from Python is important on Raspbian, because many of the system processes and devices are mapped into the file system.

Opening a File

To read from or write to a file in Python, you need to open it using the built-in function *open()*. In its basic form, *open()* accepts two arguments:

```
open(filename [, mode])
```

If the file is not in the same directory as your Python script, you need to specify the full path to the file.

Mode is optional and if you do not specify it then Python opens the file in read-only mode. This means that you cannot change the file, only read data from it. The most-common values that are used here are:

Mode	Description
r	Open the file for reading.
rb	Open the file for reading in binary format.
w	Open the file for writing only. This overwrites the existing file or, if it does not exist, creates the file.
wb	Open the file for writing only, in binary format.
a	Open a file for "appending". Anything you write is added to the end. This overwrites the existing file or, if it does not exist, creates the file.
ab	Open a file for appending binary data.

Python makes a distinction between working with a text file and working with a binary file. The key difference between the two is that with text files Python deals with the text encoding and line break formats for you. In binary mode, you have access to each byte that makes up the file, and it is up to you to decide how to process them.

When reading and writing to a text file, you can only use *string* objects. When reading and writing to a binary file, use *bytes* and *bytearray* objects.

Reading from a Text File

To read from a file, open it using the mode "r", or any of the other modes that support reading. Then use the method *read()* to read a number of characters from the file.

You must remember to close files once you are finished working with them. Do this with the *close()* method. If you do not close a file then you might be unable to work with the file again, until you restart the Pi.

For example, to read the "message of the day" (MOTD) file:

```
motd = open("/etc/motd", "r")
message = motd.read()
```

```
print(message)
motd.close()
```

If you do not specify how many characters to read, *read()* will fetch the entire contents of the file. To read only ten characters:

```
motd.read(10)
```

If you specify more characters to read then the file has left, Python reads as many characters as it can. When Python reaches the end of the file, the string returned by a call to *read()* will have a length of zero.

Writing Text to a File

To create a new text file and write a test message to it, open the file using mode "w". Then use the method *write()*. For example:

```
test = open("/home/pi/Desktop/Test.txt", "w")
test.write("Hello from Python!")
test.close()
```

If you run this example twice, you will see that the text file on your desktop still only contains one sentence.

Appending Text to a File

To add content to the end of a file, use one of the "append" modes when opening the file. For example:

```
test = open("/home/pi/Desktop/Test.txt", "a")
test.write("Another hello from Python!")
test.close()
```

If you open the file *Test.txt* now, you should see that the string has been added to the end of the file.

Renaming and Deleting Files

To rename a file, import *os* and then use the *rename()* function:

```
import os
os.rename("/home/pi/Desktop/Test.txt", "/home/pi/Desktop/Test2.txt")
```

To delete a file, use the *remove()* function:

```
import os
os.remove("/home/pi/Desktop/Test2.txt")
```

Working with Folders

The *os* module also includes many functions for creating and working with folders. Here are some of the ones you will use often:

Function	Description
mkdir(path)	Creates a new folder at the specified path.
makedirs(path)	Creates a new folder at the specified path, and any folders above it that do not exist yet.
listdir(path)	Returns a "list" of the contents of the specified folder.
removedirs(path)	Removes (deletes) the specified folder and everything inside it.
rename(path, path)	Changes the name of a folder.

6.9 Graphical User Interfaces (GUIs)

Although all of the examples in this chapter have assumed that you are running Python programs from the Python Shell or the Linux terminal, it is possible to build full GUIs in Python. To do this, you need to use a GUI toolkit (or "framework") that supports all of the different types of controls that you need – windows, textboxes, and buttons, for example.

To create a Python program with a GUI that also runs on other operating systems, you have to use a framework that is available on all of the machines on which you want to run your program. A full list of cross-platform GUI toolkits is available at *http:// wiki.python.org/moin/GuiProgramming*. Of these, the *TkInter* framework is particularly popular and is already installed on Raspbian.

7 – Controlling Input and Output Pins

One of the differences between the Raspberry Pi and the desktop computers, smartphones, and tablets that you may have used, is that the Pi is designed with a 40-pin connector that you can control from your own software. This makes it similar to development boards like the Arduino, but the Pi has the power and speed of a regular computer.

The 40-pin header is made-up of many general purpose input and output (GPIO) pins. In this context, "general purpose" means that you can use them for whatever you like – for example: turning on light-emitting diodes (LEDs); working with sensors (devices that read things like temperature and light levels); moving servos and motors; and talking to electronic circuits that you build yourself.

In this chapter, you will learn some of the techniques and knowledge that you need to build basic electronic circuits, and then see how to control the GPIO pins from Raspbian.

 Poorly designed or incorrectly assembled circuits can damage the Raspberry Pi, and may be hazardous to the person using or building them. Always seek advice from a qualified person if you are not sure about what you are doing.

7.1 Electronic Circuits, Voltage and Current

Electricity is a form of energy that flows in a circuit (a loop). It can be helpful to think of it starting from one connector on a battery or power supply, and then moving around the circuit until it reaches the other connector. Along the way, it provides power to the components that you place in the circuit. If the circuit is broken at any point, then electricity cannot flow and so nothing will receive power.

A *schematic* is a drawing that shows how different components can be connected together. For example:

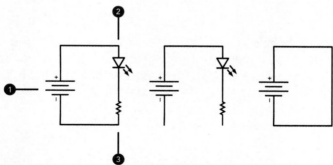

Figure 1. Three types of circuit – closed (left), open (middle), and short (right).

1	Battery or power source. This supplies the circuit with electricity.
2	Light-emitting diode (LED). When power flows, it lights up.
3	Resistor. See below.

In a *closed* circuit, electricity can flow from the + terminal, to the - terminal (*ground* in digital electronics). It passes through the LED, which causes it to glow. But in an *open* circuit, electricity cannot flow all the way around to ground so it does not move at all. In this example, the LED does not light. A switch works by opening and closing the circuit.

A *short* circuit can be dangerous. There is a direct connection between the + and - terminals on the battery. With no components in between, there is nothing to use or limit the amount of electricity that flows.

Voltage is the amount of force that pushes electricity around a circuit and it is measured in volts (V). For example, 5 V or 9 V. You will often see 3.3 V written as "3V3" in diagrams where a dot might be difficult to read.

Current is the amount of electrical charge in a circuit. It is current that makes things happen, like lighting an LED. It is measured in amps and this is shown with an A. For example, 1 A or 3 A. But electronic circuits usually use very small amounts of current, and so milliamps (mA, or thousandths of an amp) can be used instead.

The *resistance* of a circuit limits the amount of current that flows and protects components. It is measured in ohms, and written with the symbol Ω. *Resistors* have color-coded stripes that indicate the amount of resistance that they put in a circuit.

7.2 Solderless Breadboards

Breadboards (or "solderless breadboards") are easy ways of connecting components temporarily.

The various rows of holes are joined together inside the board. On a standard breadboard, there are four long rows. The holes in each row are joined together inside the board, but none of these rows are joined to each other.

In the middle of the board, the holes are divided into columns. Column 15 is highlighted on the diagram below.

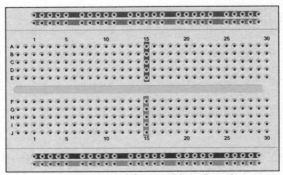

Figure 2. Layout of a typical breadboard

A15–E15 are joined, and F15–J15 are also joined. But the two groups are not connected together or to any other columns.

Connecting the Raspberry Pi to a Breadboard

In electronics, a male connector is a pin, plug, or wire that slots into a *female* connector. Female connectors are usually sockets or jacks. Unlike the designers of other development boards, the Raspberry Pi Foundation use *male* pins for the GPIO headers on the Pi. To connect the Pi to a solderless breadboard, you can either use:

- A 40-pin female-to-female ribbon cable; or
- Individual female-to-male jumper wires.

If you use a female-to-female ribbon cable, you need to use regular male-to-male jumper wires or a Raspberry Pi B+ GPIO breakout board to connect the socket on the cable to holes on the breadboard.

7.3 The GPIO Header

The 40-pin GPIO header is located in the top-left of the Pi. The pins are numbered from left to right, but odd-numbered pins are on the lower row and even-numbered pins are on the top-row.

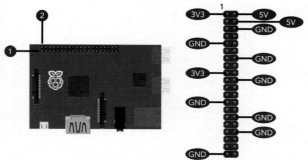

Figure 3. Location of the GPIO header (left), and the power and ground connections (right)

You can configure most of the GPIO pins as inputs or outputs and control them. But some have additional uses:

Pin #	Name	Description
3	GPIO2	Input/output. Or I2C wire SDA (I2C1_SDA).
5	GPIO3	Input/output. Or I2C wire SCL (I2C1_SCL).

158

Pin #	Name	Description
7	GPIO4	Input/output. Or provides a master clock output (GPCLK0) to external circuits.
8	GPIO14	Input/output. Or UART transmit pin (UART_TXD).
10	GPIO15	Input/output. Or UART receive pin (UART_RXD).
11	GPIO17	Input/output.
12	GPIO18	Input/output.
13	GPIO27	Input/output.
15	GPIO22	Input/output.
16	GPIO23	Input/output.
18	GPIO24	Input/output.
19	GPIO10	Input/output. Or SPI master-output wire (SPI_MOSI).
21	GPIO9	Input/output. Or SPI master-input wire (SPI_MISO).
22	GPIO25	Input/output.
23	GPIO11	Input/output. Or SPI clock wire (SPI_SCLK).
24	GPIO8	Input/output. Or SPI device select 0 (SPI_CE0).
26	GPIO7	Input/output. Or SPI device select 1 (SPI_CE1).
27	ID_SD	Reserved.
28	ID_SC	Reserved.
29	GPIO5	Input/output.
31	GPIO6	Input/output.
32	GPIO12	Input/output.
33	GPIO13	Input/output.
35	GPIO19	Input/output.
36	GPIO16	Input/output.
37	GPIO26	Input/output.
38	GPIO20	Input/output.

Pin #	Name	Description
40	GPIO21	Input/output.

The GPIO pins are rated for 3.3 V. They are not 5 V tolerant and so applying more than 3.3 V to an input pin can break the Pi.

 GPIO0 and *GPIO1* do not appear in this pinout. These functions are shared with the *ID_SC* and *ID_SD* pins, which must only be connected to a special identification EEPROM. Do not use them.

7.4 Basic Output

Blinking an LED is the electronics equivalent of the "Hello, World!" program. In this example, you will:

1. Make a circuit using an LED and 270 Ω resistor.
2. Learn how to set a GPIO pin to an output.
3. Turn the LED on and off from a terminal window, and from a Python script.

LEDs must be placed in a circuit in the correct direction as electricity only flows one way through them. One leg of an LED is longer than the other – this is called the "anode" and it is the one that receives power. The other leg is called the "cathode", and this the output leg. In Figure 4 you can also see that on the anode side, the piece of metal inside the LED is smaller.

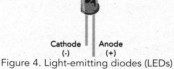

Cathode   Anode
(-)   (+)
Figure 4. Light-emitting diodes (LEDs)

It does not matter in which direction you place the resistor.

Unplug the Pi, and then build the circuit in Figure 5. If you do not have a 270 Ω resistor, then you can use a resistor of a slightly greater value. Try to avoid using smaller value resistors – if there is not enough resistance in the circuit then the LED will draw too much current and break.

 Each input/output pin on the GPIO header can only supply 16 mA of current, and the Pi can only supply 50 mA of current to all of the pins in total.

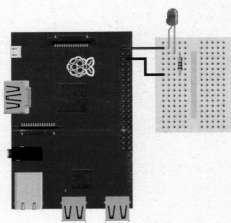

Figure 5. Lighting an LED

Check that:

1. The + leg of the LED is on the same row as the 3.3 V wire, and the - leg of the LED is not on the same row.

2. The top wire is connected to pin 1 (3.3 V).

3. The bottom wire is connected to pin 6 (ground).

Connect the Pi to its power source and the LED will turn on. If it does not, unplug the power immediately, and then check that:

1. You have placed the LED in the correct direction. The anode receives power, the cathode allows the power to flow out and into the next component.

2. You have placed the LED, resistors, and wires in the correct holes on the breadboard.

3. You have an appropriate value resistor. If the resistance is too great, you won't be able to see that the LED is on.

So far, you are using the Pi as a battery. But now that you know your circuit works, you can place the LED under the Pi's control:

1. Shutdown the Pi and unplug it from the power.
2. Disconnect the red 3.3 V wire from header pin 1, and then connect it to pin 3 (GPIO2).
3. Plug the power back into the Raspberry Pi, and allow Raspbian to load.

When the Pi boots, *GPIO2* is often brought high. A *high* signal is 3.3 V, a *low* signal is connected to ground (0 V).

Controlling GPIO2 from a Terminal Window

You can control the GPIO pins from a terminal window in Raspbian. But only the superuser can do this. For more information about users and superusers, see Understanding Linux Users and Superusers on page 37.

If you want to control the pins from the terminal, you first need to *export* the pin. This creates a special folder in the file system that you can use to change the pin from an input to an output, send the pin high, or send the pin low.

1. On the **LXDE panel**, click the **Menu** button, point to **Accessories**, and then click **Root Terminal**.
2. Type the following command and then press **Enter**:
    ```
    echo 2 > /sys/class/gpio/export
    ```
3. Type the following command and then press **Enter**:
    ```
    ls /sys/class/gpio/gpio2
    ```

The files that you see in the *gpio2* directory control the state of *GPIO2*. When exporting GPIO pins, the number you use is the GPIO number not the pin number.

To set *GPIO2* as an output and turn it on:

1. In the **Root Terminal**, type the following command and then press **Enter**:

   ```
   echo out > /sys/class/gpio/gpio2/direction
   ```

2. Type the following command and then press **Enter**:

   ```
   echo 1 > /sys/class/gpio/gpio2/value
   ```

To turn *GPIO2* off:

- In the **Root Terminal**, type the following command and then press **Enter**:

  ```
  echo 0 > /sys/class/gpio/gpio2/value
  ```

When you are done, it is a good practice to *unexport* the pin so that it is no longer under the control of the file system entries:

- In the **Root Terminal**, type the following command and then press **Enter**:

  ```
  echo 2 > /sys/class/gpio/unexport
  ```

As a final note, outputting *0* actually connects the GPIO pin to ground inside the Pi. So anything connected to that pin is also brought to ground.

Controlling GPIO2 from Python 3

From Python, you can control the GPIO pins using the *RPi.GPIO* module. This example sets *GPIO2* as an output, and then blinks the LED by repeatedly turning it on and off again. To do this, you also need to import the *time* module, which contains a function for causing a delay.

1. On the desktop, double-click **IDLE3**.

2. In the **Python Shell**, on the **Menu**, click **File**, and then click **New Window**.

3. On the **Menu**, click **File**, and then click **Save As**.

4. Save the file to your desktop, with the extension *.py*.

5. At the top of the file, type the following statements:

```
import RPi.GPIO
import time
```

6. On a new line, type the following statement:

```
RPi.GPIO.setmode(RPi.GPIO.BCM)
```

setMode() is a function in the RPi.GPIO module that sets how you are going to refer to pins. There are two options for this:

- BOARD states that when you pass the value 2 into functions in the RPi.GPIO module, you are referring to pin 2.
- BCM states that when you pass the value 2 into functions in the RPi.GPIO module, you are referring to GPIO2.

Now you need to configure GPIO2 as an output:

- On a new line, type the following statement:

```
RPi.GPIO.setup(2, RPi.GPIO.OUT)
```

The function setup() accepts two arguments: the first is the pin or GPIO number (depending on whether you use BOARD or BCM in the call to setMode()); and the second can be RPi.GPIO.IN or RPi.GPIO.OUT. To make a pin an output, use RPi.GPIO.OUT.

Now add the following code to the script and save the file:

```
while True:
    RPi.GPIO.output(2, True)
    time.sleep(1)
    RPi.GPIO.output(2, False)
    time.sleep(1)
```

The function output() sets the output pin high when the second argument is True. It sets the output pin low when the second argument is False. If you prefer, you can use RPi.GPIO.HIGH and RPi.GPIO.LOW instead of True and False.

The call to sleep() causes Python to wait one second before moving on to the next instruction. If you want to blink the LED slower, increase the value that you pass into sleep(). For example, *sleep(2)*. If you want to blink the LED faster, decrease the value that you pass into *sleep()*. For example, *sleep(0.5)*.

You cannot run this script from IDLE3, because controlling the GPIO pins requires superuser access. To run your script:

1. On the desktop, double-click **LXTerminal**.
2. Browse to your script. For example, if you saved the file as *test.py* on the desktop:

   ```
   cd Desktop
   ```
3. Type the following command and then press **Enter**. Change *test.py* to the name of your script.

   ```
   sudo python3 test.py
   ```

The LED will now blink on and off. Because the *while* loop in this script never receives *False*, the script runs forever. To stop the script, press **Ctrl + C**.

7.5 Basic Input

With the GPIO pins, input involves finding out whether the voltage that is coming into a pin from your external circuit is *high*, or whether it is *low*. In this section, you will see how to detect when a switch is closed. Any switch will work for this, but two-terminal on/off switches and four-terminal tactile push buttons are the ones that people use most often.

With four-terminal push buttons, it can be difficult to see which way round in the circuit you should place them. The top-left and top-right terminals are always joined. The top-left and bottom-left terminals are only joined when the switch is pressed. So if your circuit always detects that the switch is pressed, rotate the button 90° in a clockwise direction.

Do not wire a switch on its own between the 3.3 V power-output pin and a GPIO input. When the switch is pressed, 3.3 V flows into the input pin and brings the input high. But there are two potential problems with this:

1. When the switch is not pressed the input pin can be *floating*. When a pin floats, it is neither high nor low, and can change between the two seemingly at random.

2. When the switch is pressed, there is very little resistance in the circuit and so this can damage the Pi. It is, effectively, a short circuit.

Introducing Pull-Up and Pull-Down Resistors

In the diagram below, when the switch is open, electricity flows through the resistor and into the GPIO pin. So when the switch is open, the GPIO pin is high. When the switch is closed, all of the electricity is drawn to ground, and this creates a low on the GPIO pin. So the pin is always in one or state or the other, it is never floating.

Pulling the line up in this way is called using a *pull-up resistor*.

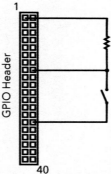

Figure 6. A switch and a pull-up resistor

A *pull-down* resistor works in the opposite way: when the switch is open, the GPIO pin is tied to ground and is low. But when the switch is closed, electricity flows into the GPIO pin and it is high.

The Raspberry Pi has pull-up and pull-down resistors built-in to all of the GPIO pins. And you can choose which ones you want to use from your software programs.

Building the Circuit

On the Pi, the circuit above has a problem. If the GPIO pin (the middle line on the diagram) is accidently set to a high output (either by the user or by the Pi when it is starting-up) then pressing the switch causes a short circuit and can damage the Pi.

Build the circuit in Figure 7. It relies on the Pi's internal pull-up resistor but also adds a 330 Ω resistor to protect the Pi if the GPIO pin is changed to an output.

If the GPIO is a high output then the electricity flows through the 330 Ω resistor and this is enough to protect the Pi. The resistor must be a high-enough value to protect the Pi but low enough so that electricity prefers to flow to ground when you press the switch, rather than into the GPIO pin.

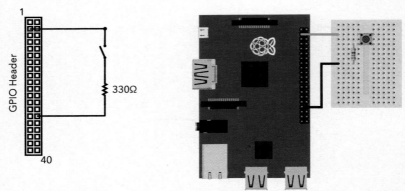

Figure 7. Basic input – schematic (left), and breadboard (right)

With the GPIO pin configured as an input and the Pi's internal pull-up resistor enabled, if the switch is open then the pull-up brings the GPIO pin high. If the switch is pressed, the connection to ground drains the electricity from the pin and this causes it to go low.

Reading a GPIO Pin from a Terminal Window

To read the state of *GPIO2* from the terminal or shell, you need to export the pin to the file system.

1. On the **LXDE panel**, click the **Menu** button, point to **Accessories**, and then click **Root Terminal**.

2. Type the following command and then press **Enter**:

   ```
   echo 2 > /sys/class/gpio/export
   ```

To configure the pin as an input and enable the internal pull-up resistor:

1. In the **Root Terminal**, type the following command and then press **Enter**:

   ```
   echo in > /sys/class/gpio/gpio2/direction
   ```

2. Type the following command and then press **Enter**:

   ```
   echo 0 > /sys/class/gpio/gpio2/active_low
   ```

To read the pin, you can use the *cat* command, which is used to read files and display them in the terminal:

1. In the **Root Terminal**, type the following command and then press **Enter**:

   ```
   cat /sys/class/gpio/gpio2/value
   ```

2. Type the following command but do NOT press the Enter key:

   ```
   cat /sys/class/gpio/gpio2/value
   ```

3. Press the switch (hold it if you are using a push button), and then press **Enter**.

When you are done, unexport the pin so that it is no longer under the control of the file system entries:

- In the **Root Terminal**, type the following command and then press **Enter**:

  ```
  echo 2 > /sys/class/gpio/unexport
  ```

Reading a GPIO Pin from Python 3

As for output pins, you can use the *RPi.GPIO* module to read from an input pin, and the *setMode()* method to state how you want to refer to pin numbers.

1. Create a new Python script and save it with the extension *.py*.

2. At the top of the script, type the following statements:

```
import RPi.GPIO
RPi.GPIO.setmode(RPi.GPIO.BCM)
```

Now you need to configure *GPIO2* as an input and enable the internal pull-up resistors:

- Add the following statement on one line:

```
RPi.GPIO.setup(2, RPi.GPIO.IN,
pull_up_down=RPi.GPIO.PUD_UP)
```

The *pull_up_down* parameter can be one of three values:

Value	Description
RPi.GPIO.PUD_UP	Activates the internal pull-up resistor.
RPi.GPIO.PUD_DOWN	Activates the internal pull-down resistor.
RPi.GPIO.PUD_OFF	Disables the pull-up and pull-down resistors.

Add the remainder of the code to the script:

```
while True:
    if RPi.GPIO.input(2) == RPi.GPIO.LOW:
        print("Switch pressed.")
        break
RPi.GPIO.cleanup()
```

This script loops until the switch is pressed and *GPIO2* goes low. At that point, it prints a message to the user, *breaks* from the *while* loop and then releases its control over the GPIO pin.

7.6 Communication between 3.3 V and 5 V Devices

Even though the Pi has a 5 V power supply, it is a 3.3 V device and 3.3 V is the maximum voltage that you can safely connect to its input pins. However, most other popular development boards, sensors, and components are 5 V devices.

To connect 5 V outputs to an input on the Pi, you will need to convert the voltage levels so that high signals are only 3.3 V.

 The high signal from the Pi is usually enough to ensure that the 5 V device detects the line as high. This section is primarily concerned with protecting the Pi's input pins.

If you need to convert more than a two or three signals, then a bi-directional logic level converter chip is a useful purchase. But if you only need to convert one or two signals then there several methods you can use. Two are shown here.

1. Using a Voltage Divider

In the example below, the two resistors form a potential divider. This divides the voltage and allows enough of it to pass to ground so that the GPIO pin only receives around 3.3 V. The exact resistor values are not too important – but the first resistor must be slightly over half the value of the second resistor or the divider does not work correctly.

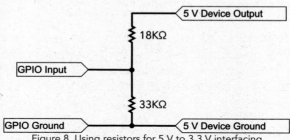

Figure 8. Using resistors for 5 V to 3.3 V interfacing

2. Using a Diode and Pull-Up Resistor

Diodes are passive components that only allow electricity to flow in one direction. On schematics, they resemble an arrow and this indicates the direction in which electricity can flow. On an actual diode, there is a thick line that corresponds to the vertical line on the schematic symbol.

In Figure 9, when the output on the 5 V device is low then it is actually connected to ground. This means that the electricity from the 3.3 V supply passes through the diode and into the 5 V device, pulling low the GPIO pin on the Pi. When the 5 V device outputs a high signal, the diode blocks the voltage. But because the diode is blocking, the 3.3 V cannot flow to the 5 V device and so it flows into the GPIO pin on the Pi – creating a high signal.

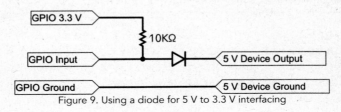

Figure 9. Using a diode for 5 V to 3.3 V interfacing

7.7 Serial Peripheral Interface (SPI)

Serial peripheral interface (SPI) is a serial data protocol that is used by microcontrollers and small electronic devices to exchange information. The term "serial" means that each bit of a binary number (for example, the number 255 is made up of eight bits in binary – 11111111) is sent one at a time, on the same wire.

SPI divides devices into two categories: *masters*, and *slaves*. The master is the device that starts the communication. The slave receives instructions from the master and does what it is told. A master can talk to many slave devices, but usually only one at a time.

To use SPI, you need four pins:

Pin Name	Description
MOSI	Master output, slave input. The master uses this line to send information to the slave.
MISO	Master input, slave output. The master uses this line to read information from the slave.
SCK	Serial clock. Each bit is read on the "edge" of the clock signal.

Pin Name	Description
SS	Slave select. Use one of these for each slave device in the circuit. The master uses this wire to indicate which slave device should listen and respond to instructions.

When the master sends information to a slave, it usually:

1. Pulls the *SS* line low for the selected slave.
2. Brings the *MOSI* line high if the bit it is sending is *1*; or brings *MOSI* low if the bit is *0*.
3. *Pulses* the *SCK* line. For example, if the clock line is low when SPI is not being used, then pulsing the line involves briefly bringing the clock line high and then bringing it low again.
4. Repeats this process until all of the bits are sent.
5. Brings the *SS* line high.

When the master reads information from a slave, it usually:

1. Pulls the *SS* line low for the selected slave.
2. Pulses the *SCK* line.
3. Reads whether the *MISO* line is high, or low.
4. Repeats this process until it has all of the information that it is expecting.
5. Brings the *SS* line high to end communication with the slave.

With some devices, the master sends a command to the slave device to tell it to send data. In these cases, the master moves between the sending and reading phases without changing the *SS* line.

There is some variety in how different SPI devices expect these two processes to work. Some require that the clock line is high when it is not in-use, and others require it to be low. Some SPI slave devices expect their *SS* line to be high when the master wants to communicate with it, and others expect the *SS* line to be low.

Enabling SPI on the Raspberry Pi

You can use any of the GPIO input/output pins for SPI since it only involves bringing pins high and low, and reading input in the same way as described earlier in this chapter. This approach is often called "bit-banging". However, five of the Raspberry Pi's GPIO pins have alternative uses for communicating over SPI. By using these pins you can use prebuilt libraries and tools instead of writing as much code.

The SPI pins on the GPIO header are: MOSI – pin 19; MISO – pin 21; SCK – pin 23. The header has two slave select pins – pin 24 and pin 26.

By default, the SPI functions of these pins are disabled in Raspbian. To enable them:

1. On the Raspbian desktop, double-click **LXTerminal**.

2. Type the following command and then press **Enter**:

   `sudo raspi-config`

3. Press the **Down Arrow** key seven times to select **Advanced Options**, and then press **Enter**.

4. Press the **Down Arrow** key four times to select **SPI**, and then press **Enter**.

5. Press **Enter**.

6. Press **Enter**.

7. Press the **Right Arrow** key twice to select **<Finish>**. Then press **Enter**.

8. Type the following command and then press **Enter**:

   `sudo nano /etc/modules`

9. On a new line at the end of the file, add the following text:

   `spi-dev`

10. Press **Ctrl + O**, and then press **Enter**.

11. Press **Ctrl + X**.

12. Type the following command and then press **Enter**:

    ```
    sudo shutdown –r now
    ```

When the Pi restarts, the SPI modules load automatically.

Using SPI from Python 3

To use SPI from Python, you need to install the *python3-dev* libraries, and a module for Python that makes the SPI devices accessible.

1. On the Raspbian desktop, double-click **LXTerminal**.

2. Type the following command and then press **Enter**:

    ```
    sudo apt-get install python3-dev
    ```

3. When the installation is complete, type the following command and then press **Enter**:

    ```
    git clone git://github.com/rpodgornypy-spidev
    ```

4. Type the following command and then press **Enter**:

    ```
    cd py-spidev
    ```

5. Type the following command and then press **Enter**:

    ```
    sudo python3 setup.py install
    ```

When connecting the Pi to SPI devices, the GPIO pin *MOSI* (master output, slave input) connects to the *SI* (slave input) pin on the external device. Similarly, the GPIO pin *MISO* (master input, slave output) connects to the *SO* (slave output) pin.

Figure 10 shows how to connect the Raspberry Pi to a 64 Kb SPI SRAM chip from Microchip Technology, Inc. The 23K640 is a 3.3 V, 8-pin device that you can use to store a byte in each of its 8192 slots (or "addresses"). This means that the chip has 8 KB (64 Kb) of volatile storage.

> ▼ Volatile memory chips lose their contents when you disconnect
> them from the power. Non-volatile memory chips, such as "flash"
> memory technologies, retain their contents.

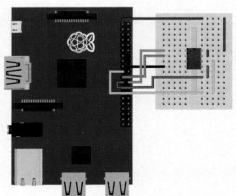

Figure 10. Connecting a 23K640 SPI memory chip to the Pi

To use SPI in Python:

1. On the desktop, double-click **IDLE3**.

2. In the **Python Shell**, on the **Menu**, click **File** and then click **New Window**.

3. Type the following at the start of the script:

    ```
    import spidev
    import time
    ```

To create an instance of the *SpiDev* class and open a connection, add the statements:

```
spi = spidev.SpiDev()
spi.open(0, 0)
```

The first parameter to *open()* is the device number. Only one SPI master device is available on the GPIO header and so this is always zero. The second parameter is the slave select pin that you want to use. *0* tells the module to use pin 24, and *1* tells it to use pin 26.

To write a byte to the SPI device, you can use the *xfer()* method. For example:

```
spi.xfer([2,0,0,8])
```

The *xfer()* method accepts one argument, and that is an array of bytes. When you call this method, the slave select pin is brought low and then it sends the values in the byte array to the SPI device. The clock signal is generated for you.

To write a byte to the 23K640, you send the WRITE command (2), followed by two bytes that form a 16-bit address, then the value to be stored (8):

```
[2,0,0,8]
```

You also use the *xfer()* method to read from an SPI device. The slave device expects the master to generate the clock pulses that it needs to transmit data. So you may need to include extra bytes in the call to *xfer()*.

For example, if an SPI device expects the master to send the sequence 3,0,0 before it sends back a byte then you would pass an extra 0 into *xfer()*. This generates the additional clock signals for the value that the device is sending.

```
spi.xfer([3,0,0,0])
```

The code below is a short, but complete, example of how to use SPI to read and write to a 23K640 SRAM.

```
import spidev
import time

spi = spidev.SpiDev()
spi.open(0, 0)

def Read23K640(addr1, addr2):
    vals = spi.xfer([3, addr1, addr2, 0])
    return vals[3]

def Write23K640(addr1, addr2, value):
    spi.xfer([2, addr1, addr2, value])
```

```
Write23K640(0, 0, 8)
print(Read23K640(0, 0))
```

You can use several properties of the *SpiDev* class to change how the SPI methods work. This is useful when you are using SPI devices that do not follow the usual process.

Property	Description
cshigh	When *True*, a high signal is used to tell the slave device that it should listen and respond. When *False*, a low signal is used. *False* is the default.
max_speed_hz	Not all SPI devices can run as fast as the Pi. Decrease the value of this property to slow the SPI transmissions down.
mode	Sets the clock polarity and phase. Can be 0–2.

7.8 I2C Communication

I2C (pronounced eye-too-see) is another serial communications protocol, but it uses fewer wires. The master device controls I2C communications, and you connect all slave devices to the same wires. Each slave device has a unique number (called an "address") and it only responds to messages that it receives which specify this address. This means that you cannot use two slave devices that have the same address.

The two I2C lines are called *SDA* and *SCL*. You need to use a pull-up resistor on these lines. The value of the resistors is not very important, but around 10 KΩ is generally suitable.

I2C can be convenient on the Pi because you only have to convert the logic level of the SDA wire to interface with 5 V devices (regardless of how many 5 V slave devices you actually connect to those lines).

Any GPIO pins can be used for I2C, if you want to write all of the code. But it is a more complicated protocol to implement from scratch. To use prebuilt I2C libraries and modules, the two I2C wires are pin 3 and pin 5 of the GPIO header.

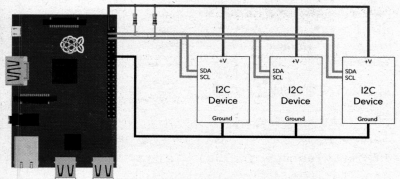

Figure 11. I2C communication between the Pi and multiple devices

Enabling I2C

On Raspbian, I2C is disabled. To enable it, you must first remove I2C from the module "blacklist". This is a file that stops Raspbian loading certain modules. To remove I2C from the list:

1. On the desktop, double-click **LXTerminal**.

2. Type the following command and then press **Enter**:

   ```
   sudo nano /etc/modprobe.d/raspi-blacklist.conf
   ```

3. If you see lines in this file that read *blacklist spi-bcm2708* or *blacklist i2c-bm2708* then add a # symbol at the start of the lines. This makes the line into a comment so that Raspbian ignores it.

4. Press **Ctrl + O**, and then press **Enter**.

5. Press **Ctrl + X**.

To add the *i2c-dev* module to the list of modules that Raspbian loads when the Pi is started:

1. In **LXTerminal**, type the following command and then press **Enter**:

   ```
   sudo nano /etc/modules
   ```

2. On a new line, add:

   ```
   i2c-dev
   ```

3. Press **Ctrl + O**, and then press **Enter**.

4. Press **Ctrl + X**.

Now you need to install the *i2c-tools* package and build the *py-smbus* module:

1. In **LXTerminal**, run the following commands one by one:

   ```
   sudo apt-get install i2c-tools
   sudo shutdown -r now
   ```

2. In **LXTerminal**, type the following command and then press **Enter**:

   ```
   sudo apt-get install python3-dev
   ```

3. Run the following commands:

   ```
   sudo apt-get install libi2c-dev
   cd /home/pi/Desktop
   ```

4. Type the following command on one line, and then press **Enter**:

   ```
   wget http://ftp.de.debian.org/debian/pool/
   main/i/i2c-tools/i2c-tools_3.1.0.orig.tar.bz2
   ```

5. Run the following commands:

   ```
   tar xf i2c-tools_3.1.0.orig.tar.bz2
   cd i2c-tools-3.1.0/py-smbus
   ```

6. Type the following command on one line, and then press **Enter**:

   ```
   wget http://www.vilros.com/vfiles/
   smbusmodule.c
   ```

7. Run the following two commands:

   ```
   python3 setup.py build
   sudo python3 setup.py install
   ```

Using I2C from Python 3

At the top of your Python script, you need to import the module *smbus* and create an instance of the *SMBus* class.

In the following example, the code sends the value 88 to the I2C device that has the address 23:

```
import smbus
bus = smbus.SMBus(0)
bus.write_byte(23, 88)
```

To read from an I2C device, use the *read_byte()* method and pass the device's address as an argument. For example:

```
v = bus.read_byte(23)
```

7.9 Serial UARTs

A universal asynchronous receiver/transmitter (UART) is a chip that translates the parallel data used by a microprocessor or microcontroller to serial data for use with communications ports.

Serial ports are *asynchronous*, which means that you can send data at the same time as receiving it, and both devices can initiate connections and send data when they want to.

On the Pi, the GPIO header has two UART pins for making connections to other devices using a traditional serial port. These are pin 8 (UART_TXD) and pin 10 (UART_RXD). The TXD pin of the Pi is connected to the RXD pin of the other device, and the RXD pin of the Pi is connected to the TXD pin of the other device. And to make electricity flow, you also need to connect a wire between the ground of each device.

 The Pi's serial port uses 3.3 V logic levels. You need logic level converters to connect the Pi to the 5 V ports used by most USB serial port adapters.

In Raspbian, the Pi's serial port is */dev/ttyAMA0*. This device is usually configured for console input and output, and so if you want to control the port from your own programs then you need to change two configuration files:

1. On the Raspbian desktop, double-click **LXTerminal**.

2. Type the following command and then press **Enter**:

   ```
   sudo nano /etc/inittab
   ```

3. On the line that reads *TO: 23: respawn: /sbin/getty –L ttyAMA0 115200 vt100*, add a # symbol at the start of the line. This makes the line into a comment so that Raspbian ignores it.

4. Press **Ctrl + O**, and then press **Enter**.

5. Press **Ctrl + X**.

6. Type the following command and then press **Enter**:

    ```
    sudo nano /boot/cmdline.txt
    ```

7. Remove all references to */dev/ttyAMA0* so that the line reads:

    ```
    dwc_otg.lpm_enable=0 console=tty1 root=/dev/
    mmcblk0p2 rootfstype=ext4 elevator=deadline
    rootwait
    ```

8. Press **Ctrl + O**, and then press **Enter**.

9. Press **Ctrl + X**.

10. Type the following command and then press **Enter**:

    ```
    sudo shutdown –r now
    ```

Making Serial Communications from Python 3

To send and receive data from the serial port in Python, you can use the *pySerial* module:

1. At the top of your script, include the following line:

    ```
    import serial
    ```

2. Create an instance of the *Serial* class, using the line:

    ```
    ser = serial.Serial("/dev/ttyAMA0", 19200,
    timeout=0)
    ```

3. Use the *write()* method to send data. For example:

    ```
    ser.write("Hello")
    ```

The first parameter of the call to *Serial()* is the name of the serial port device. */dev/ttyAMA0* is the serial port that is available on the Pi's GPIO headers. The second parameter is the connection speed (also known as "baud rate"). The other device needs to open its serial port at the same speed.

The remaining settings that you need to use on the other device are:

Parity: None
Data Bits: 8
Stop Bits: 1
Handshaking (hardware flow control): Off

To read from the serial port, you can either call the *read()* method with no arguments to read a single byte, or pass the number of bytes that you want to read into the method. The *timeout* parameter that you specified earlier defines how long the Pi will wait to receive data. If *timeout* is zero then *read()* will wait until it receives all of the bytes that you request.

For example:

```
value = ser.read()
values = ser.read(10)
```

To wait until the other machine sends a specific number of bytes before you attempt to read from the port, you can use the method *inWaiting()*. This returns the number of bytes that your script has not yet read.

When you are finished with the serial connection, you should close the serial port by calling the *close()* method of the *Serial* class.

8 – Building an IP Camera

IP cameras are a type of camera that you do not need to connect to a computer in order to view the videos and images that they record. Instead, they connect to your local network router and make the output available over Internet protocols (IP). This allows the videos and images to be viewed across the Internet.

Because the Raspberry Pi is small, and has good Internet connectivity, it is well-suited for building this type of camera. In this chapter, you will see how to connect a Pi camera module to the Model B+ and configure Raspbian.

You need:

1. A Raspberry Pi (any model) running Raspbian.
2. An Ethernet or Wi-Fi connection setup on the Pi.
3. A Raspberry Pi Camera Module.
4. Administrator access to your network router (to make the video accessible over the Internet).

8.1 The Pi Camera Module

The Raspberry Pi camera module is a small, high-definition video camera that connects to the Raspberry Pi using the camera serial interface (CSI) connector.

It has a fixed-focus, 5-megapixel sensor, capable of taking still images in resolutions up to 2592 pixels wide and 1944 pixels tall, and video in resolutions up to high-definition 1080p at 30 frames per second.

Connecting the Camera

The camera module uses a long, flexible cable, and this is useful when you need to fit the camera and the Pi into a case. However, this type of cable can be damaged easily. Do not bend or twist the cable excessively, and do not use it as a weight-bearing support.

To connect to the camera module to the Pi:

1. Ensure the Pi is unplugged.

2. Open the CSI connector on the Pi by grasping the top of the CSI connector and pulling it upwards.

3. Take the flexible cable and gently push it down into the CSI connector. It will only push in by a few millimeters. The blue stripe on the Pi end of the cable should face the Ethernet port.

4. Hold the flexible cable in position and then press down on the top of the CSI connector to close it.

5. Reconnect the Pi to its power supply.

Figure 1. Connecting the camera module to the Model B+

Enabling the Camera

By default, the camera is disabled in Raspbian. To enable it:

1. On the Raspbian desktop, double-click **LXTerminal**.

2. Type the following command and then press **Enter**:

   ```
   sudo raspi-config
   ```

3. Press the **Down Arrow** key four times to highlight **Enable Camera**, and then press **Enter**.

4. Press the **Right Arrow** key to highlight **<Enable>**, and then press **Enter**.

5. Press the **Right Arrow** key twice to highlight **<Finish>**, and then press **Enter**.

6. Press **Enter**.

Disabling the LED

The Pi's camera module has a red light-emitting diode (LED) on the board. To disable it:

1. On the Raspbian desktop, double-click **LXTerminal**.

2. Type the following command and then press **Enter**:

   ```
   sudo nano /boot/config.txt
   ```

3. Use the **Down Arrow** key to move to the end of the file, and then add the following text on a new line:

   ```
   disable_camera_led=1
   ```

4. Press **Ctrl + O** and then press **Enter**.

5. Press **Ctrl + X**.

6. To restart the Pi, type the following command and then press **Enter**:

   ```
   sudo shutdown —r now
   ```

8.2 Motion

Motion is a command-line tool that is designed for working with cameras from Linux. It takes still images, records videos, detects movement, and streams live video feeds across the Internet.

Motion-mmal is a version of Motion that is designed to work with the Pi camera module. To install Motion-mmal, you must first install several files and pieces of software that it works with.

1. On the Raspbian desktop, double-click **LXTerminal**.

2. Type the following command on one line, and then press **Enter**:

   ```
   sudo apt-get install —y libjpeg62 libjpeg62-dev
   libavformat53 libavformat-dev libavcodec53
   libavcodec-dev libavutil51 libavutil-dev
   ```

```
libc6-dev zlib1g-dev libmysqlclient-dev libpq5
libpq-dev
```

3. Change to your desktop folder. For example:

   ```
   cd /home/pi/Desktop
   ```

4. Type the following command and then press **Enter**:

   ```
   wget https://www.dropbox.com/s/
   xdfcxm5hu71s97d/motion-mmal.tar.gz
   ```

5. Type the following command and then press **Enter**:

   ```
   tar zxvf motion-mmal.tar.gz
   ```

6. Type the following command and then press **Enter**:

   ```
   sudo mv motion /usr/bin/motion
   ```

7. Type the following command and then press **Enter**:

   ```
   sudo mv motion-mmalcam.conf /etc/motion.conf
   ```

8. Type the following command and then press **Enter**:

   ```
   sudo chown root:root /usr/bin/motion
   ```

Steps 6–8 above move Motion into a system folder and change its owner.

Configuring the Software

Before starting Motion, you should check its configuration settings. When you start Motion with no command-line arguments, it reads its configuration settings from the file */etc/ motion.conf*. To open this file:

1. On the Raspbian desktop, double-click **LXTerminal**.

2. Type the following command and then press **Enter**:

   ```
   nano /etc/motion.conf
   ```

There are many settings that you can change, but the key ones are:

Setting	Description
width	The width of still images and video frames in pixels.

Setting	Description
height	The height of still images and video frames in pixels.
framerate	The maximum number of frames to capture per second.
rotate	You can use this setting to rotate the image. Acceptable values are 0, 90, 180, and 270.
target_dir	The folder where Motion saves images and videos.
stream_port	The port number you want to use when accessing the live stream from other devices.
stream_maxrate	The maximum number of frames to send per second to devices viewing the live stream.
output_pictures	Set this to *off* if you do not want to save pictures when Motion detects movement.
ffmpeg_output_movies	Set this to *off* if you do not want to record video files when Motion detects movement.
ffmpeg_video_codec	If you have difficulty viewing the video files that Motion records, change this to use a different video codec. For example, *msmpeg4*.
max_mpeg_time	The maximum length of video that Motion saves to each file before starting a new one.
webcontrol_port	The port number for accessing the control panel from a web browser.
webcontrol_localhost	When this is *on*, only web browsers running on the Pi can access the control panel.

When taking images or recording video, the larger the image size (*width* and *height*) and the number of images taken (*framerate*) greatly affect how much space the files will use on the SD card. If you are streaming the video feed to other devices, the *width*, *height*, and *stream_maxrate* settings affect how fast each image or frame is sent to connected devices.

The default image size of 1024 x 576 is a little large for the Pi to stream to connected web browsers. The size suggested in *motion.conf* of 352 x 288 works much better and at higher frame rates.

If you only want to access the live video feed, it is recommended that you set *ffmpeg_output_movies* and *output_pictures* to *off*. Otherwise you may run out of space on the SD card very quickly.

To change the configuration of Motion:

1. On the Raspbian desktop, double-click **LXTerminal**.
2. Type the following command and then press **Enter**:
    ```
    nano /etc/motion.conf
    ```
3. Change any settings.
4. Press **Ctrl + O**, and then press **Enter**.
5. Press **Ctrl + X**.

Password-Protecting your Camera Stream

If you want to stop others from accessing your video stream, you can configure Motion to require a username and password.

To do this:

1. On the Raspbian desktop, double-click **LXTerminal**.
2. Type the following command and then press **Enter**:
    ```
    nano /etc/motion.conf
    ```
3. Change the setting *stream_auth_method* to *1*.
4. On the line that starts with *;stream_authentication*, remove the semi-colon and change *username* and *password*.
5. Press **Ctrl + O**, and then press **Enter**.
6. Press **Ctrl + X**.

Starting Motion

With the default settings, you start Motion from the command line. Once the software is configured how you want it, and you have tested it, you can set Motion to start automatically when the Pi starts and loads Raspbian.

To start Motion manually:

1. On the Raspbian desktop, double-click **LXTerminal**.

2. Type the following command and then press **Enter**:

    ```
    motion
    ```

When you want to stop Motion, press **Ctrl + C**.

To configure Motion to start automatically:

1. On the Raspbian desktop, double-click **LXTerminal**.

2. Type the following command and then press **Enter**:

    ```
    nano /etc/motion.conf
    ```

3. Change the setting *daemon* to *on*.

4. Press **Ctrl + O**, and then press **Enter**.

5. Press **Ctrl + X**.

6. Type the following command and then press **Enter**:

    ```
    sudo nano /etc/rc.local
    ```

7. Before the line that reads *exit 0*, add the following text on its own line:

    ```
    motion
    ```

8. Press **Ctrl + O**, and then press **Enter**.

9. Press **Ctrl + X**.

10. To restart the Pi, type the following command and then press **Enter**:

    ```
    sudo shutdown -r now
    ```

Viewing the Live Stream from Devices on your Network

To view the video from a device on your local network, ensure Motion is running and then open a web browser on the device.

You need to know the IP address of the Raspberry Pi. For more information, see Finding the IP Address on page 41.

Type *http://* followed by the IP address of your Pi, then a colon and the port number (*stream_port* in *motion.conf*) into the address bar of the web browser. Then press the Enter key.

 Internet Explorer on Windows is not able to open the stream this way, but other browsers can. You can also use VLC (*http://www.videolan.org*) to open the stream using its address.

Viewing the Live Stream over the Internet

To access the live stream from devices outside your local network, configure your router to allow incoming requests on the port *stream_port* (in *motion.conf*). To do this, you will use the Pi's IP address and so it is helpful if the Pi is using a static IP, see Using a Static IP Address on page 42.

You need to create a rule that allows incoming traffic on a TCP port of your choosing (for example, 8081), and states that this traffic should be forwarded to the Pi on port 8081 (or the value of *stream_port* in *motion.conf*).

To access the stream over the Internet, you need to know the external IP address of your router. Open a web browser on a device connected to your network and visit *http://www.whatsmyip.org*. Then you can open the live stream using an address that begins *http://*, followed by the external IP address of your router, a colon, and then the incoming port number that you set in your router's port forwarding.

 When your router restarts or reconnects to the Internet, your IP address may change. Using a dynamic domain name system (DDNS) service provider, you can map your IP address to an Internet domain name and use this domain name to access your live stream.

9 – Building a Smarter Doorbell

A doorbell is a push-button switch that closes a small electrical circuit when a visitor presses the button. With the circuit closed, electricity flows into components that make the chime or buzzing sound.

With a Raspberry Pi, you can make a much smarter doorbell – one which is capable of doing a lot more than playing a sound. Anything that the Pi can do, you can do in response to someone ringing the doorbell.

In this chapter, you will see how to make a prototype Raspberry Pi-powered doorbell.

You need:

1. A Raspberry Pi running Raspbian.
2. A set of speakers. For more information about suitable speakers, see section 9.2.
3. A door chime sound effect as an MP3.
4. A doorbell ("bell push") or momentary push switch.
5. Some wire.
6. One 330 Ω resistor.
7. A solderless breadboard, perfboard, or stripboard for attaching wires and components.

 The doorbell on the front of your house is usually wired into the "mains" electrical supply. Do not connect the Pi doorbell to the mains supply, and consult a qualified electrician before attempting to remove your current doorbell.

9.1 The Button Circuit

The push-button circuit used in this project is the same as you can see described in section 7.5 Basic Input on page 164.

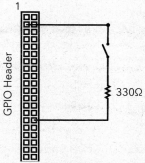

Figure 1. Basic button input

You can use a push button for this project, or a standard doorbell switch. Doorbells usually have two screw terminals inside, which make electrical connections by tightly holding wires onto metal contacts. To connect a wire to a terminal:

1. Loosen the screw by turning it counterclockwise.
2. Strip 25 mm–35 mm of insulation from the wire.
3. Wrap the exposed part around the screw.
4. Tighten the screw by turning it in a clockwise direction.

Repeat the process for the other terminal.

The direction that you connect the wires to your circuit does not matter.

1. Connect one wire from the bell to *GPIO2* (pin 3).
2. Connect the other wire from the doorbell to one leg of the 330 Ω resistor.
3. Connect the other leg of the resistor to a *ground* on the GPIO header.

9.2 Speakers

There are two types of speaker that work well for this type of Raspberry Pi project: stereo, desktop PC speakers; and speakers that have an HDMI input and built-in amplifier.

Speakers that have an HDMI input extract the audio information from the HDMI signal. If you are using the HDMI output then you do not have to change your configuration to use these speakers.

Stereo PC speakers come in two varieties: passive, and active. Active speakers have their own power supply and can play sounds at a much greater volume. Both types usually have a 3-pole 3.5 mm stereo plug that you can connect into the Pi's 3.5 mm output jack.

By default, if you connect an HDMI cable to the Pi then any audio signals will also use that. You can force the audio out through the 3.5 mm output jack with the *amixer* command:

1. On the Raspbian desktop, double-click **LXTerminal**.
2. Type the following command and then press **Enter**:
   ```
   sudo amixer cset numid=3 1
   ```

9.3 A Basic Doorbell

To make a doorbell, you can use a Python script to detect when the button is pressed and then play a sound.

To begin:

1. On the desktop, double-click **LXTerminal**.
2. To make a new folder for your doorbell project, type the following command and then press **Enter**:
   ```
   mkdir Doorbell
   ```
3. On the desktop, double-click **IDLE3**.
4. In the **Python Shell**, on the **Menu**, click **File** and then click **New Window**.

5. On the **Menu**, click **File** and then click **Save As**.

6. Save the file to your folder, as *doorbell.py*.

7. Add the Python code below, and then save your
    script again:

```
import RPi.GPIO
RPi.GPIO.setmode(RPi.GPIO.BCM)
RPi.GPIO.setup(2, RPi.GPIO.IN,
pull_up_down=RPi.GPIO.PUD_UP)

def Ring():
    pass

while True:
    if RPi.GPIO.input(2) == RPi.GPIO.LOW:
        Ring()
```

This code detects a button press in the same way as described
in Chapter 7 – Controlling Input and Output Pins on page 154. It
then calls the function *Ring()*, which does nothing yet.

To play a sound file from Python, you can use *mpg321*. This is a
command line tool for playing MP3 files on Raspbian, but you
can start it from a Python script. To install mpg321:

• In **LXTerminal**, type the following command and then
  press **Enter**:

```
sudo apt-get install mpg321
```

Copy the sound effect *.mp3* into your *Doorbell* folder.

Add the following import directive to the top of the script:

```
import os
```

Then in the *Ring()* function, remove the *pass* statement and add
the following code; replace the file name of the MP3 file if
necessary.

```
os.system("mpg321 ring.mp3")
```

The *system()* function in the *os* module runs command line tools
from Python scripts. To run the script:

- In **LXTerminal**, type the following command and then press **Enter**:

```
sudo python3 Doorbell/doorbell.py
```

Press the switch to hear the audio file play. If you hold the button down, the script repeatedly plays the sound.

To stop the script from looping the sound, you can make sure that the button is released before the script checks for another press:

- Add the following statements to your script file, in the *Ring()* function, after the call to *os.system()*:

```
while RPi.GPIO.input(2) == RPi.GPIO.LOW:
    pass
```

The *while* loop continually runs the *pass* instruction (which does nothing) until the button is released and *GPIO2* goes high.

Starting the Doorbell Script Automatically

If you want your doorbell script to run when the Raspberry Pi starts up, you can use a feature built-in to Linux called *cron*. Cron is a way of starting programs in the background.

First, create a shell script that starts your Python program:

1. In **LXTerminal**, type the following command and then press **Enter**:

   ```
   nano Doorbell/doorbell.sh
   ```

2. Add the following text to the file:

   ```
   #!/bin/sh
   cd /home/pi/Doorbell
   sudo amixer cset numid=3 1
   sudo python3 doorbell.py
   ```

3. Press **Ctrl + O**, and then press **Enter**.

4. Press **Ctrl + X**.

5. Type the following command and then press **Enter**:

   ```
   sudo crontab -e
   ```

6. At the end of the file, add the following text on a new line:

   ```
   @reboot sh /home/pi/Doorbell/doorbell.sh
   ```

7. Press **Ctrl + O**, and then press **Enter**.

8. Press **Ctrl + X**.

9. Type the following command and then press **Enter**:

   ```
   sudo shutdown -r now
   ```

Step 6 tells cron to run the command *"sh /home/pi/Doorbell/ doorbell.sh"* when Raspbian starts. To stop the script from starting when the Pi starts up, repeat step 5 and remove the line.

9.4 An Enhanced Doorbell

In this section, you will see a short example of how you can extend the Pi doorbell script so that Python takes a picture from the Pi camera module when a visitor presses the doorbell.

The Python *picamera* module contains the functions for accessing the camera. *Time* contains functions for working with the date and time. Add the following import statements to the top of your *doorbell.py* script:

```
import picamera
import time
```

Then create an instance of the *PiCamera* class:

- Underneath the two *RPi.GPIO* functions, add the following statement:

   ```
   camera = picamera.PiCamera()
   ```

To take a picture from the camera module, use the method *capture()*. This method accepts one argument – the file name where the image is to be saved. In the next example, the current date and time is combined with the string "Ring .jpg" to create a unique file name each time the doorbell is pressed.

Add a call to *capture()* above the *os.system()* call. For example:

```
camera.capture("Ring %s.jpg" % time.strftime("%Y%m%d-
%H%M%S"))
```

 The string passed into *strftime()* determines the format of the date and time string. For more information about the *time* module, see *http://docs.python.org/3/library/time.html*

The full Python script should look like this:

```
import RPi.GPIO
import os
import picamera
import time
RPi.GPIO.setmode(RPi.GPIO.BCM)
RPi.GPIO.setup(2, RPi.GPIO.IN,
pull_up_down=RPi.GPIO.PUD_UP)
camera = picamera.PiCamera()

def Ring():
    camera.capture("Ring %s.jpg" % time.strftime("%Y%m%d-
%H%M%S"))
    os.system("mpg321 ring.mp3")
    while RPi.GPIO.input(2) == RPi.GPIO.LOW:
        pass

while True:
    if RPi.GPIO.input(2) == RPi.GPIO.LOW:
        Ring()
```

10 – Making Free Phone Calls with Google Voice

Google Voice is a form of voice over Internet protocols (VOIP) that is now available in Google Hangouts. You can use it to make free phone calls to numbers in the US and Canada[1], and it gives you a landline number that others can use to call you – either from their Google account, or from a regular phone.

You can use Google Voice from the Google Mail website, or the Google Hangouts apps for smartphones. However, if you set up your Raspberry Pi as a private branch exchange (PBX) then you can allow any SIP-compatible phone or softphone to make and receive calls using your Google Voice account.

In this chapter, you will learn how to install the RasPBX distribution and configure it to let SIP phones use your Google Voice account.

You need:

1. A Raspberry Pi, and either an Ethernet connection or a USB Wi-Fi dongle.
2. A spare microSD card.
3. A SIP phone, SIP app for your smartphone, or a SIP softphone for your desktop PC.

10.1 SIP and Softphones

Session initiation protocol (SIP) is a VOIP standard that defines how phones and softphones (software that runs on your computer and pretends to be a phone) communicate with the servers that route phone calls over the Internet. Unlike regular phones, SIP phones connect to a local area network using Ethernet instead of connecting to a phone line. A PBX server often connects to a phone line and to computer networks, and it routes landline calls to the SIP devices.

---

1. You can make international calls, but these are not free and require you to add credit to your account.

If you do not have a SIP phone, there are many softphones available for Windows, Linux, and Mac OS X desktop PCs, and there are also SIP apps that run on smartphones. It is beyond the scope of this guide to review all of the softphones that are available. However, as a starting point, you may want to download Linphone (*http://www.linphone.org*) or Zoiper (*http://www.zoiper.com*).

There are also hosted SIP service providers that give you a landline number which is associated with their SIP servers and PBXs. You can connect your SIP phone or softphone to these servers and receive free incoming calls. However, outgoing calls usually incur charges. Using Google Voice means that you do not have to pay for outgoing calls to numbers in the US or Canada.

The registration process for Google Voice requires that you give them a phone number where you can be reached. If you do not have one then you can get a free number and SIP service that you can use for the registration.

To do this:

1. Open a web browser and visit *http://sip.pregi.net*
2. Click **Create Account**.
3. Complete the registration form (you do not need to enter a value for the phone number field), and then click **Register**.
4. Check your email and confirm the registration.
5. In your web browser, visit *http://www.ipkall.com*
6. Click ***Sign-Up***.
7. In the **SIP URI username** box, enter your sip.pregi.net username.
8. In the **SIP URI @ hostname** box, enter *sip.pregi.net*.
9. Complete the rest of the form and then click **Submit**.

When you register with IPKall, they give you a Washington state phone number and associate this number with your SIP account at sip.pregi.net. To test the number:

1. Install a SIP softphone on your desktop PC.

2. In the softphone, create an account using the following details:
   Domain: sip.pregi.net
   Username: <your sip.pregi.net username>
   Password: <your sip.pregi.net password>
   Transport: UDP
   Port: 5060

3. From a landline or cellphone (if you are using a SIP app, use a different phone for this step), call the number that IPKall gives you.

If your SIP phone does not ring, check all of your settings and try again.

10.2 Google Voice

To register for Google Voice, you must: be located in the US or Canada[1]; have an existing phone number (only for the registration process); and have a Google account.

During the process, you create a new Google Voice landline number. This can be in any area code (you are not restricted to the area code that you live in) where they have numbers available.

To register:

1. If you do not have a Google account: create one at http://accounts.google.com/SignUp

2. In your web browser, visit http://www.google.com/voice

---

[1]. Once you register and obtain your Google Voice number, you can use the service from international locations to call numbers in the US or Canada.

3. Accept the Terms and Conditions.

4. Click **I want a new number**.

5. In the **Phone Number** box, enter your phone number or the one given to you by IPKall, and then click **Continue**.

6. Click **Call me now** and complete the verification process.

7. Complete the **Choose your number** process.

When you have finished the Google Voice registration process and have your new phone number:

1. On the Google Voice webpage, click the **Settings** button.

2. On the **Phones** tab, under **Forward calls to**, deselect the checkbox next to your phone number.

3. On the **Calls** tab, next to **Call Screening**, click **Off**.

10.3 RasPBX

RasPBX is a Linux distribution for the Raspberry Pi that packages together all of the telephony, server, and database software that most users need. Some of these tools are quite complicated to install, so using a prebuilt RasPBX disk image saves you a lot of time and effort.

FreePBX is one of the key pieces of software that this distribution contains. It is the server software that you use to setup extensions (equivalent to user accounts), passwords, and configure access to your Google Voice account.

To install RasPBX:

1. Download the latest RasPBX disk image from *http:/ /www.raspberry-asterisk.org/downloads/*

2. Extract the *.img* file from the zip archive.

3. Write the disk image to a new microSD card. For more information, see section 2.3 Installation of Raspbian using a Disk Image on page 21.

4. Safely eject the microSD from your PC.

5. Unplug the Pi, and insert the microSD card.

6. Reconnect the Pi.

If you are using an Ethernet cable to connect the Pi to your network, and you do not have a display, make an SSH connection. For more information, see Connecting to the Pi with SSH on page 44.

Login in to the Pi with the username *root*, and the password *raspberry*.

If you are using an Ethernet cable, configure the Pi with a static IP address. For more information, see Using a Static IP Address on page 42.

To use a USB Wi-Fi adapter, you must first install the *wpasupplicant* tool and then configure it. To do this:

1. In the terminal, type the following command and then press **Enter**:

```
apt-get install wireless-tools wpasupplicant
```

2. Type the following command and then press **Enter**:

```
nano /etc/network/interfaces
```

3. Add the following text to the end of the file[1]:

```
auto wlan0
allow-hotplug wlan0
iface wlan0 inet static
wpa-ssid <YOUR NETWORK SSID>
wpa-psk "<YOUR NETWORK PASSWORD>"
address <AN IP ADDRESS TO USE>
netmask <YOUR NETWORK NETMASK>
gateway <YOUR NETWORK GATEWAY>
```

---

1. If you are not sure about the values to enter into this configuration, look at the network connection properties of other devices on your network.

4. Press **Ctrl + O**, and then press **Enter**.

5. Press **Ctrl + X.**

6. Type the following command and then press **Enter**:

   shutdown —r now

 RasPBX is primarily a server distribution. However, you can still access the graphical desktop environment using the *startx* command. If you want to install a softphone (such as *sflphone*) on the same Pi that runs RasPBX then you can also do that.

Accessing the Admin Panel

FreePBX includes a web-based administration panel that you can use to complete this tutorial. To access it:

1. On a device connected to your local network, open a web browser.

2. Visit *http://raspbx* or *http://* followed by the static IP address of your Pi.

3. Click **FreePBX Administration**.

4. In the first box, type *admin*.

5. In the second box, type *admin*.

6. Click **Continue**.

Creating the SIP Extensions

Before you start routing the calls, you need to create extensions (the PBX equivalent of a user account) for each SIP device that you want to use.

To create a SIP extension:

1. In the **FreePBX Administration** panel, on the **Menu**, point to **Applications** and then click **Extensions**.

2. In the **Device** list, click **Generic SIP Device**.

3. Click **Submit**.

4. In the **User Extension** box, type a number. For example, *2001*.

5. In the **Display Name** box, type the name of the person who uses this extension.

6. In the **secret** box, type a password for this extension.

7. Click **Submit**.

8. At the top of the page, click **Apply Config**.

To register a SIP device on your local network to this extension:

1. In the settings of your SIP phone or softphone, create a new account.

2. In the username box, enter the extension number. For example, *2001*.

3. In the password box, enter the secret that you set in the FreePBX configuration.

4. In the domain box, enter the IP address of your Pi.

5. Check that the phone connects to the server using *UDP* port *5060*.

It can be useful to create a second extension, for example *2002*, so that you can test the server. If the SIP device on extension 2001 dials *2002* then the second device should ring. If it does not, check that both SIP devices are showing "registered". This indicates that they are communicating with the Raspberry Pi ok. To see what is happening on the Pi:

1. Make an SSH connection or login to the terminal on the Pi.

2. Type the following command and then press **Enter**:

```
asterisk -rvvvv
```

When the Asterisk CLI tool is running, you see all of the actions that occur – including when SIP devices connect to the Pi, and when they disconnect. This can be helpful in debugging.

Some SIP softphones drop off the network without warning, so if you cannot dial a device try using different softphone software.

When you are finished with the CLI tool:

- Type the following command and then press **Enter**:
  `exit`

Setting up Google Voice and Outgoing Calls

RasPBX contains a FreePBX plugin for communicating with Google Voice. This plugin is called "Motif" and it works over extensible message and presence protocol (XMPP).

To add a Google Voice account to the system:

1. In the **FreePBX Administration** panel, on the **Menu**, point to **Connectivity** and then click **Google Voice (Motif)**.
2. In the **Google Voice Username** box, type your Google Mail email address.
3. In the **Google Voice Password** box, type your Google Mail password.
4. In the **Google Voice Phone Number** box, type the phone number that you obtained from Google Voice.
5. Click the box next to **Add Trunk**.
6. Click the box next to **Add Outbound Routes**.
7. Click the box next to **Send Unanswered to Google Voicemail**.
8. Click **Submit**.
9. At the top of the page, click **Apply Config**.
10. On the right-hand side of the screen, under **Add Google Voice Account**, click your Google Voice account.
11. Check that the **Status** says *Connected*. If it does not, check your Google Voice account details.

Motif creates the outbound route for you, and all SIP extensions can now use this outbound route to make calls. The default settings allow you dial US and Canada landlines using the 10-digit phone number or a *1* followed by the 10-digit number.

FreePBX uses *dialing patterns* to specify how different styles of phone numbers are handled. To check or change these:

1. In the **FreePBX Administration** panel, on the **Menu**, point to **Connectivity** and then click **Outbound Routes**.

2. On the right-hand side of the screen, under **Add Route**, click the route that was created for you.

3. Adjust settings under **Dial Patterns that will use this Route**.

Routing the Incoming Calls

To receive the incoming calls from your Google Voice number, you need to direct them somewhere. FreePBX has a lot of features that work with incoming calls, but this guide only covers directing calls to a specific extension. To route calls to an extension:

1. In the **FreePBX Administration** panel, on the **Menu**, point to **Connectivity** and then click **Inbound Routes**.

2. In the **Description** box, type a name for this rule. For example, *Google Voice*.

3. If you want to create a rule that only applies to incoming calls from one specific Google Voice account: in the **DID Number** box, type the phone number that Google Voice gave you.

4. In the **== choose one ==** list, click **Extensions** and then click the extension that you want to connect the incoming calls to.

5. Click **Submit**.

6. At the top of the page, click **Apply Config**.

If you add multiple Google Voice accounts to your system and want to direct them to different extensions, create different rules for each Google Voice account and specify the phone number in the *DID Number* box for each rule.

10.4 SIP Phones across the Internet

If you want SIP devices or softphones to be able to access your PBX from outside your local network, you need to configure your network router to allow incoming traffic on the following ports and route them through to the same port numbers on the Pi:

Start Port	End Port	Type	Description
5060	5061	UDP	The two ports used for SIP signaling and control.
10001	20000	UDP	Ports for media (voice and video) transmission.

Your SIP devices need to connect to the external IP address of your router, not to the internal IP address of the Pi as you have used so far.

 When your router restarts or reconnects to the Internet, your IP address may change. Using a dynamic domain name system (DDNS) service provider, you can map your IP address to an Internet domain name and use this domain name to access your PBX.

11 – Accessories

One of the great things about the Raspberry Pi is the number of peripherals, expansion boards, connectors, and components that you can use with it. Here is a selection of a useful accessories that you can use with the projects and information in this guide.

USB to TTL Cable
This handy cable connects to a PC using the USB connector, and to the Pi using individual female sockets that fit directly onto the serial port pins of the Pi's GPIO header. The built-in circuitry handles voltage level conversions.
http://www.vilros.com/usb-to-ttl-cable.html

40-pin GPIO Ribbon Cable
A female to female cable for connecting external circuits to the Raspberry Pi. It can also be used to connect male to male jumper cables to the Pi when prototyping your circuits on a breadboard.
http://www.vilros.com/40-pin-gpio-ribbon-cable.html

Jumper Wires
Jumper wires (also called "jump wires") have reinforced ends that make it easy to connect components on a breadboard, or make connections with devices that have female sockets.
http://www.vilros.com/jumper-wires.html

Breadboard
A standard, 400-hole breadboard is invaluable for prototyping and testing your circuits. Their use is explained in Chapter 7 – Controlling Input and Output Pins on page 154.
http://www.vilros.com/breadboard.html

Light-Emitting Diodes (LEDs)

LEDs are components that you will use lots of. In addition to making them flash or using them as status indicators, they can be very helpful for checking which parts of a circuit are working.
http://www.vilros.com/red-led.html

Resistors

Almost all electronic circuits contain at least one resistor. Unlike other components that you may buy specifically for the project that you are working on, you will use so many resistors that it is worth keeping a stock of different values.
10 KΩ: *http://www.vilros.com/10k-resistors.html*
330 Ω: *http://www.vilros.com/330-resistors.html*

Buttons

These high-quality, push-button switches are ideal for making input circuits using the Pi's GPIO header. When the conveniently-large button is pressed and held, electricity flows between two of the switch's terminals. Exactly the type used in section 7.5 Basic Input on page 164.
http://www.vilros.com/big-12mm-buttons.html

10K Trimpot

Also known as "potentiometer" or "variable resistor", these trimpots are used when you need to change the amount of resistance in a circuit without disassembling it. For example, to reduce the brightness of an LED. These "pots" have resistance that changes as you turn the knob, from 0 Ω through 10 KΩ, and slot neatly into place on a breadboard.
http://www.vilros.com/10k-trimpot.html